MOM JEANS AND OTHER MISTAKES

TITLES BY ALEXA MARTIN

Mom Jeans and Other Mistakes

THE PLAYBOOK SERIES

Intercepted

Fumbled

Blitzed

Snapped

MOM JEANS AND OTHER MISTAKES

Alexa Martin

BERKLEY
NEW YORK

BERKLEY
An imprint of Penguin Random House LLC
penguinrandomhouse.com

Copyright © 2021 by Alexa Martin
Readers Guide copyright © 2021 by Alexa Martin
Penguin Random House supports copyright. Copyright fuels creativity, encourages
diverse voices, promotes free speech, and creates a vibrant culture. Thank you
for buying an authorized edition of this book and for complying with copyright
laws by not reproducing, scanning, or distributing any part of it in any form
without permission. You are supporting writers and allowing
Penguin Random House to continue to publish books for every reader.

BERKLEY and the BERKLEY & B colophon are registered trademarks
of Penguin Random House LLC.

Library of Congress Cataloging-in-Publication Data

Names: Martin, Alexa, author.
Title: Mom jeans and other mistakes / Alexa Martin.
Description: First Edition. | New York: Berkley, 2021.
Identifiers: LCCN 2020058108 (print) | LCCN 2020058109 (ebook) |
ISBN 9780593198896 (trade paperback) | ISBN 9780593198902 (ebook)
Classification: LCC PS3613.A77776 M66 2021 (print) |
LCC PS3613.A77776 (ebook) | DDC 813/.6—dc23
LC record available at https://lccn.loc.gov/2020058108
LC ebook record available at https://lccn.loc.gov/2020058109

First Edition: September 2021

Printed in the United States of America
1st Printing

Book design by Kristin del Rosario
Interior art: Emojis © Cosmic_Design/Shutterstock.com

This is a work of fiction. Names, characters, places, and incidents either are
the product of the author's imagination or are used fictitiously, and any
resemblance to actual persons, living or dead, business establishments,
events, or locales is entirely coincidental.

PUBLISHER'S NOTE: The recipes contained in this book are to be followed
exactly as written. The publisher is not responsible for your specific health or
allergy needs that may require medical supervision. The publisher is not responsible
for any adverse reactions to the recipes contained in this book.

To Abby,
my favorite sixth-grade locker partner,
college roommate,
and future Irish cottage co-owner.
Forever grateful for your friendship and love.

Lauren

"And just one more," our landlord, Miss Morielli, says as she hands Jude and me the final paper to sign before our town house is legally ours.

The irony doesn't escape me that I've had to sign more paper-work to live in a town house with brass hardware and popcorn ceilings than I did to take my daughter home from the hospital. I'm pretty sure being granted a tiny human should at least require a background check.

"Thank god. My hand is starting to cramp," Jude moans be-side me. "I thought people signed this stuff over the computer now? Did you know they aren't even teaching kids cursive any-more? I wonder what Addy's signature is going to—ouch!" She finally stops talking and glares at me for kicking her beneath the table. If she's expecting me to feel bad, she's going to be waiting awhile because I don't. Not even a little bit.

HGTV has really tricked people into believing that house hunting is this joyful experience where the only downside is the previous owner's terrible taste in wallpaper. And maybe it is when you have unlimited funds and don't have to worry about all the ways your five-year-old could possibly conduct a vault flip off the loft railing or mistake the terrible green paint for a chalkboard she can deface.

So after weeks of looking and lowering our standards until I'm not sure they could get much lower, the last thing I need is for Jude's complaining to throw a wrench into everything when we're one signature away from finally crossing the finish line.

"We'll sign as many papers as you want. We're just so grateful to live in your beautiful property." I sign my name on the final line and push the paper over to Jude—who is still glaring at me. I'm definitely the suck-up between the two of us. And I'm good with that. "Adelaide hasn't stopped talking about how she wants to decorate her room or asking if the cookies she had when we toured the house will be there too."

"Oh, the pleasure is all mine." She takes the document from Jude, a wide smile spreading across her face. Probably from knowing how much money she'll be making off a condo she no doubt paid off ten years ago. "It can be so hard finding the right people to rent to in this city. But the last lesbian couple I rented to was so nice and respectful, I was thrilled when your family walked through the door."

My eyes nearly pop out of my head as I register her words, but Jude, my very reactive and not at all measured best friend, almost comes out of her seat. "Oh my god, what? No!" There's no masking the shock in Jude's voice. I'm not sure if I should laugh along or be offended she's so horrified at the idea of kissing me. "I mean, not that I haven't swum in the lady pond once or twice, but never with Lauren. She's my best friend, we're practically sisters. Gross."

Okay.

Not offended. Just wildly embarrassed.

Thank god this happened after we finished signing the paperwork and the condo can't be revoked.

Poor Miss Morielli's cheeks look like we set them on fire, and I've never related to a person so much. Jude really knows how to work a person up. "Well, I guess it's a moot point, with as much paperwork as you both just signed together, you may as well be married. At least for the next twelve months."

"I'm not sure I believe in marriage." Jude stands up and rounds the table. I swear, the woman is incapable of keeping any of her thoughts to herself. She's lucky she's too far away to kick this time. "But I am a fan of sister wives . . . without the husband, of course. It's all of the support with none of the dude drama. I guess you could say that's what we're doing."

"Sister wives, huh? I think you might be onto something." Miss Morielli holds out two keys. "I hope you'll enjoy your new home."

"Are you kidding me?" Jude grabs the keys out of her hand and crosses the room, placing them next to the only photographable plant in the room. I have no doubt in about two minutes the photo will be on her Instagram feed with about a million filters. "We've only been planning this for our entire life. This is going to be the best year ever."

I think about asking Miss Morielli for her notary and making Jude sign that statement. Because as much as I've warned her and she's said I'm crazy, I have a feeling having a rule-following mom and a five-year-old for roommates is not going to be everything she thinks it will be.

But like it or not, she's stuck with us now.

ONE

. . .

Jude

Children and hangovers do not mix.

I'm sure it's common sense to most people, but this is not a problem I ever thought I'd have.

For one, my uterus is under heavy protection. And two, by the time I have kids—if I ever do—I'll be a real adult who makes grown-up decisions. You know, like one glass of heart-healthy red wine with a well-balanced meal and not the parade of low-carb vodka shots I had after eating a side salad, no dressing, last night.

But as the sticky, tiny fingers literally peel open my eyes, and my tongue is uselessly stuck to the roof of my mouth, I have the very unkind realization that this is my new life . . . at least for the next year. And for the millionth time, I hope that if a giant sinkhole were to open up, it does so underneath Asher Thompson's feet.

"Auntie Jude, Mommy made pancakes. She said to ask you if you want some before you go to your special meeting." Adelaide holds my eyelids hostage and stares into my eyes, which are no doubt bloodshot, with the most innocent expression that it almost makes me smile. *Almost.*

"Addy." I push her hands off my face and resist the urge to hit her with my pillow. But, seeing as she's only five, I feel like society and her mother might frown upon that kind of thing. "We have to find a new wake-up technique. You're going to give me crow's-feet."

Her mouth purses and her little nose scrunches, giving her these wrinkles on the top of her nose that are adorable now but might make her consider Botox in about thirty years. I don't tell her that. "You'll get a birdie's feet?" Her voice is a screech, and she honestly sounds appalled. "What happens to the rest of the bird? How will it land with no feet?"

"Oh my god." I wrap my arms around her and pull her down to me, covering her chubby cheeks with kisses until she squeals. "This is why I'm obsessed with you," I shout over her peals of laughter before sitting up with her and ignoring the slight pounding against my skull. "Crow's-feet aren't birds. They're the little lines around eyes that make your grandma Keane always look so sleepy and old."

"Oooh." She nods, but I'm pretty sure she still has no idea what I'm talking about.

"Yup." I crawl out from under the duvet I spent way too much money on, but photographs like a dream, and climb over the boxes I have yet to unpack. "And you don't want Auntie Jude to look like Old Grandma Keane, do you?"

Instead of answering and then apologizing profusely for endangering my skin, she shrugs, and I'm pretty she couldn't actually give a fuck. Rude. "Are you going to eat pancakes with me?"

"No pancakes for me." I grab her hand and walk with her down the stairs of our new townhome. "Repeat after me: carbs are evil."

"Carbs are evil," she mimics. For a five-year-old, she follows direction beautifully.

"Carbs are not evil," Lauren says from somewhere. And even though I can't see her, I know she's glaring at me.

But whatever, sue me. Someone needs to teach kids the importance of diet. That high metabolism and glowing skin they are unfairly blessed with aren't going to last forever.

"Mommy!" Adelaide drops my hand like a bad habit and takes off running to the table, where a plate of cut-up pancakes is waiting for her, complete with eggs and a healthy serving of fruit. "Wanna know what Jude taught me?"

Lauren walks around the corner, a coffee mug to her lips, looking way too hot in her mom pajamas and headscarf. The glare I knew she had is directed at me before she drops it and aims a bright smile at Addy. "Sure, baby."

"She said that Grandma Keane looks so old because of all the birdie feet on her face." She pops a grape in her mouth, completely unaware of the rising tension in the kitchen. "And what's a carb anyway?"

We're going to have to work on keeping secrets.

"Carbs give you energy to make you big and strong. And Grandma Keane doesn't look old, she looks wise." Lauren goes to put down her mug before grabbing the organic maple syrup and drizzling the saddest little sprinkling that I've ever seen on her pancakes before making direct eye contact with me. "Can we talk for a second?"

Crap.

I know that tone. It's the same one she used in sixth grade when we were locker partners and I took one of her glitter gel pens out of our locker without asking . . . and every time I've pissed her off since.

"Actually." I make a move to the coffee machine, in desperate need of both caffeine and an excuse. "I'm really thirsty."

Lauren grabs my arm and pulls me out of the kitchen with a smile that both terrifies and intrigues me frozen on her face. "Eat your food, Adelaide, we'll be right back."

I look to Addy for help since she's the one who ratted me out, but instead her eyes are closed and her shoulders are bouncing as she chews her pancakes.

Maybe I do want carbs and sugar. I'm not sure I've ever looked as happy as Addy does. And if pancakes and organic syrup are the answer, who am I to argue?

"What the hell, Jude?" Lauren snaps me out of my syrup-coated fantasy. "You can't talk to Adelaide like that. Do you understand the hell Ben will give me if she goes to visit him and she tells him we're over here talking about how old his mom looks?"

"Fuck Ben and his mom. She's a bitch and he's trash. He should really just be happy I'm not saying more." I have to fight back the rage that always tries to claw its way to the surface whenever I think of Lauren's piece-of-shit ex. I really try to be Zen- and peace-like, but that dirtbag always fucks up my chi.

Lucky for me, I guess, my anger seems to defuse Lauren's.

"What're you fucking smiling at?"

"You're just so cute when you're mad." She pinches my cheek, something she knows I hate. "Plus, my mom still defends Ben whenever he comes up, so it's nice that someone has my back."

"Well, your mom's a bitch too. But she's still goals AF when it comes to aging well, so I couldn't use her for an example with Addy." I'm sure you're not supposed to talk about your friend's family like that, but Lauren and I don't lie to each other, and Mrs. Turner really is a bitch. She never liked me and I'm a fucking delight. But I never liked her, either, so it was completely mutual. Even eleven-year-old me knew I never wanted her approval. The same could not be said for my people-pleasing best friend . . . which only made me hate Mrs. Turner more. I wouldn't mind if she shared her beauty routine, though, but I'm thinking my lack of melanin might prevent me from ever being on her level.

"I can't say you're wrong about any of this, but you still can't say it to Adelaide." Lauren fidgets with an imaginary string on the sleeve of her flannel pajamas. "You know how hard it's been for us. I just don't want her to go see him and say something that gives him an excuse to walk away from her and blame me for being the crazy baby mama."

Lauren is a spitfire. She's confident and strong and the smartest person I've ever known. Whenever I have a problem, she's the first person I tell. She gives me the best advice, and when she's done talking to me, I feel like fucking Wonder Woman. She knows what she wants in a way that both intimidates and inspires me. But whenever she talks about her douchebag ex, it's like I can see her visibly fold into herself. She shrinks right in front of my eyes and becomes this meek person I don't even know. And if he wasn't my favorite five-year-old's dad, I'd have already paid a hit man.

Well . . . I would've when I wasn't broke as a joke.

"I'll try to be better," I reassure her, but when she glares at me, I know I've failed. "Fuck. Fine." I uncross my fingers from behind my back and hold them in front of me. "I promise not to say anything about Ben or his stupid family in front of Addy."

"Thank you." She smiles and her perfect white teeth gleam against her brown skin. "And when she's not around, you can talk all the crap you please."

"I guess that's fair." I pout like Addy did the other night when Lauren told her she had to take a bath. "You know, it's still so weird to me that you're a mom. Like, you grew a fucking human! A really cute one at that. But, now when you give me the mom eye, it actually scares the shit out of me."

Even before Lauren had Addy, she would look at me like I was crazy. I do have a knack for putting myself in not the greatest of situations. I used to laugh her off and try to get her to join me (which never happened), but I guess losing countless hours of sleep and wiping butts for years just gives that look more authority, because now I cower.

"I know, and as a mom, I have to ask if you remember that you have a photo shoot in an hour?"

"Duh." I totally didn't remember. Because where Lauren is an actual adult, I just play one on Instagram.

"Mom . . ." Addy's hesitant voice calls from the kitchen. "I think I might've put too much syrup on my pancake."

"Crap," Lauren whispers underneath her breath before calling into the other room, "it's okay, accidents happen, here I come."

And on that note . . .

"You have fun with that!" I run to the stairs, not missing Lauren flipping me off before I go.

I might be living with a small child, but at least I'm not responsible for keeping her alive. Because for real? I'm not doing the best job of it for myself.

But at least I look fucking fantastic doing it.

TWO

. . .

Lauren

I know syrup is practically a staple of breakfast food for children all across America. But after spending twenty solid minutes and two rolls of paper towel cleaning up what had to be the entire bottle of fifteen-dollar organic syrup off the floor, I'm pretty sure it will now be forever banned from my house.

Well, technically not *my* house.

Our house, Jude's and mine.

When we were in high school, we always said we'd live together when we were adults. I just didn't think we'd be doing it because we were both in terrible places in our lives.

"Adelaide, please, please, *please* just put on your shoes. Your dad is expecting you, and I do not want to be late."

"But I don't know where they are." Adelaide pokes her bottom lip out and works her hardest to squeeze out a tear that never comes before plopping on the ground.

And most definitely not looking for her shoes.

I close my eyes and do the deep-breathing technique one of

Jude's yoga friends taught me to calm down. She is five and I'm the adult. I need to take charge of this situation.

One, two, three, four, five.

"Adelaide June Keane, get that butt off my floor right now and go find your shoes. Remember when I bought them? You promised to keep them in your closet. If you kept that promise, we wouldn't be having this problem. I don't make rules to be mean, I make them to avoid situations like this."

My voice starts to rise at the end of my rant, but how many times do we have to have the shoe conversation before she just listens? I mean, make it easier on yourself, kid!

She swipes a stray curl that escaped from her headband out of her face, and my heart melts a little bit looking at her. She is the perfect mix of me and her dad, inheriting the best both of us had to offer. Her big brown eyes sparkle against her golden skin, and her pink lips with a deep cupid's bow form the perfect pout. Remembering how many times we were late to preschool for this exact reason is the only thing preventing me from kissing that look off her face.

"I did put them away, Mommy." She lies straight to my face. "I think Sparkle Glitter must have moved them."

Oh dear lord.

"Sparkle Glitter did not move your shoes. She's in the North Pole with Santa, she's an elf, not a leprechaun."

Sparkle Glitter is our Elf on the Shelf. Adelaide gets a kick out of her, but I think it also scares her a little bit. Which? Fair. It's the creepiest concept, and I might hate whoever came up with it. As if the holidays aren't taxing enough, now we have to add moving an elf around every night to the list? My mom always asking why I'm not teaching her about "Jesus on the cross" instead doesn't help either.

I hope I never become that woman.

"What's a leprechaun?" Adelaide asks. Now she's just being deliberately obtuse.

"Oh for the love!" I throw my hands up in the air and spin on my heel to find her shoes. "I'll do it. I do everything," I mumble under my breath as I resist stomping up the stairs.

Be the adult. You're in charge. Be the example she needs.

It takes me two minutes to find the freaking shoe.

"I thought you said you looked in your closet." I dangle the rhinestone-encrusted tennis shoes in front of me.

"I did!" Adelaide jumps up, her pouty face and crocodile tears a distant memory. "Sparkle Glitter must have brought them back!" She snatches them out of my hand, but before I can lecture her about manners, the sound of Velcro fills the small foyer and the front door swings open, almost knocking Adelaide over.

"Auntie Jude!" Adelaide jumps up, one shoe on, one completely forgotten.

"Addy girl!" Jude drops into a deep squat and swoops my girl into her arms, peppering her face with kisses.

And it's almost too much. The free, joyous, and contagious love that they have for each other.

It's what I've always dreamt of for my daughter but was never able to give her.

To be fair, though, it's kind of hard to create a loving, stable home when your fiancé is sleeping with another woman . . . or, as it turned out, multiple other women.

Jude might be a disaster, but honestly, so am I. And Jude loves Adelaide like she loves life. Fully and unapologetically. Which is something else I needed to show my daughter. After we left my ex's house, we landed with my parents. Don't get me wrong, I'm so grateful for them. I know many women in my situation do not have the support of family to lean on. But my mom—as well-meaning as she is—is quite possibly one of the coldest people on the entire planet. Living with her when I was already depressed took me to a low I didn't know was possible. When Jude brought up the idea of living together, I latched on to it like the lifeline it was.

And now? We've created our own family.

How millennial is that?

"How was your meeting?" Addy asks when Jude finally sets her back down, sounding more twenty-five than five.

"You know." Jude sits on the ground next to her, looking her straight in the eye. I love how she treats Adelaide as an equal. She respects her opinions and never trivializes her feelings, something my mom still doesn't do for me . . . and I'm a freaking adult. "I think it actually went really well. The guy was a typical man and mansplained a lot to me, but overall, I think they liked me."

"Ugh." Adelaide rolls her eyes. "The patriarchy."

I choke back my laughter. Maybe I should tone down my feminist rants a tiny bit.

"Tell me about it." Jude keeps a straight face as she leans in and drops her voice to a whisper. "When you get home, we'll discuss it further over juice boxes and fruit snacks."

"You got a deal." Adelaide stretches her little hand in front of her to shake with Jude. "We can talk about Ruth Better Ginser. I'll bring the Goldfish."

"Ruth Bader Ginsburg, baby," I correct her, deciding at that moment that, no, the feminist rants are *exactly* where they need to be.

She tilts her chin and looks up at me through the thick lashes she did not inherit from me. "That's what I said." Skepticism is thick in her sweet voice as she stares at me like I have no idea what I'm talking about. Which is also fair.

"I must have misheard then," I say before clapping my hands together. "All right, now let's get that other shoe on. Daddy's probably staring out of his window looking for you. You don't want to keep him waiting."

I don't like to lie to her, but I also don't want her to ever question being loved. It's just that right now, I'm not sure Ben is capable of loving anybody other than himself. But at least he's finally stepped up and is having her spend the night with him when he has a break in his schedule. It's a start and I guess that means something.

"You're right. Daddy needs Addy time too." She crab walks across the linoleum to her other shoe and straps it on. "Oh no!" she shouts, jumping up from the floor like a shot. How children just casually do the workouts I go out of my way to avoid never ceases to blow my mind. "I almost forgot the pictures I made him and the bracelet I made for Stephanie!"

"Okay, hustle and go get them, I'm sure they will love them." I plaster a smile on my face, hoping to disguise the flinch I always have when Stephanie is mentioned.

I see Jude open her mouth, and I already know whatever is going to come out of it is not going to be kind. I snap my fingers at her and level her with a glare.

"Right." She deflates. "Not in front of Addy, blah blah blah," she mumbles, sounding almost identical to my five-year-old.

Adelaide runs back down the stairs, her almost pitch-black curls bouncing behind her and her purple tutu floating upward, revealing the total glory of the cat tights she picked out this morning. "Okay." Above her head she holds up the masterpieces she created, pride and confidence radiating from her tiny body. "I'm ready to go."

"Yaassss, queen!" Jude snaps her fingers, and Adelaide's cheeks, which are suddenly losing all of their chub and starting to resemble those of a little girl and not my baby, turn pink.

"Auntie Jude, I'm not a queen," she corrects. "I'm a president.

You just get to be queen, but you have to work to be president, right, Mom?"

"You're so right, sister girl." My stomach tightens and my throat constricts, the love and pride I have for this girl nearly choking me. When I was pregnant, everyone told me it was a love like I never knew. So I had an idea of what having a kid would be like, but I didn't know love could be this big. Every day I think I love her more than is ever possible, but every day, it still manages to grow.

"Well, excuse me." Jude unfolds her perfectly lean body from the ground in a way only a fitness influencer like her can do. "You're still the fanciest president I've ever seen. I thought you needed a pantsuit for that job."

Adelaide shakes her head, stuffing her pictures and the brace-let in her sequined unicorn backpack before sliding her arms through the straps. "What a person wears doesn't matter, silly. It's the inside stuff that's important." And with that mic drop, she pulls open the front door and summons me, her constituent, out of the door. "Come on, Mommy. I thought you didn't want to be late."

I follow her to the car without a saying a word. It's not like I was standing with my keys in my hand for the last thirty minutes or anything.

And now I get to see Ben.

Yay.

THREE

. . .

Lauren

Adelaide's wiggling body and my shaking hands make what's usually second nature a total and utter disaster.

"Adelaide!" My clumsy fingers miss the clasp of her car seat again. "Please, please stop moving."

"I can't, Mommy, my body is just too excited!" Adelaide's eyes are focused out of the window, looking at the brick exterior of the home where we once all lived.

The home where Ben lives with Stephanie. And it's like I can feel their gazes burning a hole through my back.

"Got it!" I shout in triumph . . . and then cower apologetically when I turn and meet Mrs. Miller's familiar glare as she walks her—maybe evil—poodle past us.

"Moooom." Adelaide's grating whine snaps me back to the present. "I can't find my shoe."

Oh, for the freaking love!

"Why in the world did you take them off?" I swear I never knew that shoes would be my downfall in life. The parenting books told me everything I needed to know about pregnancy and birth and colic, but not one of them prepared me for five-year-olds and their ability to lose shoes. Even while strapped down in a car.

"My feet were sweaty." She pokes out the bottom lip I've long become immune to. "We're so far from Daddy and the car ride was so long."

Now that? That I have not become immune to. The guilt. Holy shit. The guilt I feel, knowing she's lived in three places in two years and that most of her contact with her dad before these last few months was over the phone, eats away at me at every second of every day.

"I know, baby." The frustration over shoes is completely forgotten. "How about—"

"Junie!" A peppy voice cuts me off before I can finish, and I cringe a little hearing both the voice and the nickname. For some reason, Ben has always called her Junie instead of Adelaide. I used to think it was cute, but now it's like nails on a chalkboard.

"Stephanie!" Adelaide shoves past me and jumps into Ben's new girlfriend's arms . . . one shoe and all.

I like Stephanie.

Hand to God, I do. Before she came into the picture, I was lucky if I could get Ben to commit to seeing Adelaide more than once a month. Child support was sporadic at best. I spent my nights praying he would see the error of his ways and make a change before it was too late. And that prayer was answered in Stephanie.

I guess I should be more specific when chatting with the big man.

Because even though I like her and I know I can thank her exclusively for Ben's sudden reappearance in Adelaide's life and finally catching up on his child support payments, there's still a sick twist of my stomach every time I hear Adelaide tell me how great she is. And moments like these, when I get shoved to the side and forgotten so she can go to her other family, feel like a rusty knife stabbing me through the heart over and over again.

But my feelings don't count now, and I do what I've always done. I shove everything I'm feeling so far down that I can almost forget about it and plaster a smile I don't mean on my face.

I turn on a well-worn heel—buying new shoes for anyone except my daughter has not been on the docket these past couple of years—and greet the woman who is worming her way into my daughter's heart. "Stephanie! How are you?"

Even in workout clothes, she still manages to look like she walked right out of a Victoria's Secret photo shoot. Her blond hair doesn't have a strand out of place, and there isn't even an ounce of fat between the waistband of her spandex leggings and her sports bra. Something I haven't been able to pull off since getting pregnant.

"I'm great." Her voice is soft and melodic, and I already know from Adelaide that she tells the best bedtime stories. "Just excited to spend some time with this girl tonight." She tickles Adelaide's side, and Adelaide throws her head back and giggles uncontrollably.

Stephanie focuses her eyes on my daughter, and her bright smile grows so big that she nearly blinds me with her perfect teeth. Perfect, perfect, perfect. Everything about her is perfect. She's everything I'll never be and she's freaking perfect. It's no wonder she's living the life I wanted so badly to create.

It's such a weird feeling, being so thankful you could cry and so freaking jealous that it turns the world green and makes you sick to the stomach at the very same time.

The tears that always fall after I drop Adelaide off start to build about five minutes too early, and I can feel the facade I work so hard to keep up around them start to crumble. "Why don't you take her inside while I grab the rest of her stuff." I wave them away, climbing over Adelaide's car seat to look for her sparkly shoe, which should not be this difficult to find.

"Sounds good," Stephanie calls before I hear her talk to Adelaide again. "I can't wait to show you the stuff I got you! We're gonna have a girls' weekend. I hope you like nail polish and popcorn."

"I love nail polish *and* popcorn!" Adelaide's voice has risen about ten decibels, and even without looking, I know her brown eyes are sparkling and those sweet little creases she gets on the top of her nose when she smiles with her entire face are there.

You're still her mom. Being a constant in her life is what she will always remember.

Being a millennial might not be great for most things. You know, like home ownership and student loan debt. But if there's one thing we're good at, it's technology and prioritizing mental health, and thanks to some genius in Silicon Valley, teletherapy is totally a thing.

Also, mom podcasts and blogs. I'm not sure I would've survived these last couple of years without mom influencers. Thank the heavens for Nicola Roberts, my best mom friend . . . who has no idea I even exist.

It takes me a surprisingly long time to find her shoe, which is stuck between the passenger seat and the front door. I shove it in her backpack, which is stuffed with more than she needs, but still less than she wanted, and try to prepare myself for my least favorite part of all of this. And considering I really dislike all of it, that's saying a lot.

Each step up the pathway is a punch to the gut. I loved this tiny bungalow. We moved in at the beginning of my second trimester, not long before my pregnancy went to hell. I spent an entire weekend planting the rosebushes that are now mocking me as I walk between them—a cruel reminder that all the love I put into them will keep blossoming even if I never step foot here again. This was where, when we brought Adelaide home, Jude had decorated the entire yard with pink balloons and streamers. I thought it was where I'd watch Adelaide grow up, not where I'd watch her walk away.

Before I can even make it to the porch, which is still decorated with the flowerpots Adelaide and I painted when she was two, the front door opens and Ben steps out.

Ben Keane. The love of my life who gave me the entire world and then pulled it away just as fast.

"Hey." I hope my face looks normal. I never know what I look like when I see him. Whether my hate or love for him is showing this time. I'm sure one day it won't be a struggle to see him, but today is not that day.

"Hey." His bright blue eyes crinkle at the corners as Adelaide's smile appears on his infuriatingly handsome face. "Thanks for driving her over, I could've picked her up."

"It's not a problem." I wave him off, not wanting to admit how much I enjoy the traffic if it means getting more time with my girl. "I had some errands to run anyway."

"Good, cool . . . thanks. We're excited to have her."

"Like I said, not a problem." I've come to find this is the hardest part of Ben coming back into our lives. Every time he thanks me for something that should've been happening for Adelaide's entire life, I practically have to chomp off my tongue in order not to say the snotty remark bubbling at the back of my throat.

"Oh, and since I have you here, I wanted to ask about kindergarten for Junie."

"Okay." I draw out the word for a beat. "What about it?"

"There's a school close by, and I've heard from the neighbors that it's really good. I was thinking maybe we could enroll her there. I know we both work full-time, but Steph pretty much makes her own schedule and can watch her after school for us."

There's a lot to unpack there, but a few things come to mind right away:

1) Hell freaking no.

2) He's out of his goddamn mind.

3) If only kindergarten enrollment in Los Angeles was so easy.

"I know this is a great school district, it's the reason I wanted to buy in this neighborhood in the first place." *Because dropping off my daughter here isn't hard enough, let's rub some more salt in the wound!* "But no, she's already enrolled in kindergarten."

He pulls his shoulders back and narrows his eyebrows. The way he does anytime someone dares to tell the great Ben Keane no.

"No? Why not?"

"Because that's not how things work, Ben. I toured kindergartens and applied for a year before Adelaide got in. There were teacher recommendations, testing, and observations. It was a huge process." It was like college, but with finger painting. The entire process was freaking absurd and I get a headache thinking about it. "And you already knew about this. Don't you remember the papers you signed?"

"Vaguely." He doesn't remember, I can tell by the way he looks down at his feet when he answers. "I guess I just assumed this is a decision we would discuss together."

I want to scream.

I want to punch him in the throat and scream.

Instead, I take a deep breath.

"I would've liked that too. But if you remember, you weren't very involved for a few years there." I keep my voice measured and calm, even though it's killing me slowly. "And even if you wanted to talk about things now, it's July. Applications for schools were due in the fall and admissions were given back in March. So this conversation is moot."

I wanted to look at charter schools for Adelaide. The price of private school, even for elementary school, is mind-boggling. But my parents insisted on only the best for Adelaide, promising to cover the cost and letting me pay them back on a payment plan. I might've fought harder against it, but when Adelaide got into Remington Academy, I couldn't say no. Not only are the academics unmatched, but their art program is truly out of this world. When Adelaide shadowed a student for a day, she talked about the art teacher for weeks. She loved it. And I couldn't deny her a start in life where she loved school from the very beginning.

The color in his cheeks hasn't faded and his posture hasn't relaxed. He looks right past me and eyes the overstuffed backpack slung over my shoulder. "Is that her stuff?"

Point taken.

I'd gladly never discuss this with him ever again.

"Yeah." I take it off and hand it over to him. It's hard for me to believe that I used to consider him my best friend.

He takes the bag from my hand, careful to make sure he doesn't even so much as graze my fingertips. "Well, even if she doesn't go to school around here." He stumbles over his words and my guard immediately shoots up. "I was talking with Stephanie and we both think it would be a good idea if Junie starts coming over a little bit more."

My stomach twists into knots, and I'm afraid I might decorate those rosebushes I so lovingly planted with this morning's pancakes.

"Yeah, sure!" My voice is too high, my words are too forceful, but no matter how many calming techniques Jude's friends taught me, my panic overrides it all and I forget everything. "Adelaide would love that."

And she would. Which is why me feeling like his words are slowly ripping me apart from the inside out makes me feel like the worst mom in the history of moms. I should be happy. Right? I want my daughter to have a relationship with her dad. I want Ben to step up and be involved in her life. I freaking prayed for it! But I don't want to lose any of my time with her either. I want every good-night kiss, morning cuddle, every tickle session. I want the tantrums and snotty noses. Good and bad. I want every single second of it.

And it makes me hate Ben even more.

"Great, thanks." He at least has the decency to look somewhat nervous. And considering the roller-coaster ride this encounter has been, it's the least he could do. "I'll email you, the lawyer said it's probably best that we have everything in writing."

His sentence trails off at the same time the ground disappears from beneath my feet.

"Lawyer?" The word is barely more than a whisper.

"Oh, yeah, you know, I just wanted to make sure I go about everything the right way." His blue eyes, the ones I loved so much, look anywhere except at me.

"Ben." His name is like acid coming out of my mouth. "Do I need to get a lawyer?"

"No." He shakes his head furiously, the wavy black hair I used to love running my fingers through flopping over across his forehead. "Really, don't worry about it. You've been so great, I know we don't need to get them involved, this is just for me so I don't mess things up."

"Okay, thank you." Relief washes over me. The last thing I need is lawyer bills with the kindergarten tuition payments I'll soon be paying.

When we separated, he was a doctor and I was an unemployed single mom. I told my mom a lawyer helped me get everything straightened out, but since Ben and I never got married and I wasn't legally entitled to his money, I couldn't afford a lawyer. And the way my pride was set up, I couldn't admit to my mom that she was right to be worried. So instead, I pretended everything was fine to my parents and was grateful anytime he gave me money or graced Adelaide with his presence.

"Of course. I just want to make things good between us." He pushes his hair off his face, and then he smiles at me.

And not just any smile. Not the one I fell in love with or the one he gave me after I said yes to marrying him. No, it's the smile that came later. The one he gave me when I told him I was pregnant. The one he gave me when I told him it was fine he took an extra shift at the hospital. The one I took comfort in and trusted.

The same one he used while he was cheating on me and lying straight to my face for years.

And I know I need to get a lawyer. Which means I need to call my parents and come clean.

Just when I thought my day couldn't get any better.

FOUR

...

Jude

The best part of being a social influencer is that everyone around you wants to be one too.

I started my brand without even trying. Some random blog posted a picture from my Instagram for an article they were doing on Hollywood's hottest daughters. It was nice that they still considered my mom part of Hollywood. It was shortly after her second season on a cult-following reality show. They posted a picture of us leaving a Pilates class, and even I have to admit that my body looked bangin' in that picture. I was pulling my freshly highlighted hair out of a ponytail, and my smile was that of someone completely oblivious to the destruction life was about to rain down on her. My skin had the glow of a perfect sweat session. I looked amazing.

That night the first clothing line reached out to me. The next day, an online Pilates platform and a nutritional company. And considering I was most definitely not using my theater degree, I took this opportunity for what it was and ran with it.

That was five years ago.

I know being an influencer looks like bullshit captions and filtered pictures. Part of it is. But it's also a lot of work to stay relevant in a field that gets more and more saturated by the day. It's being conscious of everything I post online. It's seeing my life through the lens of my phone camera, projecting that sparkling image to my hundreds of thousands of followers, and never letting them see me falter. Even when my life is in a total tailspin. It's constantly pitching to brands that I'm the person they should invest in. And it's trying to expand my brand so I'm not dependent on some algorithm for my livelihood. That's what my Pilates studio was supposed to do.

Before Asher Thompson took my money and ran with it. Leaving me broke, with a "sister wife" and a five-year-old for roommates. But like I post on the 'gram, c'est la vie and some other inspirational shit.

Even though faking perfection should probably make me feel guilty or like a fraud who doesn't deserve any of the things I have, it doesn't. It does the opposite. It just proves how fucking good I am at my job. And unlike my mom, I'm making money doing this, not sending my entire family into financial ruin to keep up with the Joneses. So tonight, when I post pictures smiling with my best friend at Hudson's gallery opening, my followers will eat it up, just like I knew they would. Because I'm a goddamn professional.

Well, that's if Lauren ever gets here.

I check my phone again.

No missed calls. No text messages. Seven minutes. We're supposed to leave in seven minutes and I have no idea where she is. But unless she stopped by the mall and salon on her way home from Dickhead's house, I know she's going to need at least thirty minutes to get ready.

If she's still even going to come with me.

"Fuck it." I open my Uber app. Lauren was going to drive and I was going to cocktail my night away. Thank goodness it's an open bar, I can't afford a car *and* bar fare.

But just before I confirm my ride, the front door swings open.

"Finally!" I toss my phone on the couch and run across the living room. "Really, Lauren?" I narrow my eyes on the fast-food bag in one hand, then the giant, no doubt *not* diet soda in the other. "I've been waiting for you for an hour while you were gorging on In-N-Out? That's not even on the way home."

"I'm aware." She never drops eye contact as she lifts her (plastic) straw to her mouth and takes a long sip.

I want to lecture her about the empty calories in soda, but I notice her eyes glisten and her lips tremble around the straw. "What did that smug motherfucker do this time? I'll kill him. I've been studying all those murder dramas on CBS. I'm sure I can get away with it, they'll never prove anything." I never liked Ben. There was just something so slimy about him, but I couldn't put my finger on exactly what it was. And you can't tell your best friend to break up with her boyfriend because you hate his face. So I didn't say anything. I waver on my regret. I wish she never had to deal with him, but Addy is literally one of my favorite humans on the planet. Clearly, Lauren's DNA took the lead with her. "And if murder is out, just say the word. I can launch a social media smear campaign that will fucking ruin him."

"I think he's going to try to get custody of Adelaide." Her voice trails off at the end, but not enough that I can't hear. Not enough that I don't want to break something. Like his stupid fucking nose.

"Are you fucking kidding me?" I surprise myself when my words come out as a whisper and not the bloodcurdling scream I was expecting.

"Oh, it gets better." She drops her stuff on the kitchen counter before crossing the room and collapsing on the couch. "He slipped about getting a lawyer. I can't afford a lawyer right now. I mean, you know." She gestures to the sparsely furnished room we're standing in. And in that single movement, the haunted expression on her face, I can feel her desperation. "I didn't know what to do. I just knew I had to get ahead of it before papers showed up on our doorstep and I was left scrambling to play catch-up. I had to do it."

Realization begins to dawn on me. Lauren doesn't just look Ben frustrated. This is more. Much more. She looks ashamed and broken. There's only one person who can make her feel like that. "No." My eyes widen for a split second before I feel the wrinkles form in my forehead and try to school my expression. "You didn't."

"What else was I going to do? This is about Adelaide. I can't have some crap lawyer who doesn't care about us representing me."

"But there had to be some other option." I rack my brain, trying to think of any other alternative. "What about that one girl? Ashley? No, Amy! She's a lawyer, right? Weren't you guys sorority sisters?"

"Ava." Lauren shakes her head. "She hated me and gloated when I got pregnant. She's part of the reason I quit that sorority."

"You quit the sorority?" I didn't even know you could do that. "I thought they are like a gang and the only way out is death."

"I quit forever ago and talked to you about it before I did it." She rolls her eyes and looks at me in a way that makes my insides wither up and die. *Stupid mom glare.* "Can we focus?"

"Sorry. But Ava, she's still a lawyer, maybe she'd help. We're adults now."

"We were technically adults in college too. I don't trust her. She didn't like me. She loved Ben. Why would I think she'd have my and Adelaide's best interest during a custody battle? Plus, I'm pretty sure she's in corporate law, not family." She folds her arms in front of her chest, looking like she's trying to disappear into the couch cushions. "I had no other options."

"But your mom? She's never going to let you live this down." Have I mentioned how much I hate Lauren's mom? Yes? Okay, good.

"Maybe not, but she's one of the best lawyers there is and has connections I need." She starts to pick at her nails, a nervous habit I've tried—unsuccessfully—to kick her of for almost twenty years. "I know she doesn't always show it, but she loves me and she really loves Adelaide. That's all that matters right now."

I hate it when she's right.

I *really* hate it when she's right about her mother.

"All right." I jump off the couch because this shit is depressing and not what I signed up for tonight. "It's time to get you ready."

Her head snaps away from her now chipped nail polish, and she stares at me like I've just grown another head. "Did you hear anything I just told you? I'm not in the mood to go out tonight."

"Yes I heard you. And this is exactly the kind of night that you need to go out." I grab her arm and yank her to her feet. She forgets that even though I'm small, I'm mad fucking strong. Pilates toning strength for the win. "You're going to get dressed up, come out with me, have some free drinks, and forget about all of this for a night."

Dickhead just started committing to overnight visits in the last couple of months. Lauren hasn't had a night out in years. This will be good for her.

"I just don't think—"

"Nope." I cut her off before she can get her excuse out. "You aren't getting out of this. I already told Hudson I was bringing my superhot friend, and he'll be pissed if I show solo. You're coming. You have no choice."

"Fine, but don't complain because I'm a buzzkill and ruin the party for everyone," she whines, but still climbs the stairs with me to her room.

"Not possible. You forget who I am." I open up her closet and try to find something . . . anything . . . that doesn't look like it was sold at Moms-R-Us. "I'm fun enough for both of us. You're going to thank me, trust me."

"Infamous last words."

"*Insta*-famous last words." I toss a wink over my shoulder. "Now go shower and wash all that sadness off of you. Tonight you're not a mom, you're my best friend. And we're going all out."

Lauren lives a life of full responsibility and reality. She's in charge of not only keeping another human alive, but also making sure she's well adjusted and doesn't turn into a serial killer. That's a lot of pressure!

Fortunately for her, I can change that for a night.

It's literally what I do for a living. There's not much I can do for her to make this situation better. Because, let's be honest, it fucking blows, but I can make her forget it for a while. Fake it till you make it.

For one night, I can make her remember what it feels like to be carefree, fun, and young. Maybe I can show her that being a mom doesn't have to change her completely. That she's still allowed to be something other than Addy's mom.

I'm a good Pilates instructor, but I'm a kick-ass friend and drinking partner. And Lauren needs me now more than ever.

She just doesn't know it yet.

FIVE

...

Lauren

From the second Jude found the one miniskirt I owned and forced it on me, I knew this was a bad idea.

I love Jude. She loves me. I know her heart is in the right place, but this is literally my version of hell on earth.

"So, what do you do?" Hudson, Jude's friend who did the art for this event . . . or just hosted it because he likes art on Instagram or something, asks.

"I work at an ob-gyn's office." I don't look at him as I answer, hoping my clear lack of interest is enough to ward him off.

Wrong.

"So you're a doctor? That's hot."

Oh my god.

Please go away!

"No, not a doctor. I just work there." I take a sip of the red wine I've been nursing for the last hour. "I'm an administrator."

This is one of the topics that I hate the most.

I wanted to be a doctor. I had it planned from the time Jessica H.'s mom came to our school for career day and showed us all the pictures of the babies she delivered. I got straight A's and joined student council and played varsity soccer all four years of high school. I aced my ACTs and SATs. I could've gone to any school I wanted. But of course, I had to go to my mom and dad's alma mater. They were so proud. Their only child, doing exactly what she was supposed to do.

Everything was going to plan.

Until Ben.

And look at me now.

Another disappointment. My mom's words from earlier, and really my entire life, bounce around in my head. Always disappointing someone, always proving my mom right.

"Oh, that's cool though." He glances over his shoulder and I think I might finally get some people reprieve. "So do you do Pilates too? Or what's your Instagram brand?"

Who in the world asks that?

I love Jude.

But I think I hate her friends. What's my brand? Right now, my brand is hating everyone almost as much as I hate myself.

"I don't have an Instagram account." At my words, Hudson's entire face falls and it looks like someone just kicked his puppy or, worse, unfollowed him.

"Twitter?"

"No Twitter, I don't do social media." I already judge my life too harshly without comparing it to the seemingly perfect lives of millions of strangers online. Social media is a surefire way for me to fall in a shame spiral.

Hudson's eyebrows furrow as he tries to comprehend someone who doesn't have an online presence. "Oh, so what about Facebook?"

Oookay.

"I don't have social media." I repeat my earlier words . . . just slower.

"But, like . . ." He runs his hands through his scruffy blond hair and pulls on the ends. "How do you keep up with your friends?"

Friends? As in more than one?

"Well, I live with Jude, so we keep up pretty easily. Everyone else?" He doesn't need all the details of my lonely life. "I call them? We text. In a pinch, I can email." Holy shit. This is why people crap on millennials all the time. "We actually talk instead of me just clicking on a heart by their pictures."

"Wow." He shrugs his shoulders, and suddenly the look of confusion has cleared from his face and the interest is back. "That's really cool of you."

I scrunch my eyebrows and purse my lips. Not even Adelaide thinks I'm cool, and she's five with pretty low standards. "Is it? Is it really?"

"Yeah." His gaze drops down my body before leisurely making its way back to my face. "I love that you dedicate your focus and attention to the people you're with."

All right.

Enough of this.

"Yeah, my daughter is pretty demanding." I pull out the one thing I know is guaranteed to scare a self-obsessed twentysomething away. Kids. "She wouldn't deal well with me not giving her one hundred percent of my attention."

"Oh! A daughter! Wow, that's really . . . wow! Reproduction is dope." His eyes widen to almost cartoon size as he takes a giant step back, giving me the space I've been craving since he first walked over. "Well, you have fun tonight. I hope you enjoy the art."

He's gone before I can even say goodbye. But, if nothing else, I can have the phrase *reproduction is dope* made into wall art from Etsy, so I guess the night isn't a total wash.

"Idiot."

"Who's an idiot?" Jude wraps her arms around my waist and lays a wet kiss on my cheek.

"You better not've left lipstick on my face." After the amount of time it took her to perfect the contour on my face, it better last for the rest of the month.

"Who wears lipstick that smudges anymore?" She leans in and I get a nice, strong whiff of vodka.

Whoever said vodka has no scent clearly just drank too much of it.

"How much have you had to drink tonight?"

"Not enough." She takes my hand and guides me to a corner of the gallery filled with sculptures made from recycled materials like straws and water bottles. It's actually pretty cool, but mainly just reminds me to order a collapsible metal straw for my purse and new Tupperware for Adelaide's lunch box. Hopefully she won't throw this set away. "Now, no deflecting. Who's an idiot, and what guy are you bringing home tonight?"

"Hudson is an idiot, and you must have been drinking even more than I thought if you think I'm bringing some random dude home."

"Why not?" Her bottom lip sticks out almost comically. Even when I don't have Adelaide with me, I still deal with a pouty toddler. "I know we agreed on no hookups coming home when Addy's there, but news flash, Mom! She's not home! And anyway, when's the last time you got some?"

Well, crap.

And I thought the doctor talk was my least favorite topic.

I try to pull out of her freakishly strong grip, but it only makes her squeeze me harder. "It doesn't matter. I'm not going to sleep with some rando."

"Who said anything about sleeping?" She makes her eyebrows

dance in the way that never fails to make me laugh. Honestly, I'm surprised they can still do it with the amount of coloring and shaping she does to them.

"You're gross." I shake my head, knowing the only way to get her off me is to flip it back on her. "But you can bring someone home. Who are you looking at?"

"I know when you're deflecting. And you are so deflecting. How long has it been?"

Crap. This is why it's not a good idea to be friends with someone for so long that they know all your defense mechanisms.

"It's been a little while. Okay?"

She hugs me tighter and my lungs start to struggle to get oxygen. "How long is a little while?"

I guess alcohol makes her an expert interrogator. Something I will have to remember when Adelaide is a sneaky teen.

"Geez. Fine!" I whisper-shout, looking around to make sure nobody is streaming our conversation across the internet. "Since Ben."

"BEN!" she shouts, and if there weren't eyes on us before, they're all on us now. "That's, like, two years!"

"Closer to three," I mumble beneath my breath. But by the way her eyebrows fade into her hairline and her eyes try to pop their way into my wineglass, she heard me.

"Three years! You haven't had sex in three years?" Now she's straight-up screaming and I'm positive that everyone within a five-block radius knows the details of my sex life . . . if you can call it that.

"Jude!" I cover her mouth with my hand and then look to all the rude gawkers who can't even pretend to not be interested. "Didn't your parents tell you it's rude to stare? Look at the art. Shoo!"

What can I say? Once a mom, always a mom.

Jude peels my fingers from her mouth, and even though I'm mortified, I can't help but notice she was right. Her lipstick hasn't smudged in the slightest.

"Did you just tell people to shoo?" Her eyes are glassed over in drunk amusement.

"Did you just scream to the world about my dry spell?" I counter.

"Touché." She shrugs but doesn't apologize. Something I will one hundred percent bring up in the morning. "But three years? How? Yeah, you're a mom, but you're still hot."

"I'm not sure that's actually a compliment."

Jude has always had a way with words. Whereas I measure everything that comes out of my mouth and think of the consequences of my every action (minus getting pregnant out of wedlock and dropping out of medical school), she's fast and loose with everything—words and booze. She lives by the mantra "Act now, apologize later." Which is probably why she's so much better at saying sorry than I am.

She brushes off my comment. "Did giving birth break your vagina or something? I read some women have torn to their anus! If that happened, I'll understand. If my vag ripped to my ass, I'd never have sex again."

See! No filter!

"Seriously, Jude?" I feel the heat creep up my cheeks as I hear a few snickers from around us. I'm not sure if I'm more embarrassed or angry. "Can you please drop it?"

"Hudson!" she shouts across the room, waving her arms to summon the man I just got rid of. "Come here!"

Damn it. She's not going to stop. She knows how much I hate this kind of thing, but when Jude wants something, nothing can stand in her way. Not even me.

"Hey, Jude," Hudson sings to the Beatles tune. It's so unoriginal and predictable that I have to fight to not roll my eyes.

"Don't you think Lauren is hot?" She points at me and they both stare at me like I'm one of the pieces of art on display tonight. But not one that is outwardly pretty, one that confuses the masses and draws out everyone's uninformed opinions.

"She's stunning." His tone is serious, not mocking. And I don't know how to feel about it.

I shift beneath his gaze, hating the warmth that's rising inside of me.

I'm raising a beautiful little girl. One who I tell every day that she is smart and powerful and magical. I don't want her to focus on her outer when her inner is what will change the world.

But how can I teach her that? Authentically preach that her power comes from within, when I am practically basking in the praise that this man—one I literally just called an idiot—is showing me?

I feel the tears start to pull at the backs of my eyes, and the mortification that has been slowly rising over the course of the night skyrockets. And so does my temper.

"I think I was right, I shouldn't have come tonight." I look at Jude, who is blissfully unaware of just how uncomfortable she's made me. I put my still-not-empty wineglass on the nearest table and adjust my purse, trying to gain some semblance of self-respect when all I want to do is run out the nearest door.

"Seriously? We were just giving you a compliment!" She's still amused by all of this, and the fact that she can't even seem to acknowledge how she's made me feel, knowing what kind of day I had, is more than infuriating. It's hurtful.

I had Adelaide young, but before that, I was so focused on school I skipped the entire partying scene. Of course Jude and I have gone out for drinks here and there, but I haven't been around her drunk since freshman year of college. And I was drunk with her, so maybe I forgot this kind of behavior.

However, one thing is very clear: I'm not a fan of drunk Jude.

"I know. I'm supposed to be flattered, but I asked you to stop, and you kept going." I maintain strict eye contact, just like I do when I am disciplining Adelaide. I guess parenting books come in handy with boozy friends too. "I'm not having fun, so now I'm leaving. I know you were counting on me to drive, so when you want to leave, text me and I'll order you an Uber."

Not that forty dollars on an Uber is something I'm thrilled about shelling out. But if that's the cost of getting out of here, I'll gladly pay it.

"Lauren," she starts, but—surprisingly—Hudson cuts her off this time.

"I'll drive her home. You don't need to worry."

I look him over. His tone is steady—no slurring, his eyes are open and alert, and he's holding a bottle of water and not a mixed drink like almost everyone else. Which means he made that dope comment sober. Not sure if that makes it better or worse . . .

"If you have so much as one drink, I want her in an Uber." I narrow my eyes and point a very unmanicured nail at him.

I mean, I might not be thrilled with Jude, but she's still my best friend. I will hunt this guy down if she comes home with so much as a scratch.

He salutes me. "Aye, aye, captain."

Thankfully, motherhood is basically disciplining your child while trying not to laugh because you are actually extremely amused at whatever their latest antics are, so I'm able to keep a straight face through this. In fact, I manage to narrow my eyes more.

"Good. My mom is one of the top attorneys in the state of California, maybe the country. If anything happens to her, I will not hesitate to come for you."

"Her mom wouldn't throw water on me if I were on fire, you'll be fine." Jude undermines my entire threat.

"Really? Do you want to die?" And considering I want to strangle her at the moment, I don't know who I need to protect her from.

"Hudson's, like, the best dude ever." She rolls her eyes and takes a sip of the drink she does *not* need. "I'll be fine."

"You better be," I say to her, but look to Hudson, who is staring right back at me with a small smirk on his face. And this time I don't actually want to smack it off him. For the first time, he's not looking at me like he's preparing to go live on whatever platform he's posting on or trying to convince me he is the person he's showing the world. And I think that maybe if he came up to me like this, my night would have been slightly more enjoyable.

Strong maybe.

Oh well. It doesn't matter. I've sworn off anything and everyone in my life that does not benefit Adelaide. So even if Jude and Hudson managed to slip past my first line of defense, my dry spell will not be ending anytime soon. Maybe not until Adelaide is grown and out of the house.

What's thirteen more years anyway?

SIX

...

Jude

You turn twenty-one, and then you die.

I'm not being dramatic. Really, I'm not. But when I drank in high school, I could get pass-out drunk and wake up the next morning ready to run a marathon. Not that I would actually ever run a marathon. Who wants to run twenty-six miles? I don't even want to drive that far. I did run a half once, but that's as far as I'll go. That's beside the point. The point is that drinking without having a hangover was my superpower.

I just didn't realize that power was also called youth. Something that seems to be slowly dwindling away these days. Because now when I drink, I wake up in the morning with a headache that feels like the San Andreas Fault, a mouth drier than the Sahara, and my stomach like that one time my dad took us to Spain and I had bad paella.

Good thing last night was a fucking blast.

Sacrifices and all that shit.

Too bad Lauren flounced. Now that vodka doesn't have its

grip on me, I can maybe see why. But we were having fun and Hudson was totally into her, he told me so as soon as we walked in! I know she's a mom, but Addy wasn't even home and she needs to get some. I mean, three years? *Three!* That's like thirty-six months and . . . fuck . . . a lot of days. Plus, I've never hooked up with Hudson, but the streets talk, and the streets say he knows how to lay it down. It would've been a good sexual wake-up to get her back in the swing of things.

There's a light knock on my door and an even quieter "Jude?"

I'm not sure if Lauren's afraid to wake me up or if she just doesn't really want to talk, but I answer anyway . . . or at least I try to.

"Yeah," I croak out, my tongue sticking to the roof of my mouth.

"Oh, you're awake." She opens the door without waiting for an invitation, not that she's ever needed one. Sunshine floods my room and I instinctively yank the covers over my head.

Fuck hangovers, man.

"Awake-ish," I amend. Damn it. I'm not sure what hates me the most, my abused liver or my throbbing brain.

"Here." She yanks my sunshine shield, aka my duvet, off my head and shoves a bottle of water in one hand and four Advils in the other.

That's my fucking girl. Prescription strength only, bitches.

"You're the fucking best," I mutter before tossing all four pills in my mouth and washing them down with a single gulp of water. Let's just say this isn't my first time at the rodeo.

"Listen." She sits on the edge of my bed and stares at the pile of boxes lining my wall. I really need to finish unpacking, but I don't have the motivation. Lauren, on the other hand, has all of her stuff unpacked, pictures hanging on our walls, and has turned Addy's room into something off a Pinterest board. "Thank you for inviting me out last night. I know I don't get out often, and I really do appreciate you trying to get me out of the house. I . . . I just don't think that's my scene."

Clearly.

Even I was able to piece that together.

"I figured that out around the time you asked the bartender why they filled your wineglass up so high."

"Yeah, I guess you can't take the mom out of me." There's no humor in her voice, and I add my heart to the long list of organs in pain.

"Don't do that. I shouldn't have made a scene, and I really shouldn't have called Hudson back over. It's just, he was so into you and he's an actual, real, decent dude. There aren't many of those out there." They're basically as rare as unicorns. But since Lauren procreated with and almost married Ben, I feel like she already knows this, and I keep that skeptical thought to myself. "And you, more than anyone, deserve a night of someone pleasing you."

"Oh my god." She buries her face in her hands, but I already know her mocha-colored skin is turning pink. "Can we please not talk about sex anymore?"

"Three years!" I remind her of a fact she's well aware of. "Please tell me you at least have a sex toy in your room some-where."

"You know how nosy Adelaide is." She shrugs her shoulders, and even though it's just us having this conversation, she still looks like she wants to die. "If I had one, she'd find it. Plus, she still sneaks into my room and sleeps with me most nights. I wouldn't even have the time or privacy to do it."

My jaw falls to the floor and I just stare at her, blinking rapidly for I don't even know how long.

"You mean to tell me you haven't had an orgasm, self or man-made, in three years?"

"I mean, I've had a few. But I had a cheating fiancé and then I was single, scorned, and had a toddler. What do you expect?"

Oh dear lord almighty. No wonder my poor friend is so uptight.

"You poor, poor woman." I climb out of my covers and crawl across my bed to hug her. "I mean, we're basically already sister wives."

Her eyes go wide and she starts to pull away.

"Not that!" I push her away when I realize what she's thinking. "I meant"—I try to force out the words through my laughter—"I was going to order you some toys!"

We're doubled over on my bed laughing when my phone rings. And not just any ringtone, the obnoxious one. The one I set for the even more obnoxious person on the other end.

My laughter ends abruptly.

"Fuck," I whisper. Thankfully Lauren is still laughing and doesn't hear me. "Hold on." I gesture to Lauren to be quiet before sliding my finger across the screen. "Hey, Mom."

"Oh good, you answered for once," she greets, and it's almost laughable.

If there's one person I always answer for, it's Juliette Andrews.

And not because I actually want to talk to her.

God no.

Whenever her name appears on my screen, my stomach falls to my feet and tension weaves its way through my veins until I feel almost paralyzed with anxiety.

"Anyway," she continues, and my nerves threaten to claw out my insides as I wait to hear what she needs this time. "I'm driving to your house. I know you're probably still in bed, so get up and dressed. I don't want to wait."

"You're driving over? Now?" I look at Lauren, and the horror

I'm feeling is not at all reflected in my best friend. Instead, she's all smiles and anticipation and joy.

If she only knew.

"Yes." I can almost hear my mom's eyes rolling through the phone, like I'm the one out of line and not her for just casually dropping by on a Sunday. "And please, don't wear workout clothes today. We're going to brunch, not the gym."

Then my phone beeps in my ear, signaling the end of the conversation.

"Your mom's coming over?" Lauren asks, even though she already knows the answer.

"We're going to brunch." I don't look at her as I sign into my bank account and check my balance, trying to think of how many more Instagram posts I can commit to. I know who'll be paying for unlimited mimosas . . . and it won't be the person who insisted on brunch.

"That'll be fun. Plus, waffles and bacon make everything better, especially hangovers."

Lauren was with my family any chance her mom let her out of the house when we were kids. She loves my mom. Which, who can blame her? My mom was a blast. She shot to fame on a soap opera in the eighties, the golden era of soaps. But that didn't mean she ever neglected being a mom. She was the best mom ever.

Was.

Then my dad died.

And somehow, so did my mom. She became a stranger.

But nobody knows that. Not even Lauren.

"Don't forget the mimosas!" I try to hide my dread under fake peppiness as I peel the covers off me and slip out of bed. "You know they make them with vodka now? Hair of the dog, baby!"

Even though I don't look at her as I make my way to the bathroom, I can still feel her concerned gaze burning a hole through my back.

I turn the lock on the door and flip on the harsh bathroom lights. I can't even be bothered to hide my flinch when I see my reflection in the mirror.

Besides the mascara smudges surrounding my eyes because I was too drunk to be worried about my skin-care routine, they're also bloodshot and swollen. But that's not from last night. That's from the built-up tears I've been fighting since I saw my mom's name on my phone.

The sundress I was too unbothered to take off last night billows to the floor at my ankles along with my lacy underwear, and I step into the shower. I crank the handle all the way to hot and stand beneath the showerhead, bracing for what's coming.

The freezing water is a shock to my system, but I love it.

I *need* it.

My teeth chatter as the water transforms into needles threading through my skin, trying to sew on a costume of a daughter who loves her mom.

Then the water starts to heat and I brace.

When the scalding water attacks my skin, I welcome it. I stare at my skin, watching as it becomes so red, I wonder if I'll start bleeding soon. I don't turn down the heat until my skin becomes almost numb to it. It's what I was waiting for. The reminder that it doesn't matter where the pain comes from, eventually, I'll become numb.

Even to my mom.

Scratch that.

Especially to my mom.

SEVEN

...

Jude

For someone with so many financial troubles, Juliette Andrews sure does portray an image of wealth. From the red bottoms on her feet, to the emblem on her red convertible, to the fresh highlights in her hair that probably could've paid for the water bill I covered last month.

But fake it until you make it, I guess.

Or, more accurately, fake it until you make it *again*, or cry to your daughter until she covers all of your expenses for you . . . *again*.

"Here." My mom passes a tube of lip gloss across the table. "Put this on."

"Really, Mom?" My eyelid starts to twitch. Not constantly rolling my eyes when I'm near my mom is an ocular workout. But it's better than the hair I was pulling out when all of this started. "We're eating. It's going to come off."

"It already did come off, which is why you need more." She

shoves the tube into my hand. "And if you would've listened when I told you to put on lipstick, we wouldn't be having this conversation now, would we?"

That's when it clicks.

The smile frozen on her face. The dress code. Ordering the smallest plate possible and still not taking a bite. Her manager covering our bill. The request for a patio seat even though it's cloudy and looks like it might rain.

I groan and snatch the sunglasses out of my purse. "Please tell me you didn't call the paparazzi again."

"My publicist and I are trying to shop around a story line for the Housewives. There needs to be interest in me." She takes a dainty sip of her mimosa. "With all of the public interest you've created for yourself, us being together looks even better for me."

Because why else would my mom want to spend time with her daughter?

"No. We're not doing this again." Like my mom, I also ordered a mimosa. And like I told Lauren I would, I ordered the one that had champagne *and* vodka. But unlike my mom, I don't take a sip, I gulp that bitch.

I don't even care who judges me. If anyone was forced to sit and be photographed with the ghost of their mom, they'd need liquid courage too.

"It's not just for me, think of how wonderful it will be for you." She keeps going, like *no* is a word she's never heard before and she hasn't even the slightest inkling what it could mean. But really, I just know that her publicist gave her a speech to convince me, and my mom is nothing if not a dedicated actress. "The producers loved it when you were on the show. They want to surprise the viewers by bringing back a former castmate."

"You know how I feel about that. I don't want to be on a reality show."

"You already live your life in front of a camera, what's one more? Plus, I really need this, Ju-ju." She takes off her sunglasses as she says the nickname I used to love so much. The champagne bubbles change to rocks and settle in my gut. The familiarity of this conversation causes dread to wrap its claws around my throat. "All I want is some semblance of normalcy again. I want to be able to treat you to brunch and for you to want to spend time with me again. I know I've been different since your dad died, but I need you to stick by my side. I can't do this if I'm alone. And if I get this show, I know things will get better, our relationship will get back to what it used to be."

What it used to be . . . before Dad died. It's been three years, but most days it feels like yesterday and also a century ago.

He had a stroke. Apparently his blood pressure had been out of control. They call it the silent killer. And silent it was.

Silent *he* was.

Silent about being sick. Silent about my mom spiraling out of control. Silent about refinancing my childhood home to keep up with her spending.

At first, after he died, I knew my mom was going to be different. Her best friend, the love of her life, died. Of course that shit was going to affect her. But then, it kept getting worse. There'd be a little ray of sunshine, a glimmer of hope that she'd return to be the mom I grew up with, but then it would vanish before I even got the chance to enjoy it.

I don't think she'll change anymore.

But I also don't say no to her anymore either.

The first time I gathered up the strength to say no—after about ten sessions with my therapist—she hung up on me and sent me a text message claiming I was no longer her daughter.

The second time, she called to tell me about the pills she'd taken and to say goodbye.

There hasn't been a third, and it doesn't look like there will be anytime soon.

"Fine." Heavy resignation settles over me. I'm her daughter, this responsibility—burden—is mine to carry. "I'll do it."

Her lips curl into the first genuine smile I've seen from her in months, and like a traitor, hope begins to bloom inside of me.

"I knew you wouldn't give up on me." She taps her champagne glass against mine. "This is it, I know it is. Everything will be back to normal."

I don't say that things will never be back to normal, that Dad is never coming back. Because that feels like something a child would say. And even though I am her child, I stopped getting to act like one around her in the funeral home when she had a meltdown and I was forced to make all of the arrangements on my own.

"What do I need to do?"

"That's the best part of this plan, you don't need to do anything. Jonathon found a few new sponsors for you. All you have to do is keep up with the content you're already posting, but have more with us together." She's talking like this is no big deal, but I was agreeing to this hoping to get her off my back, not being forced to spend more time with her. "They want us to be the mother-daughter pair that everyone wants to be. Wholesome and relatable . . . yet with an air of unattainability."

This makes literally no sense. Thankfully, as I drain the last bits of my mimosa, the waitress walks by and nods when I point to my empty glass. "Only a splash of orange juice this time."

"Splash of OJ, you got it." She smiles as she grabs my glass from the table and heads back inside.

That's what I call sisterhood and true allyship.

"Relatable and unattainable, got it." It makes even less sense when I say it, but it's easiest to just nod my head and agree when it comes to Mom.

"Exactly." Her frozen forehead struggles to show her excitement, but the gleam in her eyes says it all. "Angelica's daughters are already portrayed on the show as party girls, it's really important we're the opposite of that. They need the contrast."

Angelica Sanders is a full-blown movie star. She is married to one of the top producers in the industry and is one of the original cast members on the show. For some reason, my mom thinks she's competition . . . which is ridiculous on so many levels that I can't even count that high. I'll never understand why women make it hard for other women. I feel like Addy would have the perfect thing to say in this situation. I'll grab those frosted animal cookies with sprinkles on them on my way home and talk it out with her later.

"I'm living with a five-year-old." I shove a bite of my chicken sandwich—no bun—into my mouth. "It's not like I'm going to be throwing ragers anytime soon."

"I'll tell Jonathon you're on board and he'll set up the meetings with your new sponsors." She puts her sunglasses back on and reaches across the table to hold my hand. "I know you've had a hard time since Dad died and I've been difficult to deal with. These sponsors will help us both financially; I at least owe you that much. This is me trying. I hope you see that."

I guess this is just another character to play. I always wanted to be an actress. Say what you want about soap operas, but I grew up around them. The talent of the writers and the actors and really everyone involved was just beyond. The amount of content they produce and deliver is amazing. Reading scripts with my mom, watching her when I'd have a day off school and got to go to work with her are still some of my favorite childhood memories. It was how I grew to love the craft of acting. So when I went to college, I didn't choose to be a premed student like my brilliant best friend, I chose theater. And I was good. Great, even. I started to audition for theater productions, and the directors were loving me. I could taste my dreams, they were so close.

And then my mom joined a reality show.

Even though the drama is slightly manufactured—I mean, obviously there's going to be drama when you force a group of people to spend extended amounts of time together—it's still their real lives. And my mom was my best friend, so of course there were times when I filmed with her. I just didn't realize that by doing so, I was taking my career that hadn't even started and flushing it down the toilet.

The directors I had started fostering relationships with canceled auditions. I was told I wasn't needed for callbacks I'd already booked. Everything I'd been working for vanished. How could anyone take me seriously when the only place they knew me from was the episode of *Hollywood Housewives* where Jacinda Thomas pulls off Veronica Watson's wig and throws it out the window?

But I guess without that, I wouldn't have my social media platform. Maybe I would've failed miserably at acting and this was the universe's way of guiding me elsewhere. I guess if there's one bright spot to what I'm sure will unravel into a mess of unknown proportions, it's that I could really use some extra income. And considering *Hollywood Housewives* is what got me into this mess to begin with, it feels pretty full circle.

"I know you're trying." I squeeze her hand, hoping she won't notice how flat my voice is or catch the uninterested expression I know is written across my face.

"Good. So." She pulls her hand away from me and picks up her fork, pushing around the salad on her plate without actually taking a bite. Her Emmy-winning smile is back on her face, the one that's for the onlookers, not her daughter, as I see the paparazzi flashes through her sunglass lenses. "What do you have planned for the rest of the day?"

"Lauren was going to get Addy, we'll probably just make some dinner and watch whatever Disney movie Addy is infatuated with this week." Just the mention of them eases some of the tension in my shoulders. It's almost impossible to stay upset around that little girl. Lauren was so worried I would hate living with them, but they're the only thing I know I can depend on anymore.

"That's nice." She lifts her fork for the first time since her food arrived and takes a bite of the dry lettuce. "Tell Lauren I said hi. You guys should bring Addy over to swim one day."

"That would be fun, I'll tell them."

That's a lie.

As much as I'm sure Addy would love to take her mermaid moves from the bathtub to my mom's pool, it's not an invitation I want to extend. I haven't told Lauren about any of the things happening with my mom. And, unlike my mom, Lauren is super sensitive to the people around her. One afternoon in my childhood home and she'd be relentless about figuring out what's going on between us.

I'm honestly not sure why I haven't told her. I don't know if I'm protecting her, me, or my mom. Maybe it's all three? Lauren has enough on her plate to worry about without me adding my mom drama to it. My mom would be mortified if other people knew about all of her struggles. I know that's not on me, but for some reason, it feels like it's my job to keep her secrets.

Me? Well, I'm not sure I could look anyone in the eye if they knew how I felt about my own mom. *You only have one mom*, they'd say. They'd tell me about all the sacrifices she made for me. And still, at the end of the day, my skin would still crawl with resentment. And what does that say about me?

"By the way." Mom's voice drops to a whisper, the guards I just dropped shooting right back into place. "You know I hate to ask you this, but is there any way I could borrow a couple hundred dollars? I'll pay you back. This is the last time. I promise."

This isn't the first time I've heard that promise, and I can guarantee it won't be the last.

"Sure." I pull my bottom lip between my teeth and focus on the french fries I haven't touched on my plate to ignore the stabbing ache in my chest.

Just once—once!—I want my mom to ask to see me without having any ulterior motives for it. I know I gave up hope a long time ago, so why does it still hurt so fucking bad?

Our waitress chooses that moment to come back with my freshly poured, very pale mimosa. Goddess. "Can I get you ladies anything else?"

My mom smiles at her like they're old friends. "Just the check, please."

I guess because she's gotten everything out of me that she needed, she's ready to go.

Figures.

At least I didn't have to pay for brunch today, and on that note . . . "You know what? Why not bring one more of these, please."

My mom's fake smile falters for a second, as if she's not only been counting my drinks (three) but has something to say about it. Thankfully, before she follows through, she must remember how many scenes she filmed brunching and think it will be good for appearances, so she turns to our waitress and says instead, "I'll take one more as well."

Mimosas pass the wholesome image test.

Good to know. I have a feeling I'll be needing many more cocktails as this mother-daughter bonding progresses.

EIGHT

...

Lauren

I don't know how it happened, but somehow, Wednesdays have turned into my favorite day of the week. I get off work early, do a Target run to grab Adelaide a snack before I pick her up from day care, and then we head to her favorite activity.

"No, Auntie Jude!" Adelaide's giggles fill the living room so much that even though I still need to hang up about a dozen more pictures on our "gallery wall," it feels like the homiest room in the entire world. "That's not how you do a cartwheel. Watch me."

We got home from gymnastics practice an hour ago, but Adelaide's still prancing around in the rainbow-covered leotard I got her for Christmas. My parents, who never so much as let me jump in our house growing up, gave Adelaide a gymnastic mat she insisted on being the focal point in the living room. It's her most prized possession and she somersaults and cartwheels on that thing all day long.

Jude seems to like it too.

"See? See how I kept my legs straight like this?" Adelaide lifts her arms over her head in example, just as her gymnastics instructor does. "You had noodle legs like this." She flops her arms around in an almost insulting manner. Jude's form wasn't *that* bad.

"Oh, I see." Jude nods as she watches Adelaide intently, like she's really focused on perfecting her cartwheel form. "So like this?"

She walks to the mat, strikes a pose with her arms raised in the air, and takes a deep breath before executing a perfect cartwheel.

"You did it! You did it!" Adelaide jumps across the mat and leaps onto Jude, sending them both tumbling to the ground.

This time, Jude's laughter echoes alongside Adelaide's throughout the small space. And relief washes over me.

I can't exactly put my finger on it, but something is off with her. I know Saturday night was weird, but we talked about it and she seemed fine. Then she came home from brunch with her mom, and not only was she tipsy . . . again, but she had this dead expression behind her eyes and a hollowness to her laugh.

But what can I say? Dead eyes isn't exactly solid proof . . . not to mention, a little rude.

At least now her laughter is full and real. Adelaide can do that though. I know I'm her mom and maybe a little biased, but she is pure magic. You can't be around her and not love every single piece of her. She even softened my mom. And if that's not magic, then I don't know what is.

"All right, Olympians, dinner's ready." I carry the cauliflower-crust pizza with marinara sauce I've blended zucchini and spinach into to the table before putting giant slices on each of our plates. Plates that have unicorns on them. Needless to say, Adelaide set the table tonight.

"Addy isn't an Olympian," Jude corrects me as she pulls out her chair. "She's the president, remember?"

"I can be an Olympian too. I'm good at a lot of things." Adelaide climbs into her chair, ticking off her fingers one by one as

MOM JEANS AND OTHER MISTAKES

she lists all the things she's amazing at. "Gymnastics, drawing, riding my bike, telling stories, leadership . . . stuff like that." She shrugs before picking up her pizza and taking a monster bite.

At least I know confidence isn't something she struggles with.

"Leadership?" Jude's eyes crinkle at the sides before she digs into her pizza. "Tell me about your leadership skills."

"You know," Adelaide starts, but I cut her off.

"No talking with food in your mouth."

I used to hate eating dinner with my family. They were so strict about absolutely everything. From the way we would cut our food to the subjects we could talk about. And I don't want that for Adelaide. I love that we laugh at the table and talk about whatever comes to mind. But I still have to enforce basic table manners. Mom life and all that stuff.

As soon as Adelaide swallows her food, she turns to me and opens her mouth wide as proof before launching back into her conversation.

"Mom says I have good leadership skills. 'Cause, like, when we go to the park, I find new friends and then find a game that we can all play together. Or at school, when Josie was getting pushed by Nolan, I told him to stop, and when he didn't, I told the teacher. And when the teacher told me that Nolan probably just liked Josie, I told her she was wrong. And that being mean to someone isn't how you show a friend you like them."

I had to email the teacher after that second incident.

I also took Adelaide for ice cream.

I feel like I'm failing at this parenting thing about ninety-nine percent of the time, but in moments like that, I know I'm doing something right.

"Damn, girl. You're right, you do have mad leadership skills."

"Ooooh!" Adelaide turns wide brown eyes to me. "Auntie Jude said *damn*!"

Jude throws a hand over her mouth as pink tinges her cheeks. "Sorry!"

"Mommy, what does *damn* mean?" Adelaide looks innocent, but I already know her game.

"Stop trying to figure out ways to keep saying the word. It's a grown-up word, that's all you need to know."

Also, I'm not sure I know what the actual definition of *damn* is. So I couldn't answer her question anyway.

"Fine." She pouts before taking another bite of pizza.

The rest of dinner flies by in a flurry of hand gestures and giggles. Eventually, I stop asking Adelaide to chew with her mouth closed and just let myself live in the moment, listening to my girl as she fills us in on all the latest tales from day care. Jude tells us about the photo shoot she had today and how the photographer was a woman who, like Adelaide, had phenomenal leadership skills. Then I tell them about the patient whose water broke all over the waiting room as I was checking her in. Adelaide finds it hysterical . . . Jude goes green at the word *fluids*.

Jude stands up and reaches for the plates when the entire cauliflower-crust pizza has disappeared. "I got the dishes."

I was a stay-at-home mom when I lived with Ben, and all of the household duties fell on me. I mean, I guess it was technically my job. But I don't think I'll ever forget how tired I was after Adelaide was born. It was a down-to-the-bone, crying-literal-tears tired. If he had taken even just one thing off my plate, it would've made a huge difference.

Which is why I don't take having Jude around for granted. "Are you sure?"

"Of course, you did the cooking." She waves me off, not understanding what a big deal this is for me. "I hate cooking. Which, and don't shut this down immediately—"

"Well, when you start it like that." I roll my eyes. Subtlety has never been Jude's strong point.

"I think you should start a mom blog." I open my mouth to say no, but she talks over me. "Oh! No! You should do a podcast! Just think about it! You'd be great at it and you have such a unique perspective. Plus, I know people who can help you out. It might be a fun way to get some extra income."

If a status update is too much for me, in what universe would I want to blog? And podcasting? Give me a break. Nobody wants to listen to me talk.

On the other hand . . . the extra income would be amazing, and she's made quite a name in the influencer world. So maybe? "I'll think about it."

"I know you are humoring me right now, but I'm serious. Just don't shut the idea all the way down yet."

"Fine," I grumble. I can't say no to Jude. Also, she's a nagger and I can't listen to her whine about this all night long. But, and I will never say this out loud, it is nice to finally live with someone who actually believes in me.

Growing up, I always felt like my mom was waiting for me to fail . . . which, even though she loves Adelaide, she never misses an opportunity to talk about the student loans they paid for no reason. And Ben . . . well, I don't think Ben expected anything out of me.

I have a more balanced home life with a roommate than I did with the man I was going to marry. I never had a partnership with Ben. Not ever. It was Ben's world, and he thought I was just lucky to be along for the ride. He didn't owe me anything and I owed him everything.

Never. Again.

"Sister girl." I interrupt Adelaide's latest floor routine before all of her tumbling results in the reappearance of her dinner all over the floor. "Ready for a bath?"

She spins around and plants her hands on her little hips. "Do we have bubbles?"

"Even better." We ran out of bubbles right after we moved in, and you would've thought I was trying to bathe her in a vat of acid. But I grabbed something extra for her today. "Bath bombs."

"*Yay!*" She takes off in a sprint up the stairs, peeling off her leotard as she goes.

"Go potty and I'll be up to start the bath in a second," I shout after her. I haven't really had a chance to be alone with Jude. She's here when I'm at work, we eat dinner together, but then she's usually gone by the time I get Adelaide to bed, doing some kind of influencer event.

"Okay, but hurry." Her little voice bounces off the walls, and not for the first time, I marvel at how fast she's growing.

"Being a mom is a trip. You just casually tell her to go potty and she listens. I can't imagine having to remind another human to use the bathroom." Jude's arms are covered in bubbles as she rinses off the plates before loading the dishwasher. "Also, I wish I got as excited for anything as she does for bath bombs."

"Tell me about it. But if I don't remind her to go before she gets in, she'll have to go in the middle of the bath, and then I have to clean the water from all over the bathroom . . . it's a thing." I realize I'm rambling about the bathroom . . . which could also be the name of the podcast Jude wants me to start. I take a deep breath, trying to figure out a way to broach this subject. Jude is fun and laughs, but it's hard for her to get serious sometimes. Just another way we balance each other out. "I just wanted to check in with you."

Her eyebrows scrunch together. "Check in with what? Am I

in trouble? Did Addy tell you that I let her sneak pretzels in her room the other day?"

"Well, no, she didn't. But now that you did, you're in charge when the rodents break in, looking for all her bedroom crumbs." I mean, if Jude knows I'm concerned, she's the master of playing it cool. But she's not getting me off the subject that easy. "I've just been a little worried about you. You've just seemed . . . I don't know? Off or something. If you need to talk, I hope you know I'm here. I feel like I'm always unloading my drama on you, but I want you to know you can still confide in me too. And also, I know living with us is a huge change from what you're used to. If you need space or anything . . . from me or Adelaide, I wouldn't be offended. I know we can be a lot."

Crap.

I'm rambling again. I always ramble.

"No." She turns off the water and dries her hands with the little dishtowels Adelaide made me at her school for Mother's Day last year. "It's not you at all. You know how I went to brunch with my mom?"

I nod my head but stay silent. I have a feeling she needs to get this out without me interrupting.

"Well, it's just—" she starts, but the doorbell ringing cuts her off. We both look at the door, then back to each other. "Are you expecting anyone?"

I almost laugh at that. "You know you're literally my only friend. Are you?"

"Nope . . ." She pauses and grabs her phone, probably seeing if anyone texted or called her. "At least not that I remember."

"I'll get it. If it's one of your friends, do you want me to tell them you're not here?" Considering Jude is in her pajamas and has pizza sauce smeared across her cheek, I'm assuming she won't want company right now.

"Please!" she whisper-shouts before hiding in the kitchen.

I bite back my smile as I pull open the door, fully expecting to see one of her annoyingly attractive friends.

Instead it's a man who is attractive, but if he's one of Jude's friends, I've never met him before.

"Lauren Turner?" the man asks.

"Yes?" My spine stiffens even as my stomach drops.

He nods once before reaching a hand behind his back, and all sorts of terrible, worst-case scenarios run through my mind. If I survive this, I'll start saving for a camera doorbell immediately.

To my relief, when his hand is back in sight, he's only holding an envelope, not a deadly weapon.

"Lauren Turner." He hands me the envelope. "You've been served."

Though in reality the envelope is probably only a few ounces, it feels as though he just placed the weight of the world in my palm. I don't have to look at the papers to know who they're from. I don't have to read them to know they will unequivocally turn my life upside down.

When I played soccer, there was this one time I wasn't paying attention at all. One of my teammates kicked a ball as hard as she could, and because I was inspecting grass, I didn't see it before it hit me. I swear, the soccer ball nailed me directly in the lungs and they were collapsing inside of me. I was dying, I was sure of it. I fell to the ground, trying to inhale as the panic started to out-weigh the physical pain. The burning in my eyes matched that of the lava flowing down my throat as I gasped for air that just would not come.

And it's happening again.

Except this time, nobody touched me.

But the world is crushing me.

I'm suffocating.

Dying.

"Lauren!" Jude runs to me, my panic mirrored in her voice. "What's wrong? Are you hurt?" Her eyes roam my body, no doubt looking for blood.

But I still can't speak. The razor blades in my throat are preventing the words from coming.

So instead, I hold the envelope up for her to see for herself. She snatches it out of my hand without hesitation and tears it open. She scans the letter for a split second before her face turns bright red and all traces of worry disappear, and all that's left is the pure fury I'm too scared to feel.

"Custody papers!" she shouts, and confirms what I already knew. "Just say the word. Just fucking say it, Lauren, and I swear to god I'll kill the motherfucker myself."

I want to reassure her that I'll be fine, but for the first time in my entire life, I'm not sure I will be. Rage and fear like I've never felt before roar between my ears. Even though Jude is standing beside me, her voice sounds miles away.

I turn to face her, my eyes suddenly feeling too large for my face. The pressure building in my head grows with every failed inhale.

"I . . . I . . ." I try to force the words out, but I can't.

Unable to blink, I see the moment the anger flees and concern replaces it. She closes the door and links her fingers with mine, pulling me gently across the room and depositing me on the couch. I don't know how long she's gone before she's back by my side, pressing a glass of water against my lips.

"Take a sip," she says in a hushed tone I'm not sure I've ever heard from her. "We're going to come up with a plan. This feels like a blow and you have every right to feel everything that you are feeling. But I promise you, when this is over, Ben is going to regret it. These papers are irrelevant. You are the strongest, smartest, kindest person I know. This is going to backfire on him, Lauren."

I take the glass from her with trembling hands. Letting her words penetrate the panic clouding my mind, I cautiously allow hope back in. "Do you really think so?"

Jude jokes a lot. She is goofy and silly and almost always hides her emotions behind sarcasm and jokes.

This is not one of those times.

"I fucking know so."

For some reason, the sincerity behind those words coming from the one person in this world I've always been able to count on allows my lungs to fully expand for the first time since that envelope was placed in my palm.

"Mommy!" Adelaide's impatient shout from the top of the stairs filters into the living room. "What's taking so long? I'm ready for my bath bomb!"

I lean back against the couch with my hands on the top of my head, the way my coach instructed me to all those years ago. I focus on the brass light fixture hanging from the dated ceilings and take deep, measured breaths, letting Jude's words play on a loop in my head. I try to anchor myself to what matters most right here and now: Adelaide is with me. I'm her mom. Ben can't change that.

Jude's right. These papers don't matter.

All that matters is Adelaide . . . and her bath bomb.

"Let me do it." Jude pushes off the couch. "I'll give Addy her bath and you just chill down here with a glass of wine."

"I love you so much for offering, but I need to do this." I stand and pull her into a quick hug. "Thank you for talking me down, but if anything is going to keep my head together, it's Adelaide."

"All right, well, I'm down here if you need me."

"Thank you." I squeeze her hand in mine. "And we'll finish our conversation from earlier when Adelaide goes to sleep, okay?"

Jude waves a dismissive hand in front of her face. "No, it's not a big deal at all. Don't worry about me. Right now, we're going to figure out a way to bring Ben down to his pathetic fucking knees. The fucking scumbag. I didn't think I could hate him any more than I already did, but he showed me."

"You're the best." I seriously love her so much. I hate that this happened, but I'm so grateful she was the person with me when it did. "And you're right, Ben just woke up the sleeping giant, and he's going to regret it."

"Yes!" Jude gives me a high five. "I fucking love feisty Lauren!"

I love feisty Lauren too. And it's been too long since I've seen her.

As I make my way across the small living room and up the stairs to my perfect little girl, who I took care of and loved while Ben was off doing whatever the fuck Ben wanted to do, I remind myself that this isn't a surprise. I knew this was coming and I know Ben.

But Ben doesn't know me.

Not anymore.

And the only one of us who is about to be surprised is him. The timid, weak woman who was afraid to cause waves is long gone. I'm a fighter and there is nothing I will fight harder for than my daughter.

So yeah, he's going to fucking learn. Lauren Turner is not going to roll over for him.

Not this time.

NINE

. . .

Lauren

Every time I pull into the driveway at my parents' house, it's hard to remember that for the majority of my life, seeing the bright red door, perfectly manicured hedges, and white siding brought me comfort.

This house is where I skinned my knees and cried until my mom put on a Band-Aid I probably didn't need. I blew out the birthday candles on the homemade birthday cakes my dad insisted on making me every year. I had my first-ever sleepover with Jude. I took pictures on the first day of school and before dances.

But now, it's also the place where I told my parents I was pregnant and my mom stormed away, slamming the door so hard, one of her precious black porcelain figurines shattered across the spotless floors. It's where I came to tell them I was dropping out of med school so Ben could focus on his career. It's where I came crawling back after Ben and I broke up and Adelaide and I had nowhere else to go.

It's been three days since I got the custody papers from Ben. And now it's where I'll go to try to keep my daughter.

Proving, once again, what a giant disappointment I am.

"Nana!" Adelaide nearly comes out of her skin when she sees my mom's head poke through the curtains. "Hurry, Mom! I have to show her my new dance! Nana loves my dances, Auntie Jude."

"I'm glad something brings her joy." Jude flinches when I pinch the back of her arm. "I mean, of course she does!" The extra pep in her voice is a little much, but I'll take it. "Everyone loves your dances."

"Better," I mumble before unbuckling my seat belt and opening my door to go free Adelaide of her five-point harness.

This time when I open the back door, Adelaide has both shoes on and the top buckle of her car seat unsnapped. "Is Papa home too? I made him a song."

I don't have any proof, but I'm pretty sure I'm the least creative person in the entire world. I aced all my math and science classes growing up, but art? I struggled . . . hard. And art tutors aren't a thing, my mom checked. So how I got this child who is rainbows, glitter, and show tunes is beyond me.

"Yup, he's here too. You're going to play with him while Mommy, Auntie Jude, and Nana have a quick meeting, okay?" I push the bottom button of her car seat, which might as well be a launch button with how fast she jumps out.

"Okay, Mommy!" she shouts over her shoulder as she rushes up the walkway to the porch, where my mom is now waiting for her. Her little body barrels into my mom, wrapping her little arms around her legs. "Nana! I missed you! Wanna see my dance?"

"My sweet girl." My mom peels Adelaide's arms from her legs and lifts her up. The severe angles always apparent on my mom's beautiful face soften, and laughter makes her harsh voice almost sound gentle and melodic. "I have to talk with your mom, but as soon as we're done, I'd love to see your dance. Anyway, Papa's got a surprise for you in the backyard."

I don't have to see Adelaide's face to know she has wide eyes and an even wider smile. "Surprises are my favorite."

"Then let's go see what he got you." She takes her eyes away from Adelaide, and just that quickly, every shadow is apparent on her wrinkle-free face as she makes eye contact with me for the first time. Her mouth tightens and she gives me a quick nod before turning on her heel and heading inside, closing the door behind her.

"Holy shit." Jude appears at my side, reminding me that she came along and I'm not the only one who'll cause my mom's jaw to clench today. "Who was that woman? Because it was not the Gloria Turner I know."

"Right? It freaks me out every time I see them together. Adelaide has magic woven into her DNA. Nobody can stay mad around that girl." I reach into the back seat, grabbing my bag with the custody papers in them off the floor. I still haven't read them all the way through. Each time I sit down to do it, my stomach turns and my head spins. Hopefully having my mom and Kim—the lawyer my mom hired—going over them with me, they won't seem as scary.

Hopefully.

Adelaide made the walk to the front door look so easy, but all I feel is dread knowing what's waiting for me inside. "And please, don't try to get my mom all worked up today."

"Me? Work up your mom?" Her eyes widen and she holds a hand to her chest, an affronted caricature. "I would never."

"You would and you do so often. It's just . . ." My hand freezes, hovering above the doorknob. "Just not today, okay? I really need you to have my back in here."

The laughter that's always just beneath the surface with Jude disappears. She grabs my wrist with her long, slender fingers and levels me with a look I haven't seen since I told her about Ben's affair . . . I mean, *affairs* (plural). "I'll always have your back. I'm not sure you understand how much I love you and Addy. There's nothing I wouldn't do for you two"—the mischievous glint returns to her bright blue eyes—"including leaving your mom alone for an afternoon. But all bets are off tomorrow."

"That's all I ask." I shake my head, my eyes rolling without any of the intended irritation behind them.

A little bit of the pressure I always feel when I have to talk to my mom eases from my chest, and I open the door feeling more confident than I did before.

Sure, living with Jude wasn't part of my master plan, but maybe it should've been. Having her on my side is what I needed. She might've been onto something with the whole "sister wife" thing.

. . .

"Full custody?" I'm not sure how many times I've said those words, but they still aren't really registering. "I mean . . . full custody?"

"How is that possible?" Jude takes charge of the conversation I lost control of as soon as our lovely and extremely competent lawyer, Kim, finished reading the custody papers and told me what Ben was asking for. "He wasn't even involved in her life for what? Three years? And even before then, it's not like he helped while they were still together."

"Because there's no paper trail proving otherwise. This is why I asked you if you had a child support agreement in place when you first left him." My mom levels me with a glare that makes me want to shrivel up and die. And even though she's trying her best to remain calm and professional in front of her colleague, I can hear the anger in her voice. She's a hairsbreadth away from losing her temper.

"I just thought that leaving him alone was the best way to go." I bring my hand up to my face and start chewing on my nails before I realize I'm doing it. "I didn't want to force his hand."

"And look where that got you!" my mom snaps. "Child support is *not* only about getting money for your child, it's about legal documentation to protect you down the line. If you would've listened to me, for once, Lauren, this could've been avoided! But instead, you lied to me, again! Now, you have to go to court against your ex, a white doctor. What do you think he's going to do? Because I already know. You're going to be the angry Black woman, the vindictive baby mama who kept his daughter away from him. And you're not going to have any proof that you aren't."

Okay.

I was wrong.

Now I want to shrivel up and die.

Nobody can make me feel as small as my mom does.

I keep chewing on my fingernails, not saying anything as I wait for the burning behind my eyes to subside. I will not cry. I will not prove to her just how weak I am.

"Okay, well." Kim shuffles the papers on her desk and avoids making eye contact with my mom. I'm sure Kim is shooketh to see the always contained Gloria Turner lose it, but if she sticks around long enough, I can guarantee it won't be the last time. My mom doesn't lose her temper often, but when she does, it always seems to be reserved for me. "There's nothing we can do about the past, but what we can focus on are these upcoming months."

My mom closes her eyes and takes a deep breath, visibly trying to regain her composure.

Is this what Adelaide sees when I do it? Because if it is, I really need to find a new calming method.

"You're the expert, Kim." My mom takes a seat in the chair next to me, her voice calm and measured again. It's almost like the outburst never happened. "What strategies have proven most successful in the past?"

"First things first. Any paper trail you have, Lauren? We need it. Old texts, emails, day care bills, bank statements. Anything that can prove Ben was truly absent and unreliable up until very recently."

I don't tell her that I tried to call more than I emailed or texted. I had hoped that hearing my voice or Adelaide's voice would make him more likely to step up.

I'm such a fucking idiot.

"Okay, I can do that." I nod, trying to keep the guilt out of my voice.

Out of the corner of my eye, I see Jude taking notes on her phone. Like she promised, she hasn't done anything to rile my mom up. Actually, I'm not sure she's been silent this long in her entire life.

"Next, we need to think of ways we can prove that you aren't vindictive or angry. You are a loving mom who has done nothing but focus on providing the most loving environment for your daughter. References from your daughter's teachers. Have you been class mom? Do you volunteer frequently? Playdate groups? Anything that we can use to show you in a glowing light."

"I volunteered in Adelaide's classes whenever I had the opportunity, but it was hard to do too much because of work." Even though I moved in with my parents, Los Angeles is still expensive. I couldn't live in the school like some of the stay-at-home moms I know. "I did sign Adelaide up for playgroup with kids from her new school. Maybe her gymnastics teachers could vouch for me? Ben has never even stepped foot in the gym."

Kim taps her clear-coated nails against the table. "That's a good start." She throws a nervous glance at my mom before looking to me with eyes full of sympathy. "I don't want to be alarmist, but your mom isn't wrong. It is going to be easy for Ben to spin things in his favor. I'm not sure a couple of volunteer hours and a gymnastics teacher are going to be enough. We need more. Something that Ben can't control. Something that shows you as the dedicated and loving mom who has sacrificed to provide for her child."

A hush falls over the room as we all contemplate what this means.

Jude's fingers, which have been flying across her screen, suddenly pause. "Umm . . ." She clears her throat. "I think I might have an idea."

My mom mumbles something beneath her breath before speaking for the entire class to hear. "Not now, Jude. This is important."

"Yeah, I know." The words fly out of Jude's mouth before she turns her attention to Kim. She can pretend like my mom's disdain for her doesn't bother her, but Gloria Turner's side-eye is legendary and nobody can escape its wrath, not even the perpetually confident social media influencer Jude Andrews. "I have built a very successful social media platform. I focus on fitness, but I know quite a few mom influencers. I mentioned it to Lauren before, but what about a mom podcast? I can even do it with her and use my contacts to get her in touch with different parenting experts. She can use it to direct the narrative in her favor."

Even though I told Jude I would think about doing it, I had pretty much decided against it. But now, looking at the way Kim's smile is practically taking over her entire face and even my mom looks impressed, I know I'm going to have to give in.

"I love that idea!" Kim practically shouts, her words reverberating off the wainscoted walls. "Mommy influencers are all the rage these days. Having a powerful platform like that behind you could really move things in your favor. But, and this is a very big but, you have to carefully cultivate the image you portray. As easily as it can be used for you, it could be used against you."

"No need to worry about that," I say with false confidence. "If this is what will keep Adelaide with me, it will be the best podcast in the world."

Kim hits the table with both hands. "This is a great start. I'm feeling really good about this."

"Yeah." I ignore my mom's gaze burning a hole into the side of my face and Jude's smug smirk as she taps away on her phone again. "Me too."

This is going to work.

It has to.

TEN

...

Jude

The high from Mrs. Turner having to admit I'm not a complete idiot had me walking on clouds for a solid week. It looked like she sucked on a lemon as she thanked me.

It was fucking glorious.

But you know what they say about being on top. The only place to go is down.

And meeting with my mom and her agent isn't a little slope. No.

It's like a death drop. With fire and explosions and carnage. So much carnage.

"Jude." My mom is using her "professional" voice during the meeting. It's like her regular voice but about five octaves higher, and she enunciates each word so slowly I almost doze off during the three-syllable ones. "What do you think?"

"Think of what?" I haven't been paying attention, but what can I say? I don't want to be here.

"She's such a jokester. Just like her dad." She sounds a little hysterical as she laughs me off and waves a hand at Jonathon. I don't know why she still puts on this act in front of him. He's been her manager for the last three years. Clearly he knows what a fucking disaster we are. "I know you wanted to start your own gym and the noncompete clause with Fit Flow Studios is a little strict. It's just that after what happened last time, we figured you'd be waiting awhile anyway and it wouldn't really matter."

After what happened. Well, I guess that's a nice way to dance around the fact that Asher Thompson stole all of my money and set me back years.

I was finally at the point in my career where my sponsors were lining up and my followers were wanting more than pictures of me doing Pilates. They wanted in and I wanted to give that to them.

I started small. Posting YouTube tutorials, creating classes they could do at home. From those, local studios began reaching out and asking me to guest teach. It was kind of like a pop-up shop. I would announce on the day of the class where and when I would be teaching. Each time, the studios were overwhelmed by the amount of people trying to get into my classes. And every time I'd get rave reviews, not only from the people who took the class but from the studio owners who got an influx of new members signing up.

Then I met Asher.

He was an investor in one of the studios I taught at. He reached out after attending one of my classes. He was so goddamn charming. And what can I say? I am my mother's daughter, I love a compliment. He wasn't bad on the eyes either. He told me how he'd been watching my social media grow and respected the way I was building my brand. I was so thrilled someone noticed the work I was putting in. When he asked me out, I was a goner. He moved in with me a month later.

I was putty in his slimy hands.

"Let's build an empire together," he said as we were lying in bed together one night. That was it. One line and he had me. The very next day, we started planning the first Jude Andrews studio. Because he'd been involved in studios before, he convinced me to let him take charge of the business stuff. He would do the things I hated, finances and legal jargon, and I'd stick with what I loved, branding, aesthetics, and Pilates.

It was perfect.

Until I was the idiot you see in every movie who signs the paperwork without having a lawyer look at it first. We were in love. Why would I need a lawyer?

Well, probably because I basically handed him my entire savings account and gave up any rights to sue once he took off while I was teaching a class only a few weeks later.

Thinking back on it, I'm still not sure if my mom was more upset that I was heartbroken or that I couldn't afford to loan her money for a couple of months.

And even though I'm getting back on my feet, it will take me years to get to the point I was at before Asher took off. Years.

"Fit Flow Studios is fine. They have a lot of locations and I'm good with only working out there for a while. What I don't understand is the contract for the subscription box. The moral clause is ridiculous. No drinking? I'm not doing that. Who cares if I have a cocktail"—*or five*—"when I'm out with friends? I'm of age, this shouldn't be a thing."

"Don't worry about that." Jonathon's patronizing voice gnaws at my nerves. "I talked to them about it. They don't mind you having a drink, they just don't want their brand partners being seen drunk in public. They are a wellness company, after all."

"I'm aware of what they are, Jonathon. I've been working in the fitness and wellness category for years. But if they mean they don't want me drunk in public, the contract should say that."

Jonathon takes the contract in front of me and scribbles out *no drinking* and replaces it with *no public intoxication* before pushing it back to me. "There. Better?"

I think everyone here has forgotten that I didn't want to do this shit in the first place. I could be at home with Lauren and Adelaide watching a *Frozen* marathon and making craft crowns, for fuck's sake! Plus, I saw a link somewhere that paired drinks with Disney movies that I really wanted to try.

I don't even attempt to make my smile look real. "You know what would be better? If you—"

"Okay!" my mom interrupts. "Can you please just sign it, Jude? You know how much I need this. I don't understand why you insist on making things so difficult. Jonathon had the lawyers look over it. I'm your mother! Do you really think I'd lead you into a deal where you're not protected?"

Considering she hasn't acted like my mother in years . . .

"Of course not." I pick up the pen on the table and scribble my signature across the line. I hate that I keep putting myself in these situations. But there's no backing out now unless I want my mom to break into hysterics and ice me out of her life until the next time she needs money. It's not the icing that bothers me. It's the limbo of not knowing when she's going to barge back into my life and how much trouble she'll be in when she makes her grand reappearance. "There. Happy?"

"Very. I have the best daughter in the world." She walks around the table and wraps her bone-thin arms around me. "Isn't she the best daughter, Jonathon?"

"She's a gem." Jonathon's tone could not be drier, but at least now I know I'm not the only one in the room at Juliette Andrews's mercy.

"Oh! And one more teeny-tiny thing," she says, and the hairs on the back of my neck stand up because I know, without a doubt, that this isn't going to be a teeny-tiny thing. "We worked out a deal with *StarGazer* magazine. It's not a big deal, they'll just assign a couple of people to us. All we have to do is make sure they're the only ones we call before we have big events."

She knows how much I hate paparazzi. I'm not famous. This isn't even something I should be dealing with! Not only does it make me look like a desperate hack to call the paps, it's worse to have them assigned to me. It's fucking creepy to have strangers knowing where you live and taking pictures of you.

And now it's not even just me.

Fuck.

Welcome to Juliette Andrews ruining the only good thing I have going in my life, episode 758.

I close my eyes and try to gather all my strength to do the one thing I never do.

"No."

Her arms go stiff around me before she drops them and uncurls her spine. "What?"

"No, Mom." I repeat the word I shouldn't dare utter to her. "I won't get drunk. I'll take Pilates classes with you at Fit Flow every week. I'll start taking whatever vitamins you want and spamming my followers with them, but I can't do the paparazzi thing. That's my line in the sand."

"I . . . I don't understand." Her voice begins to wobble as her eyes gloss over with the crocodile tears only a soap actress could conjure up so fast. "You know that paparazzi are part of the deal. I can't get back on *Hollywood Housewives* without them."

"And you should do paparazzi, I'm not stopping you. But I live with Lauren and Addy and they aren't signing up for this. They have enough going on without strange men standing outside of our house taking pictures of them."

"They won't be taking pictures of them." She swipes away the stray tear rolling down her cheek. "You know I would never put Lauren or Addy in danger. I love them."

I'm sure my mom does love them. But the way my mom loves now is so convoluted and dysfunctional. She's so caught up in her own hurt that she doesn't register the pain she inflicts on others. On me.

"I know you wouldn't, it's just that we're still adjusting to living together and it's going really well. I don't want anything to mess with it. Especially with Lauren having to deal with her ex." I don't really understand why I have to explain not wanting strangers stationed at my house or why I'm using my gentle voice to do it, but somehow I always end up here with my mom. "Things are just very delicate right now."

The quiet, pretty crying she was doing moments ago is a thing of the past. Her face crumples and she collapses into a chair and begins to sob. "And I'm just a burden. I'm always such a burden. I don't even know why you bother with me anymore. Even when I try to make things right, I still ruin everything for you."

"You know that's not true, Mom. You're not a burden." I've seen her cry on demand hundred of times. Logically I know this is too big a reaction for what's happening, but that doesn't stop the guilt from infiltrating every cell in my body. "I guess as long as they promise only to get shots of me and not to get too close to the house, it'll be okay."

She sniffles, slowly unfolding in the chair. "Are . . . are you sure?"

Mascara stains run down her face, and her nose is bright red. She looks as awful as I feel.

"Yeah, I'm sure it will be fine. I'll run it by Lauren and if she has any questions, I'll give her Jonathon's number and she can ask him all of her questions." I look at Jonathon just in time to see him roll his eyes. He only gets paid if my mom gets paid, so technically he owes me for all of this. Which reminds me. "Hey, Jonathon. Actually, since I have you here and we're talking about Lauren, we're starting a podcast together. Since you're so good at finding sponsors, could you keep an eye out for good ones for a mommy-type show? I mean, if she's going to get pulled into all of this, it really is the least we could do."

"You and Lauren are finally doing a project together? I love that so much! Of course he can help!" My mom volunteers Jonathon just like I knew she would. "He's the best at that kind of thing. Right, Johnny?"

His head snaps to my mom, and color rises up his freshly shaved cheeks. "Um, yeah, sure. That shouldn't be a problem."

He looks pissed and it brings me so much joy. Just another brick in my pathway to hell. *Not so fun to fall victim to Juliette Andrews, is it, bud? Ha!*

"My mom's right about you, you really are the best . . . Johnny."

My mom isn't watching, so she misses his glare. I bask in it. If I have to suffer through all of this, it's only fair that someone joins me. I know I would normally post about misery loving company and how we should rise above. But I'll save that for tomorrow's Instagram.

Today, petty reigns supreme.

"I'm going to head out and get all of this paperwork faxed over, but I'll give you an update soon." He stacks up all the paperwork and puts it in his briefcase. I stand up with him, ready to get the hell out of here. That Disney cocktail is calling my name.

"Ju-ju." My mom's hand on my arm stops me, but she doesn't say anything else until she waves her farewell to Jonathon. "You know I hate to bother you, especially when you're already doing so much for me. And I wouldn't ask if I had any other choice."

Of course.

Because agreeing to let paparazzi infiltrate my life wasn't enough for her. I don't know why I assumed I was free and clear from an extra favor today.

"What do you need, Mom?" Any sympathy I had during her crying outburst fizzles away with the heat of anger that constantly lingers just beneath my skin.

"It's just my phone bill, so not too much. And I promise I'll pay you back."

"I know you will." She won't. "Just text me with the amount and I'll figure it out." Somehow.

Her smile is real as she wraps me in a tight hug. "How'd I get so lucky?"

And how the hell do I get out of this?

ELEVEN

. . .

Lauren

"I feel like I need a cocktail."

I don't know why I'm so anxious about starting this podcast with Jude. It's just a podcast. It's not like anyone will see me, and there's a good chance nobody will even listen. I mean, why in the world would anyone want to listen to me, a bona fide hot mess who's not only a med school dropout but also a single mom in the midst of a custody battle, and Jude—not a parent at all, also a bona fide hot mess—for parenting and life advice?

"You know I'm always down for a cocktail, but you don't need one." Jude sits on the couch, watching me with more than a little amusement as I pace back and forth across the living room. "We aren't recording, today is just a brainstorm session. We'll get everything in order, a name, website, content calendar, brainstorm ideas, that kind of stuff. Then we'll figure out days when to batch all of our content so we don't fall behind."

"I only understood like twenty percent of what you just said.

What's a content calendar? What does batching mean? And how do you know so much about podcasts?"

She shrugs and takes a sip of the giant water bottle she always has close by. Besides booze, the only other thing she chugs is water. "It's just a different medium than my website and socials. I don't know the technical things, but the organizational stuff that goes into it is the same. The content calendar will be our plan for the next two or three months. We can plan monthly themes like back to school or nutrition and stuff like that. We'll list the dates we'll release a new podcast. We can do it as frequently or spread out as you want, but I think once a week is the sweet spot. Then we'll pick a day to batch our content. Once a month, we'll schedule back-to-back interviews and get them all done in one day. That way we won't ever feel rushed to create a new podcast. It'll keep us organized and our stress minimal."

"Holy crap." I give our rug a break and sit next to Jude. "I mean, I knew you were killing it with your influencer gig, but I didn't know how much went into it. You're, like, really good at this."

She turns to face me, tucking her legs crisscross-applesauce-style. Something I haven't been able to do comfortably since Adelaide wrecked my pelvis and hips during pregnancy. "If I wasn't good at this, there's no way I would've brought the idea up to your mom and Kim. Kim thinking I'm an idiot is one thing, but I would never give your mom that kind of satisfaction."

"Okay. No, you're right." I know this. Even without proving my mom wrong, Jude would never get me in over my head and leave me hanging. "I think I'm just nervous to put myself out there. You heard Kim, this could be great or terrible. Ben was always telling me what a know-it-all I was with Adelaide. What if I come across as condescending and people hate me?"

"Fuck Ben. We don't take his opinion into consideration because it's trash, just like him." Her cheeks go red like they always do when Ben is mentioned. "Speaking of the jackass, don't you all have a meeting with your lawyers or something?"

"Yeah, September fourteenth." A month and a half away. The date is burned into my mind. Every time I close my eyes, it lights up like a giant billboard. I just hope the light is more of a spotlight and not the headlights of a train getting ready to plow me down. "I want to say I'm hopeful we'll get things worked out, but I know Ben. He's never been told no, and I'm not giving him full custody, so we'll see how it goes. Do you think we'll be able to have the podcast running before then?"

"I think we can get the first one posted by the first week of September. That's what? A month away? I'll ask my podcast person when they get here just to be sure. Which"—she grabs her phone off the coffee table and looks at the time—"should be any minute."

My nerves start to flutter back to life. "Who's coming again?"

Jude starts to fidget with her phone and avoids looking at me. "You'll see."

Before this very moment, I thought Jude didn't tell me who she asked to help us because I wouldn't know who they were even if she gave me a name. But now? Now I know she's doing something sneaky.

"Jude Elizabeth Andrews." I stand up and put my hands on my hips. If she thought I'd given her my mom glare before, she had no idea. "What are you up to?"

"Me? Whatever do you mean?" She's laughing at me. My mom stance and glare didn't even affect her! This is worse than I thought.

"Oh no. What did you—"

Unfortunately for me I'm cut off by our doorbell. Thanks to Jude, the gentle fluttering of butterflies in my stomach has transformed to freaking fighter jets . . . and I'm pretty sure one just knocked out my kidney.

Jude jumps off the couch and skips—*skips!*—to the front door.

"Ooooh! I wonder who that could be?" She pulls open the door without looking through the peephole. It would serve her right if it's a missionary trying to save her godforsaken soul. But it's not. "Hudson! I'm so glad you could make it." She grabs his hand and pulls him into the house without waiting for a response. "Lauren, look who it is! It's Hudson. You remember Hudson, don't you?"

The guy she tried to get me to sleep with after announcing my dry spell to the entire world? How could I forget?

"From the gallery, right?" I try to play it cool, but after pretty much only socializing with other moms and small humans for the last five years, my ability to hold a conversation with other adult humans is pretty much nil. Another thing the baby books don't warn you about.

"Yeah, you threatened to have your mom put me in jail." He smiles, and I don't know if it's from fondness of the memory or the cringe I'm unable to hide.

"So!" I clap my hands and run to the kitchen. "Do you want anything to drink before we get started? We have . . ." I pull open the fridge and look inside. "Ummm, we have juice boxes and water. But Jude has booze somewhere."

"Water'd be great, thanks."

I busy myself looking for a glass that doesn't have a cartoon character on it while Jude brings Hudson into the living room. I vaguely hear them talking about what the plan is for today as I procrastinate in the kitchen. But when I can't take any longer—I mean, how long can it possibly take to get someone a glass of water?—I make my way to join them.

I don't know if it's the lighting or that he's in a T-shirt instead of a button-up, but he seems so different than he did when we first met. He's not outright movie-star gorgeous by any means, and I'm sure someone has called him average before. Ben was movie-star gorgeous. Hudson doesn't have a megawatt smile that you'd see on a toothpaste commercial. It's small, even hesitant. It lacks the cocky tilt that all men in LA seem to have. His body lacks the bulk most of Jude's fitness-fanatic friends have; instead there is a softness, the quiet confidence of a man who doesn't have to try to be someone else. Everything about him screams gentle and it stirs something inside of me that hasn't been stirred in a long time.

"So, Hudson"—I hand him the water—"I didn't realize you did podcasts. I thought you were an artist."

"I have a podcast centered around becoming more green and living a more sustainable lifestyle. I was just the host of the art show. Unfortunately, my artistic skills max out at stick figures."

Jude cracks up at that. "Looks like you two have that in common. Lauren's the only person I've ever known who could ace a chemistry test with her eyes closed but fail art."

"It's true." I try to laugh off her words, suddenly very conscious of what Hudson might be thinking of me. "And my poor daughter loves all things arts and crafts, I've been told many times that I'm a terrible assistant."

"Write that down!" Hudson reaches in front of Jude and snatches her laptop away from her. "That right there is what we need for the podcast."

"Really?" I feel my eyebrows scrunch together and see Jude prepare to reprimand me for force-feeding wrinkles onto my face, but lucky for me, she doesn't say anything in front of our company. "How is my lack of art skills going to help the podcast?"

"Because it's real and it's authentic. That's what people want." He slides the laptop back onto the coffee table. "We all know that the influencer/podcaster/blogger space is oversaturated. Standing out in the crowd is hard. You're slightly above the ground level because Jude's your cohost, and on the Venn diagram of life, some of her followers will be your target audience. But listeners today know when they're being spoon-fed shit and told it's caviar. They won't listen if all you two do is talk about what you think they want to hear."

"I guess that makes sense, but I'm not sure they'll want parenting advice from me either. I don't necessarily have all my ducks in a row." *Understatement of the century.*

"I hate to break it to you, Miss Perfectionist, but nobody has their shit all the way together. Thinking it's possible is life's oldest and greatest fucking con," Jude says. "Even with my platform, I have to talk about my stumbles sometimes. I have to let my followers know that I struggle, too, but that even if it's hard, there's always a way to grow and learn. If I was just telling them how wonderful I was and how everything came so easy to me all the time, nobody would follow me."

"Exactly." Hudson breaks back in. "And I'm not a parent, but what I've learned from friends who are is that nobody wants them telling them how to parent their kid. They want people they can relate to and commiserate with. You don't need to be an expert. You just need to be open and honest. Plus, you and Jude already have this great built-in story. Childhood best friends living together and raising a kid? It's honestly podcast gold."

Apparently, Jude has filled him in on our situation. I'm not sure if I'm relieved or irritated by that, but it doesn't matter, because I'm too focused on everything else they just said. And they're right.

I know they are.

Because when I think about the mommy influencers I follow or the podcasts I listen to, it's not because they know more than me. It's because I feel like they're my friends. I read the posts about the art projects they had to come up with so they could get a moment of reprieve. I laugh at the podcasts where they bitch about drop-off lanes and the new stain on their carpet. None of it is because I want to listen to an expert tell me all the ways I'm screwing up my child.

This should make me feel better. I won't have to try to pretend to know everything and be something I'm not.

But it does the opposite.

I don't know how to be open and honest about parenting. It's so personal and scary. When this podcast was just us working together to conduct expert interviews and give ideas for lunch, it was boxes I could check off. Nothing had to get deep, I didn't have to reveal myself to strangers. I could carefully craft what they saw.

This? Well, this scares the crap out of me.

But the payoff, making sure Adelaide stays with me? That outweighs everything.

"All right." I take a deep breath and sit up straight. "Then I guess we're going to need at least one episode on why it's so hard for kids to wear shoes."

There's no turning back now.

TWELVE

. . .

Jude

Lauren grabs the giant bag she packed out of the trunk and hoists it onto her shoulder before getting the picnic basket—yes, a real picnic basket and not a plastic bag, because Lauren is that much of an adult—and shoves it into my hands.

"Hand." She says the one-word command like everyone should know exactly what she's talking about. But by the way Addy curls her fingers tight around Lauren's as we cross the parking lot and doesn't dare let go until we're safe and sound on the sidewalk, it's clear the only person who needed to understand the command got it.

"Yo, that mom magic shit is fucking wild," I say when Addy is far enough in front of us that I won't get scolded for my liberal use of "grown-up" words.

"Well, it took a lot of repetition and fear tactics to ingrain it into her cute little head." She adjusts the bag and keeps her eyes on Addy. "Thanks for tagging along today, but you know you really didn't have to," she reassures me.

For the fifth time.

"You're starting to give me a complex. Did you not want me to come?" Because it's not like the road trip to Irvine for a play-group at an "adventure park" is the way I planned on spending this lovely—and blistering—August Saturday. But when she mentioned it, I figured it'd be good to see what happens with mom groups.

Research for the podcast and stuff.

Obvi.

After our little meeting with Hudson, Lauren did what Lauren does best. She took all the information Hudson and I gave her and learned as much as possible. She never wants to be seen as the weakest link, so thanks to her, the three of us have shared Google Docs with all the information we could possibly need. She signed us up for a web domain and then figured out how to DIY a simple yet awesome website and get an email list going. Things that took me years to master, Lauren picked up in weeks. Because that's just how she operates.

She's also been asking about Hudson in a way that is too nonchalant to be nonchalant. I've been pretending like I don't notice, because she spooks easily, but I fucking notice!

And since Hudson has also been texting and calling me way more than he ever did before, also asking about Lauren, I feel like Lauren's dry streak could soon be coming to an end.

"Of course I wanted you to come, it's just— Adelaide, slow down! Not too far ahead!" she yells as Adelaide tries to disguise her running as skipping as she makes her way to the masses of kids not too far away. I always find it so impressive how Lauren can jump in and out of two conversations so easily. "It's just that I know this isn't exactly your scene and . . . well . . . never mind."

"No. No never minds." I stop and grab her arm. "What were you going to say?"

"I don't really know how to say it, it's just, mom groups are kind of savage." She glares at me when I start to laugh. "I'm serious, Jude! I just started meeting with these moms, their kids are going into kindergarten at Remington Academy with Adelaide. There's a lot of pressure to fit in for her sake and I'm already kind of the odd one out. So just . . . no more f-bombs, okay?"

"I got it. I'll be on my best behavior." I raise my free hand in front of me, pinkie out. "Promise."

Without hesitation, Lauren links her pinkie with mine. We kiss our thumbs, then smoosh them together, and when we're finished, she looks infinitely less stressed. There you have it: the power of a pinkie promise does not fade with age.

She starts walking toward the park again. "Thank you. And don't judge me for what's about to go down."

"Why would I judge you?"

Lauren is the shit. I would never judge her.

"Oh, you'll see."

That sounds way too ominous for a playgroup at the park, but she has successfully piqued my interest. Maybe this drive to Irvine will be worth it after all.

· · ·

I'm never having kids.

Don't get me wrong, the mini-humans running around are adorable and everything. It's having to deal with the parents that has completely turned me off the idea.

When Lauren said she was the odd one out, I assumed she meant it was because she's a single mom and probably a lot younger than most of them.

I didn't think it was because she was the only one without a massive stick up her ass.

These moms.

They've done nothing but humblebrag about their little angels since we arrived. Like, I get it, Karen, your kid's a genius and can paint like Picasso. Nobody gives a fuck.

Poor Lauren just sits there, nodding politely and laughing at their jokes that are def not even a little bit funny. If I'd known it was going to be like this, I would've snuck some wine into the picnic basket.

On the bright side, however, I've been able to see Addy's playground leadership skills in full effect. And let me tell you, they have not let me down. She's totally going to be president.

Thankfully for me—not the child—a high-pitched scream pulls all of our attention away from the mind-numbing conversation about class moms and the future field trip chaperone schedule.

"Mommy!" A little girl with curly brown hair and overalls runs over to Beth—one of the moms who doesn't seem to be terrible. "Declan took my fruit snacks and put them in his mud pie!"

Tears are running down her dirt-stained face as she wraps her little body around her mom. And even though it's sad, it makes me nostalgic for the days when losing my fruit snacks was the worst thing that could happen to me.

Beth turns and looks at Whitney—one of the awful moms, who I'm assuming the little jerkface gummy-stealing Declan belongs to.

Whitney shrugs and gives Beth the most patronizing smile I've seen outside of my own mother. "Boys will be boys."

Ewwww.

I bet Asher's mom said shit like that and it's why he grew up to be such a giant fucking scumbag.

"Being a boy doesn't make it okay to be mean, they should be nice too," Adelaide, the rock star of my life, says as she approaches the crying girl. "It's okay, Marlow, we brought extra gummies, if your mommy says it's okay, you can have some."

The stupid smile falls right off Whitney's face once she realizes she's been schooled by a five-year-old. And even though I know Lauren is proud, she also looks like she wants to crawl beneath the table and die.

"Thank you, Adelaide, *you* are a very good friend. Marlow would love gummies." Beth's voice is sugar sweet, but the way she turns to shoot daggers at Whitney is not.

Is it wrong that I hope the playground brawl I see today is between the moms? Because I so do.

"Here you go." Lauren hands Marlow one of the baggies of fruit snacks that have hidden vitamins in every bite—Lauren's words, not mine.

"Thank you!" Marlow takes the bag, tears long gone, and has a huge smile that shows all of her tiny teeth.

It's not long after Gummygate that the kids finish their lunches with minimal drama before throwing away their trash and running back to the slides.

"So, Jude," Jennifer says from across the picnic table we've all congregated around now that the kids have dispersed. "How do you know our Lauren?"

Lauren practically glows when Jennifer says *our Lauren*. My sweet, beautiful friend only sees the best in people and so deeply wants to fit in with these moms.

But here's the thing: I hated Jennifer on sight.

Her blond, layered hair doesn't have a strand out of place, and her bright pink lipstick and perfect contour were undoubtedly applied by a glam team. Whatever. Fine with me, I get wanting to look good. She's wearing a bright, floral Lilly Pulitzer dress, and her daughter is wearing shorts with the same print, which is weird, but still not the reason I hate her. (Okay, maybe it's part of the reason. Who wants to match a five-year-old?) It's not even the way she keeps yelling at sweet little Lake for playing in the mud feature this park is apparently known for because she doesn't want her to ruin her stupid shorts.

No. It's none of that.

I hate her because when we first arrived and Lauren pulled Addy to the side to put sunscreen on her, I saw the way Jennifer took off her overly embellished sunglasses—that I do actually really like—and pointed at Lauren before she started snickering with her little group of bitches. And maybe it's because I only associate with people who aren't the worst, but I thought the whole mean-girls thing was over. I definitely didn't expect it from a group of moms who should know better.

But because I promised Lauren I'd be on my best behavior, I'm nice to the bitch. "We've known each other since third grade and now we live together."

"You live together? How fun!" Her bleached teeth nearly blind me, but still don't distract me from how fake her smile is. "I can't imagine having a roommate, but I'm sure you both make it work."

"It's actually been really great." I force my smile to mimic hers. "I imagine it's just like having a husband, but with more help around the house and none of the terrible sex or mansplaining."

I purposefully look away from Lauren and thank my lucky stars she's not close enough to pinch me under the table.

I know, I promised my best behavior, but seriously. Fuck that woman. Anyway, way more moms laugh than gasp, so I know I'm not the only one who doesn't like the mean-girls clique. Maybe some of them aren't so bad after all.

"I would die to live with my best friend," Sabrina says. "Don't get me wrong, I love Zach more than anything, but he'd rather eat every meal on paper plates than help me with the dishes. And the golf. If I have to spend one more Sunday watching golf with him, I'll scream."

See, Lauren, be friends with Sabrina. I'm doing you a favor by weeding out the terrible moms with no sense of humor.

Plus, Sabrina's daughter, Winnie, is so cute and so funny. She and Addy are both covered in mud and loving every second of being messy and wild. Poor Lake is just watching from the side as they take turns running over to her and giving her toys from the mud zone.

"It has been great," Lauren speaks up, and I'm so proud of her. I know how uncomfortable she gets during these things. She's an introvert to the core and needs to be invited to feel welcome to anything. "Plus, Adelaide loves Jude. It's so nice to have someone she wants to spend time with so I can make dinner or shower in peace."

"Wait," one of the moms whose names I don't remember cuts in. "You mean you can take a shower without her asking you for snacks? I swear, my husband will be sitting in the kitchen and Jaxon will still come and get me out of the shower for food. It makes me nuts!"

She's met with a choir of *me too*s and *same*s. The only people not laughing or joining in are Jennifer, Whitney, and Colleen.

Color me shocked.

"I'm so glad I'm not the only one that happens with." Lauren's shoulders are finally relaxed, and the tension lines around her mouth have disappeared. "Jude, we have to write that down for the podcast."

"A podcast?" says Lucy, who I remember because she has bright red hair just like Lucille Ball. "How fun! What about?"

Even though Lauren does her best to play it cool, I know she's mortified being the center of attention right now and is kicking herself for mentioning the podcast.

"It's about being a millennial mom in the city," she says. "But Jude's doing it with me, so she'll add her perspective as a single woman with no kids. Plus, she's really into fitness—she's pretty much a Pilates master and has tons of good workout advice too. It should be fun, we start recording soon."

"Oh my god! I knew you looked familiar," Colleen, who was giving me a strong stink eye only seconds ago, is now grinning like a fool. "You're Jude Andrews! I follow you on Instagram and went to one of the classes you taught. I thought I was in great shape, but my legs were sore for almost a week after. It was the best."

Even though Colleen is one of the mean girls, I can't help but bask in the glow of her compliment. And Jennifer looking as if she just gulped spoiled wine doesn't hurt either.

"She really is the best at everything she does," Lauren says. She's my number one fan. Even though she would rather die than ever brag about any of her many accomplishments, she's the first to shout mine from the rooftops. "She's even been doing little classes with Adelaide, and Adelaide is completely obsessed."

"Kids' Pilates?" Beth reaches into her purse and pulls out her iPhone. "I would love to do Pilates with Marlow! What's the name of your podcast? I'm going to subscribe now."

I look to Lauren and nod since—despite telling everyone how uncreative she is—she came up with the best name ever.

I can see how nervous she is to share this, which I understand. It's scary to share anything personal with other people. But because she's Lauren fucking Turner, mom and friend extraordinaire, she pulls back her shoulders and puts a little extra oomph into her voice. "*Mom Jeans and Martinis,*" she tells the table. "It's not out yet, but you can still subscribe."

"Oh my god!" Sabrina shouts, pulling out her phone as well. "I love that! I'm totally subscribing too."

The other moms—minus Jennifer and Whitney—all do the same, pulling out their phones and hitting that subscribe button as they gush about our name and buying new yoga pants.

I knew our podcast was going to be a hit, and I think Lauren is starting to finally see as well. And if she's not, I have no problem forcing her and the rest of these uptight LA moms to let loose and enjoy themselves a little while they figure it out.

Even if I have to ride to Irvine in Saturday traffic to do it.

THIRTEEN

. . .

Lauren

Adelaide wanted to spend the day with my parents.

They spoil her something fierce, so this is a common occurrence. But because of the lingering fear of losing time with her, it's been hard for me to let her go. I probably wouldn't have agreed at all if it wasn't for Jude pressuring us to record our podcast. Ever since the playgroup two weekends ago, she's been on my case, constantly reminding me of how excited the other moms were. She's been reminding me that if we want to get the first episode out by the first week of September, it's pretty much now or never. She softens her reminders by saying we should strike while the iron's hot, but I think she really just wants to do it before I inevitably panic and change my mind.

Thanks to her and Adelaide having matching pout faces and saying please about a thousand times, I gave in.

I'm such a freaking sucker.

So now Adelaide is off at my parents'—probably loading up

on as much sugar and caffeine as she can get her hands on—and I'm sitting on my couch with my leg profusely bouncing and my stomach doing Olympic-style flips.

"Don't worry, Lauren," Hudson says as he adjusts the mic in front of me. "This isn't live. If there's something you regret saying, we can edit it out. Just try to let loose and be yourself. You're impossible not to like."

My stomach twists again, but this time it's not because of nerves.

I don't know the precise moment when I stopped viewing Hudson as the idiot who said, "Reproduction is dope," and started seeing him as much, much more, but all I know is that now, he makes me so freaking giddy I can't control myself. I don't know what it is about his floppy hair and Southern California vibe that just does it for me, but it freaking does it for me. Maybe it's because he's so laid-back that just being near him eases my anxiety by half or that when he smiles, he does it with his entire face. Or maybe it's because he's such the polar opposite of Ben that I have to believe he must be perfect?

All I know for sure is that I need to check it. Because awkward giggling definitely isn't what we're going for here.

Plus, I'm pretty sure a single mom who's nearing thirty and living with a roommate isn't exactly on Hudson's wish list. And while unrequited love is wonderful and gloriously angsty on TV, it never is when you're living it.

"Are you sure you don't want me to make you a cosmo?" Jude points to the pinkish concoction sitting in front of her. "Martinis *are* part of our brand, so you could rationalize that drinking is a work necessity . . . at least that's what I'm doing." She shrugs before picking up the glass and taking a sip.

Usually I'd be a firm no—day drinking really isn't my thing—

but I'm not usually in close proximity to a man I find extremely attractive and about to record myself talking about the thing I'm most self-conscious about, so I do consider it for a second.

"No," I say when I finally come to the decision. "We both know my tolerance is pretty much nonexistent, and I don't think slurring would be the best look for me."

"Responsibility is on brand for you, so that makes sense." Jude shrugs before picking up the glass and taking a sip.

I waver on my decision for a split second when I see how much Jude seems to enjoy her drink, before getting my head back in the game. I focus on Hudson sitting on the other side of our dining table, wearing headphones and looking at his computer.

"Okay." I square my shoulders and take a deep breath, knowing this is the point of no return. "Where do we start?"

"This is all the fun stuff." Hudson hits a few keys on his computer before turning to me, and maybe it's just my imagination, but I swear his smile gets bigger when he does. "First we'll record the intro and outro you wrote, and then we'll just start recording. I think you had . . ." He looks back to his computer, clicking around a few times. "Yeah, the content calendar has five different podcast topics for today. We can try to knock them all out or just wait and see how you're feeling. There's no rules. Just whatever works best for you."

See. It's that.

That's what's making me like him so much.

With Ben, it wasn't—and still isn't—what worked best for me. It was all about him, all the time. And maybe some of that was my fault? I bent over backwards for him. I let him matter more than me. His job, his feelings, his time, everything was superior to me . . . and I'm still trying to come back from it.

"I say we record all of them today," Jude says when I don't answer right away. "We'll aim for thirty-to-forty-five-minute episodes, then we'll do it again next month. I'd just rather be ahead of the game in case anything comes up for any of us."

I nod my head yes even though nothing will come up for me. If anything, I might have more time on my hands soon . . .

I squeeze my eyes shut and try to rid the lingering thought from my mind. This is supposed to be fun. I can't think about the possibility of losing Adelaide before we record.

"Are you all right, Lauren?" Hudson's voice breaks through the fear trying to cloud my mind.

When I open my eyes and look at him, the easygoing, happy Hudson I'm so used to seeing isn't looking back at me. No, this man is intense and serious and worried . . . *about me*.

The good thing about seeing him like this is it forces all thoughts of Ben and custody right out of my head.

The bad thing about seeing him like this is it forces all thoughts of spending time with Hudson and him only ever looking at me this way right into my head.

"Oh yeah . . . me? Yeah, no." I stumble over my words, temporarily ignoring Jude's laughter but making a mental note to yell at her later. "I'm good. Totally good. Sorry."

"Totally good?" Jude mocks my tone. "Like totally. Who even are you? Valley Lauren?"

I cross *yell at her* off my mental checklist and replace it with *kill her*.

"You're the worst, and because of that, now you get to read the intro and outro." I resist the urge to stick out my tongue as I find the script in the three-ring binder I've obsessively pieced together and shove it in front of her. "I already timed myself reading it. They're both right around thirty seconds."

Where I've been silently freaking about being the opening voice of the podcast, Jude's a freaking rock star and isn't even a little nonplussed by it. She scans the script for a few seconds, taking her pen and adding a couple of notes before nodding at Hudson. "Got it."

He nods back and hits a few buttons. "Ready."

I knew it was coming, but the way Jude's voice transforms from the teasing, slightly bored tone she's been using all morning to the peppy, motivational influencer her followers love her so much for being still takes me by surprise.

"Welcome to *Mom Jeans and Martinis*. I'm Jude Andrews."

She stops talking and I pick up on the cue. I try to forget all those times I've heard my voice on a voice mail or a video that Adelaide has taken of me and pretend like I have confidence. "And I'm Lauren Turner."

"On the surface, we couldn't be more different. I'm a fitness influencer with a penchant for a good martini, Lauren's a single mom who finds joy sneaking veggies into desserts, but we're still best friends. *Mom Jeans and Martinis* is for millennial women trying their hardest to navigate this crazy life. Whether you're single, married, divorced, have kids or don't, this podcast is for you. Each week, we'll dive into our wins and losses while helping you avoid the latter. So come on over! Here, the only thing stronger than the drinks is the friendship."

Hudson clicks something before giving a thumbs-up like a nerd, which makes him even cuter. "Got it. That was great!"

"Thank you." Jude looks entirely too smug taking a sip of her martini.

I can't help the way my eyes roll to the heavens. Modesty is definitely not in Jude's vocabulary.

"Let's not forget who wrote the script so you could sound amazing." It's not much, but it's all I have. I know Jude is going to upstage me on every aspect of this podcast . . . which is honestly part of the reason I agreed.

But she can't know that. Her head is already big enough.

"It was actually amazing," she says, shocking the ever-loving crap out of me. "The last line, 'the only thing stronger than the drinks is the friendship,' was so, so good!"

I wasn't expecting this at all, so I don't really know what to say . . . a feeling that only burgeons when Hudson pipes in. "It really was. I can't believe this is your first time doing this. I've met people who've been in the podcast game for years and still can't write a precise, catchy intro."

"Aw, shucks. Thanks." Warmth fills my stomach and cheeks as I try to wave them off. "You're both too kind. It was only one paragraph." The praise coming from both of them reminds me of Adelaide's favorite movie, and I realize why Olaf likes warm hugs so much.

"Huds," Jude shouts much too loud for someone who's only a couple of feet away. "Add an episode dedicated to allowing women to accept praise to the content calendar. And by women, I mean Lauren."

His chuckle washes over me just as the embarrassment hits. *Yup. Totally killing Jude later.*

"Whatever." I try to ignore both of them. I don't know how long until my mom brings Adelaide back, and I want to get more than the opening recorded. "Let's record something before a small child returns and makes it impossible."

Jude gives me a massive side-eye. She knows my game, but she also knows I'm not wrong.

There was a time I thought being a stay-at-home mom was all I wanted, but as I stayed home with Adelaide, I knew that as much as I adored my child, I needed to work. So then I thought working from home was the epitome of living my best life . . . until I tried to get work accomplished with her at home. That was the moment I discovered work-at-home parents are either saints or superheroes, because I wanted to cry by noon.

"Good call. You know I love my Addy, but I have a feeling her asking for snacks every five minutes would make the editing a little challenging."

That's the understatement of the century.

I flip through the binder until I find the notes I made for the first episodes. "Are you still good with talking about transitioning and adapting in the first episode and then making it a little lighter and talking about health and wellness for the second one?"

"Sounds good to me." Jude nods her head. "And thank you for taking charge of all the behind-the-scenes details. I really appreciate it."

"Well, we are doing this to help me, so it's probably the least I could do since I wrangled you both into this."

"I don't know about Jude," Hudson says, speaking up before Jude has the chance, "but I wouldn't want to be anywhere else. I love doing podcasts and watching other people fall in love with it too."

Something about Hudson talking about falling in love causes my lungs to malfunction and my heart to stop beating. I'm so glad he's helping us, but I honestly don't know how I'm going to survive working this close with him. He's slowly—and unintentionally—breaking through every wall I've built around myself since Ben. And I don't appreciate it.

• • •

I don't know why, but podcasting is exhausting.

Sure, all I did was talk to my best friend for a few hours, but we talked about things that actually mattered. I was forced to say, out loud, to the world, how hard it was to transition from being a fiancée with no worries to a single mom whose entire life was filled with uncertainty. We talked about my crazy desire to belong, Jude's even crazier desire to stand out, and how—whether you have kids or not—the growing expectations on children these days is out of control. I could've talked about the process of finding a school for Adelaide for hours. Even Jude was shocked by it. We also talked about sneaking veggies into food, and Jude gave tips on starting a fitness routine. A lot was said, and I really hope somebody ends up listening to it.

I'm about three seconds away from asking Jude to make me one of the cocktails she's sipping when a knock at the front door grabs my attention.

Ever since the custody papers were delivered, my stomach falls to my feet when someone rings the doorbell or knocks. I didn't think something like that could cause trauma, but it definitely did. Thankfully, before I can panic too much, Adelaide's voice breaches the door and fills the living room.

"Mommy! Hurry! I gotta go potty!"

As I unlock the door, I think I hear my mom telling her this is why she should've saved her juice boxes until she got home.

"Hey, sister girl!" I bend down and swoop her into my arms, smothering her face with kisses. "Did you have fun with Nana?"

"So much fun!" She squeals and pushes out of my embrace. "I'll tell you all about it after I go potty."

I put her down and she takes off, shouting, "Hi, Auntie Jude! Hi, other person!" as she runs up the stairs.

My mom peeks around me, her eyes widening when she gets a good look at Hudson. The ever-present twelve-year-old inside of me whenever I'm around my mom panics like I got caught with a boy in my room. I rush to answer the question that most definitely wasn't asked. "That's Hudson, he's helping us with the podcast."

My mom purses her lips and levels me with the same look that's brought fear into my life for the last twenty-eight years. "Mmm-hmm . . ." Only she's capable of filling a sound with so much judgment. "Well, I'll get out of your hair." She hands me the canvas grocery bags I didn't even notice she was holding. "We stopped by Target on the way home and she picked out a few little things. But I got you those granola bars I know you like and a few face masks I've heard good things about."

My mom always spoils the heck out of Adelaide, so I'm not surprised when I look in the bag and see a new leotard, two Barbies, and the sticker books she loves. But I am surprised she thought of me.

"Wow . . ." I don't really know what to say. "Thanks, Mom. That was really thoughtful of you."

"You're welcome." She waves her hand in front of me, and her low-cut nails, which are always painted clear, are now a very glossy baby pink. I can't help but smile thinking of what Adelaide must've said to get her to agree to that. "It's just a little something."

"Well . . ." I start, but a little ball of energy blasts back down the stairs, interrupting my train of thought. "Adelaide, come give Nana a hug and thank her for your new goodies and having you over."

"Thanks, Nana!" She barrels into my mom's legs, wrapping her arms around her and squeezing tight.

"You're welcome. Thanks for my manicure," my mom says, confirming my earlier assumption. "Don't stay away from me and Papa so long, we missed you."

"I know," Adelaide says. "I kept telling Mommy that you needed Addy time too."

"You did." I can feel my smile stretching in the way it only does when I'm with Adelaide. I love her confidence. I love that she knows how loved she is. It's moments like these when I don't feel like I'm completely screwing up this motherhood thing. "We'll call Nana and set up another day soon, okay?"

"Okay," Adelaide says, and then, like a five-year-old with an attention span of ten seconds, she pulls the bag from my hand. "Can I go show my new toys to Auntie Jude?"

"Of course you can!" Jude yells from the kitchen. "I hope you got more Barbies for our rock band. Jade's slacking on the drums and needs a replacement."

If I didn't know better, I'd think it was amusement and not irritation in my mom's eyes when she watches Adelaide run off to show her new treasures to Jude.

My mom adjusts the strap of her purse on her shoulder. "She hasn't had dinner yet, just lunch and a few snacks after."

I know *snacks* is code for candy and other sugary treats, but I don't care. I'm glad Adelaide has this relationship with my parents. I loved my grandma so much, and when I was pregnant, I was so worried Adelaide wouldn't get that relationship.

"I'll get dinner going then." The tension between us grows with Adelaide gone. "Thanks for bringing her back."

"You're welcome. Call me soon and update me on everything with custody."

"I will." I don't want to, but I will. "Bye, Mom."

"Bye." Lines strain around her mouth, and I know she wants to frown, but instead she offers a weak smile before turning and going back to her car.

I lock the door behind her and walk toward where Adelaide is talking a mile a minute to Jude and Hudson.

"I'm going to get started on dinner," I say, interrupting her as she's describing all the ways her new toy can be played with. "Is everyone okay with lasagna roll ups?"

"Yeah!" Adelaide and Jude shout in unison.

The first time I offered this meal, Jude almost had a heart attack. Carbs are the equivalent to the devil in her book. She didn't relax until I told her I use zucchini instead of noodles.

I look to Hudson, who doesn't answer. "You're staying, right?

The least we can do is feed you after you listened to us talk for so long."

"Um, yeah. Sure." Color rises in his cheeks, probably from being put on the spot, and I kick myself a little. "That sounds good."

"Are you sure?" I try to walk back my offer. He's probably so sick of us. "I won't be offended if you don't want to stay."

"He wants to stay," Jude says. "Hudson needs your lasagna rolls. Everyone needs to experience them."

"Okay then." I glare at Jude but try to fix my face when I look at Hudson. "I'll get dinner started."

"And I'll show Hudson all my toys." Adelaide says this as if it is the most exciting thing ever, and I cringe a little for the evening Hudson doesn't even know he's in for.

By the time I pull dinner out of the oven, Adelaide has been entertaining Jude and Hudson for well over an hour. Last I heard, they were discussing who'd be lead vocals for the rock band.

Poor Hudson had no idea what he was agreeing to when he chose to stay. I'm not sure my lasagna is going to be worth it for him. Hopefully it doesn't make him quit coming to help us.

I put the lasagna on the table with the salad and bread basket before going upstairs to get everyone.

Once I reach the top, the lack of noise is almost concerning. After the amount of sugar I'm sure Adelaide consumed today, I'm surprised she's not bouncing off the walls. I start tiptoeing, more curious than anything to see what's happening, when Hudson's voice floats into the hallway.

"Ready, Addy?" he asks. "*The Addy Show* take five in three . . . two . . . one."

"Welcome to *The Addy Show*!" Jude's voice is just as bubbly as it was when she recorded the intro to our podcast. "Here's the star you've been waiting for, Addy June Keane!"

Applause of way more than two people starts to play, and my curiosity is at an all-time high when I peek in Adelaide's room.

And what I see takes my breath away.

Hudson is sitting on the floor, his computer in front of him. His camera with a microphone is on a tripod, aimed at Adelaide, who's on her bed with her Barbies and stuffed animals all around her. A sign that says "The Addy Show" is taped on the wall behind her in handwriting I don't recognize.

I push the door open a little wider, accidentally pulling Adelaide's attention from the activity at hand.

"Mommy!" She leaps off her bed, causing some of her stuffed animals to tip over. "Look at what Hudson let me do!" She grabs my hand and pulls me farther into her room. "It's *The Addy Show*! He let me pick out special music on his computer and even made me this pretty sign! Isn't it so awesome?"

"It's so awesome," I say, because it is. It's unbelievably freaking awesome. "But I think we're going to have to take a quick dinner break."

"Yay! Lasagna!" She drops my hand like a bad habit, racing over to Hudson and wrapping her little fingers around his wrist. "Come on, Hudsie. You can sit by me!"

Hudsie.

Oh my freaking god.

"Sounds good." Hudson stands up, his smile not faltering in the slightest. "After we eat all of our food, we'll come finish and I'll show you how I edit it, and you can pick some cool visual effects like rainbows and sparkles to add to your show."

"Rainbows?" Adelaide breathes out the word like she can't believe her luck. "Hurry! Let's go eat!"

She starts running, never easing up on his wrist as she pulls him out of her room.

But when they walk past me, I swear time stops. His smile is like a slow-motion film as he looks at me. I see it as the creases around his eyes deepen and his smile gets just a fraction wider. Then I watch as his free hand moves toward me, my entire body tightening in anticipation until he reaches me and gives my hand a squeeze that causes every nerve ending in my body to light up in a way I've never, ever felt before.

Then time starts working again and they're out of the room, Adelaide's voice echoing up the stairs as she tells him what chair to sit in, and I'm staring at the empty doorway, wondering what in the hell just happened.

"What did I tell you?" Jude startles me out of my Hudson trance. "I told you he was the shit."

I don't say anything to her. I don't have to. She knows she's right. And I know I'm screwed. Because as much as I like Hudson in this moment, I also know nothing can happen.

I have one thing to focus on and until that's done, not even *The Addy Show* can distract me.

Thanks a lot, Ben.

FOURTEEN

Jude

When I ran the podcast by Lauren, I thought it would take a lot more time and effort on my end since she was for sure not sold on the idea. But I underestimated Lauren's desire to be the best at everything and Hudson's desire for Lauren. Between the two of them, all I've had to do is sit on the couch, sip a martini—or two—talk with my best friend for a few hours, and watch as she gradually developed a massive crush on Hudson. That's how I want to spend my days anyway.

Besides reaching out to a few fellow influencers who already owed me favors to promote our show, I've had nothing to do. And since I already had blocked out the last two weeks of August for the podcast, I decided to take over the one thing I knew I could do best: throw a banging-ass launch party!

"Where's the bar going to go?" I ask Olivia Enis, the owner of Bougie Britches, the cutest boutique in Silver Lake, where our launch party is taking place.

She points to the empty space in the corner of the boutique. "Right over there. I didn't want it too close to the dressing room or to the front door. This should balance out the high-traffic areas so it doesn't look too crowded."

"Perfect, and the jeans will be set up around the room?"

"Yes, all around." She points to the empty tables her employees are starting to fill up. "I even reached out to a friend with a vintage store for some of their jeans to use."

I figured since we are *Mom Jeans and Martinis*, both things needed to be well represented at the party. We're even doing a little fashion show that will be the evolution of the mom jeans. It's going to be great. The martinis are obvious. Not a chance in hell I would ever throw an event and not have alcoholic drink options.

Even though I hate to admit it, I wouldn't have been able to throw this together without my mom's magazine deal. It's much easier to get a sponsor to donate last minute when there's a publicity guarantee. You know, return on investment and all that jazz.

"This is going to be so great, Olivia. I really can't thank you enough." Olivia has been a pretty good friend for the last few years. Hers was one of the first brands that wasn't just Pilates-focused to reach out to me. But even when I'm not getting paid, I still promote her stuff often, so she was more than happy to loan us Bougie Britches after hours. "Lauren is going to die, she's never been the center of anything like this before. And Addy—her daughter—starts kindergarten this week. She's been a fucking mess. Hopefully a martini will calm her down."

Olivia starts to laugh. "I don't think I'm about that mom life. This store might be the only thing I ever birth."

"Same, girl. Hard fucking same." We start walking to the door. I have to head home and change while Olivia puts the finishing touches on everything. "Living with Addy's a blast, but mainly because Lauren does all the important shit. I just get to play dress-up and do cartwheels in the living room. Being a 'fun aunt' is my full capacity of dealing with a child."

"Oh my god, that reminds me!" Olivia's eyes go wide and she grabs my hand. "I have those matching necklaces you wanted in the back. Can you wait for just one second while I grab them? There's no way I'll remember them tonight."

I glance at my phone. I should probably get going, but a few minutes won't hurt anyone. "Not a problem, thank you for ordering them."

I found these adorable necklaces that were almost like the friendship necklaces we used to buy at Claire's in fourth grade, except way nicer. The ones I ordered are a brushed rose gold instead of glitter-coated plastic, and instead of a fractured heart, these necklaces have a very simple triangle attached to the chain. Alone, they're pretty, simple, and something any adult would be happy wearing . . . even though—let's be honest—I would still rock the shit out of a plastic glittered heart necklace.

But what really makes these necklaces so special are the names I had Olivia get engraved on the inside: Lauren, Adelaide, Jude. I found them right after I watched *Boss Baby* with Addy. Even though I know it's just a kids' movie, now I can't see a triangle without thinking of the three of us joining together, creating the strongest shape in nature.

I really hope they'll love them as much as I think they will. Well, at least Lauren. Addy has no standards. She legit got excited the other day because I let her keep the ribbon from a product I was sent.

Olivia waves off my thanks, the signature crystals on her long acrylic nails glittering under the recessed lighting. "You know I live for personalized gifts, and they turned out so cute, you're gonna die." She spins on one of her high heels and runs to the back room.

I make my way to one of the chairs that has been brought in for tonight, silently thanking the heavens I fell into the influencer niche where flip-flops, tennis shoes, and bare feet are expected.

I pull out my phone, using these spare minutes to respond to comments on my pictures and send a few messages to followers I've had for a while. I do it all the time, but people still seem surprised when I do. Like I'm some untouchable rainbow cloud shining down on them. Like, no, girl. I'm a hot-ass mess who almost had to move back in with her mom . . . but her mom couldn't afford it. I'm lucky you let me grace your inbox! But I guess it just means my platforms are successfully portraying what I want them to see.

Part of the beauty of Instagram is that in pictures, there's no difference between water and vodka.

I'm adding one more emoji than necessary when the front door squeaks open. I glance up from my phone, hoping it's the bartender and I can give him the personalized swizzle sticks I absolutely didn't need but still wanted. However it's not the man who will supply me with drinks who walks through the door.

Nope, it's the woman who makes me drink.

"Mom?" I drop my phone in my purse. "What are you doing here?"

I know my mom is trying her best to become relevant again, but Bougie Britches is so not her scene. There's no way she would be caught dead wearing anything so easily accessible to the public.

Oh . . . did that sound rude?

Sorry.

What I was trying to say is that my mom is a fucking snob. Champagne taste with a Boone's Farm budget.

"Jude! My love!" Her tone is airy and light, a stark contrast to the terse one she had last night when I told her I was busy today and couldn't join her for a paparazzi-trailed Pilates class and dry lettuce lunch. "I was just walking in this adorable little neighborhood and saw you! It's so cute here! Why don't I come over here more?"

I'm assuming this is rhetorical, because again, fucking snob.

I'm trying to keep my shit together, but sometimes I feel like my mom is just a wrecking ball waiting to crash into me every time I'm starting to feel good about things.

And I felt good about tonight.

"Yeah, so cute. But, um, what are you doing here?"

She takes a seat on the velvet bench in front of what will be turned into our swag station. "I wanted to see the progress you and Lauren made. Can't I just be proud of you girls?"

Even though she's made it really hard for me to count on her the last few years, she was totally that asshole mom who showed up at school performances hours early to make sure she was able to block off the best seats for her, my dad, and whoever else she had convinced to come cheer me on. She even started saving seats for the Turners once Lauren and I became friends. I think it might be the only good thing Mrs. Turner has to say about my family.

Plus, she loves Lauren as much as Lauren loves her. And, she did actually seem genuinely excited when I told her about the podcast. She even asked about it the other day when we went on one of our magazine-sponsored brunch dates. The fact that she remembered something that didn't revolve around her felt like a small miracle. And she hasn't asked for money since her phone bill. Maybe this is her trying?

"Of course you can." I sit down next to her, feeling cautiously optimistic. "You know Mrs. Turner isn't going to come. I think it will really mean a lot to Lauren if you're here . . . and to me, too, obviously."

"I'm glad to hear that." She looks down and starts to fidget with the zipper of her designer bag. "My feelings were a little hurt that I had to hear about this from Eliza and not you."

"I'm sorry, I should've told you. I guess I just got so wrapped up that I forgot. I'm really glad Eliza told you."

Eliza is our handler at *StarGazer*. It's not that I wanted to call her. As per my contract, I *had* to call her when I knew I was going to throw the launch. But—and as much as I hate to say it—having her backing me and confirming national press coverage has really taken this party to a level I wouldn't have accomplished without her.

"You have no idea how relieved I am to hear you say that." She turns to face me, a blush I haven't seen in ages coloring her cheeks and making her look so much younger. "I have a tiny confession."

Oh lord.

Here it comes. I wonder what the favor is this time or how much the loan that will never be paid back is for.

"I didn't actually happen to just be in the neighborhood. I called *StarGazer* and they told me you'd been here for a while," she says, and shocks the crap out of me.

"That's your confession?"

"Yes." She reaches for my hands. "Please don't be mad. I promise I'm not keeping tabs on you. I just wanted to talk to you before tonight. I didn't want to just turn up at your event and ruin it if you didn't want me there. I know how—"

"Mom," I say, cutting her off. Once Juliette Andrews starts to ramble, she doesn't stop. A trait that very well may be hereditary. "It's fine. I already figured that's what happened and you weren't randomly strutting around Silver Lake."

Her shoulders fall in relief, and guilt that I didn't even realize she seemed stressed courses through me.

"I did mean it when I said it's cute here. I passed a coffee shop a few blocks back that looked wonderful. Maybe we can grab a drink there sometime soon?"

"Yeah, Mom," I say. "I'd love that."

And I actually mean it this time.

Maybe this plan of hers is working and my mom is slowly coming back to me.

"Okay!" She claps her hands together and her TV-perfect smile lights up her face. "I'm so excited for tonight. I'm going to run home and freshen up and then I'll see you back here in a few hours. Seven o'clock, right?"

"Right," I confirm.

She wraps her thin arms around me and pulls me in for a quick hug. "Proud of you, Ju-ju," she whispers in my ear before walking out of the door and leaving me staring after her, speechless. Tears prick at the backs of my eyes, and for the first time in a long time with my mom, they're happy tears.

I think the thing that makes our mother-daughter relationship so hard is that even when I want to hate my mom, I want to love her more.

Even when it hurts.

Maybe especially when it hurts.

I want my mom even if it feels like a knife to my chest. I'll take the pain if it means one day getting to love my mom without the hurt lingering just below the surface.

This must be why they say love is like a drug. Knowing just how destructive it can be, but willing to risk everything for a momentary high when all you feel is good.

"Is it safe for me to come back out?" Olivia whisper-shouts from the back of her store.

"Yeah, of course, sorry about that. It was just my mom, I didn't know she was coming." See, the rambling? Definitely genetic. "Anyway, yeah. Please don't hide in your place of business because of me."

"It's totally fine." She hands me a bag with three beautifully wrapped boxes inside. "Trust me, I once walked in on three people having sex in the dressing room, this was nothing."

"Three?" I debate whether or not to ask for more details but realize how much I still need to do. "I need details about this, when I take you out for drinks soon?"

"Definitely," she says. "Now go! Get glam and let me take over things here. It's going to be great."

She's right, this *is* going to be great and I can't freaking wait.

FIFTEEN

Lauren

The last party I went to was Bryson Tripp's fifth birthday. There was a bounce house, a face painter, and gluten-free carnival food. Adelaide had a blast and immediately crashed in the car afterward, so I was blessed with an hour of silence during the drive home. I didn't think any party could top that glorious day.

Then I walked into Bougie Britches.

Jude's been staring at me since she told me to open my eyes and finally revealed everything she's kept so secret. She's been watching me silently as I take in the fabulousness she's orchestrated.

"You're fucking killing me here! I don't know what that face means. Do you love it? Do you hate it? Do you need a martini? What about a mini-manicure? Some hors d'oeuvres?"

Apparently she's reached the end of her quiet rope.

"It's freaking fantastic," I say, putting her out of her misery and pulling her into a giant hug as I do. "It's better than anything I could've even imagined."

It really is.

I'd be lying if I said the perfectionist—or control freak, whatever—in me wasn't dying to plan every little detail of anything that had to do with our podcast. But my mom always told me how important it is to know not only my strengths, but my weaknesses as well. And parties are not my thing. I'm more numbers and structure. Jude is all creative and living life to the fullest. It's why we work so well together.

"Really?" She pulls out of my massive bear hug. "You're not just saying that to make me feel good about myself?"

I don't know if she's asking because she's really not sure or if she wants me to stroke her ego a little more, but either way, she deserves some ass pats for pulling this all together. "I'm not. This is honestly amazing and I have no idea how you managed to do this so quickly. You're magic. Party-planning magic."

Jude doesn't try to mask how thrilled she is to hear this, and now that I know I have properly stroked her ego, she pulls me straight to where else? The bar.

"Two Juice Boxes, please!"

Her smile is brighter than I've seen it in a long time, and I know it's from more than the vodka-brand-sponsored bar we're standing at. And even though I lost my doubts about this podcast a long time ago, seeing her so happy and how much fun we're having doing this would've totally convinced me. Plus, even though I talk a lot about motherhood on the podcast, I feel myself finding pieces of myself that I lost when I had Adelaide. It's been a wonderful and unexpected upside for me to cling to whenever the embers of fear start to light back up. Because as glamorous as tonight is, in the back of my mind, I'm still reminded that the only reason I'm here is because I might lose my daughter.

Jude hands me the pink cocktail with a purple-sugared rim,

preventing me from diving headfirst into the panic spiral I'm about to fall into.

I lift the drink to my mouth, but she halts my hand before it makes it all the way to my lips.

"Picture first." She plants one hand on her hip and lifts the drink close to her face, but not close enough that it blocks any of her smile. I try my best to mimic her, but whereas she looks care-free and natural in her pose, I'm pretty sure I look like a wide-eyed robot when the flashes start to go off. "Now take a sip," she says without her smile slipping, the flashes still rapid-firing as she takes a small sip and then throws her head back like she's laughing.

I try my best to keep up but make a mental note not to look up any of these pictures online.

"I can't see anything anymore. My vision has gone white." I say the words while trying to keep the smile on my face but am positive I'm only looking more nuts with every click.

"You're a natural! You're doing so good." The lie slips effort-lessly out of Jude's pink-painted lips.

This is just one more benefit of hanging out with adults. Ad-elaide is very honest. Which is wonderful . . . and almost brutal. Kids are fucking mean.

Almost as mean as vindictive ex-almost-husbands . . .

Once the photographers are satisfied with the pictures, they nod their thanks before finding other things to photograph as people start rolling through the door. Jude finally ditches the baby sip she was taking for the camera and takes the deep gulp she's wanted. "Oh my god. It's so good." She grabs my martini glass–holding hand and lifts it to my lips. "Isn't it so good?"

I take a bigger sip than intended thanks to Jude's "help" and feel my eyes go wide. "It really is good!"

Martinis aren't usually my favorite. They're always too strong and I don't love the taste of alcohol. This one is almost like juice. Ha. Now I get why they called it Juice Box. But now that I know how fast I could down these babies, I decide this will be my first and last of the night.

I haven't been drunk in years.

Not since the first night Ben had Adelaide after we separated. The next morning was so miserable that I vowed it would be my last-ever hangover. I've kept my promise so far and don't intend on ending it tonight. Especially not in a room filled with cameras to document it.

I focus on the front door, which is propped open as the constant stream of people flows through. I was really worried no one would come even though Jude assured me that wouldn't be the case. As always, she was right. I guess it doesn't matter that I'm a nobody when my rock star best friend is my cohost. I search the faces for any of the moms from Adelaide's school but don't recognize anyone yet.

"Stop, they look great." I grab Jude's attention from fixing the tissue paper in some of the guest bags. "And I need you to talk to me so I don't look like a loser in the corner. What time did your mom say she was going to get here?"

She rolls her eyes. "You do not look like a loser in the corner, but even if you were huddled in a corner, all you'd have to say is you're an introvert and people would get it." She reaches into her tiny purse and pulls out her phone. "My mom didn't say when she'd be here, but between her personality and traffic, it could really be anytime."

I love Jude's mom so much. She was a staple in my childhood, and I could always count on her to help me relax when the expectations from my own home became too stifling. Since we moved in with Jude, I thought I'd see her much more. But besides the few times she's come to get Jude for their brunches, Pilates, and all those other things normal moms and daughters do together, I haven't seen her at all. I feel like something is going on between them, but I don't have any proof, so I've kept my mouth shut.

"Well, whenever she decides to grace us with her presence will be great. I'm excited to finally get to really see her, you know, without Adelaide interrupting and while I'm wearing real clothes."

Mrs. Andrews is never anything short of stunning—often just teetering on the edge of ostentatious. It will be nice to see her tonight and not have to apologize for my stained T-shirt or the headscarf I hadn't taken off.

"Well, while I go get ready for our welcome speech and you're waiting for Juliette, I think I know someone else who might enjoy checking out your real clothes . . ." She lets the sentence fall off and does a quick chin jerk toward the door.

Considering the only people I invited to this party were the moms from Adelaide's kindergarten class, I know by the smirk on her face that I'm going to be face-to-face with Jennifer, aka Ms. Preppy Prints, aka the mom who is always matching her daughter.

I'd rather be alone in the corner.

I try to arrange my face into what I hope looks like a smile and not a grimace before I turn around. But my efforts are futile because when I do turn, it's not Jennifer's whitened teeth and flamingo-print dress that I see.

It's Hudson.

The last time I felt flutters of any kind in my stomach, I was pregnant with Adelaide. Even though I thought everything was okay with Ben until the day he walked away, I stopped getting butterflies from him long before.

I hoped I could talk some sense into myself after the whole *Addy Show* thing and gather my wits. I prayed I wouldn't feel like this. So when I feel them as Hudson's hazel eyes go soft, the delicate lines around his eyes crease, and his crooked smile tugs on

the corner of his mouth, it's not a feeling of excitement or giddi-
ness that follows.

It's fear.

And maybe even a little anger.

"Hudson, hi!" I try to gather my wits so I don't make a fool
out of myself even though all I want to do is duck the hell out.

"Hey." He takes a step closer, dropping one arm around my
shoulder and giving me a quick side hug, which doesn't just make
the flutters come back. No, it makes them take over. "This all
turned out great."

"Yeah, thanks. I didn't have anything to do with it. But you
knew that. Anyway . . ." His smile gets wider as he watches me
stumble over my words and fiddle with the drink in my hand, the
liquid courage I need but also need to avoid splashing onto the
floor. "I didn't realize you were coming tonight."

And honestly. Why didn't I realize he was coming tonight? Of
course he was going to come tonight! The guy has single-handedly
provided us with all of our tech and is teaching me how to edit—by
watching him do all of the actual editing. All of this rambling is to
say that while living with Jude has been a godsend in many ways,
it has *not* helped get my talking-to-adults game back on track.

"I figured I'd swing by and see all the work Jude has been telling us about." He shoves his hands in his pockets and rocks back
on his heels. "It's just too bad that you're here, taking away from
all the work she's put in."

What the hell?

I've never been a person who gets angry easily. Over the last
few years I've dealt with a cheating significant other, my mother,
and a small child who loves to push my buttons, so now it takes
a whole lot to rattle me.

But Hudson managed to do it in a second.

"Excuse me?"

"Oh shit. No." His eyes almost double in size and his cheeks go cherry red. He takes his hands out of his pockets and waves them in front of his chest. "That's not what I meant! I swear, in my head it sounded so much better."

I find that hard to believe.

Yes, Hudson has really grown on me, but he is still the same idiot from the gallery.

"Then, please"—I gesture for him to continue before my hands find their way to my hips—"explain how that sounded in your head."

I should just walk away, go talk to one of the many other people who are here to support us. Maybe hit up the manicure station since I haven't had a manicure in years. But instead, I'm standing here, needing Hudson to prove that even when men have kind eyes and crooked smiles and sit patiently with your daughter, they're still trash.

"I just meant that you look really gorgeous and it's hard to see past you." The color in his cheeks somehow deepens as he starts to study his shoes. "I wanted to tell you you're pretty. That's all."

Well.

What do I do with that?! Besides love his eyes and smile even more?

Even without the fear of a custody battle lingering over my every move, I swore off men after Ben.

Not only to avoid the drama that comes with starting a new relationship, but because I've watched enough crime shows to know when something goes bad, it's *always* the mom's boyfriend.

So why the hell does my entire body go soft and why is my stomach all knotted up? This is freaking treachery.

And how dare treachery feel so dreamy!

"Oh, um." I try to think of something, anything, to say. "Thanks, I guess?"

Yup.

Thanks, I guess?

That's what I came up with.

The music stops playing on the speakers, because of course the only thing this moment was missing was uncomfortable silence.

But, in a stroke of luck that never happens, Jude's voice comes over them a moment later. "Lauren Turner, get your MILF ass up here ASAP!"

Okay.

So not that lucky.

But if I have to decide between public humiliation at the hands of Jude Andrews or quiet and personal humiliation with Hudson, I'll take option one.

"Um, sorry," I say, not sorry at all to be escaping this awkward interaction. "Better get to her before she starts to lose it. But chat later?"

"Yeah, Lauren, later sounds good." He obviously knows I have no plans to talk to him later because all hints of embarrassment leave his face and instead he looks amused—amused!—as he watches me walk away.

"Hudson!" Jude's voice booms over the speakers again. "I see you giving Lauren flirty eyes! Just wait five minutes and you can have her back."

Okay. I've changed my mind. I would definitely prefer private humiliation over this.

You know where stuff like this never happens? At home. Screw pretty nails and martinis. I'm never leaving my couch again.

SIXTEEN

...

Jude

I was already thrilled with the way the party has turned out, but seeing the look of pure mortification on Lauren's face as she walks to the front of the room and our makeshift "stage" officially makes this the best party I've ever been to.

In my fucking life.

She gets to embarrass Addy. I get to embarrass her. Nobody embarrasses me. It's called balance.

"I'm going to murder you," she mutters through the fakest smile I've ever seen as she finally takes her place beside me.

I hold the mic down so I'm not accidentally broadcast throughout the store. "Not scared. We both know I'm the scrappy one." Before she can respond, I uncover the mic and bring it back to my mouth. "Hello, everyone!"

Cheers and whistles echo throughout the tight space, and lightning shoots through my veins. This is the feeling I love, what I still crave after years of not being onstage. Yeah, social media helps and I have a large following, but there's no feeling like being live and in front of a crowd. Too bad Lauren's hands balled into tight fists and the way she is chewing on her bottom lip indicate she feels the polar opposite.

Another way we balance each other out.

"Thank you so much for joining us tonight!" I shout even though I have a microphone. "For those of you who don't know us"—I turn and gesture to Lauren, who still looks like she might vomit—"this is my gorgeous best friend, Lauren Turner, I'm Jude Andrews, and we're the hosts of *Mom Jeans and Martinis*. The fab new podcast that gave us a reason to get dressed up and drink tonight."

I lift my martini glass in the air and take a quick sip and watch as the people in front of me do the same. "As you can see, I'm clearly the martinis part of this duo." I laugh with the crowd before moving onto the speech I semi-prepared. "Lauren's the peanut butter to my jelly, the Beyoncé to my Jay-Z, the filter to my photos, and the mom jeans to my martini. We met in the third grade while I was being reckless on the playground and my wonderful friend rushed to me when I fell on my head after dangling upside down on the monkey bars. From that day on, we were inseparable. We were even college roommates. Then Lauren went and met a man and had a baby. And me? Well, I worked out and took pretty pictures for the 'gram.

"Even though on the outside, our lives couldn't look more different, we're still best friends. And when things went south for us both over the last few years, we were each other's cushions. So now we're roommates again . . . except this time, Lauren traded in the mason jars filled with flavored vodka for a swear jar I've contributed to more than I'd care to admit, and we have another roommate, the love of both of our lives, Adelaide June.

"*Mom Jeans and Martinis* was started because we wanted to create a place where women could get together and support each other. It's for moms to find the person they were before they had children. It's for single women to love their lives without wanting to rush to the next step. It's female friendship amplified. It's motherhood raw. It's the life of two millennial women just trying to live our best lives out in these wild streets. And we're so happy to have you come along on this ride with us."

I told Lauren I would do most of the talking but she'd still need to say a little something. Even with that warning, she doesn't look the littlest bit prepared as she wraps her trembling fingers around the mic as I hand it to her.

"Um, yeah, like Jude said, thank you for coming tonight. I'm definitely more comfortable behind the scenes than I am standing in front of all of you beautiful people. I'm not sure I would've had the courage to start this podcast without Jude, and I definitely wouldn't have thrown together such an amazing event."

Even though she's holding a mic, she's still managing to pick at her nails with her free hand. But since I've already publicly embarrassed her once tonight, I don't scold her.

"Like Jude said, we're two women living completely different lives. Jude is a white woman with no kids and a fitness influencer. I'm a Black woman, a single mom, work at a doctor's office, and avoid any and all physical activity. On the surface, we have nothing in common, but life is so much deeper than the surface. Our differences have made our bond so much deeper." She turns to me and takes a deep breath before continuing on. "When I got engaged, people were always telling me how my fiancé was my soul mate. It never felt right, but I didn't know why."

"Probably because he's a dirtbag." I don't mean to cut in, but Addy's not here and it's basically impossible for me to bite my tongue when it comes to that douche-canoe.

Lauren laughs with the crowd, and her grip on the mic finally loosens. She shakes her head, her glorious smile probably stealing the breath of everyone here right now. "No. It's because you're my soul mate. You've been there for me at my best and my worst. I couldn't think of anyone else I'd want to do this with. So thank you for always pushing me to be better. I hope I do the same for you."

Fuck fuck fuck.

I don't cry.

Not out of anything except anger. My heart has been ripped up and patched back together so hastily that I'm still not sure it's functioning properly.

But because I never cry, I don't bother with waterproof mascara. And now Lauren has scored a direct hit to my feels and that burning behind my sinuses starts up. If I start blubbering in front of this crowd, someone's going to take a picture and my ugly cry face is going to be printed all over *StarGazer*. Guaranteed.

Fuck.

I take a step toward Lauren, closing the small gap between us, and wrap my arms around her, using her body as a shield for my face. "How dare you try to make me cry," I whisper in her ear. "Now you have to tell everyone to enjoy themselves so I can run to the bathroom and contain myself."

"You're so dramatic." Even though I've never been more serious, Lauren's body is shaking with laughter. "But fine, you run away and I'll keep pretending like I don't feel like throwing up from talking in front of everyone."

"That's all I ask." I squeeze her a little harder before turning on a heel and bolting away.

I hear Lauren fumble with the mic a little more before her voice comes over the speaker.

"Thanks for coming, everyone, now please, go! Drink, buy some jeans, get your nails done, whatever you want, just enjoy yourself. And thank you again for all of your support now and in the future."

I don't know why she was so nervous. She's a natural at pretty much everything she does and she's so fucking beautiful that no-body can take their eyes off her when she speaks.

One day, she's going to realize just how fucking powerful she is and she's going to rule the world. I won't rest until it happens.

Thankfully, because everyone was up front for our little speech, the single-person bathroom is unoccupied and I don't have to stand in line before I get my moment of privacy.

I push into the well-lit bathroom, making sure to lock it—we've all made that mistake before—and hanging my little purse on the hook behind the door. I close my eyes and slowly breathe in and out like I do at the end of each of my Pilates classes. Only once I feel like I've regained my composure do I open my eyes and look in the mirror. And not to be cocky or anything, but I still look great. The tears that welled up didn't mess with my mascara, and my winged eyeliner still looks fab. I reach into my purse to grab my sponge to get rid of any shininess I have, but when I see my phone lighting up, I grab that instead.

My phone is usually an extension of my arm, so having all of these missed call notifications is a bit of a novelty. Four missed calls, all from my mom.

I swear, only she could manage to get lost going to a place she was at only hours ago.

I swipe it open once it recognizes my face and hit my mom's contact to call her back.

"Hey, sweetheart," she greets after the third ring.

"Hi, Mom, do you need directions?" I grab my sponge and start blotting my T-zone. "Lauren is so excited to see you."

"Well actually," she starts, and my hand freezes on my fore-head. "You know how badly I wanted to come tonight, but Jona-thon found out that Angelica Sanders is hosting a party in the Hills. You know how important it is that I show my face there, right?"

"Yeah, of course." All of the emotion I was feeling only moments ago is gone. The love and appreciation and gratitude just dissipate, and those familiar feelings of anger and hurt and loneliness take over. "Wouldn't want you to miss that."

My tone has gone flat and I'm sure any other mom would notice, but not mine. "Oh good! I knew you'd understand," she says. "I can still stop by later this week. It's not like you two don't live together."

Her laughter through the phone makes my eyes twitch and my entire body tense. I know it's not normal to feel like you want to punch a wall when you hear your mom's laughter. It's why the only thing able to break through my rage is shame. This is just who she is. I need to learn to accept it. It's my fault for expecting a different result this time.

I'm pretty sure it's the literal definition of insanity.

"Yeah, of course. You're welcome anytime." I offer the open invitation knowing damn well she won't take me up on it . . . which is the only reason I extended it.

"Well, do give Lauren my love. We're pulling up now, so I have to go."

I'm met with dead air before I can even respond.

Typical.

I throw my phone and sponge back into my purse without another glance in the mirror.

The only good thing about my mom making me crazy tonight is that she did it while I'm in the vicinity of an open bar. And if anything can get me over Juliette Andrews, it's a free fucking martini.

Or five.

• • •

All of the martinis started to blend together about an hour ago.

I'm sure for most people, that would be concerning, but for

me, it means I've really hit my stride. Not being able to taste the difference means I can ditch the sugary juices and go straight to shots. And since I organized the event, the bartenders have no problem pouring me a vodka shot every time I slide past them.

Not all superheroes wear capes, folks.

"Jude, right?" Someone calls my name just after I toss back another shot.

The heat is still settling in my chest as I turn and come face-to-face with Matchy McMatcherson mom from the park.

"That's me! Jennifer, right?" I don't know if I would've remembered her face, but she's in another hot-pink-and-green-floral collared shirtdress, and it jogs my mind instantly. I forgot Lauren invited the Shady Moms Club.

"Yeah." She smiles. "I wasn't sure you'd remember."

"I could never forget those dresses." Oops. Sometimes vodka fucks with my filter. Thankfully, Jennifer's face lights up and I can tell she took my comment the wrong way.

Lucky for me. Lauren would murder me.

"Thanks!" She smiles freakishly big. Like, I can see her molars. "It's Lilly Pulitzer. I actually got one just like this for Lake."

Of course she did.

"How fascinating." I decide to switch topics before I say something I can't get myself out of. "Are you enjoying yourself?"

Safe, easy small talk that centers around the guest's feelings. Miss Liddell, my etiquette teacher back when I was in elementary school, would be so proud.

Well, minus the drunk thing.

"I didn't know what to expect when Lauren invited us, but it's wonderful." She holds up her purple martini. "It's like the perfect moms' night out. I'm honestly surprised Lauren did it."

Normally, this is the moment I would stake the claim to the glory of creating this party, but that sounded like she was trying to fucking throw shade at my girl. And that's not happening on my watch. Not ever.

"Why would you be surprised? Lauren is the most capable human being I've ever met."

"Well, you know. I know you have this wonderful following and your mom is so fabulous." She leans in closer, overestimating her safety, like I won't hesitate to slap a bitch. "Don't get me wrong, Adelaide is so sweet and Lauren seems like she's doing the most with what she has. But she's just a little . . . I don't know. Uptight? I don't know what her upbringing was like, but I'm sure being such a young, single mother has taken a toll on top of everything else she's been through."

Sober me wouldn't have handled this situation well. But drunk? *Ha!*

"I'm sorry"—*not fucking sorry*—"but aren't you the same woman who wouldn't let your daughter play in the dirt at a freaking playdate? And you're calling Lauren uptight?"

I see the exact moment she realizes she's made a huge mistake by talking to me, but it's too late for her.

"And I know people like you live in their own worlds, but you were there when we told you that we met in third grade, right? We both went to Ivymore Academy, and because I can tell you're a little racist, Lauren wasn't on scholarship. Her mom is Gloria Turner of Turner and Smith, and her dad is a newly retired neurosurgeon. So I'm not sure what upbringing you're thinking she had if it's not a wonderful one with brilliant parents, great schooling, and better friends—me, clearly."

"I'm not racist." Of course she only took that away.

"Yeah, you kind of are." She opens her mouth to defend her nonexistent honor, but I already know where this is going and beat her to it. "If you're about to tell me you have a Black friend, you can just turn your tight ass around, walk out the door, and go back home to what I'm assuming is a miserable life considering you decided to try to talk shit to me about my *best fucking friend*!"

I don't mean to raise my voice, but vodka filter. I can't help it. And also? Fuck this bitch.

Too bad that's also the moment Lauren happens to walk closer to us.

She looks at me, her eyebrows furrowed together. "Um, hi, you two. Everything okay here?"

Before I can answer, Karen, president and CEO of the Karens, beats me to it. "Actually no, everything is not okay here." She glares at me, defying the laws of Botox. "When you invited me, I didn't think I was taking time away from my family to come and be insulted."

I roll my eyes so hard that I can hear my dad's old warning of "they're going to get stuck like that" floating through my mind.

"Insulted? What?" Lauren asks, and I don't even have to look at her, I can feel the heat of her anger radiating off her. "I'm sure there was a misunderstanding. We're both so grateful you came."

"I don't think her calling my life miserable could be interpreted in any other way." Jennifer aims her stupid, smug smile my way like she bested me.

"Don't forget racist," I say. "I also called you racist."

"Do you see?" Her face turns so red that I think she might actually explode. "I'm sorry, Lauren. This is unacceptable and I hope you decide to do something about this. She's clearly unhinged and she will not be welcomed at playdates until something is done."

"Oh god. No playdate! What will I ever do with my free time if I can't go to playdates?" I mock, rolling my eyes again, even knowing that Lauren is likely plotting where to bury my body.

"I'm so sorry, Jennifer. This isn't how she normally behaves."

Lauren growls out the end of the sentence and I know I'm in such deep shit.

But even knowing that, I still can't keep my mouth shut. "She's right. I don't. I only act like this when someone deserves it, and you deserved it. Don't come for my fucking girl and there won't be any problems."

In the infamous words of Jamie Foxx: "Blame it on the a-a-a-a-a-alcohol."

Jennifer doesn't say anything to that. Instead she just stomps off, tossing her hair over her shoulder as she goes.

"What a bitch," I say to her retreating form. I don't know why Lauren invited her in the first place. Sure, Addy has to invite all the kids in the class to her party, but we're grown as fuck. We can be selective!

Lauren's long fingers grip my wrist and she starts to drag me through the thinning crowd. Because of the slightly more-than-is-advised amount of booze I've consumed, staying on my feet as she pulls me along is a challenge. When we reach the dressing rooms, she shoves me inside before jerking the velvet curtain closed.

"What the actual fuck were you thinking, Jude?" She hisses the words out, but this time it's not the tone or the glare that makes me worried. Lauren cussed. Lauren never cusses. It's like her mouth is physically incapable of forming the words. Especially an f-bomb.

And it sobers me up almost instantly.

"I'm sorry, but you should've heard the—"

"No!" She cuts me off, also very un-Lauren-like. "I don't care what she said. You ignore it and bitch about it later. You don't call her miserable and a racist!"

"But she was being racist. If you would've just heard her—"

She cuts me off again. "I know she's racist, Jude. I'm a Black woman in America. Do you think I don't deal with racist shit

every single day of my life? Because I do. But I have to interact
with this woman for the next six years, so I ignore her and I play
nice while taking her number, remembering what she said, and
keeping her an arm's length away." The rigidness to her shoulders
starts to melt away, and she slides onto the little bench at the back
of the dressing room. "Adelaide loves Lake. And unless Jennifer
said something that directly affected Adelaide, I was going to ignore it. But now, thanks to you, I'm going to have to placate her
feelings and listen to how she voted for Hillary or donated to the
NAACP once upon a time when I should be focusing on my
daughter during her first week of school."

I hate how stressed and upset she is, but I can't pretend like I
regret the things I said to that woman. Maybe next time she'll
think before running her stupid mouth. But I do have enough
sense to read the (dressing) room and not say that to Lauren.

"I'm sorry that I made things awkward, but you know me.
There's no way I'm just going to let someone come and talk shit
about you to me. You protect Addy. I protect you. That's how
things work in this sister wives circle of life."

"I do appreciate you always having my back, just next time,
please take it down a notch." She stands up and hugs me, which
I take as a good sign that she's not planning on breaking the lease.
"Especially when it comes to the moms in Adelaide's class. I warned
you mom groups were vicious. Maybe next time you'll listen."

This is why I love Lauren. I'm not perfect. Not at all. And even
though she doesn't hesitate to call me on my shit, she also forgives
really fast. I never feel like I need to grovel with her or earn her
love. We both know that even if we're mad at each other, we'll
always have each other's backs. Always.

We pull apart and open the curtain.

Besides the little tiff with Jennifer and my mom—unsurprisingly—
not showing, the party was amazing. And now that people are

beginning to leave, the aftermath to Olivia's cute boutique is obvious.

The other obvious thing? The way Hudson is still lingering around and not so subtly checking out my friend. I might have blown it with the mom from hell, but I think I can help out here.

"I'm going to stick around and help Olivia clean up." I hook my arm through Lauren's and start to slowly guide us toward where Hudson is tinkering with his phone in the corner. "I know we were planning on catching a ride home together, but since I know you need to get some sleep before Addy comes home tomorrow, why don't you go without me?"

"You set up, I can help clean." She says what I already knew she would. She's too nice. Why she chooses to be my friend is a mystery. "I'm used to not having much sleep."

"No, seriously, you should go," I tell her, and when we get close to Hudson, I drop all pretense of trying to be discreet in my motives. "Oh my god! Hudson? I didn't even see you standing over here! But how lucky that you're still here!"

I feel Lauren trying to pry her arm away from me, but thanks to my killer Pilates routine, she doesn't even gain an inch.

"Um, yeah, still here." Poor, earth-loving Hudson looks so confused. One day he'll become immune to my antics, they all do. "I just wanted to say bye to La . . . to both of you." He corrects himself and not smoothly at all.

"Well, why don't you say goodbye to me and take my Lauren here home? She needs to get back, and who knows how long I'll be here. It could be hours, really." It won't be hours. I give it thirty minutes tops. I hired a cleaning crew to come in before opening tomorrow. We just have to clear the big things so they can clean. But Lauren and Hudson don't need to know that. "You'd really be doing us both a huge favor."

"I mean, if you're good with that?" He looks at Lauren and

his eyes do this weird/cute thing they weren't doing when he was looking at me seconds ago.

"If it's not too big of a hassle, I'd really appreciate it," Lauren says.

I don't care how many times she tells me she's not into him, her voice, expression, and body language all say something different.

"Not a hassle at all. You're on my way home." A huge grin pulls at Hudson's lips and he looks like Addy when I sneak her candy when Lauren's not looking.

He's so into her. Plus, I've been to Hudson's place before. We are not even close to being on his way.

I finally release Lauren's arm and give her one more quick hug before she walks over to Hudson.

"Now, you crazy kids, don't get too wild!" I yell after them, ignoring the not-so-nice finger Lauren holds up as she walks away.

When they're gone, I head over to my favorite bartender of the night.

He has a shot waiting for me.

I wonder if my mom saw pictures from tonight or if she wished she'd come here instead of the Hills.

I throw that shit back, not even flinching as the burn hits the back of my throat. Then I go to find Olivia. Time to clean up my mess.

Well, at least one of them.

SEVENTEEN

...

Lauren

"I don't get it." Jude shoves a bite of scrambled eggs in her mouth. "Is it her first day of kindergarten or is she starting her work as a congresswoman?"

Okay. To be fair, one could say that I've gone a little overboard for Adelaide's first day of school. But one could also say that she's my freaking baby, she's growing up, and "overboard" is actually just the right amount of excitement and fanfare.

They could also say that I'm in the middle of a custody battle and everything I do for her feels like it could be the last and I'm an emotional wreck just trying to freaking survive. So yeah . . .

Overboard is just going to be the norm until this mess is over.

Adelaide giggles as I adjust the bow on her head while she finishes her breakfast. "You're so silly, Auntie Jude."

"Kindergarten is a big deal, right, Adelaide? You're going to learn so much and make so many friends. Remember all the special art projects you'll be able to do this year?" Adelaide is a social butterfly who has never had a hard time adjusting, but I've still been working overtime trying to make kindergarten sound like the best thing that's ever existed.

I also realize that I'm doing this more to convince me than her.

It's just *such* a big change.

When she was in preschool, it was half days and I would pick her up during my lunch hour and take her to my parents' until I got off work. This is a whole new world. She'll be in after-school care because Remington Academy is too far from my parents. It's full days, a new school, a new teacher, and, even though we've gone on the playdates, new friends.

Also Lake and her mother . . . which is something I've been working very hard not to think about.

Safe to say, I'm freaking the freak out.

"I guess." Jude stands up and takes her plate to the kitchen. "I'm pretty sure when I went to kindergarten my mom maybe snapped a picture and pushed me onto the bus."

"A bus?" Adelaide turns to me, toast crumbs stuck all over her little lips. "Can I take a bus?"

"Remington doesn't have buses, so you get to ride with me." I grab the napkin and wipe her face through her trying to jerk her head away. "Plus, buses smell weird."

She seems satisfied with the answer. She shrugs and hops out of her seat. "I'm going to get my new shoes! Then you can take pictures of me with my special sign. Okay?"

Clearly this is Adelaide's world and I'm just living in it.

"Sounds like a plan." I tap the screen of my phone to check the time. "But hustle, we need to leave in ten minutes."

We really have twenty minutes, but I've learned that it's better to give her and Jude a shorter time frame. Otherwise we'd never be on time for anything.

Adelaide runs up the stairs in her adorable plaid jumper, her curls bouncing with each step. As soon as she's out of sight, Jude breaks up the silence.

"Lauren, what in the fresh hell is this?" she asks, holding up Adelaide's opened personalized lunch box that matches her personalized backpack, courtesy of my parents. No way was I shelling out that kind of money.

"Uh . . . Adelaide's lunch box . . ." My eyebrows furrow together. I know Jude bought lunch most of the time, but even she knows what a lunch box is.

"Well, duh, I'm not a total idiot." She rolls her eyes and unzips it. "I mean, what even is this lunch?"

"What do you mean? It's just a sandwich, fruit, and cheese puffs." I feign ignorance. I know exactly what she means.

"Yeah, but the sandwich is cut like a flower, the fruit is arranged according to color so it looks like a rainbow. The organic cheese puffs are in a . . . what is this?" She pulls the cheese puffs out of the unicorn bento box I put inside her lunch box. "A cupcake wrapper? And she has a thermos with her name on it. What happened to Lunchables?"

All right.

So here's the thing. It's a struggle being a mom in the age of Pinterest. It makes you feel like unless you are going above and beyond, you're failing. So I might have gone above in making her lunch. But it's the first time she'll be eating at school and I wanted it to be special for her.

Again, am I overcompensating because of fear?

Possibly.

I know a judge isn't going to look at pictures of school lunches, but if they do, I'll for sure win.

"That's a very well-rounded, visually pleasing meal that Adelaide will love, thank you very much." I ignore the way she rolls her eyes at me—because she's totally right, it's nuts—and grab my phone and the huge Canon camera Ben bought for me for Mother's Day one year, and throw the strap over my head. It dangles around my neck like the suburban mom equivalent of Flavor Flav's clock. "Grab her sign, please?"

I ordered one of those personalized "First Day of School" chalkboards from Etsy. It has her name on it and then places you can fill out what grade she's going into, her age, the date, her teacher's name, what she wants to be when she grows up, and things she loves. And, because I'm me, I didn't just scribble everything down, I bought a hand-lettering book and made sure it looked beautiful. I mean sure, I could've just typed it up and printed it out for her to hold. But again, this is special! She only starts kindergarten once.

"Okay, Mommy!" Adelaide flies down the stairs with her new navy glitter Keds on. I swear, this might be the first time ever shoes weren't an early-morning fight. She was so excited to finally wear that she found a special spot in her closest and then checked on them every night. "I'm ready for pictures!"

"Addy June! Why are you the cutest, flyest kindergartner on the face of the earth? I can't even deal!" Jude runs from the kitchen and picks Adelaide up, swinging her in circles.

Adelaide squeals in delight. Her headband falls off, but her cheeks are flushed and her eyes are gleaming when Jude puts her down. This is just another reason why I know that living with her is what we needed. She loves Adelaide almost as much as I do, and Adelaide loves her. Nothing feels missing when we're all together.

Sure, I still kind of want to kill Jude for what she said to Jennifer the other night, but I know her heart and why she did it. If someone tried to bad-mouth Jude in front of me, I probably would've had—almost—the same reaction.

Jude bends down to look at Adelaide eye to eye. "Did I tell you I got you something for your first day of school?"

"No! What is it?" Adelaide starts bouncing and clapping her hands. My girl loves surprises and gifts so much that sometimes I wonder if she might actually be part Jude's kid too.

Jude grabs her hand and pulls her to the entryway closet. She lets go of Adelaide and reaches to the top shelf, pulling out a little bag that has three tiny boxes, each one with a different-color ribbon. She hands Adelaide the one with the pink ribbon, gives me the one with the gold ribbon, and she takes the silver-ribbon box.

"When I count to three, we can take off the ribbon and open it, okay?"

Adelaide nods her head, and I swear her entire body is trembling with excitement. I'm just really curious. Jude is a notoriously terrible gift giver. Not in thought, but in timing and keeping secrets. She usually gives me my Christmas gifts in November . . . and that's after she's already told me what they are. But she hasn't mentioned a word about these.

"One . . . two . . . three!" she says, and we're all ripping off the ribbons and giggling like crazy.

Then I open the box.

And my giggling stops.

Somewhere I hear Adelaide's gasp of excitement at the shiny necklace Jude's just given her, but I can't pull my gaze away from the small box in my hand. My thumb grazes over each of our names engraved on the triangle attached to the delicate chain.

"See?" Jude says to Adelaide. "There's your name, Mommy's name, and my name. All on the strongest shape. So no matter where you go, you'll always be able to remember how much we all love each other."

"It's so pretty. I love it!" Adelaide leaps into Jude's arms, causing them both to fall on the ground as Jude covers Adelaide's face in kisses.

To Adelaide, I know this is a fun, pretty necklace, but to me? It's so much more.

I love Jude to the end of the freaking universe. She's loyal—almost to a fault—my biggest encourager, and lives life with a zest I can only hope will rub off on me. What she is not is emotionally open. Never has been. But since her dad died, it's gotten progressively more noticeable. And every time I try to dig in, breach the walls she's built around her, she jokes me off. Or, as I've seen lately, drinks in excess.

I know her mom not showing at the launch party hurt her. I know something is going on between the two of them. I'm pretty sure I know Jude better than she knows herself. So even when she thinks she has successfully thrown me off the scent of her pain, I'm really just retreating to figure out what the hell my Trojan horse is going to be. And this necklace, this thoughtful, meaningful necklace that says more than maybe she even intended, just reinforced everything I was already thinking.

"Jude." My voice is hoarse with unshed tears. "This is amazing."

"Right?" She ignores the way I'm obviously on the verge of tears and starts to untangle her body from Adelaide's. "I saw them and knew we had to get them, like those BFF necklaces we used to buy, but better. I got Addy a shorter and stronger chain, though, because I love you, Addy June, but you play rough AF and I knew you needed extra strength."

Adelaide pushes off the beige carpet, her little jumper wrinkled and crooked, but looking so cute and happy that I can't even care. "What's *AF* mean?"

I bite my lip and look to Jude to see how she works her way out of this one.

"Oh, it means . . . it means awesome forks." She says this with such authority that I know with one hundred percent certainty I'm going to get a call from Adelaide's teacher for her constant usage of *AF* every time she thinks something is cool.

Because I'm still emotional AF from the necklace, but also impressed with how quickly she worked that one out, I let it go.

"Adelaide, pick your headband up and go grab your backpack and clip your lunch box on like Nana showed you, okay? I'm going to talk to Auntie Jude real fast."

"Okay, Mommy." She starts to walk toward the kitchen, then halts her steps and swings back around, pointing a light pink polished finger at me. "And *then* can we take my pictures?"

Leadership skills, leadership skills, leadership skills.

I always want her to be so strong willed and ready to speak her mind, but sometimes it's a serious struggle living with it.

"Yes, then we'll take your pictures and go to school and I'll take more pictures."

I told my office I'd be in late today. I want to make sure I get as many pictures as possible and then linger by the classroom door until her teacher asks me to leave. And I took Friday off. I'm going to pick her up from school and I have a whole evening planned to celebrate her first week of school. We're going to go to this warehouse that's full of bounce houses and have dinner at a restaurant with milkshakes that are unreal, and then we're going to come home and have a spa night while watching a movie. She's going to love it and I can't wait.

She turns back around and continues her way to the kitchen, so I think my answer seems to appease her. Even though I think I might hear her mumble, "Finally," beneath her breath.

Sassy.

Once she's out of sight, I walk over to Jude just in time to see her exaggerated eye roll. I swear, she's like an adult Adelaide.

"Don't you come over here getting all emo on me. It's a necklace. That's all."

"Bullshit," I whisper so only she can hear, and her eyes go wide. Life lesson: when you don't swear often, it has a greater effect. "You know these are more than just a little gift and don't even try to pretend with me."

"Lauren, really—" She starts, but I cut her off.

"No. Don't Lauren me." I make a zipper motion in front of her mouth. "I know that I've been preoccupied with everything from Ben to the podcast to Adelaide, but don't think I haven't noticed that something serious is going on with you. I don't know what it is, but this necklace means something. Our unit means something to you."

She unzips her lips with her hand before talking. "Well, duh, you know how much I love you and Addy."

"I do. But I also know you aren't letting me in. You're always there for me. Literally, always. And I know you think that by being strong and not confiding in me, you're protecting me. But you're not. How can I be your friend if you won't let me in?" I wanted to yell at her a little bit, but the words come out as a plea instead. "I can see that you aren't okay. I know something is going on with your mom. Please, just let me be there for you like you are for me."

Jude is a great actress. Starred in our high school plays, majored in the arts, lives her life out on social media without blinking an eye. She never breaks character. Not ever. But right now, the strong, carefree facade she's been trying to sell me finally starts to crumble. Her bright blue eyes start to gloss over and her chin quivers.

It's the closest I've seen her come to crying since her dad's funeral.

And of course, it's the moment my little ray of sunshine barges in between us, grabbing both of our hands and yelling, "Time for pictures! I can't be late on my first day!"

I look over at Jude, her bright smile back in place along with all of her walls.

I was so close.

"All right, girlfriend." Jude opens the front door and helps Addy position herself with her sign on our little front porch. "Big smiles and strike some poses!"

I start snapping pictures, not letting my finger off the button, hoping at least one shot will capture a fraction of the joy I can feel in this moment. Fighting back the fear that next year, I'll have an empty sign and no Adelaide on her first day of school.

Adelaide smiles her huge, totally fake smile, holding her sign with one hand and putting her free hand on her little hip. "Like this?"

"Yes, queen slash president!" Jude says, probably a little too loud outside this early in the morning. "New pose! Yasss! Work it, work it!"

Thanks to Jude and her antics, Adelaide's fake smile is gone and the smile that lights up my whole entire world is bright and wide. Her curls frame her face, highlighting her eyes, which are sparkling with excitement.

And I know that if I could create this magnificent little human? If after all the uncertainty she's faced in her short life, that she can stand here full of confidence and joy? Jude doesn't stand a chance against me.

I'll crack her wide open. No matter how hard she fights it.

EIGHTEEN

. . .

Lauren

From: Lauren
Date: September 6
Subject: Cheers to that!

Hey!

Today's the day! The first ever episode of *Mom Jeans and Martinis* is officially LIVE! Because I'm behind a computer, you can't see me, but if you could, you'd know I'm full-blown channeling Eminem via *8 Mile* with my sweaty palms. But I've been sitting here, trying to figure out why I'm so nervous and I think it might be because we don't really know each other yet. And since you're here and I'm here, I figure now's about as good a time as ever to change that!

I'm Lauren, a single mom to a 5-year-old firecracker named Adelaide. I grew up wanting to be a doctor and was on track to do so until I found myself unexpectedly pregnant at 23. Even though I would do it all over again for Adelaide, pregnancy was not fun . . . it was actually miserable. So while I was on bed rest, my fiancé and I decided it would be best that I stay home and focus on the baby while he finished getting his medical degree. Yeah, no need to go back and reread. I'm single. That plan didn't work out all too well for me.

I'm sure some of you are thinking, "Whoa there, Lauren! We just met! Slow it with the oversharing already." And that's probably fabulous advice, but since we're friends now (I called it already, no take-backs!) and you're going to be listening to *Mom Jeans and Martinis*, it's best you know up front . . . we're oversharers. Me, because I have spent the last five years of my life with a small human and have forgotten how to properly interact with adults. Jude, my cohost/best friend/roommate/unofficial sister wife, has no kids. She overshares because she's your typical millennial who posts everything on social media and therefore has no concept of boundaries.

Between the two of us, you're in for a ride—like to Target or your favorite coffee shop, not hell or anything. It will be fun, I promise. We aren't perfect and just because we have a microphone and editing equipment available doesn't mean we pretend to be. We started *Mom Jeans and Martinis* to be an open dialogue. To talk about motherhood without the fear of judgment and talk life without the expectation of knowing everything already. Because nobody knows it all. That's part of the fun.

Jude and I live wildly different lives, but we're still best friends. And we hope that by joining us today and every Tuesday from here on out, you'll realize how sometimes it's the differences between us that create the most magic.

Cheers! 🥂
Lauren

PS In case you haven't already, don't forget to subscribe! And maybe leave a review . . . but only if it's a good one. Kidding. Kinda.

I reread the email until the words blur together into one giant blob of text. As a person who has only sent very professional emails for the last three years, everything in me wants to delete this. It's too personal and informal. I mean, I used a freaking emoji! And thanks to Jude and her other social media maven friends, our email list is bigger than I would've ever imagined . . . and so is the pressure. It was already a decent size, but after everyone posted pictures of the launch to their Instagram accounts, it tripled.

But instead of hitting the delete button, I close my eyes, take a deep breath, and hit the send button.

"There," I say to absolutely nobody. Not even the sun is up yet. "Done. No turning back now."

I don't know what I thought would happen when I finally sent this out. Logically I knew a marching band and confetti wouldn't magically appear in my living room, but it still feels slightly anticlimactic. I mean, this was a big deal for me! This is the most I've put myself out there in . . . well? In forever.

I take a sip of my coffee, which stopped being hot about thirty minutes ago, and look at the screen, expecting something to happen. What? Still not sure. An email telling me I'm insane and to never email them again? Possibly. A response thanking me for this amazing email and my superb usage of the champagne glass emoji? Also possible.

I just want something to happen.

I wonder if this is how Jude feels every time she posts a picture on Instagram. Just waiting for likes and comments to roll in? I would lose my mind. Thank goodness she's in charge of the social media part of this podcast.

After refreshing our podcast email account approximately a thousand times, I close my computer, drain the last of my coffee, and walk to the kitchen so I can make Adelaide's lunch and obsess over something—or someone—else.

Ben.

We have our first meeting next week, and I can't help but think it's going to be even worse than I thought. I need this to work and be over. I don't know what I can say that will make me sound like the better parent. Ben is a doctor, I'm in administration. Ben owns a house, I have a roommate. I'm just so scared that by trying to be easygoing, I screwed myself over.

When I picked Adelaide up from his house last weekend, he seemed fine. Stephanie was nice as ever. They gave her a really cute sequined pencil case for school filled with all sorts of goodies. I just don't trust it. But I guess that makes sense given our history.

I grab one of the banana-zucchini chocolate chip muffins I made while Adelaide was gone and put it in her lunch box along with turkey roll ups, carrot sticks, and heart-shaped cucumber slices. I pull out my phone and take a quick picture like Jude has insisted I do each morning after she gave me a hard time about Adelaide's flower-shaped sandwich yesterday. I open our junk drawer, which is actually pretty organized, and pull out the pink card stock and silver glitter pen I bought. I write out a quick note telling Adelaide I love her, complete with lots of hearts, before I put it on top of her unicorn bento box and zip up her lunch box.

"It's so early." Jude's groggy voice comes from behind me and scares the crap out of me.

"What the heck!" I jump, holding a hand over my rapidly beating heart. "You scared me."

Her eyes are barely open as she grabs a mug out of the cabinet. She drags her pedicured feet across the vinyl kitchen tiles to the coffee machine and fills her mug to the brim, taking a deep sip without adding cream or sugar.

Gag.

"I still don't know how you drink your coffee like that." My coffee is basically half vanilla creamer, and that's how it will always be.

"I save my sugar for better things than coffee." She closes her eyes and takes another sip, inhaling the caffeine like it's the only thing keeping her alive. "Unless I go to a fancy coffee shop, then I'll try whatever sugary, fun, overpriced latte they have if I think it will photograph well."

Influencers are so freaking weird.

"So I'm guessing you don't want one of the muffins I made?" I didn't add extra sugar . . . besides the chocolate chips, and I used a light hand.

"Are you crazy? Of course I want one." Her voice kicks up a notch, like the coffee is finally settling in her system. "You added zucchini. That's all I needed to know to convince myself it's guilt-free. And send me the recipe so I can add the link with the picture I'm posting of the muffins later this week."

I hand her a muffin and she takes a giant bite, groaning as she chews. "I'll email it over to you later."

She gives me a thumbs-up, washing her muffin down with bitter coffee.

We sit in silence for a few moments. Me still enjoying the final moments of silence, Jude getting rid of the final residues of sleep.

"Why are you up so early?" I ask once she's tossed her muffin wrapper in the trash and rinsed out her mug. "The only time I've seen you awake before the sun comes up is if you haven't gone to sleep yet."

"I have a photo shoot while teaching a Pilates class, and then I have meetings with some of the sponsors my mom's agent set up." The edge always present in her voice when she mentions her mom is stronger than ever. I want to dig, but it's too early . . . even for me. "She helped secure some sponsors for both of us and I have a meeting with a few of them today. It's looking like they might want to expand our work together."

"Of course they want to work with you more! You're amazing and so good at what you do."

"Thank you. I do work really hard." Unlike me, Jude has never had a problem accepting compliments. "The only thing is this company has a moral clause, which I already broke a little at the launch party. So if we expand, I'm going to really have to check how I act when I go out in public."

"Well, I have faith in you."

This weekend was kind of a disaster, but she felt genuinely terrible after. She may be a hot mess sometimes, but she's dependable and I know she wouldn't break a contract just to get drunk.

"Thank you." She stops and her eyes bulge out of her head before she slaps my arm. "Oh my god! I can't believe I let it slip my mind. It's podcast day! Are you so excited?"

She's bouncing from foot to foot, and if she was still sleepy before, she's not now.

"I'm not sure yet. Right now I'm just nervous." I start to pick at my nails but drop my hands to my sides when Jude glares at me and raises her hand like she's about to pop me . . . which she might. "I sent the email just before you came downstairs. It feels really official now. I'm just nervous that maybe Kim was wrong and this is the opposite of what I should do."

I don't know if I've always been a worrier or if I just can't remember what life was like before I became a mom, but I feel like my nerves are constantly frayed. I'm sure my turbulent pregnancy triggered it, but the calm I expected once I held Adelaide in my arms never came. I've always been so afraid of losing her that what's happening with Ben feels like a self-fulfilling prophecy. What if everything I do is only making matters worse? What if nothing I do can stop Ben from getting her?

"Lauren." Jude takes a step closer to me, resting her hands on my shoulders. "All you do is talk about how much you love being a mom. Sure, you're real about it getting hard, but nobody could listen to you talk about Addy and not hear the love that emanates from you. It's going to be great."

I close my eyes and let Jude's words sink in.

She's right.

It's going to be amazing. I know it.

• • •

I know nothing.

This podcast is a disaster and is going to be the absolute death of me.

After our big recording day, Hudson helped me edit them and told me how to schedule the publishing dates. Literally, all I had to do was send an email and publish the podcast.

The email? Sent. Easy-peasy.

The podcast? It's still not up.

I just *ass*umed it was up and running all morning, and went about my business as usual. It wasn't until I dropped Adelaide off at school and decided to listen to it on my way to work that I realized it wasn't live. And of course it happens on a day when Jude is booked all morning and can't help out.

Proving even more that Lady Luck hates my freaking guts, my usually laid-back job working the front desk and doing admin at an ob-gyn's office went crazy when not one but *two* women's water broke while they were waiting for their checkups.

What are the freaking chances?

I managed to text Hudson after the first waterworks show to see if he could help, but I haven't been able to check my phone since. I feel like a leech. He's such a good guy and I feel so bad constantly asking him to help with things I could probably just google.

"Lauren." Jackie, one of the nurses, calls my name. "It's your lunchtime, why don't you head out."

The office I work at is composed of all women. Something I, and our patients, appreciate immensely. If I'd known about this office, I would've for sure gone to them when I was pregnant with Adelaide. I'm not saying all male doctors are terrible, but mine was. He was so condescending and dismissive.

Being a Black woman in America is hard. Being a pregnant Black woman in America is terrifying. I'm almost certain that if it wasn't for Ben, Adelaide and I both would've died. Just another statistic of a Black woman who died with pregnancy complications.

Beside Adelaide herself, it's the only thing I'm grateful to Ben for.

I look at the clock and see that Jackie is right, it's actually ten minutes past my break time. Thanks to the pandemonium of the water shows, we're running behind and I didn't even realize how late it had gotten. "Thanks, Jackie." I grab my purse from beneath the front desk. "I'll be back soon."

"No," Kristen, my favorite doctor, says. "Take your entire break for once. You always come back early and today was a mess. Literally. You need a real break. Actually, you know what? Take an extra thirty minutes. We can handle it without you for a bit."

"But—" I start, but she does the zipper motion in front of her mouth . . . and I see why it's so effective with Adelaide.

"No. We'll kick you out if you come back early."

Ew. Doctors are so bossy.

"Fine, I guess if you don't want me." I pout, hoping to channel the look Adelaide gives and break some of their resolve.

"Not for an hour and a half." Kristen shoos me out the door. "Bye, go. Leave."

"Geez." I throw my purse strap over my shoulder. "I'm going, I'm going."

The door to the office closes with a soft thud behind me, and I look at the time on my phone. I see a few notifications from Hudson and relax a little. I still don't know what I'll do for an hour and a half, but at least now I can call Hudson and hopefully work out the podcast.

Our office is located on the first floor of the hospital we deliver at. It's super convenient for the doctors and the patients . . . especially those whose waters break in the office. I usually eat lunch in the hospital cafeteria. They have a really good salad bar and it's cheap, but I guess now that I have so much time, I can go to a real restaurant.

The bright, sunlight-filled lobby comes into my sights as the quiet murmurs of hushed conversations start to get a little louder. I reach into my purse, trying to find my keys somewhere in the mess of receipts, crayons, and unused tissues. I'm a pretty organized and neat person, but my purse? That's another story. I stop near the lobby entrance, shaking my purse, trying to lure my keys to the top of the pile, when a hand lands on my shoulder and scares the ever-loving hell out of me.

I jump away from the hand, a little scream falling out of my mouth that echoes among the quiet voices around me.

"Shit," a familiar voice says behind me. "Sorry, I didn't mean to scare you."

"Hudson!" I put my hand on my chest and take a deep breath to slow my racing heart. "What are you doing here?"

Between Jude scaring me this morning and now this, I probably just lost a full year of my life.

"Oh, um . . . it's just . . . I . . ." He stumbles over his words, and I realize how rude I must've sounded.

"Not that I'm not thrilled to see you," I say, trying to recover, "I just wasn't expecting you."

"You seemed freaked about the podcast and I know how stressful those first ones are . . ." He fidgets with the straps of his backpack, still seeming a little nervous. "Jude told me your lunchtime. I texted you. I guess they didn't go through."

"No . . . I mean, yeah. They did come through." I pull out my phone and show him the notifications on my screen. "Today was just so hectic in the office. I was going to read them when I got to my car."

"Word." He exhales and seems to finally relax a little bit. He always seems so cool and collected, it's weird seeing him so fidgety and awkward. "Well, I brought my laptop with me if you want to go somewhere and get the podcast all figured out?"

"Oh my god!" I launch myself at him, wrapping my arms around his neck and hugging him tight. "Yes, please! You're a lifesaver!"

I reluctantly let him go—I want to feel his arms around me for much longer—and his cheeks are bright pink as he adjusts the straps of his backpack I knocked off him in my hug, which was accidentally very aggressive.

"There's a little place close by," he says. "They have good food and Wi-Fi, if you want to head there? You can just ride with me if you want."

Considering I think my purse ate my keys, this is perfect.

The ride in Hudson's Prius to Locally Grown is quick and quiet. Both of which I appreciate after a crazy morning. Once inside, we head to an empty table in the corner and place our orders with the überhandsome hippie, boho waiter who undoubtedly moonlights as an actor.

Hudson pulls out his laptop and opens the files of our podcast that he—thankfully—didn't delete, and has me sign into our Libsyn account so he can figure out how I screwed up something that's basically impossible to screw up. And after typing a few words and a couple of clicks? *Mom Jeans and Martinis* is up and running.

"Holy crap." I pull out my phone and open my podcast app to see that it's live. "Thank you so much!"

I want to hug him again, but he's across the table and my arms aren't that long.

"You don't have to thank me." His shy smile makes his eyes curve up like little moons. I love it so much. "I told you I was here for you and I meant it."

I know he's just talking about the podcast, but besides my dad—who can also be iffy depending on my mom's mood—I've never been able to rely on a man. I mean, sure, I haven't tried since Ben. I got burned once, I don't need it to happen again before I learn my lesson. But Hudson? He's just so different. He's amazing at what he does, but he almost completely lacks ego. Which seems to be a stark contrast to the way most influencers behave.

The Addy Show is now up to three episodes. He still sits with her, no matter how long it takes or how many times she changes her mind, letting her have control and patiently answering the hundred and one questions she throws at him. I hoped maybe the novelty would wear off, but it's still so sweet that my heart aches a little bit every time it happens. And when I say bye to him, I can't help but get jealous of the woman out there who's going to avoid the pain I went through when she snatches him up.

"I feel so bad. That was so easy for you to fix and you drove all the way out here." If I'd just checked my damn texts, he could've avoided traffic and having to entertain me during my absurdly long lunch break. "You know you don't have to stay, right? I can just grab a Lyft back to work. I won't be offended."

"No," he says right away. I can tell he didn't mean to say it so fast by the color rising in his cheeks again. "I mean, you don't need to feel bad, I came out here on my own. Plus"—he looks down, twisting the corner of the fabric napkin around his finger—"I really like spending time with you."

All of my insides turn to Jell-O, and I can feel the goofiest grin spread across my face. He's just *so sweet*.

"Really?" I bite the inside of my cheeks to try to stop smiling like a crazy person, but even so, the doubt rings clear in the single word. I'm not the most fun person to be around.

He looks up, his eyebrows furrowed together and his hazel eyes assessing. "Yeah, really. You're smart and determined and"—his face goes bright red—"really beautiful. Why wouldn't I love spending time with you?"

Now my cheeks are heating, but hopefully my melanin prevents him from noticing.

Nobody has ever said anything like that to me. Ever. Between me and Jude? I'm never the person people want to spend time with. Jude is hilarious, easygoing, spontaneous, and drop-dead gorgeous. And me? Well . . . I overthink everything to death, I'm uptight and too serious.

"Um, thanks." Now I'm the one fidgeting and unable to make eye contact. "That's nice of you to say."

"It's not me being nice." He sounds more confident than I've ever heard him. "It's me telling the truth. And actually, I was hoping that maybe we could eat together again soon? Maybe for dinner? And go to a movie or something?"

My head snaps up and my mouth falls open.

Did he just ask me on a date?

"Like . . . like a date?"

"Yeah, exactly like a date." He holds my stare. His gentle brand of confidence radiates across his kind and beautiful features. "I really like you, Lauren. I want to get to know you better."

My lungs freeze and breathing feels impossible.

The last time I was asked out on a date was when Ben and I started dating.

And I want to say yes.

Holy shit do I want to say yes. So bad.

But I can't.

It took me too long to pick up the pieces after Ben, and I can't risk that happening again. Not when Adelaide is finally beginning to feel settled. The only relationship I can trust myself with is with Jude. And now, with the custody battle looming over my head, I'm afraid a relationship is something else Ben could use against me.

"Hudson." I say his name, hoping the words I don't know will just follow naturally . . . but they don't.

He must see my answer—or my fear—written across my face, but instead of getting angry or offended, a soft smile pulls at the corners of his mouth.

"It's okay if you're not ready or even if you don't want to." He reaches his hand across the table and holds on to mine. "I know Addy is your priority now, as she should be. I just want you to know that I like you . . . a lot. When and if you're ever ready to date again, I'd love to have a chance. Because I think you're incredible."

All of the feelings flow through my body at his words.

Happiness, gratitude, sadness.

But one feels stronger than the rest. Anger.

Anger that even though Ben left me, even though he's the one who betrayed our relationship, I still seem to be the only one paying for it.

I just hope that with our meeting next week, some of the uncertainty around him will come to an end. And maybe, just maybe, I'll be able to move on. Maybe I'll even accept a date from a gentle and kind man who might see more in me than I see in myself.

NINETEEN

. . .

Jude

This week has been a freaking ride.

I've had to apologize—multiple times—for getting wasted at the launch and yelling at matchy-matchy, and slightly racist, Jennifer. Adelaide had her first day of kindergarten. Our podcast launched with some small glitches that somehow led to Hudson finally asking out Lauren . . . which she turned down.

But the main thing that went down this week is that I showed Lauren weakness. And now I'm fucked.

I don't know how I let it happen. I've been expertly disguising my sad mommy issues for years. Then, *bam*! Four months in the same house with Lauren and she's onto me like fucking Scooby-Doo! I hoped with everything we have going on in our life, Lauren would lay off a little bit.

The opposite has happened.

How she has time to work, help Addy with homework—yes, in kindergarten—make gourmet-quality breakfast, lunch, and dinner, and still concentrate on my problems is beyond me. All I know is I don't appreciate it. I need time to rebuild some of that wall she knocked down and she's not giving me any space to do it. Even when we're all sitting on the couch watching Addy's measly thirty minutes of screen time, I can feel her eyes on me, analyzing and trying to figure out how to break me.

It's rude.

Like, let me fucking struggle in private!

Sure. I would never let her do that to me and I would cuff her to the banister until she broke, but this isn't the same.

She took today off so she can take Addy on some grand adventure for finishing a week in kindergarten. I can't even imagine what it's going to be like when that child graduates high school.

Lucky for me, though, she wasn't able to ambush me like I know she wanted to because there's an influencers' convention—yes, that's a real thing—and I'm speaking on a few panels.

I was so lucky to get more than one leg up in this industry. Anytime I get an opportunity to help other people trying to come up as influencers, I jump at it. So many people think there can only be a few people on the top, but that's such bullshit. As long as you're being yourself and not trying to mimic someone else, there's room for everyone. We all have unique voices and experiences that should be showcased.

It's gaining visibility and learning how to make money that's the hard part. But lucky for everyone who's coming today, I'm pretty good at teaching both of those things.

"Jude!" Spencer Foster shouts my name from across the room before her long, lean legs dodge the crowd as she runs over to me. "Bitch! I've been looking for you all day! Where the fuck have you been hiding?"

I love Spencer. She's one of the first people I met when this entire influencer journey of mine began. We were both kind of getting started. When it comes to our brands, on the surface, we're almost completely opposite. I'm muted, light tones and she's over-the-top neon. I do Pilates, she's into kickboxing. My blond hair is always braided or in a bun, she's got masses of black hair always pulled in a high pony.

But at our core? We're so similar it's scary.

Her dad invented some crazy workout device that had a huge following in the eighties, but had a comeback when one of its infomercials resurfaced a few years ago. She was able to piggy-back off his fifteen minutes of fame and build a super-loyal fol-lowing of her own, just like I did.

And even more, we're both fucking disasters. Her more so than me . . . and that's saying a lot.

"I went to one panel about podcasting and then I've been walking around to meet some new vendors." Finding new spon-sors is always a good idea. Plus, I'm really good at networking. Getting to do so much peopling is one of my favorite parts about this job. "Why didn't you call me?"

"I fucking tried! There's no service in this place." She pulls out her phone and shoves the screen in my face to prove her point. "Who plans a fucking influencer convention in a place with no reception? And how did you not notice that? You're always glued to your phone."

I shrug. "I just haven't looked. I've been taking business cards instead. It's so much easier than punching everything into my phone."

"Ew." She shudders a bit. Nobody can say Spencer isn't dra-matic. "That's so nineties."

The business card thing is new to me. She's not lying when she says I'm always glued to my phone.

I've just been avoiding my mom since the launch party. And even though I keep telling myself that it's okay for me to take a break from her so I can gather all my thoughts and get my emotions under control, each time I intentionally ignore her call, my stomach twists into knots, and guilt causes my throat to tighten. Sure, technically, keeping my phone in my purse with the ringer off is to avoid answering her phone calls, but it still absolves me of some of the guilt.

"Whatever. Look how pretty they are." I pull one of my cards out of the front pocket of my purse and hand it to her. "Plus, they make me feel mad fucking professional. You should see how some of the execs act when I pull the cards out."

That gets her attention.

"Really?" She inspects the heavy-weight card with gold-foil lettering. "These are really nice."

"Right? And I worked out a deal with the printing company to do three mentions for them and got them for free."

It saved me about three hundred dollars. Whoever thinks influencers are dumb clearly hasn't been around us. We work smart and we work hard . . . well, some of us.

"Damn it. Now I want some. Anyway . . ." Spencer shoves my card in the back of the pouch on her lanyard with all of her credentials in it. "Wanna skip out of here really fast and go grab a martini or three?"

Okay.

So where Lauren is the angel on my shoulder always telling me to make good decisions? Spencer is the devil.

I was lucky. My mom didn't go batshit crazy until I was an adult. Spencer's mom ran away with their family accountant when Spencer was nine. Her dad did steroids during his time as a fitness celebrity and is majorly fucked up from it. She grew up in dysfunction, while I'm just trying to avoid it.

I'd never admit this out loud, but sometimes it's nice to be around someone else who is also fucked up. Sure, Lauren's situation sucks and fuck Ben until the end of time. But Lauren still has a serious job, she's a great mom, and even though Mrs. Turner is a bitch, at least Lauren can depend on her. She still has support.

I'm out to drift and it's fucking lonely.

Spencer gets it because it's the same for her.

I check my watch and see how much longer until my panel. "Fuck, I have to be at my next panel in thirty minutes."

"What panel?"

"Poses and Yoga Pants." I try not to cringe at the name. I'm ninety-nine-point-nine percent sure a man came up with it. "We're doing the Growing Up Boss panel together, right?"

"Yup. We can both talk about our wonderful parents and how lucky we are to benefit from their wealth of industry knowledge." Her voice drops to a whisper. "Meadow Blake is on it, too, which means we'll have to listen to her baby voice cut us off every two seconds."

"She is?" I try to suppress my shudder, but I can't stand Meadow. "I didn't see her name on the list."

"Yeah, Jasinda pulled out for some reason and they replaced her with Meadow."

I get along with most people in this industry. Meadow is the exception.

Her dad is this vegan chef on one of those cooking channels. He basically just goes around appropriating cultures and profiting off them. Like, no, Hank—which is his real name, not fucking Ziggy like he says—we know you didn't discover fucking turmeric, ya jackass.

And Meadow is worse. Can you say white savior complex? She's always traveling to Black and brown countries, feeding them vegan foods, and posting pictures of children too small to consent to their images being plastered all over the internet. I tried to gently explain to her how problematic her content was after I met her a few times. Of course, when I did, she cried and turned herself into the victim. A few days later, every sponsor we had in common dropped me.

So yeah, fuck Meadow.

"I feel like I have to be sober for that panel, otherwise I'll say some stupid shit that'll make me lose sponsors." And I'm not losing more money at the hands of Meadow fucking Blake. No way, no how. "But after I'm going to need more than a couple of cocktails."

Spencer raises her hand in the air and keeps it there until I slap it. "That's my fucking girl."

. . .

September in Los Angeles is still blissfully warm. As Spencer and I wait outside for our Lyft to pick us up to take us to our favorite happy hour, we're not coated in sweat like we would've been if it was still August or July.

Fall is for sure my favorite season. I'm basic AF. Give me all the pumpkin-spiced goodies, oversized sweaters, and UGGs you have. I want them all. Standing outside and feeling the chill start to come at night gives me a little boost that I don't usually have when looking toward the future.

"The panel wasn't too bad," Spencer says, but her words lack conviction.

"Are you messing with me?" I look around me to make sure nobody is lingering nearby, and when I see the coast is clear, I let it out. "It was a total fucking shit show! Who in the actual fuck does Meadow think she is? And did you see the look she gave me when I talked about consent? I still don't understand how people just give her free pass after free pass to post pictures with these kids who have no authority in their faces being plastered all over the internet to make her look good. Plus." I lean in closer to make sure nobody hears my good gossip. "You know she hired one of my photographers for one of her trips? He told me that they stayed in a five-star resort and only left once, purely for picture purposes. She's gross and so transparent."

Spencer was nodding along while I was talking but breaks into laughter as soon as I stop.

"I was just messing with you!" She wipes away the nonexistent tears on her cheeks. "It was a total disaster! I just love it when you get worked up over her. Your face gets all red and your hands curl into a ball, it's fucking hilarious." She throws a toned arm around my shoulder and pulls me into her side.

"God." I shake my head but can't help laughing along with her because she's right. "You're such a bitch."

"Takes one to—" she starts, but doesn't finish when a voice that sounds more childlike than Addy's cuts her off.

"Hey, girls, so that was fun, don't you think?" Meadow Blake appears next to us. She's wearing her typical look of a maxi skirt paired with a crop top with billowy sleeves. She'll say it's from some small village she found on her travels, but I'd bet money she bought that shit at Anthropologie. Her handwoven purse falls off her bony shoulder like it, too, hates being this close to her lying face.

"Yeah, it was great." Spencer smiles politely, not giving it away at all that we were just talking about her. "Robyn was a great moderator. I had fun."

I, on the other hand, used all my phoniness sitting onstage with her and can't be bothered. So I just roll my eyes and mutter, "Meadow," before pulling my phone out of my purse, hoping to the god I'm pretty sure abandoned me years ago that our Lyft is almost here.

Of course, thanks to LA traffic and whatever curse has been placed on me, it's still fifteen minutes away.

"So, Jude," Meadow says to me even though I'm clearly not

interested. "I feel like you were trying to say something to me onstage tonight, but I'm just not sure what. I figured I'd ask. I met with a healer on my last trip to Mexico and she really stressed the importance of good, clean energy and I just feel, like, a really dark vibe coming from you."

I could not hate her more.

The deep sigh my body emits is enough to make me go light-headed. "Seriously, Meadow?"

"Of course." She tilts her head to the side, tucking a piece of her extra long, wavy brown hair behind her ear. "I really don't understand why you seem to have such problems with me. I would really like to be friends."

Maybe she hit her head and has amnesia or something? That's the only reason I can think of that she would be out here asking me this question she already knows the answer to.

"If you wanted to be friends, maybe you would've thought twice before you went crying to the sponsors we had in common and getting me dropped." I look down at my phone again, needing to escape, hating how I just let this bitch suck me into whatever drama she has planned.

"I have no idea what you're talking about. And I don't have the power to get anyone dropped, so if they let go of you, that was probably more to do with you than me." Her voice goes even softer and I want to scream. If that was really her voice, fine. But before we had our falling-out, I was around her at parties and this is *not* her voice. "I really think you need to look within."

I really, really try not to fall into her hands. After last weekend with Jennifer, I promised myself I would start checking my reactions and not let people get me worked up. It's just *so hard.*

"Whatever, Meadow." I take a few steps away from her. "You can leave now."

She doesn't.

Instead she closes the space I just created.

"If I was able to forgive you for the things you accused me of, you should be able to get over whatever this imaginary grudge you're holding is." She looks at me with a grin on her face that lets me know exactly what she's doing.

I take the advice I give to all my friends. I close my eyes and take a few deep breaths. She's so lucky I decided to wait until after our panel to drink.

But that still doesn't mean I won't put a bitch in her place.

Just quietly and with a bit more discretion this time.

"I didn't accuse you of anything, I let you know the things you post scream white savior and are problematic. That's not an accusation, that's an opinion. An opinion a lot of people seem to share considering people are always discussing the way you delete comments criticizing you for this very thing." She opens her mouth to respond, but I talk over her. "What I said on the panel wasn't directed at you"—*it totally was*—"and if you felt like me stating that consent, especially concerning minors and vulnerable youth, was targeting you? I think you really need to examine why that is."

Could I say more? Definitely. I could be here all night listing my problems with her. But considering her eyes are already starting to well with tears, I know nothing I say will get through to her.

"There's nothing wrong with me posting pictures of children and gaining attention to help them." The tears start falling down her face, and instead of feeling bad, I just want to slap her more. "Just because I'm white doesn't mean I shouldn't help people who don't look like me."

"I'm white too!" I yell. Damn it. This is why I can't deal with her. "I'm just self-aware. And the fact that you're crying and making yourself the victim . . . *again* . . . is another reason on a long list of why you're problematic as fuck. You should stop antagonizing me, go home, and educate yourself. Maybe then you can actually help the people you say you want to help instead of just helping yourself."

I know I'm not a perfect person or a perfect ally. It's almost impossible to be one. But because Lauren is my best friend, I listen to the things she tells me, even when it's hard for me to hear. Growing up as one of the few Black girls in our elite private school, she dealt with things that were invisible to me. But over the years, especially in college, she opened up to me about the challenges she's faced and woke me up to some of the things I did that I didn't even realize were racist. White-women tears, like Meadow is so apt to do, were one of the things. It was hard to hear, and even though I wanted to be defensive, I knew I had to listen. One of the things I know I can do is call out the racist things I see—whether it be with Meadow, Jennifer, or anyone else who crosses my path.

Meadow's wet cheeks turn fire-engine red, and even though she always gives me the stink eye, this is another level. I'm almost curious to hear what she has to say. But by a stroke of luck I don't often get, my phone starts to vibrate in my hand.

"Oh." I hold a finger to her almost cartoonishly angry face, sounding as unbothered as I can. "Let me get this real fast."

I swipe open my phone without looking at the screen.

"Hello!" I might sound a little too cheery, but really, I'm just so fucking pleased with how the tables turned in this situation that I can't help it.

"Ju-ju!" my mom says from the other end. "I've been trying to get in touch with you all week."

Damn it.

I knew this call was too good to be true. But because Meadow is still watching, I make sure I keep up appearances even if I really want to tell my mom I'm busy and hang up.

"I'm sorry, I've just been *so* busy." I stress the words, loving the way Meadow is getting more angry by the second. "How are you?"

"I'm great, which you would know if you answered your phone more often." She chides me again, and I should get some kind of trophy for the way I manage to not only keep the smile on my face but keep my eyes from rolling to the fucking heavens. "Anyway, I'm having Jonathon set up a brunch for us at the Ivy this Sunday. The car will pick you up at ten."

I love the way she completely ditches me and then demands my presence without even acknowledging that she might have hurt me.

So fucking typical. She can't see past her own nose.

"Sounds perfect! I can't wait," I lie, my acting skills still so on point.

I'm about to hang up when her voice comes over the line again. "And make sure you wear a dress, no jeans and definitely no yoga pants."

Forced brunch and a dress code, just your average mother-daughter outing.

"Can't wait." This time, the words are kind of forced out. I can't help it. My mom manages to get under my skin like nobody else. Even Meadow is a walk in the park compared to her.

I hang up the phone, thinking the call wasn't as lucky as I thought and knowing after even the shortest call with Juliette Andrews, I don't have the energy or patience to deal with Meadow's ass.

"Why are you still here?" I ask her. "Go read a book and learn something."

When I turn my back on her and move closer to Spencer, her smile is the biggest I've ever seen it. "That was fucking awesome."

That's debatable.

I'm almost certain that Meadow won't listen to anything I said and will, in turn, post even more problematic, racist content.

Finally, before Meadow can gather her wits and come back over, my phone buzzes in my hand, and a notification that our Lyft driver is pulling up lights up my screen at the same time a red Camry comes to a stop in front of us.

We slide into the back seat, buckling our seat belts and leaving a red-eyed Meadow alone on the sidewalk.

I lean forward, poking my head between the front seats. "I will tip you twenty dollars if you can get us to happy hour in the next ten minutes."

Our driver doesn't say anything, but he does peel away from the curb so fast that his tires screech against the pavement.

I couldn't be more grateful.

Because a margarita or two with extra tequila is exactly what I need.

TWENTY

...

Lauren

I get to Adelaide's school thirty minutes before the final bell rings to make sure I get a spot in their tiny parking lot. The other parents started filling up the pickup lane soon after I arrived, so I didn't feel too crazy for my enthusiasm.

She's been going to after-school care all week, which, thankfully, she loves. It was the thing I was feeling most nervous—and guilty—about. It seems like such a long day for her, but they play and do crafts and she always sprints to me, showing me her latest creation. Plus, because she's a kindergartner, the older girls in after-school care have seemed to swoop her up as their own little sister. She loves the extra attention. But none of that is to say she hasn't been practically jumping out of her skin for our night together.

I mean . . . I might have hyped it up a little bit—or a lot.

I glance at the clock on my dash and even though I still have fifteen minutes, I decide to close the app on my phone and make my way to the door she'll be coming out of. I emailed her teacher to make sure she'd walk her outside instead of taking her to after-school care today, but I want to be the first person she sees.

Remington Academy is beautiful. The landscaping is perfection with lush green grass that if I didn't know better would think never grew because it's always cut low. Window boxes overflowing with bright flowers line every window. In the back of the school, there's a garden complete with lemon, avocado, and plum trees. The students help maintain it, and once a week, the cafeteria provides a meal using the literal fruits of their labor.

I'm the first parent to stand in front of the kindergarten exit. I'm pretty sure most parents just use the carpool lane, but it intimidates me. Every morning, my heart rate increases, my blood pressure skyrockets, and my shoulders tense as the teacher volunteers blow their whistles at us and yell to "hurry, hurry!" I'm pretty sure they want the kids to jump out of moving cars. It's intense. And of course, Adelaide giggles through it all.

I lean against the fence blocking off the bushes and preventing the kids access to the flower boxes and pull open my email. I've really enjoyed all aspects of the podcast, but the newsletter has become my second baby. I'm not sure why that is, but I love it so much. I still obsess over every email—too many exclamation points? Not enough exclamation points? No emojis . . . or maybe one emoji? Do I sound uptight and will it turn people off?—but it's still so satisfying every time someone emails us back, letting us know they relate to everything we're talking about.

I hear footsteps approaching and contemplate for a second before deciding to put away my phone and try my hand at being the peppy school mom. I just really hope it's Sabrina . . . or really anybody other than Jennifer. I saw her on Monday and things were fine . . . but not great. And I'd rather avoid any awkwardness today.

I shove my phone in my purse and look up with what I think

is my friendly smile plastered on my face, prepared to say hi, when I realize I should've wished for Jennifer.

"Ben? What are you doing here?"

This has got to be some kind of a cruel joke. Just two months ago he didn't even know the name of the school Adelaide was attending, now he wants to show up without even contacting me or my lawyer? Of course he does it here. Not that I like to cause scenes anywhere, but there's no way I would create one outside of our daughter's school. Which he knows.

"Lauren, hey." He gives me an awkward wave that's so unlike him. His movements are always sure—confident. "I didn't know I'd see you here."

"Well, it's kind of where Adelaide goes to school, so I'm not sure what you expected." His eyebrows raise, and even I'm a little taken back by the irritation lacing my words. I guess Jude has been rubbing off on me after all.

"Oh yeah." He stops a few feet in front of me, shoving his hands in his pockets. "I guess I just thought you'd be at work; Junie told me she's been going to after-school care. I thought since I was off today, I'd just grab her."

I've always let Adelaide call Ben whenever she wanted, but because of the upcoming custody meetings, Ben now has to answer. We set up three times a week when Adelaide FaceTimes him and fills him in on everything happening in her life. Of course, this week, that included talking nonstop about her new school, showing him every craft she made, and telling him she was in after-school care.

"You thought this without checking with me first?"

Peak Ben. Classic freaking Ben. Does what he wants, when he wants. Screw everyone else.

"No . . . I mean, of course I wanted to check with you. My

lawyer said it would be okay if I did this because the custody is still open. We were going to call you in the car. I figured since I was supposed to have her next weekend, we could just switch. I'll take her tonight and then she can spend the weekend with me. And next weekend she'll stay with you." He takes a small step closer to me before he stops. "I missed her first day of school, I want to make up for that . . . and everything else I've missed. I made us reservations at this little tea party place and got tickets to see the Broadway production of *Frozen*."

I don't know if I'm more irritated that Ben was practically going to kidnap my daughter or that even knowing this, I still feel a twinge of guilt for not being able to give Adelaide everything she deserves. A tea party and a Broadway show? She'd love that and there's no way I can afford it.

Ben must take my silence for no, because he starts talking again.

"Listen, I know I really fucked up with this lawyer stuff," he whispers, looking over his shoulder to make sure we're still alone. "But you know my mom. She just pushed me into it and I didn't stop her, I should've stopped her. I know you're a great mom and I don't want to take Junie from you. Hell, my schedule's so crazy right now I'd still barely see her if she was with me all the time."

I hate the way Ben makes me feel.

It's always been like this. If he hadn't left me, I probably would've stayed and tried to forgive him for cheating. The second he apologizes, it's like my brain malfunctions. Every instinct I have telling me to stand my ground and tell him no vanishes.

"I don't know, Ben," I say, but any of the force I felt when I first saw him is gone. My words are weak and so is my resolve. "I planned a night with her, too, and we've really been looking forward to it."

"Please, Lala." He uses the nickname he started calling me

soon after we met. I loved it so much. If I'm being honest, I miss it. "I'm trying to step up here, I want to be a part of her life. I know I let you down years ago and then I let you down again with the custody stuff."

"I want you to be involved too. I always have, you know that." My voice wavers just as my sinuses begin to burn. Every time he would miss her call or cancel when he was supposed to get her, my heart broke. All I've ever wanted is for Adelaide to know she's loved by both her parents.

"I know. And you've always been great about letting me spend time with her. I'm not going to go after full, I never was. I only put that in the papers because the lawyer and my mom agreed it was the best way to start negotiations. When we have the meeting, I was already planning on changing it to weekends or something you're more comfortable with. I promise. I just want to be involved. That's it."

The relief I feel hearing he doesn't want to go for full custody is palpable. I've been living in constant fear since I was served those papers. Every move and every decision I made were with the possibility of losing my daughter in the back of my mind. But I know Ben. I know his ego. So maybe if I just keep doing what I've always done for him, just let him be . . . he won't change his mind.

And then I can plan another night with Adelaide, because she'll be with me. Yes, I've been looking forward to tonight all week, but I've been loving Adelaide for her entire life and we can make so many more memories. She'll have fun with Ben . . . and then he'll realize how easy co-parenting can be if we just talk. Without lawyers.

"Okay." I know it's for the best, but the simple word tastes like acid rolling off my tongue. "She can go with you, but I just want to see her, let her know the plans have changed."

His smile lights up his beautiful face as he closes the gap between us and wraps me in a giant hug. "Thank you. You have no idea how much this means to me."

But I do.

It's about Adelaide, so it means everything.

She's everything.

When he lets me go and takes a step back, I realize we aren't alone anymore and a small crowd of moms who are dressed to be seen, not just sit in their cars, are congregated around us. Thankfully, none of them look familiar.

Before I can think too much of it, the bell rings and it's only a few seconds later that the sidewalks fill up with a swarm of navy, red, and white. The double door in front of us opens and Adelaide's teacher, Mrs. Allen, appears, holding hands with a little boy with red eyes and tearstained cheeks. She holds on to him as she lets the rest of the class file out of the door, repeating a reminder of "don't run" every five seconds or so.

When Adelaide appears in the doorway, her little eyes light up. Seeing me and Ben together is not a common occurrence in her life. And despite her teacher saying not to run, she takes off into a sprint, colliding with me and Ben, trying to wrap her little arms around both of us.

"Hey, my love!" I squat down and pull her into me, soaking her up, breathing in her scent. She smells like sunshine and dirt. "How was school?"

"It was so fun! We got to go to the garden and pick a piece of fruit from one of the trees to take home." She peels her backpack off her shoulders and drops it to the ground, making quick work of the zipper and pulling out an avocado. "I picked this for Auntie Jude because she likes them so much, but always says that stores are ripping her money."

Jude does complain about stores ripping her off a lot. But if she stopped shopping at Whole Foods all the time and woke up early enough to come to the farmers' market with me and Addy, she wouldn't be.

"That was so thoughtful of you, Jude is going to love it so, so much." I pull her in for another hug, peppering her face with kisses.

"Mommy!" She pulls away from me, trying to look mad, but her giggles give away her real feelings. "Stop kissing me!"

"But I love kissing you." I stick out my bottom lip in an exaggerated pout, and because she's the sweetest girl in the entire world, she leans in and gives me a quick kiss on the cheek.

My heart constricts.

I'll never get used to the way it feels to love somebody so much.

"Daddy." She looks up at Ben. Her cheeks are bright red, her curls are a mess on the top of her head, and there's faded paint staining her little hands. Proof of a great day at school. "Are you coming to play with me and Mommy? We're going to have a girls' night, but since you're a daddy, you can come too. Right, Mommy?"

I look at Ben and he nods, letting me break the news to Adelaide that I think only I'm going to be sad about.

"Actually, Daddy's here because he has a surprise for you." Just like I knew they would, her eyes go wide and her already big smile grows at the mention of a surprise. "He's going to take you for a tea party and then guess what?"

She's bouncing on her toes, like her body can't physically hold all of the excitement. "What?"

"Then you are going to see *Frozen* with the *real* Elsa!"

The squeal that comes from her body is almost enough to puncture eardrums, but there's so much joy in it, I can't help but laugh as she jumps into Ben's arms.

"Does that mean you're excited, Junie girl?" Ben asks, his beautiful smile aimed at Adelaide, his eyes shining with love. For a moment, I forget everything he's put me through and only see the man I fell in love with, wishing more than anything that we could still be a family.

"I'm so excited!" She's still shouting, but thanks to all the kids running around, it just kind of blends in with the noise. "Is Mommy coming too?"

Ben's smile fades just a bit and he looks to me.

"Not tonight," I tell her, trying as hard as I can to keep the smile on my face. "Tonight you're going to have a special time with Daddy. Then you get to spend the night with him and Stephanie, and I'll come get you on Sunday. But I want you to call me tonight and tell me everything about it, okay?"

"Okay!" Her smile doesn't falter a bit at the news. She pushes against Ben's tall, lean body, signaling for him to put her down, and comes back over to me, wrapping me up in one of her best hugs. "I'll call you tonight and tell you everything! You should go watch the *Frozen* movie so you know what I'm talking about." She says this like she didn't watch *Frozen* for two months straight and I couldn't forget the movie even if I bleached my brain. "And will you give Auntie Jude her avocado?"

"Of course I will." I take the avocado, which is as big as her hand, as she pulls it out of her backpack again. "I love you, okay? Have so much fun with Daddy."

"I will!" She holds her arms up and I pick her up, smothering her face with kisses again as she wraps her legs and arms around me. I close my eyes, trying to memorize this moment, the weight of her tiny body in my arms, the sound of her voice, hoping it can hold me over for the weekend. "Love you, Mommy," she says as I put her down.

She zips up her backpack and I help her get it back on her shoulders before she skips over to Ben. He holds out his hand and she wraps her little fingers around it. Turning around as they start to walk away and shouting, "Bye, Mommy! I love you!"

I know I can't say it to her retreating form without breaking into tears, so instead I just blow her kisses and wave until she turns around and looks up at Ben, her little mouth moving a mile a minute. I stand frozen—no pun intended—to my spot on the sidewalk, watching them until I don't see them anymore before I turn and make my way back to my car.

Alone.

It's not that I want Adelaide to be sad we're not spending the evening together, but I kind of want her to be sad? I don't know. I feel crazy. I think I am crazy. Because I'm so happy she's going to get to have this wonderful experience with her dad, but I'm also so sad because I won't be there to see it. Missing these moments with her is the thing I think I'll die regretting.

But there's nothing I can do about it, so I do what I'm good at. I pretend. I pretend I won't spend the weekend wanting to cry. I pretend that even one fewer night with her doesn't shatter my heart and make me want to crawl into bed and not get out until I get to see her again.

I pretend I'm not broken.

I unlock the door to my car, trying to remind myself that giving up this one moment will give me so many more in the future. It will prove to Ben that I'm willing to be flexible and this whole nightmare can be over at our meeting.

But then, out of the corner of my eye, I see the bright pink gift bag next to Adelaide's car seat that I filled with goodies for our special night.

The tears I always hold back fall and the ache in my chest becomes uncontrollable. Alone in my car, in the parking lot of my daughter's school, I break.

. . .

TWENTY-ONE

Jude

Spencer is definitely a terrible influence.

And I'm okay with that.

Our "happy hour" turned into a sleepover, which turned into club hopping, which turned into *another* sleepover. And even though I've been pounding Pedialyte and water intermittently since Saturday morning, I still feel like death.

I'm getting too old for this shit.

I texted Lauren on Friday night not to expect me home, and all she sent me was a thumbs-up emoji. I know she had a super-special night planned with Addy. She was probably relieved I made myself disappear for the weekend. I know they love me, but I also know I get in the way sometimes and they need time alone.

Plus, with my impending brunch with Juliette Andrews, I would've been on edge and Lauren would've broken me. Guaranteed.

So yeah, what I'm saying is that I hid.

Sue me.

I walk down the path to our house, my hair a mess, and wearing some of Spencer's neon-green biker shorts, a black hoodie, and sunglasses that hopefully cover the dark circles under my eyes. I look a hot-ass mess. It's the perfect visual representation of both my life *and* my mental state.

What the fuck does my mom need this time?

I slide my key in the door and twist open the knob, bracing myself for the impact of Addy hurtling her little body at me. It's only nine a.m., but that girl is an alarm clock that never fails. She never sleeps past seven.

But when I take a step inside, there's no sign of Addy anywhere. No breakfast on the table, no early-morning cartoons, no giggles or singing. No cartwheels upstairs making the ceiling shake.

Instead, Lauren's laid out on the couch watching some depressing-looking shit on TV. The remote is on the floor surrounded by empty soda bottles and an empty pint of Ben & Jerry's. Even her hair, which she has meticulously wrapped in a headscarf every night from the time I met her, is wild and matted like she hasn't moved from this spot in days.

Oh.

Shit.

"Hey." She doesn't even lift her head off the pillow. "Didn't expect you back so early."

"Ummm . . ." I look around, not knowing what happened or what to say. Which is practically a first for me. "Are you okay?"

Stupid question.

She is very clearly *not* okay.

"Oh yeah, sure." She sits up, her foot falling from the couch and knocking over the empty ice cream container. "Just relaxing and enjoying the quiet, catching up on some Netflix."

"Netflix is always fun." I walk over to the couch, keeping my steps slow and even like she's some alley cat who will pounce. When she doesn't jump up and run from me, I sit down next to her.

"Totally," she says.

Lauren might be a quiet little introvert to the rest of the world, but not to me. To me, she's a talker. We share everything. We talk about everything. What we don't do is give one-word responses.

"Soooo . . ." I decide I have to point out the obvious since she's clearly not going to. "Where's Addy? I thought you two were having your superfun girls' night slash weekend?"

I barely get the sentence out before tears start rolling down Lauren's face. Not small, dainty tears. Big, ugly tears. With a snot nose and noises. I mean, she's full-on sobbing.

"Oh my god." I reach over and wrap my arms around her, pulling her into my body. Seeing her cry was already enough to break my heart, but feeling her body shake as the sobs roll from what feels like her soul, I'm ready to commit murder. "What happened? Do I need to hurt somebody?"

She starts to take some deep breaths to slow the tears and control her breathing. When she finally stops shaking, she sits back and stares at me with bloodshot eyes and a watery smile.

"Nothing happened, really," she says, what feels like ages later. "I'm just being so dramatic."

That's all she has to say to let me know who is at the root of whatever happened while I was gone.

"What the fuck did Ben do this time?"

Her swollen eyes widen just a smidge. "How'd you know it has to do with Ben?"

"Because he's literally the only person on this planet who makes you doubt yourself like this." Maybe because she's so obviously hurting right now, I should pull my punches. Or maybe, this is the time for me to finally say what I've been thinking for years. "Even with your mom, you fight back. But with Ben? You question your entire being. You let him get away with any- and every-thing and then blame yourself for his shit. So, Lauren Honor Turner, I'll ask again. What the fuck did Ben do?"

She takes a deep breath and looks down at her poor, battered manicure. "He showed up at Remington after school on Friday." Her voice is barely above a whisper.

Mine is not. "He what?!"

"He made reservations to take her to a little tea party place and had tickets to take her to see the Broadway production of *Frozen*," she says, still avoiding eye contact with me.

"And you told him to go sit on the tea spout and fucking spin, right?"

I hate that man with a fiery passion.

"I looked up tickets for *Frozen* when it first came to town, they were so expensive." Her voice is beginning to shake again. "I couldn't prevent her from having that experience. It would've been selfish. You should've seen her when she FaceTimed me after. She was *so* happy."

I can feel my temper rising more and more with every word that comes out of her mouth.

"Listen, Lauren. You know I love you, right?" I ask, and she nods her head, still not looking at me. "I need you to look at me. I need you to really hear this." She turns her head to the side and finally makes eye contact with me. "Ben is a manipulative piece of shit. You have a temporary custody agreement right now, don't you?"

"Yeah, but—"

"No buts." I cut her off before she can try to explain or defend him. "So he knew this was your weekend with Addy. He know-ingly made reservations and bought tickets for a night he *knew* was yours. He could just as easily have done both of those things with her next week when it was his time with her."

"I mean . . . maybe."

"No, Lauren. Not fucking maybe." I'm trying really hard not to take my anger out on my sweet friend when something else dawns on me. "Wait . . . did you say he showed up at Addy's school?"

She slowly nods her head up and down. "He came up to me while I was waiting outside of Adelaide's school, waiting for her to get out."

Holy shit. Holy fucking shit. That piece of trash!

"And he knows Addy goes to after-school care." This is a statement, not a question. I've listened as Addy told him and Stephanie all about her new school . . . which includes after-school care. "So he was planning on going up to the school, thinking you were at work, and taking Addy with him without you knowing."

"He said he was going to call. That his lawyer said it'd be fine."

"Lauren! Wake up!" I don't mean to yell, but fuck! I want to shake her! "No lawyer would ever say that basically kidnapping a child is fine because that's *fucking crazy*." I draw out the last two words. "I need you to see how horrible this is. Like really see it. If this happened to anyone else, if their ex showed up behind their back to take their kid when they weren't supposed to have them, would you think it was okay?"

And that's when the thread of composure she had gained snaps.

"I'm so afraid I'm going to lose her, Jude! So, so afraid. She's my whole entire world." Her words are barely understandable through the onslaught of tears, and my heart breaks into a million pieces. "He told me that he just wants to be involved, not get full custody, and will say that at our meeting. So I couldn't say no. I couldn't do anything to make him change his mind because I. Can't. Lose. Her." She buries her face in her hands.

I take a moment to make sure my voice is intentionally gentle. I don't want to do anything to add to her pain, but I don't believe anything that shithead says. "If he doesn't want full custody, then why go through all of this? Why the lawyers and court? It doesn't make sense."

"He said it was all his mom, that she pushed him to go for full even if he wasn't going to do it."

That I kind of believe. His mom always had it out for Lauren. She makes Mrs. Turner look like a fucking saint. But still, Ben is a fucking adult and he can't put all of the blame on his mommy.

"So you had him put this in writing, right?" I ask, but know the answer when she looks away from me again. "Lauren, you made him put it in writing, didn't you."

She starts picking at her poor nails, which honestly can't take any more of her abuse. "We were outside of the school. It's not like I had a pen and paper ready."

"So then you emailed him this weekend, recounting the conversation and he confirmed everything?"

Her silence is all the answer I need.

"Fuck, Lauren." I stand up and start pacing the room. "When are you going to stand up to him and stop letting him walk all over you?"

"This will all be over soon and I won't have to worry anymore." She stands up and walks over to me. "Once this is over, it won't matter what he says and I'll be able to move on with my life."

I'm not sure who she's trying to convince, though, me or her, but I know she doesn't need me to talk sense into her. She needs her friend. In this moment, the only thing she needs is for me to be there for her and tell her everything is going to be okay.

"You're right." I grab her hands, as much to comfort her as to stop her from messing with her nails. "Everything is going to be fine. And even if Ben tried to go for full, he wouldn't get it. Because you're an amazing mother and Addy is all the proof you need. You created that amazing girl and she's the magical being she is because of you. Because you fight for her and lift her up and do everything and more that a mom should do."

Her eyes start to well up again, but this time, the smile on her face is real. "Thank you."

"You know I have your back." I touch her necklace, the one I gave her and Addy. "We're stronger together. Always."

And it's at that exact moment that there's a knock on the door and I realize what time it is.

"Fuck." I let go of Lauren's hand and go open the door to greet whatever driver my mom sent to get me. "Hi! So sorry, I'll be out in a second."

I ignore the disapproving once-over the man gives me that says I'll need much more than a minute and close the door in his face.

"What's that about?" Lauren asks, her problems behind her now and her curiosity piqued.

"Nothing, just meeting my mom for brunch." I try to keep my tone light and conversational. The last thing I need is to have all that concern I focused on her flipped back on me.

But when Lauren's eyes laser in on me, I know I've failed. Massively.

"Oh, no, ma'am. Do not think that because I had a momentary breakdown that I forgot there's something serious going on with you and your mom."

All traces of sadness have dissipated, and she sounds like her normal self . . . but more determined. Which really sucks for me.

"There's nothing—" I start, but this time *she* cuts *me* off.

Oh how the tables have turned.

"No. Not a chance. I've let you skirt around this for too long because I've been so preoccupied by everything with Ben. But that stops now. When you get home, you're telling me everything. Whether you're ready or not." Her hands are on her hips and she's using her scary mom voice. I couldn't say no even if I wanted to.

There's no way around this.

I purse my lips and grumble, "Fine."

"Good." She bends down and starts to clean up the depressing mess on the floor. "And go take a shower, you smell terrible."

Rude!

You help your friend out and this is how they treat you.

But she's right, my hair is so greasy and I'm pretty sure my pores are leaking tequila. Plus, I need to armor up for my mom.

TWENTY-TWO

. . .

Jude

The driver rolls up to the Ivy twenty minutes after our reservation time.

My mom is sitting on the patio—because of course she is—and her practiced smile is pasted on her face as she looks over the menu. I let myself roll my eyes one time before I open the car door and weave my way through the light crowd.

As much as I hate when my mom drags me out of the house for her own gain—which is the only reason she ever sees me anymore—and as much as I hate being paraded in front of cameras, it could happen at a worse spot.

The Ivy is cute as hell.

True to its name, ivy drapes from the roof and climbs up the exterior walls. Flowers, both fresh and in print, cover every single surface. Vases overflowing with bright, multicolored roses and whatever other flowers they chose for the day sit in the center of the tables. Even with the LA smog, you want to breathe deeper as soon as you approach the little picket fence surrounding the patio. Their signature pottery, covered in floral prints, tops every table, while floral cushions and throw pillows make the metal chairs look homey and welcoming.

She sees me approach the table and her smile grows wider.

"Jude!" Her voice is much, much too loud for a public space as she stands and circles the table to greet me. She pulls me into a hug and whispers in my ear, "Twenty minutes? You couldn't even be on time when I sent a driver?"

All of my nerves go haywire. Do I want to scream? Do I want to laugh? Do I want to turn my happy ass around and go the fuck home? Yes to all of that.

But I've been trained better. I'm not the person in this relationship with a free pass to hurt, use, and disappoint. So instead of hiking it out of this paparazzi hot spot and disregarding her like she did to me at my launch, I focus on the flowers and take a seat.

The other wonderful thing about the Ivy? The service. Which I'm reminded of when a waiter walks over and places a glass of champagne in front of me like the godsend he is.

God bless the fucking service industry. They're mad undervalued. There's honestly no way I, a person who posts pictures on an app, should get more love than the people who literally keep this world moving.

"Thank you so much." The desperation is clear in my voice.

"Of course. I'll be back to check on you soon," he says, and I swear I see sympathy in his eyes.

But considering where we are, I'm sure we're not the first tragic mother-daughter duo he's helped out today.

Because the Ivy is not only visually beautiful but also perfectly located, it has become destination numero uno for many pseudocelebs to dine and be photographed. Even if my mom didn't already have her own team of camera people following her around, she'd still end up in a magazine or two just sitting here. This is where you come to be seen.

My mom ignores the waiter, staying quiet until he leaves. Her giant, bedazzled sunglasses cover her beautiful blue eyes and make her already delicate features look even daintier. She might make me absolutely crazy, but there's a reason she was the soap queen during the golden era. She's beautiful. And actually very talented when she tries.

Which isn't often anymore.

"So, Mom"—I unwrap my silverware and place my napkin in my lap—"what's going on? Why the summons to paparazzi land?"

I see the twitch in her jaw, and for some reason it gives me a massive amount of pleasure. At least I'm not the only one feeling irritated at this table. What's the saying? Misery loves company? Well, yes, I do.

"Can't a mother just want to have a nice brunch with her daughter?"

A mother? Yes.

My mother? Not a fucking chance.

"Sure, but this is pretty fancy." I gesture to our surroundings. "I just figured it was for something."

"Okay, there is something." She leans forward and her smile changes to one of her real, beautiful smiles that have been so rare since Dad died.

Even with everything that's happened between us, when she smiles like that, I smile too. It reminds me of the times I could rely on her, when she was my best friend. It reminds me that she's hurting, too, and maybe if given time, she can heal and return to the person I grew up loving. No matter how much I try to protect myself from her, she's the only person who can knock down all of my defenses with a single smile.

"Why all the suspense?" I lean forward, feeling like a little kid learning a secret. "Tell me!" I whisper-shout.

She pulls her lips between her teeth, like her face muscles need a break from using muscles that have gone so unused, and reaches across the table to grab my hands. "I got a call from the *Hollywood Housewives* producers," she whispers, but I can still hear her excitement lacing through every syllable. "They asked me to be a full-time cast member! I'm back!"

As soon as she says it, I'm out of my seat, rounding the table and wrapping my arms around her.

"Congratulations, Mom," I say into her ear. "I'm so, so happy for you."

I know I wasn't on board with this plan, and I honestly still have my doubts considering the rabbit hole she fell down when she was initially cast. But she seems happy, genuinely happy. And this is the first thing she's really followed through with since Dad died. Her first real income.

As selfish as it is, I'm hoping this finally gives me the break I need too. I can build my savings again without having to worry about her bills. I can pay for the therapist I desperately need, because Dr. Vodka is really starting to fall down on the job.

I'll be able to breathe again.

I let go of her and go back to my seat.

"Thank you, Ju-ju." She lifts her floral napkin to her cheek and dabs away the few stray tears she let fall. "I couldn't have done it without you. I hope you know how much I appreciate you."

I didn't.

But hearing her say it and actually feel like she means it helps heal something inside of me.

"Thanks, Mom."

Just then, the waiter comes back. "Are you ready to order?"

"Are you?" my mom asks me.

"Sure, you go first though." I figure by the time she orders her salad and tells him everything she wants them to leave off, I'll know what I want.

"Okay . . ." She purses her pink lips and looks at the menu once more. "You know? What the heck." She tosses the menu on the table. "I'll have the crab Benedict."

My jaw damn near falls to my lap. I haven't seen my mom eat more than lettuce in public in years.

"Seriously?" I ask, thankful that my sunglasses are hiding the way my eyes are probably bulging out of my head right now.

"Yeah, why not?" she asks. "We're celebrating today."

"Okay then." The smile on my face is starting to hurt. Maybe this really is the fresh start we need. "Then I'll have what she's having . . . and one more glass of champagne."

Because while Dr. Vodka has been slacking, celebratory champagne has never let me down.

Once we thank our waiter and he walks away, my mom reaches for the champagne flute in front of her that's almost gone, and raises it in the air. "The Andrews women," she says, and her smile wobbles a bit. "And to George, for loving us."

"To us and Dad." I tap my glass against hers, fighting back the tears that always appear when my dad is mentioned. "Proud of you, Mom."

"Love you," she says.

And then she doesn't say anything else. For the first time in what feels like forever, there are no strings attached to her love. The weight I've been carrying on my shoulders for years starts to lighten.

Best. Brunch. Ever.

And it wasn't even because of the complimentary champagne . . . even though that certainly didn't hurt.

. . .

The best part of my mom getting this job and seeming to finally find her footing in this world again is that when I step back through the front door and see Lauren waiting to give me the third degree, I'm not dreading it. And I'm not even drunk! All of this is more than a small miracle.

"Good, you're home," Lauren says in greeting. "I have to leave to get Adelaide in two hours, so I'm not putting up with your attempts to misdirect me or get out of this. Got me?"

Wow. Hard-ass Lauren is pretty impressive. If only she'd do this to Ben.

"Got you." I walk across the living room and sit down on the couch next to her.

Confusion mars her gorgeous face. "You're not going to fight this?"

"Nope," I say, even though I know I'd be singing a different tune had brunch not gone the way it had. "You opened up to me, I need to do the same. I don't need you worried about me when Ben is acting like an ass."

"Okay, yeah . . . good." She was obviously expecting a fight and is trying to regroup. "What's going on with you and your mom? You used to be so close, but now you shut down whenever I mention her."

"You know I love my mom." For some reason, I feel like I have to preface this story with loving her. "It's just . . . she changed when Dad died."

Lauren takes my hand in hers. "Your dad was the best."

"He really was." I don't like talking about him. It makes me feel like I'm not in control. I don't think I ever really came to grips with his death. I've been so busy taking care of my mom that I've had to push my grief to the back of my mind. Add that to the long list of shit my future therapist gets to help me work out. "And I didn't realize how much he was holding together"—*and hiding*—"until after he died."

Lauren's eyebrows furrow together. "Like what?"

"My mom was just a mess. She was so preoccupied with keeping up with the other women on *Hollywood Housewives* that she was spending money they didn't have. And my dad being my dad tried to hold everything together, but did that by not telling my mom she'd gotten out of control. So when he died, he did it in debt."

I've never told anyone about this, but instead of the shame and embarrassment I thought I'd feel, it's actually a relief to share it with someone. To share it with Lauren.

"My mom flew through the life insurance money, and for the last few years, it felt like the only time she ever wanted to see me was when she needed money." I left brunch feeling better, but it still doesn't take away the sting when I think back on the way our relationship has suffered. "It was really hard not to be resentful, you know?"

"I had no idea." Lauren's eyes gloss over. The last thing I want is for her to cry. Part of why I never told her is because I didn't want to just be another burden to her. "I'm so sorry."

"No." I shake my head and squeeze her hand. "Do not be sorry. You couldn't have known. And things are better now."

Those are words I never thought I'd be able to say.

"They are?" She looks skeptical, and rightfully so.

It was just last weekend that my mom blew me off and I took some of it out on stupid Jennifer . . . even though I still stand by my decision. She deserved it.

"I don't think I really told you, but my mom's manager made a deal with a magazine to get her name out there. It's part of how

I got so many sponsors for the launch." I give her the super-abbreviated version of the story. "The goal in the uptick of media was to get her back on *Hollywood Housewives* because she's been struggling to get a well-paying job since my dad died. She found out a few days ago that she got the job!"

I thought Lauren would be just as excited by this news as I am, but instead, she looks more concerned.

"Didn't you say that her first time on this show is when she started to lose control? Do you think this is the best thing for her?"

I understand her concern. Especially because it was my first thought when my mom initially ran this plan by me.

"I was worried at first too," I admit. "But you should've seen her today. She was actually smiling and laughing. I didn't realize it until today, but I haven't seen her like that since before my dad died. I think she needed this. She needed something to remind her that she still has to have a life after my dad."

Plus, I have to believe that after struggling financially for so long and not having my dad to depend on, she'll be smarter this time. And if she's not? I've done my part and she's an adult. She'll have to figure it out on her own.

"If you're happy, then I'm happy," Lauren says. "I just hope you remember that no matter how much I love your mom, I love you more. I'm team Jude until the day I die."

"And I'm team Lauren." I point to my necklace. "I'm sorry I worried you, but I'm good now, honest. Now we can focus on you taking down Ben. I want to see him cry."

Lauren bites her lip, trying to hide the mischievous smile she rarely ever gives. "I kind of do too."

I slap her leg, so excited to finally hear her ready to go toe-to-toe with Ben. "Hell yes you do!"

They say hell hath no fury like a woman scorned, so imagine how fucked Ben will be with both of us coming for him.

TWENTY-THREE

Lauren

Everyone says that hospitals have a funny smell, that they smell like death. I always thought they were crazy. I think they smell like life and miracles and love.

But lawyers' offices? Now *they* have a terrible stench.

I've been coming to them since I was a little girl, visiting my mom for lunch or trailing her around on Take Your Daughter to Work Day. But the smell, I've never been able to get used to it. It's like there's blood in the air and a bunch of hungry sharks are hiding in their offices, preparing to attack. The bitter scent of fear lingers on every surface. It taints the air and poisons your lungs, making it impossible to breathe.

"Everything's going to be fine." Kim squeezes my hand as we sit in the most uncomfortable chairs lining one side of the long conference table and wait for Ben and his lawyer to arrive. "If we don't come to an agreement today, it's still okay. The only way something will be finalized is if we all agree. There's no need to be nervous."

My foot hasn't stopped bouncing since we sat down. I keep looking out of the window-lined walls, waiting to see Ben make his appearance.

"It will be finalized today though," I say. "Ben said he didn't want to go for full custody. I'm okay with every other weekend and switching holidays."

I'm not okay with switching holidays.

The thought of Christmas morning without Adelaide makes me want to curl up in a corner and cry until I die from dehydration.

"I know. Remember, Lauren, we've talked about this." Kim's voice is quiet and gentle. I'm guessing this is also the way she'd talk to a skittish animal. "And I know what Ben told you, but we have to prepare for what comes next if that changes."

"It won't change. He just told me on Friday. It hasn't even been a week." I don't know if I'm reminding her or convincing myself.

I play back the conversation from Friday and will my nerves to chill the freak out. This is going to be great. This is going to be a fresh start, and maybe once it's over, Ben and I can learn how to co-parent respectfully.

Yes.

I close my eyes and take a deep breath, holding it for five seconds before exhaling just as slowly.

This is for the best and it's going to be great.

"All right"—Kim taps my leg—"here they come. Are you ready?"

My eyes snap open. I look through the glass and see Ben trailing behind a man I'm assuming is his lawyer. His lawyer nods his head, greeting his coworkers as he guides Ben through the office and into the conference room where we're waiting. He pushes the door open and motions for Ben to walk in.

Kim and I both stand, extending our hands to shake with Ben and his lawyer before we all take our seats.

I immediately hate Ben's lawyer. Ethan Caputo looks to be in his early to midforties, but considering how overtanned his skin is, I'm thinking he could be younger than that. From his jet-black, slicked-back hair to the Gucci tie around his neck, everything about him screams asshole. I'd bet good money he drives a yellow sports car.

Of course this is who Ben would choose to represent him.

I look at Ben and offer him a small smile as we sit, but when he avoids my eyes, the panic I had been working hard to squelch comes back with a vengeance. I want to get his attention, make sure we're still on the same page, but Kim has gone over today ad nauseam and I know I have one job: stay quiet.

I lay my palms on top of my thighs, trying to stop my legs from starting to bounce again as Kim gets this meeting rolling.

"Mr. Caputo, Mr. Keane, we all know why we're here today, to do what's best for our clients' five-year-old daughter, Adelaide." Her voice is calm but determined, and I thank my lucky stars that my mom helped me get such a capable lawyer. "Mr. Keane filed for full custody, but I think we all know that after being absent from such a large portion of his daughter's young life, that's not what's best for her."

"Kim." Ethan tilts his head to the side, not returning Kim's respectful way of addressing him. There's a glimmer in his eyes and his smile looks greasier than his hair. "Everyone in this room, whether they want to admit it or not, knows that Adelaide would be better off in the custody of my client and his wife."

My vision swims and the room feels like it starts to spin.

"Wife?" I know I dodged a bullet when Ben broke up with me. He sucks. I'm better off without him. Still, knowing he's married feels like someone found my voodoo doll and stuck a hundred needles through my heart.

While Ben ignores me completely, Ethan must smell my shock

and pain like the shark I knew he was. He zeroes in on me, and Kim's hand reaches for mine. I don't know if it's to remind me she's on my side or that I need to stay quiet. Either way, I know I need it.

"Yes, Mr. Keane and Stephanie Parson were married at the beginning of the month." He informs me of something Ben should've told me weeks ago . . . or at least on Friday when we were talking freaking face-to-face. "Obviously, living with two married adults who love each other is a better, more stable home than the sorority house Miss Turner is living in."

I think that was supposed to get a rise out of me, but instead I have to suppress my laughter with how far he's reaching. I've known Jude for almost twenty years. Ben met Stephanie less than a year ago. Plus, Ben's a freaking resident. He works all the time and has no seniority to get days off. However, I can't tell Jude any of this because she will straight up murder Ben and Greasy Hair. Which won't look great for me.

"If your client has been married for that amount of time and we're just now finding out, I think that goes to prove our point that he lacks the capability to properly communicate with Miss Turner." Kim's voice has an edge to it, and I don't know what to make of it. "We should've been made aware of this before this meeting took place."

"No"—Ethan settles back into his chair, amusement written all across his sun-damaged face—"what it goes to prove is that your client is unreasonable and my client didn't feel safe to reveal this information until he had representation present."

My leg begins to shake again, but this time it's not from nerves. It's from anger. Pure, unadulterated, steaming-hot rage.

He didn't feel safe? What a lying piece of shit.

"I think that's a laughable excuse at best." Kim still sounds calm and collected. I try to take comfort in that. She's seen this before. None of this will throw her off balance . . . I hope.

"How so, Kim?" Ethan leans forward, resting his elbows on the dark wood tabletop. "My client stayed in a relationship with Miss Turner out of obligation and fear of retaliation for years. And when he finally gained the courage to end their engagement, she left and took their daughter, refusing to let him see her for years."

I open my mouth, to scream or laugh—not sure which one yet—at how fucking absurd this all is, but Kim's firm hand on mine stops me.

"Mr. Keane had multiple affairs while engaged to Miss Turner, some of those taking place while she was on bed rest with their child. That doesn't sound like a concerned and loving father or partner to me."

I don't love the reminder that Ben was a cheating piece of crap during one of the scariest and darkest moments of my life, but I'm glad Kim is throwing it out there. I don't have the most faith in Ben as an overall human being, but I can't believe he's letting his lawyer sink this low.

"And instead of going to therapy like a healthy adult, Miss Turner practically stole Adelaide away from my client, not letting him be involved for years."

"Where is your proof that my client wouldn't let Mr. Keane see Adelaide?" Kim asks. "You don't have any. We have emails and call records from my client to yours. In no way does your narrative fit with the evidence we have."

I keep expecting Ben to speak up. Just last week he said he didn't want full custody. Now he's not only still fighting for it, but insulting me in the process.

"Your evidence won't hold up," Ethan says. "Not when we have character witnesses who will attest to my client's claims. Miss Turner is controlling, uptight, and vindictive. She has done whatever she could to maintain control of their daughter. The courts will vouch that control is not love, but a form of abuse."

I couldn't quiet the gasp that falls from my lips even if I wanted to. Abuse? They're going to claim I'm emotionally abusive to the little girl I love more than anything in this world? That I'd hurt the child I've given up my entire life for and would literally die for? Are they insane?

"And we have character witnesses who will state the opposite. Witnesses like teachers and pediatricians who have never had a single interaction with Mr. Keane but know Miss Turner well."

"Do those witnesses know that Miss Turner picked an elementary school without giving my client a say? Do they know that she bulldozed my client into giving their daughter a name he despised so much that he only calls her by her middle name? Miss Turner's control issues don't stop with my client, they're leaking into their daughter's life."

Something inside of me shatters.

I don't know what it is. The pain is radiating throughout my entire body, and I can't pinpoint where it's coming from. I don't know if I'm angry or heartbroken. I don't know anything anymore.

I know the name Adelaide wasn't Ben's first choice, but he knew how important it was to me. It was my grandmother's name, and before we even knew we were having a girl, I asked him if we could name our daughter Adelaide. He asked to pick the middle name since I chose the first name. We both said yes and that was the end of it. To hear him say he despises her name? It makes me want to vomit. She's five. How can he hate her name that much? It's part of her.

And the school thing again? He can take the first fucking train to hell with that.

"Ben." I try to keep my voice steady, but with everything that's been said swirling through my mind, I can't control the way it breaks. "You know that's not true. How are you letting him say these things? You just told me you didn't want full custody on Friday, why are you doing this?"

Ben barely looks at me. The spineless, worthless piece of garbage.

"Speaking of Friday," Ethan says, and the way he does causes chills to race down my spine. "She went off of the assigned schedule, leaving my client to cancel important meetings to spend time with their daughter. Thankfully, Mrs. Keane has a flexible schedule and was able to provide care for when Mr. Keane couldn't be home."

Ben fucking played me.

I've done everything I can to make it so easy for him to be involved in Adelaide's life. Including bending over backwards to drive her over to his house, which is an hour away from me, whenever he decided to step up for a day or two and giving up my plans with her so he can spend time with her.

So the other things suck and are hurtful, but this? Knowing that I gave up a night when I had special plans with her, not so he could treat her to *Frozen* and bond with her but so he could use it against me today? That's what makes me lose my ever-loving mind.

"How dare you." My voice is barely above a whisper, but I gain everyone's attention. "If I hadn't called off of work on Friday, you were going to practically kidnap Adelaide. You showed up at her school without ever contacting me, and I let you have the weekend with her. Not because I'm controlling or manipulative— no, those words only describe you—but because I'm desperate for our daughter to live a happy and healthy life with both of her parents. And instead of thanking me for my kindness, you fucking lied to my face!" My voice has steadily increased, and I don't know how it happened, but I'm screaming now. "You told me you didn't want custody. You told me you were too busy with work!

And now, in front of this freakin' slimeball, you want full custody again? For what, Ben? To convince Stephanie she didn't marry trash? Because that's what you are. Trash. I feel bad for Stephanie, because she's lovely and has no idea what she just got herself into. Because you'll try to ruin her too. It's what you do. You ruin people. I'll do everything in my power to keep your toxic ass from screwing up our daughter like every other member of your insane family."

When I finish, I'm out of breath and my heart is racing like it did the one time I took a spin class with Jude. I know I should probably regret what I said . . . maybe all of it . . . definitely the part when I called him a toxic ass. But I can't find it in me. All I feel is the relief of finally saying what's been building inside of me for the last three years. If that feeling wasn't enough to make me feel better, the shell-shocked expressions on Ben's and his lawyer's faces are.

Jerks.

"Well then." Kim gathers all her papers from the table and tucks them back in her folder. "I guess that's all for today. I'll get the next meeting with a court-appointed mediator scheduled."

She stands and I follow her lead. We walk out of the room, neither of us mumbling a goodbye to the assholes still sitting quietly in their chairs. I trail slightly behind her, neither of us saying anything until we're alone on the elevator and the doors slide shut in front of us.

"I'm so sorry, Kim." I know I messed up. My one job was to stay quiet. "I don't know what happened. I never lose my temper and I just—"

"Lauren." Kim cuts me off and I notice the giant grin on her face. "That was amazing. Ben needed to know that you aren't just going to lie down and let him run all over you anymore. And I hate Ethan. Actually, *hate* isn't a strong enough word for how I feel about him. Seeing them both just staring with their stupid mouths hanging open? Brilliant."

"Really?" I don't think she'd lie to me, but it's hard for me to believe she isn't pissed that I broke the lone rule she gave me.

"Really." She nods her head and grabs my hand again. "But when the court-appointed mediator is there next time, then you have to hold it in. No matter what."

I was really hoping everything would be over today, but in a way, part of it is.

I finally understand that I can't change Ben. It doesn't matter how nice or accommodating I am, it won't matter.

I have to live my life for me and Adelaide.

He's a nonfactor.

TWENTY-FOUR

. . .

Lauren

From: Lauren
Date: October 11
Subject: A mom, an influencer, and a cow walked into a bar . . .

Hey!

All right, so maybe the title of this email is a little misleading, but there will be a story about a mom, an influencer, a cow, *and* cocktails in this week's podcast. Is your interest piqued? It should be.

What is that? You want a sneak peek? Why, I'd love to!

When I enrolled my daughter in her school, one of the things I loved most was their emphasis on hands-on learning. In kindergarten, they go on field trips every other week, the older grades go at least once a month, but they have weeklong camping trips in the fall and spring. I was so excited for the opportunities and experiences Adelaide would get at this school. What I forgot about was that I would have to be a chaperone for a large majority of these.

And let me tell you, teachers deserve to make like . . . a billion dollars a year.

My first chaperone duty was going to Underwood Family Farms for World Farm Animals Day—which is actually a thing. My ears are still ringing from the bus ride and it's been over a week. And the bus is just the tip of the iceberg. There were also tears at lunch from the kids who had meat products, a bathroom accident that wasn't nearly as entertaining as the one in *Billy Madison*, and a poor child who had an intense fear of pigs that only got worse when the farmer insisted that petting the pig would help.

I'm not a drinker, but after that, I needed a drink. Thankfully, Jude always has me covered and after (rudely) laughing at me, she whipped me up what she called a Baa Baa Berrytini. It was delicious and helped me loosen up before recording this week's episode of *Mom Jeans and Martinis* where we discuss the pressures parents and students face these days. (I mean, when I was in kindergarten, I was learning ABC's and playing house, not reading full chapter books and picking a second language.) Jude helps dissect the need to be perfect, how it coincides with the rise of social media, and her opinion on how to help combat it . . . which may or may not include so many profanities that we had to give the episode a content warning.

As a mom who works really hard to look like I have everything figured out, this was a conversation I both hated and needed. Plus, for all you nonparents out there, Jude has a lot of tips on not only how to build a social media platform that will be authentic, but how to monetize it from simply being you.

Cheers! 🥂
Lauren

PS If you want to drink with us, here you go!

JUDE'S BAA BAA BERRYTINI

1 ounce strawberry vodka
½ ounce Chambord
2 ounces cranberry juice

Pour all ingredients in a cocktail shaker, fill with ice, shake, pour in a martini glass, and enjoy!

PPS Drink responsibly!

"You're adding the martini recipe?" Jude says as she reads the email over my shoulder. "I can't believe you're already so good at this! That's the perfect freebie incentive. I'll post our selfie with them tomorrow and then direct people to subscribe for the recipe."

I want to roll my eyes and brush off her compliment, because really, I'm just writing silly emails, but I can't. Flexing the creative muscles I've abandoned for most of my life has been crazy fulfilling. Knowing that Jude, the social media queen, is impressed means more than it probably should.

"Thank you. I read that adding a PS to the bottom of emails is a good idea and a recipe is always fun." I schedule the email to go out at midnight and close my computer. "Oh! And did I read you that one email I was telling you about?"

I've done more research on growing an email list than I ever thought possible. I wasn't sure it would pay off, but we've already gotten so many response emails from people telling us how much they're enjoying the content and even forwarding them to friends. Our list has grown by twenty percent, something Hudson told me is super impressive.

"You told me about it, but then Addy spilled her milk and you forgot."

Yup. That's what happened.

"Okay, then I'm reading it to you now, let me pull it up." I tap away on my phone until I find the email I saved last week. "All right, here it is. 'Hi, Lauren and Jude, I don't normally respond to emails like this, but I couldn't help it. I look forward to your emails and podcasts every Tuesday. You've quickly become like my new best friends. I had my son earlier this year, and while he's the greatest thing I've ever done, I'd be lying if I said I haven't felt extremely lonely. Listening to you changed that. I finally feel like my struggles and my joys are represented. I wait until he's asleep every night and pour myself a martini before tuning in. I have laughed and cried while listening. I really hope you both never stop, you've filled a void in my life that I didn't know was there and I'm sure I'm not alone. With love, Valerie.'"

"Holy shit." Jude is almost slack-jawed when I finish reading the touching email.

"Right!" I tap on my phone and find the other one that just made me laugh. "And look at this one. It's just a bunch of fire emojis."

"You're seriously kicking ass at this. I knew you'd be good, because you're you and you're good at everything, but you're kind of blowing me away." Jude adjusts herself on the metal bench overlooking Adelaide's gymnastics class. "I'm terrible at my newsletter, I might need you to help me."

"I'd love to." I don't know if she's blowing smoke up my butt because I've been a little . . . fragile . . . since the meeting with Ben and Ethan, but I'll take it either way. I'm craving positive feedback like Jude's poor plant craves water. "You know where to find me."

"I swear, the list of perks to living with you grows every day."

Okay.

So she's definitely blowing smoke.

"You don't have to keep doing that, the complimenting me all the time." I slide my computer into my backpack and turn to face her. "I promise, I'll be fine."

The promise might be a stretch. Depending on how this custody battle ends up working out, fine might be highly optimistic.

"One, I'm not doing anything. I really do suck at email marketing and you're really good at it . . . I mean, look at that email you just read me! And two, Ben's a fucking dickbag and I'll give you nothing but compliments until they're filling up your brain and there's no room left to remember that dumb shit he said."

"Jude!" I whisper-yell, looking around to make sure the other parents in this gymnastics class aren't close enough to hear Jude's foul mouth. "You can't talk like that at a kids' gymnastics class."

"Why the fuck not?" She waves a hand to the mat in front of us. "None of the kids are close and their parents are big enough to have heard the words before. Plus, you know if I even think about that shithead ex of yours, foul language is the only language I know."

This is true.

It was true before, but it's even more true since I filled her in on the meeting.

"Still . . ." I start to tell her she has to watch her mouth around these parent groups, but Ethan's words start to bounce around my head again—*control freak*, *uptight*, *manipulative*—and the words die on my tongue. "Never mind."

"No. No 'never mind.'" The mischievous glint that's ever present in Jude's eyes is replaced by a determination that can only mean horrible things for me. "What were you going to say?"

"Nothing, really." I shake my head. I'm not going to dictate what an adult can or should say. I'm not her mom. "It's not a big deal."

"It's actually a huge deal if something that idiot said about you is making you doubt yourself like this."

I avoid looking at my well-meaning best friend and focus on Adelaide as she makes her way through the floor exercises they're working on. Her curls are tucked into little buns to stay out of her face as she cartwheels and somersaults across the mat, her smile so big that even though my mind is a mess, I can't help but smile along with her. I lift my hand and wave to her even though she's paying zero attention to me, but I know if I look at Jude, I'll either want to cry or crawl beneath the bleachers. "It's not that I'm doubting myself as much as I'm trying to be more aware of my behavior."

"That's bullshit and you know it," Jude, still not mincing her words, says with more force than I've heard come from her in a long time.

"It's not and *you* know it." As much as it pains me to admit it, not everything Ethan said was wrong. I am a control freak. I always was a little bit, but it's gotten worse since Adelaide was born. Logically, I know I wasn't the reason Ben cheated, but I can't seem to escape the fear that I'm going to push away everyone I love. "I mean, I just was telling you what not to say like you were Adelaide. You're an adult, how much longer are you going to want to deal with me mothering you?"

"Are you crazy?" Jude's brows knit together and her neck juts out. "Lauren, I'm a fucking disaster ninety-nine percent of the time! You're literally the only person I know who helps me hold my shit together."

"That's not true." I shake my head, thinking of how Jude has been there for me over the last five . . . or fifteen . . . years of my life. "You've done so much for me and all I do is lay my burdens on you."

"Okay, enough." She grabs my hand and yanks me down the bleacher steps and keeps pulling me until we're standing outside of the building.

"What the heck?"

"I'm not going to sit there and let you shit on yourself because that fucking jackass says anything to get to you." She's glaring at me and I finally get what she means when she says my mom looks scare her, because I'm not loving being on the receiving end of the look. "You asked me to stop swearing in a children's gymnastics class. That was not an unreasonable request."

"But you're an adult. I can't tell you—" I start, but don't finish.

"That I should watch my mouth in circles that you frequent but I just occasionally observe?" She widens her eyes as she waits for a response, but I don't really have one.

"Well, sure, when you put it like that it doesn't sound so bad." I know I'm looking like Adelaide's twin right now because I can *feel* the pout overpowering my face.

"Because it wasn't bad." She lets out a deep sigh and her entire posture changes.

I instantly brace.

Jude is the fun one.

Until she isn't.

She doesn't get serious on me often, but when she does, it tends to shake me to the core. I already know I'm not going to like whatever she's about to say . . . no matter how much I need to hear it.

"How much do you love Adelaide?" she asks, and my head jerks back. This is not where I was expecting her to go.

"I'm not sure it's measurable. She's my entire world, you know that."

"I do know that." She nods her head. "What is it about her that you love so much?"

I feel like this is a trick question. What don't I love about that little girl?

"Everything." I shrug my shoulders, a smile tugging at the corners of my mouth as I think about everything that makes Adelaide June the most wonderful kid in the entire world. "I love her kindness and her joy. I love her tenacity and the way she isn't afraid of anything. I love her mind. She's so smart and views the world in this way that fascinates me and puts me in awe. She stands up for what's right and loves so huge, it's all-encompassing. She's magical."

Finally, some of the seriousness slides off Jude's face. Because like I said, Adelaide is magic. Even thinking about her makes it impossible not to smile.

"She really is magic." Jude grabs my hand and holds it tight. "And if she ever doubted her magic because of a man? If she ever tried to dim her light to appease a man who has hurt and abandoned her? What would you say?"

Well . . .

Crap.

Direct freaking hit.

I squeeze my eyes shut and press my lips together as the truth of Jude's words filters through my body and digs its way into my mind . . . and heart.

"You're right." The words are barely a whisper, but it's not easy for me to admit the way I've completely lost myself to Ben. Even after I promised myself I wouldn't. "I don't know why I let him do this to me."

"Because you loved him and the line between love and hate is a thin one. You both created this magical being, and as much as I hate his fucking guts and will for all of time, I can't fault you for needing to see the good in him and remembering that he was a huge part of your life." She moves me away from the door as another woman and little girl in a sparkly leotard approach the doors before she drops her voice even lower. "But when you do that, even subconsciously, you're assuming the things he says have some modicum of truth to them and aren't what they really are: another way to manipulate and control you."

For the second time in the span of just as many minutes, I don't know what to say. Jude knows me better than anyone, but she's never said anything like this. "Since when did you become the wise one in this sister-wife relationship?"

"I mean . . ." The seriousness leaves her face, and the smug look that only she can pull off appears. "Between you and my therapist, I was bound to pick up a thing or two."

Jude called a therapist after her brunch with her mom. She's only gone twice, but the change has already been pretty incredible. She seems so much happier and more relaxed . . . compared to where she used to be, at least.

More little kids in leotards and gym shorts start to arrive, so I know Adelaide's class is about to come to an end. I nod my head in the direction of the door, and Jude slows her always frantic pace to fall in step beside me.

"You might need to pass me her number, because I clearly have more problems than I'd care to admit." Many, many more. Ben, my mom, completely losing my identity and all grasps on who I am outside of a mother, to name a few. "But really, thank you. I told myself I wasn't going to let him get to me, but it's so much easier said than done."

"You're preaching to the choir." Jude pulls open the door, and the peaceful quiet from outside immediately disappears as little kids chase each other up and down the hallway, waiting for their class to begin, and parents—and nannies—chat with each other or get on their phones now that their little ones have a distraction. "There is one other thing I think would help get he who shall not be named out of your head . . ."

The way she trails off at the end of the sentence is all I need to know that I do not want to hear what she has to say next. But considering she's on a bit of a roll and the rest of her advice has been spot on, I make the mistake of not keeping my mouth shut. "What else do you think I should do?"

"Do you really want to know?"

I look at the mat and see Adelaide and the rest of her classmates sitting on the edge of the gymnastics floor, waiting—not so patiently—as the teachers riffle through the basket by the door to get the stamps and stickers for a job well done. "Class is almost over, so hurry up and tell me before I change my mind."

This is apparently all the encouragement she needs, because a smile so like Angelina Jolie's in *Maleficent* lights her perfect face, it makes me instantly regret wanting to know.

"Call Hudson, accept the date, bang the hell out of him, and let him worship you the way I know he wants to."

She says it so fast, it takes me a moment to comprehend what words actually came out of her mouth. My cheeks heat at the same time my stomach does that wonky flip it always seems to do when I think of Hudson. But this time, thanks to Jude and her filterless mouth, I feel something a little lower too.

"I . . . I don't know." I keep my eyes glued on Adelaide as she chats her life away with the little girl sitting next to her on the mat, and I try to remember for a second what it felt like to be so innocent. "I just . . . is it too soon? Shouldn't I just focus on Adelaide at least until the custody is finalized?"

"Too soon? Ben got fucking married!" She's whispering, but it still doesn't mask her feelings . . . at all. "Adelaide likes Hudson. You like Hudson. Go on a date with the guy."

She pulls out her phone and taps away before holding it out to me. I shouldn't be surprised, because Jude is not a person to be ignored, but the way my body convulses when I see she's calling Hudson cannot be helped.

"Jude!" I hiss, but it does nothing. Instead she just shoves the phone against my ear and walks away, leaving me a stuttering mess when Hudson's deep, podcast-perfect voice comes on the other line.

"Jude, my dude!" Hudson says the same greeting that makes Adelaide giggle hysterically.

"Oh, um . . . hey! Not Jude, it's actually Lauren. Hi. Hey." I close my eyes and shake my head, wondering how in the world people flirt because I'm clearly incapable.

"Oh! Lauren, hey! How are you?" The tone of his voice changed, but I can't put my finger on how exactly it did. Maybe it's a little softer? More gentle? More caring?

I don't know.

All I know is it makes my heart squeeze in a way I haven't felt in years . . . maybe ever.

Jude's right. Hudson's a good person, and no matter how hard Ben tries to convince me otherwise, I deserve that. So with the courage I'm beginning to learn that I have, I put myself out there . . .

"So, um . . . is the date still on the table? Because if it is, I'd love to go on one with you."

It only takes him a second to respond, but that second feels like a million years.

"Really?" He sounds as shocked as I feel. "Are you sure this isn't Jude messing with me and getting my hopes up?"

"I'm sure. Jude's helping Adelaide get her shoes out of her gymnastics cubby." A laugh somehow manages to force its way out despite my nerves, but I don't know why I'm surprised. Hudson always manages to set me at ease. He's just *such* a good guy. And hot too.

And for some reason, he wants to date me.

Take that, Ben Keane, ya jerk.

"Then yes, the date is still on the table. It was never going to leave the table," he says, and I have to bite my lip to prevent my massive smile from taking over my face. "I wouldn't want you to have to give up time with Addy, so let me know what days work for you and I'll plan around your schedule, if that's good."

God. Such a good guy!

"I'm free next weekend, if that's okay?"

"Yeah!" he shouts in my ear. "I mean, shit. Sorry. See, you got me all worked up and excited and I can't even play it cool. You scramble my brain, Lauren. What I meant to say is I'll plan something and let you know tonight the details if you'd like."

"Yeah." I nod my head like he can see me somehow, feeling like a giddy teenager who just got asked to prom. "That sounds good. I'm really excited."

"Me too . . . and, Lauren," he calls just before I'm about to hit end. "Thanks for giving me a chance."

Jude's holding Adelaide's hand, staring at me as Adelaide's little mouth moves nonstop, no doubt telling her all the titillating details of level-one gymnastics. She widens her eyes, asking about a million questions without saying a word. I smile back, hoping it gives just as many answers.

"I feel like I should be the one thanking you."

There's silence for a second before his soft voice is in my ear. "Then you'd be wrong. I'll call you tonight, okay?"

"Okay."

I hit end, knowing I can't take any more of his sweetness unless I want to dissolve into a puddle of tears on the slightly padded floors.

Adelaide finally spots me as I weave my way through the crowded hallway, and lets go of Jude's hand and sprints toward me.

"Mommy!" she cries as she jumps into my arms, her little body not nearly as light as it was a year ago. "Did you see my roundoff? I was so good!"

"You were amazing." I grunt as I lower her back to the floor. "I'm so proud of you!"

"I know." She waves off my words. "You're always proud of me."

"And I'm proud of your mom." Jude takes her phone from my hand and slides it back into her bag.

Adelaide looks at Jude, her face scrunched up with those adorable little wrinkles on the bridge of her nose that I used to kiss when she was a baby. "Why?"

"Because she's really brave." Jude says the words like they mean nothing, but I feel them down to my soul.

"Of course she's brave, she's my mom." Adelaide shrugs before intertwining her fingers with mine as we approach the parking lot, like she didn't just shift my entire world.

Because she's right. In the blunt honesty that only a five-year-old can deliver, she reminded me that I'm her example for this life. If I want her to grow up to be a strong and happy adult, I have to show her what a strong and happy adult looks like.

No matter how much it scares me. No matter how hard I have to fight for it.

TWENTY-FIVE

. . .

Jude

I'll never understand how in the hell I let Lauren convince me to do some of the shit she makes me do.

After she got her license, she talked me into going camping with her for the weekend. Of course, she told her mom she was just staying at my house and I told my parents that I was going to hers. This was a brilliant plan until we got there and realized we had no fucking clue what we were doing. I, the smart and reasonable sixteen-year-old I was, said we should ditch it and just go crash at a hotel overlooking a lake instead. Genius, right? Well, Lauren wouldn't do it. And we ended up eating cold hot dogs and sleeping in a tent that continuously collapsed on us all night long. It was a disaster and I swore I would never go with her again.

Until she asked me a month later and, like an idiot, I said yes.

But because Lauren is Lauren, she spent that month reading about camping and then grilling the employees at some camping store. So when we went back, it was literally the best time ever.

I guess my faith that she wouldn't let me suffer through the same thing twice is how she convinced me to come to another playgroup meetup.

Well . . . that and the fact that Addy gives a really good pout face when she says please.

"Honest to God," I lean over and whisper to Lauren as we wait in line for the bounce house the kids just *had* to get in. "You owe me so fucking hard for this, Lauren. I can't believe I let you talk me into this shit."

Instead of looking the least bit apologetic, the bitch laughs. *Laughs!*

The audacity.

"Oh, come on." She opens her arms wide, gesturing to the hellhole also known as Mr. Bones in mid-October. "When's the last time you went to a pumpkin patch? This is fun."

Clearly, we have very different definitions of fun.

"I guess fun is subjective." I look straight ahead, counting the number of heads we have until our group can have their turn in the bounce house.

Apparently, I'm the only person who seems to be worried about the sanitation of a bunch of children—and it's a scientific fact that children are gross—climbing into a bounce house and most likely losing and/or taking off their socks at some point. Disgusting.

But beyond nasty kid feet, there are about fifty other reasons I can think of for today not being "fun."

One, we had to buy VIP passes for this outing. To a pumpkin patch. I love my city, but that is so LA it makes me want to vomit.

Two, and more importantly, it's a day I have to spend with Jennifer and her band of merry witches . . . which is not a Halloween pun.

In a cruel stroke of fate, Lake and Adelaide have apparently become best friends this year. So I was lectured more than Addy was on the car ride over. It felt excessive, but then I got my first glimpse of Jennifer and Lake and realized how necessary it was.

Because I learned that matching wasn't just a fun summer activity. Jennifer was equipped with a mother-daughter fall wardrobe as well. And if I ever thought the bright floral dresses were the most obnoxious things in the entire world, I was instantly proven wrong when I saw Jennifer and Lake in matching Gucci cardigans.

Fucking gag.

Allover logos are tacky as hell, and that's a mountain I will gladly die on.

Outfitting yourself and your fucking five-year-old in logo-covered, five-hundred-dollar cardigans makes me feel punchy. I'm not a violent person, but I swear to god, when I saw Jennifer, my palm started to twitch.

And poor little Lake, she just wants to roll in the fungus-coated bounce house, ride the smelly ponies, and get her face painted. All activities Jennifer has curled her lip and begrudgingly agreed to only if Lake took off her sweater.

Like maybe don't put your kindergartner in a fucking Gucci sweater to go to a pumpkin patch and let her breathe, bitch.

But thanks to Lauren's lecture fresh in my mind and my new therapist, Chloe, all of this stayed tucked inside as I forced a smile on my face and didn't say a word. Like a goddamn champion.

Or a reasonable adult.

Same thing.

We get to the front of the line, and Addy takes her shoes off in a split second before her group of five is racing through the tiny, oval-shaped entrance. We move to the side, watching through the netted siding as they jump and flop all around. Their giggles grow with every second, and my cold, hardened heart can't take it. They're so damn cute and their joy is contagious. Before I even know it's happened, I'm laughing along with them and taking an obscene—and maybe creepy—amount of pictures of children who do not belong to me.

"You're breaking." Lauren nudges my shoulders, not even trying to disguise the smugness in her voice . . . or on her face. "I knew you'd have fun eventually."

"Again, I think you're playing it a little fast and loose with that term." I roll my eyes and tuck my phone back into my little cross-body bag. "But I'm not hating it, and as always, Addy makes everything better. You made the cutest damn kid."

"Thanks, I worked really hard on her." She laughs as she says it, but whenever anyone mentions her pregnancy, I can see the ghosts cross her face. Not only did she almost die, but it's also the time she saw her relationship start to fall apart. "But she was worth it. C-section scar and all."

"Yup"—I cringe thinking of the horror stories she told me about her organs being outside of her body and then the way she could barely move for weeks after—"never fucking having kids. Addy's it for me."

"Then it's a good thing we're practically married, I guess."

"Truer words." I follow her to the front of the bounce house as she gathers Addy's shoes and gets out of the way for the next stampede of kids when their time is up.

All of the moms shepherd their children out of the flow of traffic and keep them surrounded until their shoes (and, as predicted, socks) are back on.

"I vote we grab food and then go pick our pumpkins," Sabrina, still my favorite Remington mom, suggests. "I think they have Mexican food over there. Some of us can hop in line and the rest can reserve tables."

Besides this place being overpriced and overcrowded, the one thing they do have going for them is excellent taste in food trucks.

Considering we've been here for two hours already, I figure it should almost be time to wrap this party up. Plus, if they don't feed me, I'm gonna get hangry, and I can't go there again.

Whitney's lip curls in disgust, and I assume she's only just now realizing her evil leader is wearing a Gucci sweater. "Food trucks? I'm sorry, but I am not feeding my child from a food truck."

Even though I'm trying really hard to stay on my best behavior, there's not a chance in hell—or the valley—that I could prevent the way my eyes roll. Thankfully, from all the deep sighs and moans I hear going around, I'm not the only one who finds her completely unbearable.

"Well, then you can be one of the people who saves the seats," Lauren . . . *Lauren!* . . . says. "And the ones of us who are okay with our kids eating from the gluten-, dairy-, and egg-free food truck can go do that."

My head snaps toward my quiet, polite, mild-mannered best friend. I don't know if I want to high-five her or leap on her and smother her with kisses. Like, honestly, who even is this fucking bombshell, boss bitch next to me? She's still the best mom and friend, but now she's making plans for dates and coming up with snappy, but still kind, responses for the wicked witches of Remington!

Hell yes! Look at us, just rubbing off on each other and becoming better people.

God. Chloe is going to be so proud of us.

"So that's settled then," Sabrina says. She's got a shit-eating grin on her face that makes me like her even more. "Kids, you're going to sit with Miss Whitney, Miss Jennifer, and Miss Colleen while we go get your food. Be on your best behavior, okay?"

She's met with an adorably in-sync round of yeses. Addy, Lake, and Winnie all hold hands together, following behind the moms who got roped into supervision duty.

"Do you want me to hang back and keep an eye on Addy?" I ask Lauren. It's not that I don't trust Jennifer . . . no, sorry, that's a lie. It's def that I don't trust Jennifer, and by the way Lauren's shoulders sag in relief at my offer, it's clear she doesn't either.

"Yes, thank you." She grabs my hand and squeezes it once. "Want me to get you tacos?"

"Is Jennifer's sweater the most obnoxious thing ever? Obviously I want tacos." I know, I'm stuck on the damn sweater, but I just really fucking hate it! Until today, I didn't know that brand-name cardigans were my most irrational pet peeve, but here we are.

She rolls her eyes and shakes her head, but she does not disagree that Jennifer's sweater is, in fact, the most obnoxious thing ever.

She turns away, catching up with Sabrina, Brandi, and Lucy, and I trail behind the kids, making no effort to engage in conversation with the aging mean girls leading the charge. They head to the secure area where they stored their lunch boxes before going to the seating area.

Now, I'm not saying that they actually are witches, but I *am* saying it's crowded as hell, and as soon as they got close to the tables, two magically opened up. That could be a coincidence, but it could also be a spell they placed.

Either way, I'm glad to be off my feet and drinking the free water that came with our sixty-dollar VIP passes.

Only in Los Angeles.

Jennifer directs all the kids to sit at one table, and—with great reluctance—I join the adult table. I know Addy is way more entertaining than any of these women, but she's living her best kindergarten life with her friends and I don't want to cramp her style. *Even though I am very much the cool aunt and she would be lucky to have me at her side.*

I sit quietly, minding my own business as the moms who were too good for the food truck unpack lunches for their kids. Because they were so high and mighty about the food options here, I assumed they'd have gourmet meals complete with all-organic, maybe even vegan options. Instead, I bite back my laughter as they hand their kids Lunchables, sports drinks that are pretty much all sugar, and a few pieces of fruit.

Oh, the irony of it all.

"So, Jude," Colleen, the only one of these women I can kind of deal with, grabs my attention. "How's the podcast going?"

I ignore the way Jennifer's cheeks go red at the mention of the podcast. *I guess she's not over the launch party after all . . .*

"It's going great." I'm not a person to humblebrag—or really be humble at all—but I'm definitely not going to hold back singing Lauren's praises to these women. "I knew it was going to do well, but it's surprised us all with just how quickly it's taken off. The mommy influencer arena is pretty saturated, but everyone is loving Lauren. She's really been the big draw. People love her honesty, realness, and humor. Because of her, we're already fielding sponsorship offers."

I should've reached out to this damn pumpkin patch and offered an Instagram post and ad during the podcast in exchange for our passes. I probably could've saved us almost two hundred dollars. I'm slipping.

"Well, I'm sure your name and platform played a huge part in the success too," Whitney offers. "I have a vlog, and gaining an audience before you can monetize takes ages."

The urge to roll my eyes is so strong that I'm afraid they'll start to bleed if I don't give in.

"My platform got us a few listeners in the very beginning, but all the work Lauren has put into building our email list and coming up with relatable and authentic content is what has skyrocketed our success." Did Jennifer not tell these women that I'm not gonna sit back and let them get away with their passive-aggressive jabs? "Most influencers are stagnant because people aren't authentic. They're trying so hard to appeal to everyone or present this picture-perfect facade that nobody can relate to. Audiences are a lot smarter than most content creators give them credit for, and they can see right through the bullshit. If your vlog is struggling, I'd suggest you do an audit and go over all of your posts. See which ones have the most engagement and which ones didn't do well. Then you need to sit down and really think about what *you* have to offer instead of just going off what you think you need to be."

Whitney doesn't really deserve my help. She's awful. But maybe she'll realize she's been awful and do a video about being a recovering mean girl and leave her dark, evil ways behind her. And while Jennifer's rolling her eyes at my really fucking good advice, Whitney's eyes are a little wider and I can see she's really taking in everything I've told her. I might not be great at many things in life, but I'm damn good at my job. She'd be right to listen to me if her vlog is something she's truly passionate about.

"Thanks." She pulls out her phone, and I assume she's taking down notes on what I told her. "I never thought about doing a content audit. That's a really good idea."

I want to say duh, but again, like an adult, I don't. "I find them really helpful. I do one at the beginning of the year and again in June or July."

Before Whitney can respond, shrieks of excitement are heard from the kids' table.

"Mommy!" Addy shouts like she didn't just see her mom ten minutes ago.

Lauren's smile lights up, her love for Addy written all over her face, and it makes her—impossibly—more beautiful. So much so

that a few guys turn their heads and watch her as she goes by. I
know she's still struggling with the custody battle and the things
Ben said about her, but something has shifted inside of her and
everyone is taking notice. Even strangers.

"Are you hungry?" Lauren asks as she gets closer, holding a
bag of food in one hand and drink tray in the other. Her steps
falter a little when she sees the lunches already on the table, and
she pulls her lips between her teeth, no doubt fighting the smug
smile I know she wants to let free.

"I'm starving, Mommy," Addy, who may or may not be even
more dramatic after living with me for a few months, says. "I can
feel my muscles shrinking, I need food to keep them strong."

Yup.

Definitely more dramatic.

And I refuse to apologize. It's adorable.

"Well, I wouldn't want your muscles to disappear," Lauren
says with a straight face. "Will tacos help?"

Addy's eyes light up and she jumps out of her seat. "Tacos help
with everything!"

Lauren shakes her head and looks at me. I just shrug because
Addy has never spoken truer words. She's a very wise five-year-
old who has taken very well to our strict Taco Tuesday schedule.
Some may call it propaganda, but I call it priorities. No kid of
mine (blood or otherwise) will not love tacos.

Lauren drops the bag in front of Addy, unpacking foil-wrapped
tacos and putting them on the table in front of her. Poor Lake eyes
them with envy as she chomps down on her cold chicken nugget.

"Thanks, Mommy." Addy doesn't even glance at Lauren as
she grabs her taco and takes a gigantic bite.

Lauren shakes her head and grabs the bag, avoiding colliding
with the other food truck moms, and makes her way to the spot
next to me.

"I got some vegan ones and some with chicken." She hands me a cup I know without even asking is filled with Diet Coke. "They both looked good and I couldn't decide."

"You know I'll eat anything as long as it's in a tortilla and has guacamole." This might not be the best habit of mine, but it's true. Lucky for me, tacos are kind of an institution in LA and I have lots of options.

She empties out the bag in front of us and looks to the other moms, who seem to be regretting their no-food-truck stance right about now.

"So"—Lauren takes a bite out of a chicken taco—"what'd we miss?"

For some reason, this question seems to piss Jennifer off. I have a sneaking suspicion it's because my best friend is becoming immune to her bullying tactics and is slowly—and unintentionally—encroaching on her position as the leader of the kindergarten mom pack.

And she's doing it without a stupid cardigan.

TWENTY-SIX

. . .

Lauren

I cannot believe I let Jude talk me into this.

When she turned eighteen—I'm a month older than her, something she hated then but rubs in my face now—she convinced me to go to this eighteen-and-over club.

I'm not a club person.

Shocking, I know.

Anyway, I went with her, minding my own business and bobbing my head to the music in the corner, when Jude comes plowing through the crowd like freaking Moses or something. I should've turned and run. Even under the flashing lights and between the sweating bodies, the look on her face was familiar. And it meant trouble.

She wrapped her long fingers around my wrist and dragged me across the dance floor. My ankles wobbled in the heels she'd forced me into as my body ricocheted off everyone like a freaking pinball until she slung me in front of her and we ended up in a freaking cage.

A cage.

Before I could even comprehend WTF happened, she was next to me, the door was closed, and the cage lifted off the floor. It took me a minute—or twenty—but eventually I gave in and started dancing with her. For two hours, it was me and her, putting on a show, dancing, laughing, and having the best time ever. And apparently it was evident to everyone else, too, because we were put on the VIP list and went back to that cage every single Saturday for the entire summer.

Now, ten years later, I really hope this date will be the new version of cage dancing. I could use Saturday night plans every now and again.

I check my phone, seeing it's only a few minutes before Hudson is supposed to be here, grab my purse, and head downstairs.

I've spent so much time with Hudson over the last few months, but I'm still so nervous that I have to ball my fists together to keep my hands from shaking. I don't even know why. He's a great guy—we wouldn't be doing this otherwise—and I'm sure if nothing else, we'll have fun tonight.

I thought Ben was great too . . .

I shake off that thought as I reach the bottom of the stairs. If Jude knew that was going through my mind, she'd give me one of the lectures she's become so fond of since she started seeing her therapist. The lectures could be annoying to some people, but I'm just so happy to see Jude taking care of herself—for real this time and not just for show on social media—that I happily sit through them all.

She looks up from her laptop, a giant grin spreading across her face when she sees me. "Lauren and Hudson sitting in a tree, K-I-S-S-I-N-G!"

I roll my eyes and shake my head, but I can't help but smile along with her. "You're so ridiculous."

"Well, I wanted to change it from *kissing* to *sexing*, but I didn't feel like sexing in a tree is the way you want to break your dry spell." She closes her computer and tosses it to the side like it wouldn't cost over a thousand dollars to replace. "Promise me you'll let loose tonight?"

I open my mouth to answer, but she just keeps talking.

"And by letting loose, I mean your legs," she clarifies, and I understand why she spoke over me. "Please let that man give you an orgasm."

"Jude!" I shove her shoulder, hating the way talk of sex still makes my cheeks burn. "It's our first date, that's not going to happen."

"Why not?" she whines, stomping a foot on the carpeted floor. "It's not like you don't know him already! Just fucking fuck him for fuck's sake! Your lack of orgasms is stressing me out, so I know it's got to have you tense."

I don't tell her that my sex life with Ben was never phenomenal enough to make me feel like I've been missing anything these last few, celibate, years. Don't get me wrong, the beginning was great. Everything was new and shiny and fun. But I don't want to make those mistakes again. I don't want to let the excitement blind me from the warning signs.

"I'm honestly fine." I walk over to the entryway closet to grab my shoes. "But maybe *you're* the one who needs to get some if you're so worried about my sex life."

"Well . . . you're not wrong about that." She leans against the empty beige wall, crossing her perfect, toned arms in front of her chest. "It's been too long since I've had sex. But at least I've been self-administering orgasms. You haven't had any. That's the big problem here."

"You're an actual disaster, and I don't know what I'm going

to do with you." I pull the little zippers on the sides of my ankle boots and roll up my skinny jeans a couple of times. I stand up straight and look directly into Jude's eyes before asking a question I know could go very, *very* wrong. "How do I look?"

I didn't get super dressed up. I don't even have the clothes to try to get dressed up. But I made an effort, a very valiant one, if I may say so myself. I'm wearing my best jeans that make my legs look great and my booty look better. I paired them with a deep-V black satin tunic that—thanks to Tan France—I French tucked. For my hair, I separated it into two French braids that I did half-way to the back of my head and then let my curls go crazy. And because I live with her and she's been bothering me about my nude lip gloss for months, I put on Jude's red lipstick, which I was positive was going to look ridiculous but—I begrudgingly admit—looks great.

I haven't felt this good about myself in months.

Years, actually.

"Ummm . . . do you even have to ask?" Jude looks me up and down in the most overexaggerated, obnoxious way ever. "Those legs? That ass? Your fucking boobs?! And don't even get me started on that red lip. You look so fucking hot that Hudson might literally shit himself . . . or die. He's def going to die."

Sometimes she's over the top and extra to the nth degree, but that's exactly what I need right now and it's why I love her so freaking much.

"Thank you." I let out a deep breath I've been holding maybe since Hudson asked me out, and relax a little. "This is why you're the best. I needed that pep talk."

It came just in time, because before she can even respond, there's a knock at the door.

"Coming!" she shouts, and takes off across the living room,

not even giving me the chance to prepare. She flings the door open without making sure it's him. "Oh my god! Hudson! You're here and on time and looking dapper and with flowers! I'm like a proud mom right now! Lauren, come look at the flowers your handsome date got you!"

Again . . . so freaking extra.

I make my way to them, fighting the urge to run . . . to him or away from him, it's a toss-up. But when he steps inside and I finally see him, all of my nerves disappear.

He watches me approach, and I remember exactly why I was okay with saying yes to this. He's laser focused on me, but not in a creepy way. He's looking at my face, his kind eyes and gentle smile telling me everything words never could. He's wearing jeans, too, but he's paired his with a T-shirt and sweater that accentuate his long, slender body. His scruffy blond hair is getting darker as fall sets in. Blonds have never been my thing, but as is everything with Hudson, he's just different. He's handsome, but even if he wasn't, I still think something about him would just call to me.

No matter how hard I've tried to deny it.

"Wow," he says when I reach him. "You're always beautiful, but . . . wow." His cheeks go red, but he doesn't look away or try to hide it.

I realize it's another thing I like about him. He doesn't try to mask anything from me. Sure, our first meeting was a bit of a disaster, but every time I've been with him since, he never hides anything from me. After my last relationship, where it took me too long to realize that nothing was as it seemed, this might be the thing I like most about Hudson.

He hands me a bouquet of flowers, and I really notice them for the first time. My head snaps up and I feel like my heart is trying to beat its way out of my chest. "You remembered?"

One Saturday after we recorded the podcast, Hudson met me, Adelaide, and Jude at a farmers' market. We wandered around for a couple of hours. I focused on getting fresh veggies and fruits. Jude took a million pictures and drank way too many coffees. Adelaide found every booth with treats, got a sugar high, and then ran around the play area. Hudson just lingered with us all, happy to hang. As we were walking around, we passed a vendor selling flowers. The roses seemed to be the popular option, but I told Hudson that my favorite flowers were the ranunculus. It was an offhand comment that I doubt most people would even remember, let alone buy a stunning bouquet months later.

"Of course I remembered. I'd never even heard of them before you told me about them." He shuffles back and forth on his feet, shoving his hands in his pockets. "And you told me. I remember everything you say."

"Damn, Huds!" Jude says, killing the moment. "Look at you! You haven't even left yet and I'm already giving you an A plus for the night. If you blow this, I'll murder you."

The shy smile disappears and humor lights his face, his hazel eyes sparkling in our terribly lit living room. "Lauren threatened legal action when I took you home that one night and now you're threatening murder? You two are wild."

Wild is probably the nicest word he could use to describe us, and I appreciate his restraint.

"As long as you know where you stand." Jude pulls the flowers out of my hands. "I'll put these in water. Now you two go. Have fun. And too much fun, if you know what I mean." She winks, not even attempting to play it cool. "Huds, you know what I mean, right? She needs—"

"Okay then!" I cut her off, grabbing Hudson's arms and pulling him through the still-open front door. "Bye, Jude."

She doesn't say *bye* back, but her laughter can be heard all the way to Hudson's car.

• • •

I didn't know what to think when we walked into the apartment building that offers furnished rentals. There was also a SoulCycle on the bottom. I didn't know what made me more nervous, a workout in jeans or a night in his apartment.

But as the elevator doors slide open on the fourth floor, revealing a rooftop with not only amazing views of the city, but lawn chairs wide enough for two people, and a giant movie screen, excitement replaces all of my nerves.

"What is this place?" I'm still looking around, trying to figure out what's going on. I know we're seeing a movie, but I had no idea a place like this existed. There's an old-fashioned ticket booth straight ahead, a bar and food stations in the back, and different games set up all around.

"It's a rooftop movie. They have them here on the weekends and play old movies. I figured it'd be more fun than a regular movie theater."

I hear the anxiety in his voice and stop looking at where we are and instead focus on the man who brought me here. "You're right." I take his hand in mine and thread our fingers together. "It's so much better. This is amazing."

The smile that I've found so much comfort in over the last few months changes. It turns into something new, something that I like even more. Like it's a smile just for me, one that only I can give him.

"Good," he says, his gentle voice wrapping around me like some of the blankets I see draped over the lawn chairs. "I really wanted this to be special for us."

Us.

Such a small word.

A word that has only meant me and Adelaide, and then recently, Jude. A word that I never thought would include a man again.

Until now.

I don't respond. I don't know how to. Too much is happening in my mind to even try. Instead, I don't think, I just roll onto my toes and press my mouth to his.

It's quick.

Maybe too quick. Definitely too quick.

But it's perfect. The feel of his lips against mine, the heat of his hand wrapped with mine. It's effortless but at the same time makes me want to work to make it feel like this forever. And it's not just because this is new. Because it feels like maybe this is what I've been missing. There's a familiarity lingering in our touch.

And that scares the shit out of me.

I try to take my hand away, but his fingers tighten with mine.

"Please don't." His voice is quiet amid the chatter and laughter surrounding us. "I like you so much, Lauren. Please don't pull away already. I know you feel what I do."

I do.

I close my eyes and push my lips together, hoping the red lipstick isn't smearing and making me look like the Joker.

I take a deep breath and relax my hand into his. "I'm sorry."

"Nothing to be sorry for." He leans in, dropping his mouth to my ear. Just his breath so close to me causes shivers to race up my spine. *Maybe Jude's right.* "You just kissed me and already made this the best night I've had in a long, long time."

Sweet.

So freaking sweet.

"And it's just starting." I wiggle my eyebrows, talking a way bigger game than I mean to. "Now, what movie are we seeing?"

"Just the best movie of all time," he says, and I don't know if I'm intrigued or scared by this. "But the food and drinks are themed from the movie. Want me to tell you, or do you want to try to guess?"

It's not my best trait, but I'm actually really competitive and I love games of all kinds. It's probably why I've obsessed the way I have over the podcast. It's been the first opportunity I've had in a while to be good at something other than packing lunches and school drop-off.

"I want to guess," I say, and I notice that my cheeks are hurting. I haven't smiled this hard for so long that my face muscles don't even know what to do.

"Okay, let me check in, then we'll go order."

He ordered the tickets online, so all check-in includes is Hudson saying his name. Then the person in the booth hands us two pairs of headphones and a blanket to hang over the chairs we pick to claim our spot.

Hudson takes the blanket and then hands it to me. "You pick."

I appreciate this more than he'll ever know. I'm so picky about movie seats that Jude won't even go to movies with me anymore unless I book our seats ahead of time.

I find the perfect spot, in the middle of the row just a few rows from the back. There are wide chairs for two and also single chairs. I pick a double, my stomach clenching as I think about cuddling up to Hudson for a couple of hours.

"Okay." I point to the food booths lining the back of the roof. "Now food."

We get to the booth, and as soon as I see Tater Tots and Vote for Pedro quesadillas, I squeal.

Literally.

And it's mortifying.

But I freaking love this movie and it couldn't be stopped.

Knowing Hudson loves it, too, makes me even more into him than I was a few minutes ago, and I was already *way* into him.

"You did not take me to a rooftop viewing of *Napoleon Dynamite*!" I fling my arms around him. "I'm obsessed with this movie!"

"I'm so glad, you have no idea." He squeezes his slender but strong arms around me. "Now let's eat some tots . . . and I'm pretty sure they have pin the tail on the liger somewhere."

I don't know if I was hoping this date would go just well enough that it was worth my time or that it'd be so terrible I'd never have to listen to Jude again.

But it's neither of those. It's already the best date I've ever had, and Hudson is turning out to be everything I didn't know I wanted.

Jude's totally going to rub this in my face for the rest of my life.

TWENTY-SEVEN

Jude

You don't realize how really fucked up you are until you're only slightly less fucked up.

Like, I'm still a mess, but if I'm a mess now, seeing a therapist and not having to deal with the constant stress that is Juliette Andrews, I can only imagine how big of a disaster I was a month ago.

Now I'm out here, making progress, focusing on my mental health and physical health, and being a good fucking friend. Because even if Lauren—still—doesn't want to admit it, the girl needs to get laid. When she came home from her date, way earlier than I approved of, her smile was huge and she was fucking glowing. *Glowing!* So even if she still hasn't gotten any, she already seems so much lighter. Happier. Like time with a guy who isn't a total dickbag healed something inside of her. And I get to take partial credit since I introduced them.

Plus, even after only one date, Hudson's more smitten than ever. I swear he texts me all the time to see how I'm doing, but I know he's just fishing for info on Lauren. And while I might think love is stupid, even I can't help but admit they are adorable together.

"It sounds like Lauren really experienced some growth," Chloe, my therapist extraordinaire, says. "But what's going on with you? How are things with your mom? Have you talked to her yet?"

I look around her serene office, focusing on the black-and-white prints framed on the opposite wall. "Not yet, she hasn't called. She's really busy with filming and I don't want to rock the boat. Honestly? I'm kind of loving this stretch of silence."

"Jude."

Jude. Just my name. Nothing else. But it's the tone that really hammers it home.

See, herein lies the problem with hiring a really good therapist. They don't put up with your avoidance shit. Which I guess is good because it is why I'm paying her, but I still feel attacked every time she calls me out.

"I hate when you say my name like that." I puff up my cheeks and blow the air out slowly. "Can't we just focus on how I helped Lauren? That was a big deal! I'm never the helper. I'm always the taker."

She leans forward in her seat and I know I've said too much. *Drats!*

"Why do you see yourself as the taker?" She crosses her legs and props her chin up on her fist. Having all of her focus on me like this is hugely intimidating.

"I'm just kind of a mess. I don't have a ton to offer, so if I'm not giving, I must be taking." I shrug my shoulders and for once understand Lauren's tendency to chew on her nails, because I'm super close to doing the same thing. "I feel like I'm always complaining about something even though my problems don't measure up to Lauren's. I mean, I literally just take pictures and exercise for a living. Lauren has a real job, a whole-ass daughter, and is going through a custody battle."

"You do realize that it isn't a competition, right? You can both have problems and one doesn't have to be 'bigger' or 'worse' than the other." She pauses for a second, but I can tell she still has more to say. "Has Lauren ever alluded to you that she feels like your friendship is one-sided?"

Never.

I'm almost a little offended on Lauren's behalf. But Chloe doesn't know Lauren. So she doesn't understand that even if Lauren did feel that way, she'd never say that to me.

"Well, no, but—"

Chloe cuts me off. "And has she ever asked for you to open up instead?"

"I mean, yeah, but—"

I try, but she cuts me off . . . again!

"So maybe this idea you have of being a taker is actually stopping you from confiding in a friend who wants to be there for you because you're not a taker, but instead, have been giving way more than you've let yourself receive?"

Fuck.

I hate smart people.

"I guess? Maybe."

"Yeah, I think so." She nods her head, knowing damn well that she's right. "Why do you think you haven't confided in Lauren? Do you think she's not strong enough to handle it? Or that maybe she won't support you in the way you really need her to?"

I hate this question.

It gives me a physical reaction. My fists bunch together and my stomach tightens. I don't know if it's anger or nerves or fear. I feel like over the years, those feelings have wound together so tightly, I don't know how to separate them.

"Of course she's strong enough to handle it, she's the strongest person I know." I defend my best friend's honor.

"So you don't think she will support you the way you need her to show up for you." It's not a question this time. It's a statement.

And not a wrong one.

"It's not that I think she won't support me. She will. She . . ." I try to organize my thoughts, but they're so scattered I don't even know where to begin. "This is about my mom. You know? It's not like I didn't tell Lauren absolutely everything when shit went down with Asher. This is just different. Her mom is a bitch. Like, a terrible bitch who Lauren can never please. My mom is a mess, but she loves me and she loves Lauren."

"Does she?"

I shake my head, not understanding her question. "Does she what?"

"Does your mom love you?" she clarifies, but it only confuses me more. "Is the way she has treated you how you define love?"

"Of course she loves me. She's my mom. It's just . . ." This is why I don't open up about my mom to anyone. Nobody understands. "My dad's death really messed her up and she hasn't been the same. But that doesn't mean she doesn't love me."

"Okay, but is the way she loves you healthy? Does her love cause you harm?" She leans back and assesses me with those knowing eyes of hers. "Was your dad's death not hard on you? Why are you excusing her hurtful behavior over a loss that was equally as painful for you? Plus, you said that her behavior started to change before he passed. Are you making excuses to help you, or are you enabling her?"

"That's a lot of questions," I point out . . . intentionally not answering any of them.

"It was. Which one would you like to answer first?"

None of them?

"You don't understand. You've only gotten my side of the story, and I haven't told you about how she used to be. She was the best mom, honest to God. She was so involved and so supportive. This isn't who she is."

"I don't believe you."

My spine snaps straight and my chin jerks back. It's like she slapped me, but this hurts more. "What?"

She leans forward, enunciating each word as she repeats herself. "I don't believe you. I think you're telling yourself that to make yourself feel better about your mom. I think she has always been selfish, but your dad was there to protect you from her behavior. Now that he's gone, she has shifted her needy, toxic behavior onto you, her daughter. Your dad didn't do her any favors by protecting her and you aren't, either, by making these excuses."

When I decided to see a therapist, I did it with one single intention: to bitch about my mom to a neutral party.

I needed someone to tell me that my bitterness—my animosity—toward my mom was not only valid, but warranted. I needed to get the last five years off my chest and vent it all away to someone who wouldn't judge me. I needed someone to tell me that toxic behavior isn't ever to be tolerated, no matter how much DNA you share.

This is what I wanted.

So I don't know why it's so hard to hear.

"I'm not making excuses for her." Out of everything there is to say, for some reason that's the only thing that leaves my mouth.

"You are." She doubles down. "You're making excuses for her and protecting her. Even at the cost of your own mental health and, if you're really honest with yourself, your physical health."

"What? How?" I know my mind is a straight-up disaster, but that's not *all* my mom's fault. But I'm in peak physical shape. It's literally my job.

"I think one of the main reasons you won't tell Lauren about your mom and what she's been putting you through is you don't want to change the way Lauren sees her. You're more worried about protecting her image than you are about letting in the most vital support you have in your life. You give her money at the expense of your own bills and you've had paparazzi trailing you for months, not because you wanted to, but because your mom needed you to. And when you voiced your concern over it, she ignored you and pressured you into it. And that's just the mental." She pauses and I know whatever she's about to say next is going to fucking suck. "Can you really tell me the amount of alcohol you consume is healthy."

The sharp intake of breath between my teeth is audible. "I'm not an alcoholic."

What the fuck? Am I paying this woman to just full-on attack me? None of this is even feeling helpful anymore.

"Did I say you were? Or did I ask if the amount of alcohol you consume is healthy?"

"So I drink? I'm twenty-eight, live in LA, and attend parties for a living. It's just part of what happens. It's not like I have to drink or that I can't stop. I could."

"Okay, but didn't you almost breach a contract because you got so drunk at the launch party for your podcast?"

"That was one time, and my mom . . ." I trail off, realizing that I fell directly into her trap.

Fuck.

Smart people suck.

"Like I was saying." She raises her eyebrows and smirks, leaning back into her olive-green velvet chair. "Do you think you're making excuses and protecting your mom at the expense of your own mental health? Even though your mom has exhibited narcissistic behaviors your entire life."

I roll my eyes and slouch down onto her stupid couch, eyeing the box of tissues but refusing to cry. "I guess maybe it's a possibility."

"And do you think that in protecting her, you've taken on her burdens so deeply that instead of realizing Lauren loves you, not because of your mom, but because of you, that you've not given her the opportunity to support you in not only the way you need, but also the way she wants to?"

I fold my arms in front of my chest and muster up my best Addy impersonation. "You know, I feel like I don't really like you right now."

"That's okay. I'm more concerned about you liking yourself." She takes her glasses off and rests them on the table next to her chair. "So where do you want to go from here?"

"I think I need to talk to my mom." She raises her eyebrows and I amend my statement. "I need to talk to my mom and Lauren."

"Good." She smiles, and for the first time today, there's no pity lingering behind her brown eyes, only encouragement and maybe even pride. "What are you going to talk to your mom about?"

"I'm going to tell her that I can't be her financial support anymore. I'm going to tell her that I love her, but that we need boundaries and I can't continue to change my life because she can't be responsible."

"But what if she cries again? What if she tells you that you're no longer her daughter or that she might resort to self-harm?"

I close my eyes and take a deep breath. Even though she hasn't said anything like that in some time, anytime I remember those words, the pain is just as fresh and raw as it was when she hung up on me years ago. But now I know what she was doing and I can't let her manipulate me like that anymore.

"I'm going to tell her that I'm her daughter always, but that I'm not responsible for her decisions and I won't allow her to put that on me. And then I'm going to confide in Lauren, because she's my best friend and I need her."

"That's amazing, Jude. I'm really proud of you."

I'm proud of myself too.

Therapy, man. Everyone needs this shit.

• • •

I grab my sunglasses out of my bag and slide them onto my face. The fog isn't too bad today, and the California sun seems even brighter as I walk out of Chloe's office. It's like even Mother Nature herself is thrilled with my therapy revelations.

I walk down the sidewalk, going over what I'm going to say to my mom when I call her once I'm alone. I get to my car and start it up before digging for my phone. Even though it's the end of October, the inside of my car is still burning up from sitting under the sun for over an hour.

"No more manipulation. No more financial support. No more paparazzi. No filming for *Hollywood Housewives*." I repeat the boundaries I worked on with Chloe before reaching into my purse for my phone. My nerves are going crazy. I know I need to do this and that her reaction isn't my responsibility, but the weights dropping anchor in my stomach right now don't ease up.

When I pull out my phone, intending to call my mom no matter how much I don't want to, I see that I have two missed calls from Eliza from *StarGazer*. Normally I would ignore this because . . . well, because I don't want to deal with it. But because she doesn't normally call me and I'm trying to put off calling my mom, I call her back.

"Jude!" She picks up on the second ring. "I'm so glad you called me back. I can't get in touch with your mom or Jonathon and I really wanted to talk with someone before we ran with this story."

The anxiety that had lifted only moments ago starts to bear back down, and dread forces my eyes shut.

"What story?" I don't know why I ask. I don't want to know. I want to hang up and run back to Chloe so she can tell me what to do.

There's silence on the other end for about ten seconds too long before her voice is back in my ear. "You don't know?"

Eliza is a longtime editor for a gossip magazine. I'm pretty sure she's immune to most things. So if I wasn't already nervous, the sudden surprise and hesitation in her tone would scare the shit out of me. But, because this is about my mom, I've been conditioned to expect the worst.

"What did my mom do this time?" I picture all the ways she's started drama with her castmates, hoping she didn't already get kicked off. Then my mind goes even darker and I hope she's not having an affair with some Hollywood scumbag. I can handle drama, but I couldn't handle her moving on from Dad and going to some asshole and dragging my dad's memory through the dirt. "Please tell me she's not involved in some scandalous affair. If that's it, just hang up now and let me live in ignorance for a few more days."

"It's not that . . ." I hoped she would laugh, let me know that I'm overreacting and it's not really that terrible. But instead she sounds remorseful, like the doctors did when they told us my dad didn't make it. "Well, what about the good news first?"

I'm sure she is saying this to make me feel less worried, but it only confirms that there is bad news.

"No, bad news first. I can handle it." I'm lying through my teeth. I'm not stable enough to deal with pretty much anything.

"Reports are coming in that her house is in the final stages of foreclosure and that she'll be losing it soon." The words rush out of her mouth and send my entire world into a tailspin. "It's legal stuff, so it probably won't be in print for a few weeks. If your mom calls, we might even be able to kill it, but without her, it's going to run."

Foreclosure.

My childhood home.

The house my dad quite literally killed himself to protect.

Gone.

Everything. Gone.

I gave her money. I paid her credit card bills. I paid for her cell phone. I thought she was at least paying the mortgage. It was the one comfort I had. Even if she was a mess, at least she had a roof over her head. A comfortable place to live. A place that housed the only good memories I had left of her and Dad.

Gone.

"Jude? Are you still there?" Eliza's voice startles me out of my own thoughts. "Do you want to hear the good news?"

I honestly forgot she said there was good news. I'm not sure anything can balance this out, but I'm willing to listen anyway. "Sure."

"I talked with the editor in charge of the family section, and they okayed using the pictures of you and that sweet little girl at the park and coffee shop." She says this like it isn't even more horrible than the first bit of information she threw my way. "He said that it's okay if you aren't technically related since you live together and that, actually, this looks even better for you! Isn't that great?"

"I . . ." I'm too dumbstruck to even form a proper sentence. All I want is to hang up with this poor woman who has *no* idea how massive what she just told me is, but thanks to my mom, I can't even do that. "Run the story about the house, I don't care.

But whatever you do, please, please, please don't publish the pictures of me and Addy. The only reason I agreed to this partnership is because I was promised she would never appear in any photo."

"Ummm . . . what?" The confusion in Eliza's voice only causes my anger to rise. Of course nobody told them not to snap pictures of Lauren and Addy. "Why don't I try to call Jonathon again?"

"Yeah," I snap, not meaning to do it. "Call Jonathon. I have to go."

I hang up without waiting for a response.

I squeeze my eyes shut and my head falls against the headrest as I try to come to terms with everything Eliza just told me.

Before this, I bet I would've thought it was impossible to completely decimate two different parts of someone's life in a three-minute phone call.

I would've been wrong.

The one thing I asked my mom for, the single boundary I placed on this entire deal, was to leave Lauren and Addy out of it. That's it. What might hurt the most is that I don't even know if she ignored it as much as she purposely ran right over it, proving that nothing I say matters and she's in charge of everything.

But almost as fast as the anger came, the fear pushes it away.

What will happen if *StarGazer* ignores me and publishes the pictures? What will Ben say? Could this help him gain custody of Addy? If I'm the reason Lauren loses Addy, I don't think I could ever forgive myself.

Everything Chloe told me about confiding in Lauren goes out the window. I can't even tell her this. She can't know. I just have to cross my fingers and pray to a god who clearly finds enjoyment in my despair and hope he cares about Lauren more than he hates me.

I pick up my phone from my lap, and my fingers immediately

pull up my mom's contact. I hit call, not knowing if I want her to answer or if I hope voice mail picks up, but the relief of hearing the automated voice on the end answers for me. I wait a beat after the beep sounds in my ear, not even sure what to say. "Mom, it's me, Jude," I say, like someone else would call her "Mom." "Eliza from *StarGazer* needs you to call her back. And while you're doing that, please do not call me. I'm sure she'll fill you in, but I need space."

I hang up and nearly burst into hysterics.

It's almost comical that when my mom's life is going well, I don't have to worry about her calling me. But as soon as things start to take a turn, I know I'll be hearing from her.

I almost think about going back inside the building I just left and finding Chloe, but decide against it and text Spencer instead.

Afternoon margaritas? Meet at Petty Cash?

And then I don't even wait for her answer. I throw my phone back into my purse and merge into LA traffic. Wondering why I even fucking try.

Some things never change.

And my mom is one of them.

TWENTY-EIGHT

Lauren

From: Lauren
Date: December 6
Subject: Ho ho ho . . . and a bottle of gin?

Hey!

Well, the holiday season is here.

In my old age, I've come to realize there are two kinds of people during this time of year:

1) People who love it and listen to holiday music as soon as Thanksgiving hits (and sometimes sooner).

2) People who low-key (or high-key) hate it and would rather gouge out their eardrums than listen to the iconic "All I Want for Christmas Is You" by Mariah Carey one more freaking time.

I'm in the first group. My roommate/cohost/BFF is in the second.

I think there's just something so special about the holidays with kids. It's like, for a month, magic is real. And I 100% go overboard to create this. From the Christmas tree that went up the day after Thanksgiving, to Sparkle Glitter (our Elf on the Shelf, who I both loathe and adore), to my December schedule that includes looking at lights, a full weekend of baking, ornament making, and a movie countdown, I'm into it all. Seeing Adelaide's little eyes light up during each activity makes all of the stress so worth it.

For me, creating traditions is what the holidays are about. I want to burn these memories into Adelaide's brain. For Jude, she likes the presents. She gives the most thoughtful presents every year. Her love language is definitely gift giving, while mine is quality time. However, in the Venn diagram that is our holiday preferences, our loves overlap on a white elephant party.

In today's episode, we go over our favorite memories of the holidays (which may or may not include the one time we tried to surprise Jude's mom with a pie but ended up setting her oven on fire). I give ideas to create traditions with your kids that are not only easy, but inexpensive—and will be pinned on our Pinterest board. Jude gives tips for throwing the best holiday party you'll ever go to, including easy recipes, fun decorations, and even a playlist for all you holiday-hating Scrooges.

Cheers! 🥂
Lauren

PS If you're wanting gin after that headline, here's a recipe for a festive cranberry martini!

CRANBERRY MARTINI

1 ounce gin
½ ounce lemon juice
½ ounce triple sec
1 ounce cranberry juice

Fill a cocktail shaker with ice, pour in all the ingredients, shake, strain into a martini glass, and enjoy! If you want to be extra fancy, garnish with frozen cranberries or an orange wheel.

PPS Drink responsibly!

I don't know what happened, but something's wrong with Jude.

She was doing so well and seemed really, actually happy. She was staying home on the weekends and coming with me and Adelaide to do everything. She loved her therapist and wasn't drinking as much. She was so content.

Then she wasn't.

Every time I try to talk to her about it—which isn't often because she's been avoiding the house—she blows me off and comes up with some lame excuse to leave. I've had to take her to pick up her car twice last week because she was too drunk to drive it home. And she told me she was done seeing her therapist.

I hoped it was because of the holidays coming up. She's never been huge on them, but since her dad died, it's been understandably harder on her. But I know, deep down, that it's something bigger. I just don't know what and I don't know how to pry it out of her, especially when I've been preparing for the second custody meeting.

"Everything's going to be fine." Kim's voice is strong and confident, but those words are almost like white noise at this point. She's said them so many times and we're still fighting this battle. As much as I want to believe her, I'm not sure I do anymore.

I nod my head, fidgeting with the necklace Jude gave me. Trying to find any confidence I can muster before I have to face Ben and his horrid lawyer again.

There's more pressure today. It won't just be the four of us during this meeting. Because the first meeting failed—which feels like a massive understatement—the court appointed a child-custody-recommending counselor. Basically, a babysitter who will observe and try to help us come up with an agreement today. If we can't agree, they go back to Mom or Dad, aka the judge, and give a written recommendation for a parenting plan.

This terrifies me for a number of reasons, but the main one is that I think Ben will be favored in front of a stranger. I'm a young, single, Black woman. It would be incredibly naive of me to think that with the history and the bias that has been woven into the very fabric of this country, a well-off white man wouldn't have an immediate advantage. I absolutely cannot have an outburst like I did last time. I can't do anything that might make me look aggressive, angry, or anything that could confirm whatever stereotypes and biases I have to fight. I just have to hope Ben's unexplained absence in Adelaide's life evens the playing field a little bit.

The door to the conference room at the neutral location we decided on opens and the woman I'm assuming is the counselor walks in. At the sight of her, my breath catches in my chest and tears well up in my eyes. Her curls are wild and free around her beautiful face. Her brown skin is accentuated by the red lipstick painting her full lips. Her skirt suit accentuates her curves, which remind me of my own.

It shouldn't matter.

Worrying my race would have a negative effect on keeping my daughter should never have been a thought that crossed my mind. But it was. And the relief I feel seeing this woman who will see me as a mother and not a Black mother is palpable.

The counselor must notice my instant change.

She gives me a nod, a small smile.

It's quick and so discreet I don't think Kim even notices. But that might be because Kim is white and has never really known what it feels like to be the only person who looks like you in a room. But in the space we're in, I'm almost positive this counselor has felt it. And I'm also sure I'm not the first Black person she's met with who was concerned their skin was going to hinder their case.

While she's taking her seat at the other end of the table, the door opens again and I hear Ethan Caputo's grating voice before I see him in all of his greasy, slicked-back glory. I know I shouldn't hate him for trying to do his job, but I hate him for trying to do his job.

What can I say? Emotions and logic don't always line up.

Ben's tall, lean body follows him into the room, but when he pauses to hold the door open, my spine straightens, and that little bit of relief I just felt evaporates into thin air when Stephanie enters.

I mean, I guess since they are married, it makes sense she'd be here, but it's still a shock. And on a day like today, I really can't deal with surprises. It'd be super disappointing to see her align herself with Ethan and Ben. She's smart and kind and I would *hate* if she believed their lies. But I know firsthand how convincing Ben is and I also know how stupid infatuation and love make a person.

"Relax," Kim leans over and whispers in my ear. "It doesn't matter who shows up today, this is about you, Ben, and Adelaide."

"What if them appearing together makes them look more adept at providing a family structure?" I whisper back, careful to not let the vultures on the other side of the room hear me. But even on a whisper, my voice is shaking. I couldn't hide the fear even if I tried . . . I'm sure Ethan can smell it in the air. "And Adelaide loves Stephanie, this is going to be bad for me. I can't lose her, Kim."

"You will not lose her." Kim's hand reaches beneath the table and she latches onto my hand, squeezing it almost to the point of painful. "You're a wonderful mother, and a relationship status does not change that."

I nod once, taking a deep breath, remembering the words from the acceptance meditation I did before coming today, only opening my eyes when an unfamiliar voice speaks.

"Hello, everyone. I'm Tiffany Dixon, and I'm the child custody counselor the court sent in today." Her tone is cheerful and kind, even under these terrible circumstances. "My job is to help guide you all to an agreement that makes everyone happy. If that cannot happen, I will create a written recommendation for a parenting plan and submit it to the court. Both parties will have access to the recommendation before the court date, and you'll be able to try to work out another agreement without me. Obviously, we want this to be a decision between guardians, court is the last resort. Do you understand?"

I nod my head, keeping my gaze directly on her and not letting it slip to the other side of the room no matter how much I want to.

"Yes, my client and I understand," Kim says.

"And so do my clients," Ethan says.

Clients, not client.

I have to close my eyes once more to try to control my breathing.

"Great." Tiffany looks over to Ethan, Ben, and Stephanie's

side of the table. "Since Mr. Keane is the party who initiated these proceedings, why don't you start?"

"We'd love to, Tiffany." Ethan opens the three-ring binder in front of him, not noticing the way Tiffany's eyes narrow on him when he calls her by her first name.

He's such a freaking schmuck.

"As we detailed in our past petition, Ms. Turner has gone to unconscionable lengths to keep my client away from their now five-year-old daughter." Ethan starts with a bang—and by bang, I mean a lie. "For years, she weaponized their daughter as retribution for Mr. Keane ending their relationship. She refused to let him see Adelaide unless he paid her amounts well beyond what a medical intern could afford. Ms. Turner has a history of being controlling and manipulative. My client has had to work hard to reverse the damage she has done to their young daughter by spewing poisonous rhetoric about Mr. Keane."

Unlike last time, I keep my mouth closed while Ethan rattles off one lie after another. I try my hardest not to react, but even though I know nothing he's saying is true, to hear someone say such terrible things about me . . . and more so about my parenting is torturous.

". . . living with her parents, now with a social media influencer, and who knows where she'll end up next. Now, especially with my client's new wife, who has a flexible work schedule, it's clear that Mr. and Mrs. Keane are a more stable environment for Adelaide to live full-time." Ethan finishes with one last, strong knockout punch, and the hiss of breath that comes from it is audible.

But it's not mine.

"I'm so sorry," Stephanie says. Her eyes are on Tiffany as she pushes her chair away from the table. "Can I please speak with my husband and Mr. Caputo in the hallway for a moment?"

Tiffany doesn't hesitate. "Of course. Take as much time as you need."

"I don't think—" Ben starts, but stops when Stephanie's eyes slice to him.

"No, Ben." There's a bite in her voice that I've never heard before, and even though she's on the other side of the table, it makes me—begrudgingly—like her even more. I never stuck up for myself to Ben, and I love that she challenges him. "The hallway. Now."

She doesn't wait to see if he's following before her back is to him and she's throwing open the door.

"Ben—" Ethan says, and that cocky arrogance that's always on his stupid, smug face has diminished just a bit.

The Ben I was in a relationship with would've let me stew in the hallway—alone—until I calmed myself down and came back into the room, apologizing for daring to have my own feelings. But to my immense surprise, Ben stands up, adjusting the buttons on his suit jacket, a nervous habit he's had since I met him back in school.

"I'm sorry." Ben looks to Tiffany, color tingeing his cheeks and tension evident around his mouth. "This shouldn't take long."

His long legs make quick work of the small room, and Ethan is up and following him out seconds later.

When the door clicks closed behind them, I turn to Kim. "What in the world is going on?" I ask, even though she looks just as puzzled as I feel.

"I honestly have no idea." She pauses and glances at the door. "But if I had to guess, you have a surprise ally on the other team, and Ben and Ethan overestimated the pull Ben has on this."

My eyes go so wide they begin to burn. "Really?"

"I could be wrong"—she pulls her lips between her teeth and

nods—"but she did not look happy listening while Ethan was speaking. I get the feeling that she wasn't aware of the tactics they were using."

I pull my gaze away from Kim, and even though Tiffany is sitting quietly at the front of the room, she's looking our way and nodding in agreement with Kim.

The tension I've been carrying since Ben walked in the room leaves my shoulders. I don't know if it's because Tiffany seems to know Ethan is full of crap or if it's because of Stephanie.

I know in the majority of cases, the stepmom gets a bad rap, but I always liked Stephanie. So much so that Jude thinks I'm a little crazy. I'd be lying if I said finding out about her didn't sting in the beginning. I was still mourning my relationship, living with my parents, and struggling to come to grips with my life as a single mom, only to find out Ben had already moved on. But then Ben started calling when he said he would. He wouldn't cancel on his time with Adelaide like he did before. I started getting child support checks that had his name on them but definitely not his penmanship. She treated my daughter well and did this while having Adelaide paint me pictures or make me cookies.

If she wasn't Ben's new girlfriend . . . and now wife, I would've wanted to be her friend.

Which is why seeing her waltz into the room earlier hurt like hell. Because even though I knew she was on Ben's team, I still thought she respected me not only as Adelaide's mom but as a woman. And even though Ben is straight trash and probably bad-mouthed me to her, I thought she was above all that.

Now I'm praying that I was not wrong.

I don't know how long they stay in the hallway, discussing who knows what, but it feels like hours before the door opens and Stephanie struts back into the room with her shoulders back and a look of pure determination on her face. I don't know her well enough to decipher what this means, but my stomach twists with hope I know better than to have that this will mean good things for me. And when I see Ben and Ethan walk in a minute later, Ben with his shoulders slumped and Ethan with a bright red face and fists pulled into a ball, I let that hope bloom.

I sit up straight, my hand going to Kim's beneath the table.

"Sorry about that," Ethan says as he slides back into his chair.

"Not a problem at all." Tiffany's white teeth shine bright against her red lips. "I hope you were all able to get on the same page and come to an understanding."

Ethan opens his mouth to answer, but it's Stephanie who speaks. "We did." She looks away from Tiffany and looks directly into my eyes. "We're all in agreement that Junie is a wonderful little girl in part because she has a wonderful mother. A mother who, despite my husband's crazy hours and demanding job, and even a prolonged absence that he's trying very hard to make up for, has been the most accommodating, even making a two-hour round-trip drive so their daughter can spend weekends with us." She turns away from me and levels a glare at the men sitting next to her before looking back to me with soft eyes and a softer smile. "Junie is a loving, happy, and smart little girl who loves her dad and adores her mom. We would never want to take her away from Lauren."

I've spent so much time telling myself to be stoic. To fight back all my feelings and not show any emotion during this meeting. I refused to give Ben the satisfaction that he could still get a rise out of me. I was going to be cold and unyielding. His lies were so meaningless that they were going to bounce right off me. I had nothing to prove to him and he wasn't even worth eye contact.

What I did not prepare for was kindness. The walls I barricaded myself behind crumbled with every kind word Stephanie aimed at me, but told Tiffany, pretty much guaranteeing I wouldn't lose custody of the reason I breathe. So the tears that fall, the speed at which I round the table, and the strength with which I wrap my arms around this unlikely ally cannot be helped.

"Thank you," I whisper into her ear. "Thank you so much."

"I wanted Ben to be involved, and I'm so sorry I didn't know the means he was going to use to do it." Her voice hitches, and I realize I'm not the only person crying right now. "I'm so sorry I pushed him to this. You're the best mom, and I would never want to hurt you or Junie. I just thought having an agreement in place would protect all of us."

I want to warn her that she didn't push Ben to these techniques, that was Ben. Behind his mesmerizing eyes and charming smile, he's a snake. I want to warn her to get away while she can. To find someone who deserves her beauty—inside and out. But I don't. Because I know what it's like to love Ben and—once upon a time—to receive that love right back. I'm not sure I believe Ben can change, but I have to hope that if he can, Stephanie is the one who can bring it out of him. And if she can, Adelaide will be surrounded by goodness that's only a far-off, distant daydream I have of peaceful co-parenting and blended families who spend holidays together.

I gradually loosen my arms from around her and make my way back to my seat next to Kim.

"So," Tiffany says from the front of the room. "Is there a parenting plan we can agree on?"

Instead of letting Ethan take charge—again—Kim leans forward, her confident voice ringing out loud and clear. "Miss Turner would like to resume full custody of their daughter, giving Mr. Keane every other weekend and switching holidays. She'd also like a set amount for child support and for Mr. Keane to place Adelaide on his insurance and split the cost of both school and extracurriculars."

With the foreign feeling of confidence and power flowing through my veins knowing that his lies aren't going to win and I'm going to come out on top, I look at Ben. He looks like the man I fell in love with all those years ago, but for the first time, I'm really *seeing* him. I see the anger and the insecurity and how even though he spent his time making me feel like I was the lucky one in the relationship, he was. Because as much as he tries to convince everyone around him otherwise, he's confused and wandering through this life searching for purpose and contentment he's never going to find.

Contentment and purpose I get every single time I look at Adelaide or hear her voice or feel her arms wrap around me.

The anger and hate I've felt for this man vanish and are replaced with pity as he nods his head to Ethan and deflates in his seat.

"We agree to those terms," Ethan says without any of the grandstanding I'm so used to from him.

"Wonderful." Tiffany types away on her computer before stopping and looking to both Kim and Ethan. "Is there anything else?"

"No, ma'am," Ethan says, a far cry from the man who called her Tiffany at the beginning of the meeting. "That's all from us."

All of Kim's teeth are showing when she smiles at Tiffany and says, "That's everything from us, thank you."

I'm not positive, but even though I think Kim is happy for me, I think she's happiest to see Ethan looking so despondent.

After all the lies he spewed about me, I can't say I'm not enjoying it too.

"Well then." Tiffany closes her computer and stands at the front of the room. Even though she's addressing everyone, I can't help but notice the way her eyes seem to only focus on me and Stephanie. "I love when a resolution is worked out. Adelaide is a very lucky girl to have people in her life who love her enough to be civil and work out an agreement between themselves."

She's right. Adelaide is lucky . . . but so am I.

Now that this is finally over, I can move on with my life and start living without shadows chasing me.

It's been a long time, but I can't wait.

TWENTY-NINE

. . .

Jude

There's no place to hide.

Between having to plaster on a smile for Instagram and pretend I'm living this elevated, enlightened life where I drink green juice and do Pilates, then go home and put on that same happy face for Lauren so she won't start hounding me with questions she doesn't want to know the answers to, I feel like I'm going to break.

The most fucked-up part is that I don't even think I care anymore.

I know I'm no saint, but I think I'm a decent person. I'm a good friend, I've tried my hardest to be a good daughter, I care about people, I don't steal, and I would never intentionally cause pain—small exception for Ben, but that goes back to me being a good friend. And nothing ever comes of it. I'm still here struggling while shit people get reward after fucking reward.

Why do I keep trying to climb this damn mountain when all that ever happens is a hard shove back to the bottom? What's the fucking point?

I'm pretty sure there's no point. We try to make sense out of life. Find our purpose, make our mark on the world, but it's all bullshit. Life is a series of struggles and then you die.

That's it.

So while I'm struggling, I might as well try to enjoy myself too.

"You're going out again?" Lauren asks from the couch.

I know she doesn't mean to sound judgmental. She's concerned. I see that. She's happy and she wants that for me too. She means well, but she just doesn't understand that unlike her, my wins are few and far between, and when they happen, I'm still alone.

"Yeah, I'm meeting Spencer at Perch for an ugly sweater party. Obviously." I point to my sweater, which I sewed a stocking onto as a bottle holder. "You should come."

"I don't know . . ." She looks around the room, and I know she's trying to think of an excuse not to come.

"I do. Addy's with Ben. Hudson is visiting his family in whatever bumfuck nowhere town he's from. If you don't come, you're just going to sit here watching Netflix and coming up with ideas for that creepy-ass elf."

"Was not," she says, but her eyes go wide and she closes her laptop, so I know she's a big liar and was googling elf ideas already.

No matter how much she complains about that damn elf—Sparkle Glitter—she's more obsessed with it than Addy. Last week, she created a Barbie-themed elf week. One day Sparkle Glitter and Barbie were taking a "bubble bath" in the sink with hand-sewn "beach towels" and drink umbrellas set up next to them. Another day they were riding in Barbie's convertible (she even made the elf a freaking scarf and sunglasses), and then yesterday morning, I came down to powdered sugar on the counter and Sparkle Glitter making snow angels while Barbie dolls hid behind a marshmallow wall and had a snowball fight. It's insanity. I told her to just leave the fucking elf on the damn shelf like its name says, but she said she has to "create magic."

It's a fucking mess.

Literally.

"Come on"—I pull the remote away from her and turn off the TV—"I have another sweater you can wear. It will be fun. We haven't been out together since the launch, and the Remington Witches won't be there, so you won't have anything to worry about." I see the indecisiveness on her face and decide to push it a little further. "Plus, you even said you want to start living more now that everything with Ben is in the past. So why not start tonight?"

And, if she comes with me, she won't be able to give me the stink eye in the morning because I came home so late or am still a little tipsy. It's a win for everyone.

I'd been avoiding her until I finally heard from Eliza that they wouldn't be running the pictures of Addy. I threatened not only to pull the plug on the entire deal, but to give stories to other magazines. It probably wasn't my brightest idea, but I was desperate. Thankfully for me, some actual celebs and their kids had big public outings and nobody cared about me anymore. But that didn't mean I wasn't still so mad at my mom that I couldn't even take her phone calls.

"Fine." She huffs and uncurls her legs from beneath her. "But I will not wear the sweater that lights up."

• • •

The elevator doors slide open as I reach into my purse and send my mom to voice mail for the millionth time. If I didn't know that it'd send her off the ledge, I'd block her number. I know I asked her to give me space, but she'd have to respect my boundaries to abide by that request. I don't know what Eliza told her, but I do know that I'm not emotionally stable enough to talk to her yet.

For a split second, I think about calling Chloe when I get home and scheduling another appointment, but I shoot that down. Why waste my money on a therapist when I could just accept that no matter what I do, my life's going to be a straight-up fucking disaster? Seeing Chloe isn't going to help keep my childhood home or my friendship intact if Addy's picture had shown up in the tabloids. Drinking enough vodka, on the other hand, will make me forget about it for a while, and I'd much rather put my money toward that.

Oblivion should be vodka's tagline.

I loop my arm through Lauren's and walk into the party, which is already in full swing. The best part of living in LA is that even in December, it's totally reasonable to have a party on a rooftop. The view in downtown LA is amazing, and we can see the ice rink in Pershing Square. Heater lamps pepper the space between the seating now covered in holiday-themed pillows instead of their normal boho cushions. Palm trees are wrapped in Christmas lights, and servers are walking around with tinsel dangling from their trays.

"Let's get a drink and then we can find Spencer," I say to Lauren.

I still can't believe I got her to wear the light-up Christmas sweater, but even though it's ridiculous, she somehow manages to look hot. It's like the lights are giving her the perfect glow, and I kind of want to switch sweaters.

"Sounds good to me, I'm just tagging along." Lauren's looking around in awe and I can't even blame her. As far as parties go, this one is pretty damn impressive. Plus, it's an open bar . . . which makes it even better.

The bar on the rooftop isn't as big as the one on the floor beneath us, but it's not the size that matters . . . it's the bartender's willingness to ignore the men and come straight to me. Which this one does. He hands me the drink menu, and I scan it once before placing my order.

"Hi!" I bat my lashes, ignoring Lauren snickering next to me, hoping between the shameless flirting and the cash I brought to tip that he'll continue this quick service throughout the night. "Can we get two shots of vodka, two Lolitas, and two shots of tequila . . . since this is a party."

Lauren's laughing stops as abruptly as it started.

"What the hell, Jude!" Her hand latches onto my wrist like I just ordered her death. "You know I can't drink that much!"

"Relax." I peel her fingers off me. "One Lolita is for you, the rest is for me."

I thought this would help her relax, but for some reason, her eyes narrow even further and seem to get even more serious.

"Jude . . . that's a lot." Her somber tone is even more noticeable in such a festive environment. I thought taking her out with me would negate the lectures, not bring them along. "Are you—"

"*Jude!*" Spencer screeches my name in a stroke of luck I've come to never expect. "You finally made it!"

She wraps her long arms around me, and I can smell that I'm not the only one indulging in tequila tonight. Her hair's piled into her trademark high ponytail, and her sweater has a picture of Santa doing a dead lift with the words *Merry Liftmas* framing it. I'm highly impressed she managed to find a sweater so on brand.

"Sorry I'm late, but look, I brought Lauren."

Spencer and Lauren have met a few times, but for obvious reasons, this is the first time we've all been out together.

"Oh my god! Lauren! How are you? I'm so happy you came out with Jude for once! She told me all about your dickbag ex and how you finally kicked his ass." Spencer, who's extremely friendly after a few drinks, launches herself toward Lauren and wraps her in a hug just like she did to me. "Now we can make tonight a celebration!"

"Ummm . . . thanks?" Poor Lauren is staring at me over Spencer's shoulder, obviously unsure as to how to react to the physical affection being shown to her, the fact that Spencer wants to celebrate her kicking Ben's ass, or both.

Probably both.

"Us girls have to stick together, you know?" Spencer lets her go and takes a step back at the same time the bartender slides my final shot to the front of the bar.

"Two vodka shots, two shots of tequila, and two Lolitas." He maintains eye contact with me, and his deep voice does things to me that hint at my night ending in whatever apartment he's renting.

"Thanks." I wink and put some cash down. I'm not the best at flirting, but I'm decent.

I grab a cocktail and hand it to Lauren before double fisting both shots of vodka and throwing them back . . . a drinking appetizer, if you will. And like the fucking champ that I am, I don't even fucking flinch.

"She's a beast!" Spencer's voice is a few octaves lower as she cheers me on. "Do the tequila next!"

This is why I love Spencer. She's the bad influence I need, while Lauren will make sure I make it home safely. This is my idea of a balanced life.

Well, that and also a shot in each hand.

I ignore the limes next to the tequila shots and pick up the glasses, tossing them back with the same proficiency as the vodka. No training wheels for me, thank you very much.

"Ahhh!" I cringe a little as the burn travels down my throat and warms up my stomach. I fucking love that feeling.

Spencer is still clapping, but Lauren's noticeably silent, the frown on her face saying everything she isn't.

"Oh, come on, Lauren. It's a party. This is what you're supposed to do!" I grab my glass off the bar and tap it against hers. "Live a little, I thought that's why you came. Ben's in the past, we're celebrating tonight!"

She doesn't look totally convinced, but she does take a sip of her drink, and at least that's a step in the right direction.

Her frown finally disappears, and a smile tugs at the corners of her mouth, which is the power of a well-crafted cocktail. "Is there cucumber in here?"

"Yup." I nod my head up and down. "See? You're good at sneaking veggies in food, but I get them in drinks. We're like a fucking power team."

She throws her head back and laughs . . . like really laughs. "Oh my god, that has to be our next podcast!" She wipes at the corners of her eyes. "Spencer, you have to try one of these!"

Even though I hoped Lauren would let loose and just enjoy tonight—aka not harass me about my alcohol consumption—I didn't think she actually would. But as she takes a giant sip of her cocktail and a smile I haven't seen since we were teenagers crosses her face, that hope blossoms, and I almost can't believe it. I watch as she leans against the bar and gets Mr. Deep Voice's attention.

"Can we get two more?" she asks before shouting, "Wait!" Looking over her shoulder at me, she says, "Do you want another one too?" I'd honestly rather have another shot, but this is the first time I've seen her just enjoy the moment and not worry about tomorrow, so I can't help but say yes. "Okay, three more of these," she looks at the bartender and corrects herself.

He flashes her his most dazzling smile, but she's not paying attention to him at all. She's taking another sip of her drink and looking straight at me. "Thank you for convincing me to come out tonight. I don't think I even knew how much I needed this after these last few months."

I shove down the guilt threatening to bubble to the surface for how I've been avoiding her. Sure, part of the avoidance goes hand in hand with my mom putting me in yet another situation, and some is also because I'm closing in on thirty and still don't have my shit together. But, if I'm really honest with myself, I've resented her newfound happiness. It was easy for me when we were both going through shit, but now? With her life going up and mine nosediving back to shit? I didn't know how to be around her. I thought it was hard to lay my burdens on her when she was going through problems of her own, but it's even harder to do it when she's finally getting some relief.

The bartender puts our glasses in front of her, and Spencer doesn't hesitate to grab one, lifting it straight in the air before she takes a sip. "To a night out with friends and without the dickbags who tried, and failed, to bring us down!"

Only Spencer could put the word *dickbag* in a motivational toast.

It's why I love her.

Lauren laughs and touches her glass to Spencer's, and I follow suit . . . ignoring the buzzing in my purse . . . and slamming the rest of my cocktail.

Lauren grabs her new drink and looks around the roof. "Can we go find a place to sit? If I'm going to have more than one drink, I'm going to need to be stationary."

I try not to laugh, but fail miserably. And even though I don't mutter a word, Lauren's still glaring at me because she knows exactly why I'm laughing. The first time she got drunk, we were seventeen and at Gina Robert's house, whose parents were loaded and always on vacation. Lauren went to town on the sweet wine they had. Then, as we were leaving, she tripped on a shoe and ended up putting an elbow-sized hole in the wall. She never spoke to Gina again. It's still fucking hilarious.

Spencer, either too drunk or too uninterested to care what I'm laughing at, points to the exit in the far corner of the rooftop. "If you want to go downstairs, I claimed a table on the patio down there."

I look at Lauren, who just shrugs. She's along for the ride and doesn't care where we sit . . . as long as we're sitting.

"Downstairs sounds good to me." I drop my empty glass on the bar and grab my new one before we follow Spencer to the elevator. The trip from the sixteenth to the fifteenth floor goes by in a blink and makes me feel extremely lazy, but since I didn't know where the staircase was, it was our only option. Plus, I don't trust Lauren with stairs and booze.

The doors open and Spencer leads the way to the table on the wraparound patio. The views one level down are no less spectacular. I take in downtown Los Angeles, feeling a spark of gratitude that has been noticeably missing from my life for the last few weeks. But tonight, I'm at this amazing party, taking in gorgeous views, drinking delicious—and free—cocktails, while spending time with two of my favorite people.

The rest of my life might be a total fucking disaster, but at least in this moment, I can appreciate the few good things I have left.

A waiter stops by our table, and Spencer orders a round of shots for me and her, and Lauren asks for water. Boring, but I'm still proud she went for a second drink. Getting a tolerance like mine takes patience and hard-core training.

"While we wait . . ." I reach into the stocking I sewed onto my sweater and pull out my favorite flask, which has a collapsible shot glass that screws into the side. "How about a shot while we wait for our shots?"

"Do you even have to ask?" Spencer asks the question she most definitely doesn't need to ask.

"How many shots is that?" Lauren looks between me and Spencer. I know she's trying her hardest to not mother us—or, more specifically, me—but I can hear the concern in her voice that she's attempting to keep light. "I'm tipsy after one drink!"

"Jude and I have a rule when we go out at night," Spencer says. "We don't count the three *c*'s."

Lauren's eyebrows furrow together as she looks between me and Spencer. "The three *c*'s?"

"Calories, carbs, and cocktails," I explain.

"Ah. Okay, got it." She takes a small sip of her drink. "If I don't count my drinks, I'll end up on the floor, but I never count carbs or calories, so I'm with you on those."

Spencer whips her head to Lauren so fast, her long ponytail slaps the person walking by our table. "You mean to tell me you have a kid, eat carbs, don't monitor your calories, and you still look like that?"

"Yup," I answer for Lauren, who looks like she can't decide if she's embarrassed or flattered. "It's bullshit. She also has no skin-care routine and has not a line on her face."

"What can I say?" Lauren tries to hide her smirk behind her glass. "Black don't crack. This melanin keeps my skin looking amazing."

"Then cheers to fucking melanin!" Spencer says so loud, and without any context, the tables around us all turn to stare.

We ignore all of them, happily encased in our tipsy little bubble. I unfold the shot glass and pour oversized ones for me and Spencer.

"Are you sure you don't want one?" I ask Lauren, waving the

vodka in front of her face. "This is top-of-the-line, locally dis-
tilled vodka and it's delicious."

Lauren's nose crinkles just like Addy's does when she tries to
convince her that zucchini is good. "No thanks, I'm good."

I shrug my shoulders. Her loss is my win. *More for me.*

I take the shot and screw the glass into the side of the flask,
tucking it neatly back into my stocking when I see the waiter approaching with our drinks.

"We're succeeding on not counting drinks"—well, Spencer
and I are at least—"but we need some carbs and calories to ignore. Watch my drink and I'll go grab some stuff from inside."

When Spencer was showing us to our seats, I noticed different
food stations set up inside. And at the rate I'm drinking, I'm going
to need some food to help sustain me.

"Do you want me to come with?" Lauren asks, and I don't
know if it's because she wants to come or if she's just anxious
about being left alone with Spencer. As friendly as Lauren is, she
struggles with small talk.

I would normally put her out of her misery and tell her to
come with me, but then I think about how I sat with those Remington moms and decide not to. "I'm good, you two chat. I'll be
quick."

Lucky for Lauren, Spencer's the shit.

"Oh! While she's gone, can you show me pictures of your
daughter? Jude's always talking about her and I'd love to put a
face to these stories."

Lauren's eyes light up—moms love showing pictures of their
kids, that's not a myth—as she pulls out her phone.

I push my chair out and stand up, maybe a little too quickly,
because those last vodka shots seem to have gone straight to my
head. I hold on to the top of my chair for a second, waiting for the
world to stop spinning. I move on jelly legs, weaving my way

through the crowd, laughing out loud at all the ridiculous sweaters around me until I make my way inside and the noise level multiplies.

I look around, blinking my eyes shut to clear my vision so I can find the food. Thankfully, booze doesn't affect my smell like it does my vision, and I close in on the pasta station in no time.

I fill up my plate with a little bit of every pasta they offer, justifying it by repeating my three *c*'s mantra, but also remembering that I'll share with Spencer and Lauren. Maybe. I'm scooping an extra spoonful of the lobster mac and cheese when I hear a voice that has haunted my nightmares for the last year. I squeeze my eyes shut again, hoping it's just the vodka playing tricks on me, but when I open them and turn around, I see him.

Asher Thompson.

The last time I saw him was the day before I discovered he'd fucked me over and I was broke. He took off and I was robbed of my opportunity to confront him. I've dreamt of this moment. I've visualized exactly what I'd say to him and how I'd make him grovel at my feet, begging for forgiveness and admitting to everything he's done. But when I see Meadow fucking Blake curled into his side, I forget all of it and my vision goes red.

If I was sober, maybe I'd think twice about marching over to him, but I'm not. And fuck that . . . fuck him.

"Asher fucking Thompson." I elbow my way through the circle of people fawning all over him, not knowing what a giant con artist he is. But they'll learn tonight. "Long time no fucking see."

His spine straightens and fear flashes behind his eyes. Like a fucking serial killer, seeing that fear spurs me on, it thrills me. *You should be fucking afraid*, I think to myself.

"Jude. Wow, long time no see."

"Yeah, so long!" I make my smile as big as I can, trying to keep my tone light and airy. "But I guess after you steal tens of thousands of dollars from someone, you probably tend to avoid them."

All conversations around us stop as eyes focus in on us. Which is exactly what I wanted.

Asher coughs out a laugh, his tan skin filling with color. "What? Steal your money? Come on, Jude, that's crazy."

"What's crazy is that I'm sure you've done it before and plan on doing it again." I inch closer to him until my plate knocks into his arm. "Telling people you're going to be partners, help support their dreams, and then bam! You're gone and so is the money. You know what—"

"How much have you had to drink tonight?" Meadow's stupid baby voice cuts me off. She pulls out of Asher's arm and takes a step too close to me. "You do know you can be an influencer without being under the influence, right?"

I put my hand in her face, pushing her out of my space. "Shut the fuck up, Meadow, and go run off and profit off some kids who don't know who the fuck you are."

"I can't believe you're still telling people this story about the money, Jude. It's sad, honestly," Asher says, and there are a few chuckles around us. I was so busy focusing on Meadow that I didn't realize I just gave Asher the time he needed to compose himself. "You can't run a business with a drunk. I didn't take your money, you lost it because you couldn't keep yourself together long enough to build it."

The noise around me fades, and all I can hear is the pounding of my pulse.

"Are you fucking kidding me!" I scream, the anger that's been building around him and my mom and this stupid fucking life of mine that just. Won't. Let. Up. boils to a tipping point. "Fifty thousand dollars, Asher! *Fifty!* And you took it all almost as soon as the ink dried on the contract!"

"Oh, honey." Meadow's stupid voice manages to get even higher. "You should just stop. This is sad."

"*Fuck you!* You're a fucking hack! That's not even your fucking voice! Just shut the hell up!" Before I even know what's happening, my plate covered in pasta is empty and all of the pasta is dripping down Meadow's head. "And you!" I turn to Asher, planting both of my hands into his chest, shoving him back. "You." Shove. "Stole." Shove. "*My money!*" I don't shove him this time. I pull my arm back and aim it straight for his nose.

Pain explodes into my fist, reverberating all the way up my arm and into my shoulder as the people around us seem to shake out of whatever trance they were in.

"You crazy fucking bitch!" Asher cups his nose with both hands, moaning and bending over as blood leaks through his fingers. "You punched me!"

"And I'll do it again!" I start to move toward him, but arms wrap around me, stopping me from making it to him. I scratch at the arms, twisting my body around trying to get free, trying to get to fucking Asher. "Let me go!"

"Jesus, Jude! Stop!" Lauren's voice manages to break through the rage haze. "Let's go! You have to get out of here."

My body goes slack and I look at the chaos around me. Meadow is crying, red sauce and cheese dripping down her face. Asher is on his knees as people rush to him, carrying towels and ice. And cameras.

Cameras everywhere.

Focused on me.

"Shit," I whisper. My sinuses start to burn along with the rising embarrassment that all of this pandemonium is because of me.

I don't have time to think much longer because Spencer is at my other side. They drag me through the restaurant and shove me into the elevator without missing a beat.

"What the hell was that!" Lauren shouts. She moves across the tight space, forcing me into the corner with a look on her face like I've never seen before. If I could die from a look, this would kill me. "Are you out of your mind?"

I ignore her. Not because I want to, but because I don't even know how to answer that question.

Because if I'm honest with myself, I've been out of my mind for a long fucking time and I have no idea how to get it back.

THIRTY

...

Jude

Regret and mortification adds an entirely new element to hang-overs, and I do not recommend it.

I mean, sure, I've done stupid shit while drunk before. I've accidentally flashed my lady bits. I've hooked up with people whose integrity was questionable at the very best. I've def called exes and cried to them.

What I haven't done is assault two people in front of a room full of witnesses. To that point, I hadn't assaulted anyone with or without witnesses period.

That is, I hadn't . . . until last night.

It takes me a while to figure out the pounding I'm hearing isn't coming from my head but my door. And the only reason I'm able to make that distinction is because I hear my mom's voice coming from the other end of my room.

"Fuck." I yank my pillow from beneath my head and smother it over my face.

"Jude Elizabeth Andrews, open this door right now!" Her voice grows more shrill with each word, and as much as I want to ignore her, I put Lauren through too much last night to make her listen to my mom's crazy rants so early in the morning.

Begrudgingly, I toss my pillow on the floor, peeling my comforter off me, and trying not to cringe when I see I'm still wearing my outfit from last night. My muscles feel like they're about to quit on me as they get me out of bed, and the throbbing in my head amplifies by a million. My stomach riots, flipping and turning so much that I have to stop and lean forward, resting my forehead against the cool, beige-painted wall beside my bed. Once I'm sure I'm not going to throw up all over my plush white rug, I make my way to the door.

". . . so help me god, I know how to pick a lock!" She's still ranting and raving in the hallway. Thank god Addy isn't here. Nothing and nobody gets in the way of Juliette Andrews saying what she wants to say.

My hand hovers over the doorknob as I contemplate letting her in again, when her rant turns to screeching.

"Now, Jude!"

I twist the lock and pull the door open, managing to frown at her even though it just makes my head hurt even more.

"Jesus Christ, Mom." My mouth is dry, my throat drier, and my voice is so hoarse it's almost unrecognizable to my own ears. "You do know I'm not the only person who lives here, right?"

She shoulders her way into my room, tossing her purse on my bed before turning to me and snatching off her sunglasses to level me with a glare that holds so much contempt, my stomach starts to turn again. "Oh, so you *are* capable of thinking of someone besides yourself."

I don't know if it's because I'm still drunk—which is a high possibility—or if it's my mom's words, but my vision blurs. My fingers tighten on the brass doorknob as I resist the urge to slam the door shut.

"All I do is think of other people," I mumble beneath my breath. Mere seconds around my mom and I'm already reverting to fourteen-year-old Jude.

"What was that?" She swings around and narrows her furious stare on me. If I really was fourteen, I would be a nervous wreck, but thankfully, I'm twenty-eight and my mom has screwed me over so badly these last few years that her anger no longer holds the higher ground.

"Nothing." I walk past her, not giving her the satisfaction of a reaction, and fall back onto my bed. "So to what do I owe the pleasure of seeing you first thing in the morning?"

"Don't play that game with me, Jude." I didn't know it was possible with the amount of fillers she must've had done since she was recast on *Hollywood Housewives*, but her forehead manages to crease as she points an angry finger my way. "All you had to do was hold your shit together in public. That's all. And you couldn't even do that. You ruined everything!"

Her voice has an edge of panic I'm not sure I've ever heard from her before. And as many times as I've told myself that her mental state is no longer my responsibility, hearing it causes my stomach to turn and my heart to race.

I sit up slowly, really taking her in for the first time. The dark circles beneath her eyes make her look ages older than her fifty-three years, and her size 0 jeans are loose on her already too thin legs. She looks horrible, and guilt infiltrates my defenses.

"What's going on?"

I know the answer. I've known since Eliza called me last month. But now it's staring me in the face and I can't ignore it any longer.

"The house"—her delicate voice breaks in the middle of the word—"I'm going to lose my house."

Hurt flares at the way she phrases it. Not our house, *her* house.

And I guess that's right. Who am I to say? I left her. Moved in with Lauren and practically abandoned her when her problems became too much for me to bear. Why should I get to claim ownership over something I never worked to have?

Except . . . that's where my memories live. Even if I've let her down—again—it's still where our family grew, where I last saw my dad, where I last was happy. That was my home.

And now it's going away too.

Like every single thing that means something to me.

I drop my eyes to the red spot on my carpet from when I let Addy sneak juice in my room. "I know." My voice is barely a whisper, like the shame of not doing more to help my mom is blocking my windpipe. "Eliza called and told me."

The sharp inhale should've pulled my attention away from the stupid spot I gave up on cleaning. But instead, it just makes me stare harder. No matter how hard I scrubbed and worked at the stain, it didn't matter. The mess is adhered to the fabric. It's one. There is no separating it. Even if it fades, it will still be there . . . impossible to erase.

Just like my life.

My mom's feet, covered in her designer heels, step into my vision, stopping on top of the stain. Hiding it . . . or maybe sprouting from it?

"You knew?" It doesn't matter that her voice is quiet or that her hand wraps gently around my hand, the anger and hurt in her tone and touch are practically ricocheting off the walls.

I squeeze my eyes shut before taking a deep breath and letting it all out. "Yeah." I finally gather enough courage to look at her, and regret it immediately. Because I know, until the day that I die,

I will never forget the look on her face. "I'm so sorry, Mom. It's just that—"

I don't even get to finish my sentence before she drops my hand like it was liable to ignite into flames, and scurries to the other side of the room. "You're sorry?"

My feet have a mind of their own and they move to follow her.

"I'm so sorry. I never meant for any of this to happen." I keep inching toward her, ignoring the way she's shaking her head, and trying to not let her falling tears fucking ruin me. I reach for her, clutching her limp hands in mine, needing her to understand that I didn't want to hurt her. Needing her to feel how sorry I am. "I've just been so stressed and overwhelmed. I couldn't handle it. I didn't know how to deal with losing the house too. And you're not blameless in this either. How could you ask them to publish pictures of Addy when that was my one request in this deal?"

For a split second, I think I see understanding or maybe even remorse in her bright blue eyes, but it's gone so fast, I must've imagined it.

She rips her hands out of mine and swipes at her tearstained cheeks. "Oh, stop it, Jude! Of course you're overreacting to that! Lauren doesn't care about Addy having her picture taken. You just needed to feel in control of *my* deal. I didn't realize you would be so vindictive when you found out!" She inches closer to me, forcing me to retreat in my own room. "And what do you even have to be stressed over? Is taking pictures on Instagram becoming too taxing? Is it too hard to perform the job I literally laid in your lap? I got you the following, I got you the media, I got you the contracts after you made a terrible business decision over a man. Your dad would've been so disappointed over that one." She shakes her head, rolling her eyes, while laughing a humorless laugh like she didn't just slice my heart open. "All you had to do was not be a fucking disaster in public, Jude! That's it! I had this all worked out. I was going to keep the house, but then you go and blow the one thing I'm asking of you. And poof!" She lifts her hands in front of my face, and even though she's never hit me before, I can't conceal the way I flinch. "It's all gone. The contracts. The sponsors. All gone. Because you can't do the smallest thing to help me when I'm finally almost put back together."

All of the anger I've been holding on to abandons me, and all I'm left with is sorrow. "I tried to help. I really did."

I don't know how it's possible for my heart to pound in my chest as it's shattering into millions of pieces, but it's happening.

"Bullshit," she hisses. She jabs a polished fingernail into my chest, and her beautiful face screws up so tight, it's almost unrecognizable. "If I was Lauren, you would've helped. But me, your mom? You never want to do anything for me, and I raised you."

"That's not true—" I don't know if I'm trying to defend myself or what, but it doesn't matter, because she doesn't let me finish.

"It is true! This whole thing is because you were mad at a picture of her daughter. But you know what? I don't even care anymore." She pulls her shoulders back, and the woman I idolized on her soap opera set appears before me. "You made it clear since your father died, I'm just a burden to you. Lucky for you, you don't have to worry about me bothering you now. As far as I'm concerned, you're no longer my daughter, and I hope you're happy with that."

"*What?*"

"You heard me." She grabs her bag off my bed. "I did everything for you, and now that I need you, you do this? You hate me so much, you'd let this happen to me? Well, message received. I don't need you either."

My mouth opens and closes, but no words come out.

She's done things like this in the past, but it feels different this time. Maybe because this time it really feels like it's all my fault.

I ruined everything in my life and then I did the same thing to her.

I'm like a fucking wrecking ball.

She doesn't wait for me to gain my composure.

She doesn't stop and turn when I finally manage to call her name through my tear-clogged throat.

She doesn't do anything except walk away.

It isn't until I hear her voice, as sweet and kind as if nothing just happened, saying goodbye to Lauren that it really hits me.

I'm all alone.

Always, always alone.

I move to close my door when that damn stain catches my eye again.

It has to go. There has to be some way I can fucking get rid of it. It can't just sit there forever.

My hangover makes its appearance known when my stomach turns and flips as I sprint down the stairs to find the stain remover beneath the kitchen sink. I ignore the way Lauren watches me from her spot on the couch as I sweep all of the other cleaners out of my way until I finally see the blue bottle I'm looking for.

I don't even know if my feet touch the ground as I skip the stairs and run to my room. I shove the door against the back wall so hard that not even the doorstop can gentle it. The frames on my dresser tumble over and I drop to my knees, dousing the red spot with the gel, flipping the bottle over, and scrubbing the carpet until my arms ache.

"Jude? Are you okay?" Lauren startles me out of my cleaning haze. Her voice is gentle, like it is when she talks to Addy when she's feeling sad. The way a mother should talk to her daughter.

"Water." I prop myself up on my knees and take in the now pink spot beneath the foaming gel cleaner. "I think I need water now."

She moves slowly across my room until she's on her knees beside me. She pulls the bottle out of my hands and moves it so it's out of reach. "Maybe we should forget about the stain for a second."

"No! I can't! I can't just let this stain fester in the fucking carpet!" I push up so that I'm standing. "So what? So Addy has one fucking accident and then it's just there for fucking ever? Every time she comes into my room? She has to see the reminder of the one time she messed up? No. That's not going to happen. It has to go. I won't let Addy live with that."

And then it clicks and I know exactly how to get rid of it.

I take off back through my door and down the stairs. I go straight to the kitchen, eyeing the knife block holding all of our knives. I know exactly which one I need. I pull the small but extremely sharp knife out of its allotted slot and run back to my room, waving the knife around like a knight with a sword.

Lauren's eyes double in size when she sees me walk in with the knife, but I'm too focused to notice.

"What are you doing?" The hysteria in her voice doesn't register.

Nothing registers.

Nothing matters except getting rid of that stupid fucking stain.

I fall back to the floor, ignoring Lauren's protests as I raise my fist with the knife in it and slam it into the carpet. I saw the knife around the stain, cutting and cutting until the last thread is broken and jagged edges are ripped free.

"There!" I hold up the stained carpet, letting it dangle between my thumb and my index finger. "I fucking got it!"

"Jude . . ." Lauren's big brown eyes are watching me . . . not looking at all at the carpet I just ripped up.

"No, look, Lauren! I got it!" I shove it in her face. "Addy will never have to see it again. And she'll know that I'll never let her mistakes haunt her. Not ever. I'll always be there for her. No matter what."

"Jude." Lauren takes two steps toward me and closes the distance between us. She leans in and gently peels my fingers off the knife before taking the carpet patch from me. "She already knows that."

"No matter what," I say, repeating myself, but the words don't come as easily this time.

My breathing starts to slow and awareness creeps back in. Lauren staring at me, concern and fear written across her stunning face. Right next to her, the sad, pathetic piece of fucking carpet is lying next to the knife I probably ruined.

I look away from her and find the spot where the stain used to be. My hand grazes the now empty hole in the middle of my floor. The hole that's a million times more noticeable than the red stain.

"I made it worse," I whisper, my voice breaking.

"What?" Lauren leans in to hear me.

"I made it worse." I look up, saying it a little louder this time. "I always make it worse."

Like a tidal wave, all the feeling comes back in my body. The lightness I was feeling moments ago flying through the house disappears, and a heaviness like I've never felt before takes over. My arms feel like they weigh a thousand pounds, my legs feel like they're covered in concrete, and my chest aches like I've been punched. My lungs feel as if I've been drowning for the last twenty-eight years and I just got my first taste of air.

And it hurts.

It fucking kills.

The sob that comes from the back of my throat feels like it's being torn from the very bottom of my soul. It feels like it's ripping me in half.

Then Lauren's arms are wrapped around me so tight that I can barely breathe. She's whispering words I don't even pretend to comprehend and providing comfort I can't accept.

Because I'll ruin this too. I'll push Lauren away. I'll lose Addy.

That's what I do. I fuck up everything.

And I'll be alone.

Always, always alone.

THIRTY-ONE

Lauren

There are certain things that once they happen, you know they're going to stick with you until you take your final breath. Feelings and memories that you'll hold on to forever.

I've had a few of them.

Finding out I was pregnant. Holding Adelaide for the very first time after a horrendous pregnancy and even worse delivery. I still remember the way she smelled and the feel of her baby skin . . . the way my heart exploded as I was counting her perfect, tiny fingers and they formed a fist around my finger. The moment Ben told me he'd been unfaithful and we were over.

Good, bad, and beautiful, they're all ingrained in my mind.

And now, etched right next to them is the guttural, heart-wrenching sound that came from Jude as she collapsed into my arms and cried for hours after her mom came over.

That sound. It didn't even seem human. It shouldn't be human. No one person should have that much pain welled up inside of them.

And it haunts me.

I hear it when I'm in the shower, when I'm driving. Any quiet moment I have is punctuated by the echoes of her sobs. I feel the weight of her body when she fell into me, the way her body racked with so much pain that I felt the vibrations against my skin. And the guilt of knowing how long she must've been hiding the burdens she's been buried under, the burdens that have been crushing her beautiful spirit, threatens to choke me.

Because even after all of that, even after falling apart in my arms, it was like a switch flipped at the end and she pretended nothing happened at all. "Fuck." She swiped those tears off her face and let out the weakest laugh I've ever heard before pushing out of my arms. "I am so sorry. It was not that serious. Hangovers and moms, man. Not a good combination."

And when I tried to stop her, talk to her, she said she had to take a shower, and for the two weeks since, she's been avoiding me.

"Yo. Lauren." Hudson squeezes my knee. "You good?"

"Yeah, sorry." I shake my head, trying to rid it of the thoughts of Jude for long enough to at least hold a conversation with Hudson. "What were you saying?"

His eyes go soft and he links his fingers through mine. "You still haven't talked to Jude?"

I pull my lips between my teeth and fight away the tears that have been looming behind my eyes for the last two weeks. I can't even answer his question because I know I won't be able to stop them from falling, so I just shake my head instead.

"She'll come around." He says it like it's fact, and I've never wanted to believe something so much in my entire life.

"I hope so." I tuck my ankles beneath me and lean into Hudson, bringing the glass of wine to my lips and enjoying the soft light of the Christmas tree for a little bit longer, knowing it has to come down.

I look at the pile of toys pushed into the corner of the living room. All are unwrapped, a few are still in boxes, and the dollhouse from Santa is standing tall against the wall. Suffice it to say, Adelaide is an extremely happy and entertained child right now.

Between me, Ben and Stephanie, and her grandparents, it's almost disgusting how much stuff she got. Next year, I'm going the experience route over presents. Maybe we'll drive to the mountains, rent a cabin, and go skiing. Anything other than the endless amount of crap she'll no doubt tire of by February.

"Hudsie!" Adelaide, in a voice that hasn't quieted, shouts from her room. "Can you help me? I wanna make a show with my stuffed animals!"

When Hudson came over tonight, he held a sparkly wrapped present in his hand. The only thing better than a Christmas gift is one at the end of the day when you think the excitement is over. Adelaide's little eyes lit up, and that was *before* she tore the paper off and saw the camera he got her.

It was too much. And it was perfect.

A perfect, wordless reminder that Hudson isn't like any man I've ever known. He isn't just dealing with being around Adelaide to get to me, he cares about her just as much as he cares about me. And this camera was a promise that he's going to encourage her to explore her creativity just like he's done for me.

He presses his lips against my forehead, the corners of his mouth turning up as he pulls away and levels me with a stare. "Just so you know, your daughter's the shit and we're about to go make the dopest video ever. I even downloaded new sound clips for her to use before I came over."

I never thought I'd fall for a guy who uses the word *dope* so frequently, but here we are. And I'm falling hard.

I fake a cringe. "Oh god, I'm going to have to create backdrops, aren't I?"

"You haven't already? What a slacker." He stands up, bending down and touching his mouth to mine once more before turning and taking the steps two at a time, calling, "Here I come, Adikins! Let's get this show on the road!"

Adelaide's giggles at his nickname for her float through the house, and the happiness that fills my chest is so wonderful and pure, it makes the guilt of knowing how much pain my best friend is in bubble right back to the top.

I check my phone again, seeing if she's sent another text or anything. Even though I love the time spent alone(ish) on the couch with Hudson, we were supposed to record a new holiday-themed podcast tonight. I got her eggnog and saved some of my mom's famous cheesecake for her. She said she'd be here an hour ago. I type out a quick message asking if she's okay or if she wants to reschedule, and then, even though I don't want to, I open Instagram.

I still hate social media, and I find I hate it even more every time I mindlessly drift to the app and scroll endlessly. So I try to avoid it, but since Jude is avoiding me, it's really the only peek I have into her life.

In true Jude fashion, she didn't actually address the fallout that happened with her sponsors after her . . . encounter with Asher and Meadow. Just a few quotes posted on her feed where she vaguely mentions only being able to be used and abused so many times before fighting back. And because social media is social media, that seemed good enough for her loyal followers. She actually gained followers after it all happened. I guess what they say is true: all press is good press.

I search her username and tap her profile picture, catching up on the stories she entertains her thousands of followers with. I watch the fifteen-second clips pass by, seeing her gorgeous smile filling the screen and hearing contagious laughter as she dances around, busting out Pilates poses on sidewalks. She sits in an empty Pilates studio, sipping out of her water bottle, answering the "ask me anything" questions her followers have sent her. She jokes and preaches authenticity, self-love, and acceptance.

And it's all so fake that it makes my eyes hurt.

Sometimes I forget that Jude's first love was acting. She was so, so good. The lead in all of our plays. She even got a starring role her freshman year, a first in our school's history. I guess she's so good at this influencer gig that it was easy for me to think this is what she wanted to do, and not just a road she happened down.

But seeing the emptiness behind her eyes as she showcases her straight, perfectly white teeth (that I, too, can have for fifty percent off if I swipe up and use her code) reminds me how talented she is. She's used filters and hidden behind a character she created so well that I didn't even notice.

I'm falling down the rabbit hole (that's what Jude calls it), scrolling down to pictures from years ago, reading the witty captions that made Jude the relatable best friend every person on Instagram wants to have, when I hear the front door open.

Jude strides through like she's not over an hour late and hasn't been avoiding me for the last two weeks . . . or, really looking at it, the last two years.

"Oh my god." She drops her purse on the floor and kicks off her shoes before running across the room and jumping onto the couch next to me. "You aren't going to fucking believe who I talked to today!"

I don't actually care who she talked to. Unless it's her therapist, who she stopped seeing weeks ago for reasons she—not shockingly—won't disclose to me. But this is the first time I've seen her smiling without shadows behind her eyes, and I'm so relieved to see it that I'll gladly talk about whatever it is that put it there.

"You're right, I'll never guess," I tell her. "So just tell me."

"Okay, are you ready?" She's bouncing up and down, so giddy that I can't help but smile and bounce along with her. "I don't think you're ready."

"Jude!" I whine. The anticipation over something I didn't even care about two minutes ago is so strong that I might burst if she doesn't hurry up and tell me.

And this right here? This is her influence. Right here in front of me, no matter how worried I am about her, the second she aims her energy at me, I'm putty in her hands.

"Nicola fucking Roberts!" She screeches the name in my face, and my body turns to stone, but she keeps talking. "She reached out to me because she's been listening to our podcast and loves you. She loves how open and honest you are about motherhood, but how much fun you seem to have being a mom. She signed up for the emails and fell even further in love with you."

"You're freaking lying." I breathe out the words, not sure Jude can hear over the squealing she's still doing. "She reached out on Christmas?"

This is literally the best gift ever.

"Yes, on Christmas. Holidays are the most active days for influencers. Everyone is at home, staring at their phones and wishing they weren't." She rolls her eyes like that wasn't a completely reasonable question. "I'd never fucking lie about this! And that's not even everything!" Jude yanks me closer before screaming in my face. "She wants you to do a panel with her!"

I was seventeen when I found out I was accepted into my parents' alma mater. I'd been working my entire life to get into Stanford, and opening that thick envelope to the welcome package, seeing pride evident on my mom's stern face, I finally felt like I'd accomplished something meaningful. Medical school had been even more exciting.

Then I dropped out, and besides Adelaide, I haven't felt pride like that since.

Until this very moment.

Nicola Roberts isn't just a mommy influencer. She's *the* mommy influencer. She has her own cookbook, a line of merchandise you can buy from practically any big-box retailer. She's in the midst of getting her own talk show, but while it's in development, she has a YouTube channel that garners millions of views. Features on her website don't just boost popularity, they launch careers. She's like Oprah. Her influence doesn't have limits.

And for some crazy reason, Jude is telling me she wants me on a panel with her.

Me.

"If you're lying to me, I'll never forgive you." I know how competitive this mommy influencer world is. It's why I never set my sights on making this podcast anything other than a ploy to get custody and something fun for me and Jude to do together. The little bit of money trickling in has been amazing and already more than I dreamt of.

But this? A panel with Nicola freaking Roberts? It's beyond anything my imagination is even capable of conjuring up.

"I already told you I'm not lying!" She squeezed my hands tighter. "The panel is soon, though, first Saturday in January at two o'clock, but she wants you to get there early and meet the other panelists. I told her you'd give her an answer tomorrow, but also that your answer would be yes."

"Holy shit." I'm still having a hard time comprehending how in the world this is happening to me. I unlock my phone and find the calendar, scrolling to the first Saturday in January. "Crap." I look at the note I have typed out for that day. "We have playgroup."

"Playgroup?" She says the word like she can taste it, and her entire face scrunches up in disgust. "You're not saying no to this opportunity because of playgroup. It's not even in the realm of possibility."

I know I should do this. It's once in a lifetime, but I don't know if I'm ready for that. Scratch that. I *know* I'm not ready for that. It's too soon. Making a fool out of myself with Jude and Hudson is one thing—one thing that can be edited. Doing it on a panel—*live!*—with Nicola Roberts, whatever other panelists that actually have their crap together, and an audience? No. No way.

And this is an easy out.

"It's not just the playdate. Now that custody is settled, I can't take my time with her for granted. Especially the weekends. I want to spend my time with her being as present as possible." I spew the excuses as they come to my mind. "Plus, this playgroup is at Snowfest, and she hasn't stopped talking about going sledding with Winnie and Lake. I can't cancel that."

"I know what you're doing," Jude says. "You aren't going to be able to come up with enough excuses to get out of this. I'm not going to let you self-sabotage and talk yourself out of this."

"Really?" I purse my lips and level her with what I hope is my most ironic glare. Because hello, pot, meet kettle. "You've been avoiding me for two weeks and you're gonna lecture me about excuses and self-sabotage."

She lets go of my hands and blows out a harsh breath between her lips as she deflates into the couch cushions.

"Walked right into that one, didn't I?" Her head falls back onto the couch and drops to the side so she can look at me.

"You sure did," I confirm, and she knows better than anyone that I'm not going to let this go. Not anymore. "So are you finally going to let me in on what's going on? Or are you going to keep avoiding me?"

"I'm not avoiding you." She somehow manages to say the flat-out lie with a straight face. "I've just been really busy trying to get things back on track from the sweater party catastrophe."

"The fact that you lie so well is both impressive and appalling." While I'm sure she has been busy, I'm done letting her get away with avoiding things that are very clearly affecting her. I've given her space and time before, and now I'm starting to realize that was a mistake.

Her eyes go wide; she's not used to me calling her on her shit, but she doesn't deny anything. So I power on.

"I've been a worried wreck about you for the last two weeks, and if I'm honest, a few months before that." She opens her mouth to talk, but I shake my head and keep talking. "I don't know what happened with your mom to cause you to shatter the way you did, but I know it's still eating away at you. I've given you the time and space I thought you needed, but it's not going to get better unless you talk about it. It doesn't even have to be to me, you can call Chloe again. You just can't keep burying whatever it is that is eating at you. It won't stay buried forever, trust me."

"You're right." She looks away from me, focusing on the Christmas tree instead. "I just don't know how to talk about it. I've been ignoring it for so long, I'm not even sure what the problem is or how it started. It's embarrassing when I think about how big of a mess I am."

"Girl." I turn to her and tuck my legs crisscross-applesauce. "You're talking to me. The person whose mother is a lawyer, but instead of asking for help years ago when Ben probably would've signed away everything to get rid of me, I ignored it all until I almost lost custody of my daughter."

She bites back a smile, and I'm not sure if it's because she doesn't want to hurt my feelings by laughing at the absurdity of my life or because she knows I'm right. Either way, it's something.

"If anyone is not going to judge you for going through something with your mom, it's me. You know my mom. She's perpetually disappointed in me. I'm not sure there's anything you can say to me that I won't understand."

"But you love my mom," she says quietly. "I don't want to make you feel like you ever have to choose between us. I don't want to make you think less of her when I know how close you were."

"There is no choice." My eyebrows knit together so tight that my head starts to hurt. "Sure, I thought your mom was fun, but you're my best friend, not her. I told you before and I meant it, I'm team Jude till the day I die whether you tell me what happened or not." I pause and take a deep breath, grabbing Jude's hands and hoping she can feel the sincerity of my next words. "But I really hope you tell me. I hope you let me reciprocate that love and support you've given to me and Adelaide."

And finally . . . *finally!* . . . for the first time in a long time, I see my words finally get through to Jude. Her eyes gloss over and she drops my hands before leaning across the small space between us and wrapping her arms around me.

"Thank you," she says, not even able to get those two small words out without her voice breaking. She pulls away, wiping at the cheeks that have had more tears on them in the last few weeks than they had in years. "I do want to tell you. How about you let me watch Addy and take her to the playgroup while you go to the panel. Then that night, after she goes to sleep, we'll crack open a bottle of wine, you can tell me all about your new life as an influencer, and I can fill you in on the tales of Juliette Andrews."

While I'm not sure there needs to be a deal in place for her to open up to me, I don't miss the fact that she's volunteering to spend the day with the Remington moms in order to get me to commit to a panel with Nicola freaking Roberts.

I'll give her this play.

Plus, even though just thinking about it makes me want to vomit, I can't pretend I wouldn't be devastated to blow this opportunity.

"Deal." I hold out my hand and she grabs on, shaking hard with her freakishly strong grip. Her wide, bright, *real* smile back on her face.

She opens her mouth to talk, but a little voice from behind us beats her to it. Both of our heads snap around and we see Adelaide on the stairs with her new camera aimed directly at us.

"Auntie Jude!" Adelaide shouts, her little feet barely touching the stairs as she bounces down them. "Look at what Hudson gave me! Wanna be on my show? I was going to interview my stuffed animals, but Hudson is *terrible* at the voices." She looks very put out by Hudson's lack of animated voice skills. "He said he can do it on the computer, but I don't know. Now that you're finally home, can you help? You do the best voices!"

Jude lights up. All remnants of sadness and worry flee as she hops off the couch. "Addy June!" She scoops Adelaide into her arms and peppers her face with kisses. "Are you kidding me? That's all I want to do! Tell your mom she's on snack duty. I have the feeling production is going to make me very hungry."

"Mommy!" Adelaide shouts like I didn't hear every word Jude said. "We're gonna need snacks! We're working very hard. 'Specially Hudsie, he's moving my furniture to create a set."

"He's what?!" I shout, vaguely hearing the bumping and dragging against the ceiling now that I'm not focusing on Jude.

Adelaide's eyes go wide as she looks at me before she turns to Jude, who has equally large eyes. They stare at each other for a second before they both dissolve into a fit of laughter and Jude runs up the rest of the stairs.

The sound of their laughter fades, but the feeling I had watching it lingers. So instead of caring that Adelaide's furniture is being rearranged or that she's eaten more sugar today than she has all year, I just smile and grab snacks before joining them.

And I'm not just on snack duty.

Adelaide lets me be the voice of her new rainbow zebra.

I thought Nicola Roberts was going to be the best part of my day . . . but as I watch Hudson produce *The Addy Show*—taking it as seriously as he takes working on his own projects—and Jude laughing as she gets really into her part as Twinkle Star the Unicorn, I know I was wrong.

Nicola is great, but nothing is better than this.

THIRTY-TWO

. . .

Lauren

From: Lauren

Date: January 3

Subject: New Year, new . . . never mind . . .

Hey!

We're only three days into the new year, and I don't know about you, but I'm already so over all the "new year, new you" emails spamming my inbox. Like, listen. I'm almost in my 29th year of life. I've dropped out of med school, had a kid, went through a custody battle, started a podcast, and none of those things happened because January 1 hit. Not a single one. And if it was a new me, it for sure wouldn't include me needing new jeans from Old Navy or a freaking juice cleanse. Gross.

But since we're talking about it, there was one year I made a whole list of resolutions. Jude went to some palm reader while she was on vacation in Italy. She became obsessed with astrology and crystals and talking to the universe. And because we're the same person, I got into it with her. So for New Year's Eve, I went over to her house and she decked out her entire room. And I mean her *entire room*. It looked like a freaking junior prom. You couldn't see her walls behind the metallic fringe covering them. Every single surface had crystals on it. She had stacks on stacks on stacks of magazines for us to cut up for the vision boards we were going to make, and she lit candles to cleanse the air of all bad vibes.

You want to know what happened that year? Not a thing.

Probably because as we were cutting and gluing (glueing? Both are right. Words are weird.) pictures to our poster board, Jude tossed a magazine scrap and it landed on a candle. That promptly lit on fire and then spread to the remaining scraps all around it. Of course because we were nose blind to smells thanks to that mixture of candle scents in the room, we didn't notice this until we saw smoke, and shortly after that, the fire alarm went off. This set off a series of events that ended in us standing outside in our matching pajamas while the world's hottest firefighters scolded us for our lack of fire safety (and common sense).

We never made a vision board again.

But, if I were to make a vision board, I know exactly what would be on it this year. YOU. Your gorgeous, beautiful faces pasted right next to Nicola freaking Roberts. And that would be a powerful freaking board because guess what! It's freaking happening! I'm going to be on a panel with Nicola Roberts this Saturday!!! Now all I need is to see your faces, and for that to happen, just click here to find tickets. Are you coming? Is this going to be the best year ever? Hit reply and let me know!

Cheers! 🥂
Lauren

PS Keep Jude in your thoughts. Not only is she babysitting for me while I'm on this panel, she's taking Adelaide to playgroup with the other kindergarten moms. Something Jude notoriously has no patience for.

PPS If you want to know what Jude and I rang in the new year with, it was a French 75. I was a fan. Classic and delicious!

FRENCH 75

2 ounces London dry gin
¾ ounce fresh lemon juice
¾ ounce simple syrup
2 ounces champagne
Long spiral lemon twist

Combine gin, lemon juice, and simple syrup in a cocktail shaker. Fill shaker with ice, cover, and shake until cold. Strain into whatever fancy glass you choose, top with champagne, garnish with a lemon twist, and enjoy!

PPPS Drink responsibly!

"The boots my mom got her are in the back of the closet, and make sure she wears a long-sleeved shirt and has a jacket," I tell Jude again, even though I showed her where they were last night . . . and again this morning. "And her—"

"Her gloves and hat." Jude rolls her eyes and finishes my sentence for me. "Lauren, seriously. Chill. Get it? Chill. Snow?" She laughs at her own joke—which isn't even a little bit funny—but gets serious again when she must see how much I'm freaking out. "It's going to be fine. I'm going to make sure Addy doesn't get frostbite."

"You're right. I'm sorry. You're both going to have fun. I heard this event is a blast." I feel terrible that I've been such a nag. Jude and Adelaide love hanging out together, and it's not like I'm going away for a week. I'm just a nervous wreck for this panel. No matter how I try to spin it in my mind, I'm in over my head. "I'm just freaking out about this panel. I think I made a mistake? I don't know anything about public speaking. I almost failed the one class I took for it."

"Take a breath. You're going to be great. Just like the podcast. You're going to be your smart, funny, wonderful self and everyone is going to love you. Plus, now they get to see how hot you are." She takes my hands in hers, and as much as it's for support, I know it's to prevent me from picking at my nails, which she forced me to paint. "Anyway, at least you get to go hang with Nicola Roberts. I have to spend the day with Jennifer and the rest of the bitches of Remington. Sabrina is coming, though, right? I need at least one decent mom to be around."

Welp. When she puts it like that, maybe this won't be too bad?

"Sabrina will be there, and you're right, public humiliation is still better than an afternoon of Jennifer, Colleen, and Whitney."

"You owe me so huge for this." She showcases her flair for the dramatic with the most overpronounced eye roll in the history of eye rolls. But I know there's nothing behind it. I think she wanted me to do this more than I wanted to.

Wait.

Scratch that.

I *know* she wanted me to do this more than I did.

Plus, she's still been really down about whatever happened with her mom, and I know from personal experience that spending time with Adelaide is the perfect medicine for dealing with mom drama.

"You're the best." I hug her tight, hoping she feels how much I care about her with the simple gesture. Unlike my child, who wraps herself around me like a koala when I hug her, Jude is tense throughout it all. I let her go, but only because I'm on a strict timeline. "Adelaide! Come give me a hug!"

Usually I have to yell a couple of times, but she's so excited to spend the day with Jude that she flies down the stairs at the first call and slams her tiny little body into my legs.

"Bye, Mommy!" I think I should be offended by how eager she is to get rid of me, but instead I take it for what it is and I'm just happy she's happy. Also, she sat still long enough for me to braid her hair this morning and she looks adorable. I mean, she always looks adorable, but she looks extra adorable today. "Do good talking!"

Do good talking. I freaking love this little girl.

"Thank you, sister girl." I ignore the crack of my knees as I drop down to give her all my attention. "Be a good girl for Auntie Jude, okay? And have the most fun ever. I'm going to want to hear all about it tonight."

"Okay, Mommy!" Addy grabs me by the shoulders and leans in, her face extra serious with whatever "secret" she plans to tell me. "And I'll make sure Jude is nice to the other mommies."

I try not to laugh at Jude's affronted expression because my little girl is sometimes too smart for her own good.

"Thank you," I say, and try to capture the look of pride on Adelaide's face for my memory, but my concentration is broken when a car horn sounds from outside.

I shoot up from my squat with the power of a caffeinated HIIT instructor, and every nerve I just fought returns to the surface.

"All right." I look at the door thinking maybe I could just cancel. It's not like being a podcaster and influencer was something I ever planned. So pulling out at the last minute wouldn't be that big of a deal . . . right? But then I look back at Adelaide and the huge smile on her face. Right now, she thinks she can do anything and everything. There are no limits in her life. But one day, that will change, and I'm going to have to encourage her to do something scary and huge. And what kind of example would I set for her if I quit when I got scared? "I guess this is it. I'll call you when it's over."

This lead-by-example stuff kinda sucks.

"You're going to be amazing. Seriously." Jude hands me my sweater, and I realize she's looking at me like Adelaide is. She's proud of me too. "Just enjoy it. I have a feeling this is going to be the first of many events for you."

I nod once and open the door.

No turning back now.

"Wish me luck."

"Good luck!" Adelaide's voice, which is much louder than should be possible from such a little person, bounces off the cars parked in front of our place. She's jumping up and down and keeps waving even after I'm in the back of the very tinted car.

"Cute kid," the driver says before he backs out of the parking spot.

"Thanks." I smile, already feeling the excitement of actually doing this setting in. "I'm kinda fond of her."

He chuckles but says no more, and I'm grateful to have a little time to relax before the mayhem starts.

I open my phone and check the email account linked to the newsletter and see we have more than twenty new emails from listeners. We've never gotten the amount of response emails that I did after the last newsletter I sent out. There have been hundreds. It's been mind-blowing.

I mean, I knew people were reading them. I have a spreadsheet that has the time it was sent out, the subject line, and the open rate for every single email. Like most things in my life, I'm a little obsessive about it. But this week still shocked me. Not only the number of people who actually read, but so many of them clicked the link I attached and bought tickets to the panel! I even got emails from readers out of state seeing if they could stream the event.

It's equal parts flattering and intimidating.

To know that people were going to come to the event, not because of Nicola Roberts, but because of me? What if I'm disappointing without Jude as my crutch? What if I let them all down?

But then, the little voice in the back of my head that's always trying to dream these big, impossible dreams asks what happens if I meet their expectations. What happens if I exceed them? How could this change my and Adelaide's life? Could this be the thing that sets my life on course?

Thanks to the ever-present Los Angeles traffic, I'm able to type out more than a few emails back to the readers who replied. It's important to me to respond to as many people as I can. I want them to feel like we're friends. I want those personal relationships that can be difficult to foster when you're a parent—or an adult in general.

"Here we are," the driver says as the car rolls to a stop.

I tuck my phone into my purse and then look out the window. An action I immediately regret.

You know how if you aren't feeling good and then you look up the symptoms online, the internet will tell you you're either pregnant or going to die? Well, I've made that mistake so many times, I decided not to do it with this panel. I knew if I looked it up, I'd be convinced of my impending doom and freak out more than I was already freaking out.

But as the women wearing flowy dresses, sunglasses, and trendy hats hold their phones or cameras above their heads and flood into City Market South in droves, I realize I really should've googled.

I hesitate for a minute, and when I decide it's go time, I draw in a breath deep enough to sustain me underwater for at least a solid fifty seconds and push open the car door. The door is barely shut behind me when the driver peels away from the curb, giving me the feeling I'm not the only one who was overwhelmed by the size of the crowd.

In the emails I've been exchanging with Nicola—or more likely her assistant—I know I'm supposed to meet the others from my panel in a VIP tent. I've never done anything like this before, and being a VIP at an event like this blows my mind. I crane my neck, trying to figure out who I should talk to or where I should go, but when I take a step forward, I instantly get caught in a current of influencers. I walk along with them, afraid to break free, and am transported into what is—and I say this without even an ounce of sarcasm—a magical, glorious influencer wonderland.

Different art installations cover every open wall. Giant murals with inspirational quotes from floor to ceiling dot the space for people to capture their newest profile picture. Greenery and floral backdrops with neon-light quotes highlight the cocktail stations. Vendors are packed in on each side of the aisles. There are local businesses from every market you could think of. A party-planning company has an entire section showcasing their balloon sculptures and teaching anyone who is interested how to create a garland of their own. Hair and makeup stations with selfie lights are here in hordes. Jude's favorite kombucha store is passing out samples of their tea, and a cupcake shop is handing out boozy cakes with personalized edible toppers using selfies people take when they place their orders.

It's over the top and I feel wildly out of place in my blazer, cami, and jeans. Thank goodness I'm wearing my favorite shoes. They're giving me the boost I'm desperately in need of.

And even though this is something that I would have turned my nose up at months ago, the energy flowing around me is intoxicating. Women of every age, race, and size are talking to each other, passing out compliments like confetti, and exchanging numbers with people who were strangers only moments before.

It's contagious, and I've never wanted to be so extra in my entire life.

There's a large crowd gathering not too far in front of me, and my curiosity gets the best of me. There are so many goodies being passed out all around me, I can't imagine how amazing whatever is at the center of the crowd must be.

I sneak forward, weaving with ease since I'm one of the few people who came without a friend in tow. Once I get to the front, my jaw drops because it's not a vendor. It's Nicola freaking Roberts, just in the middle of the crowd, casually conversing with everyone like it's no big deal.

But seeing her isn't what makes my mouth hang open in what has to be the most unattractive expression in the history of the universe. No. It's her looking at me, then doing a double take and shouting—in front of everyone!—"Oh my god! You're Lauren Turner! I'm so glad you could make it!"

She runs over to me. Her trademark red lipstick painted onto her beautiful smile picks up the golden hues of her skin and makes her white teeth sparkle even brighter. She's looking at me with her dark brown eyes, lined to perfection and framed with lashes that are so long, they have to be fake . . . but probably aren't. Her big, beautiful curls are out to *here*, and the highlights scattered throughout are so gorgeous that they must've cost hundreds, if not thousands, of dollars.

And she's talking to me.

For real. This is happening and it's not even my lackluster imagination trying to trick me.

"I . . . uhh . . . you're . . . I . . ." I forget what words are, and my mouth opens and closes like a fish out of water.

Thankfully, the women-supporting-women vibe is flowing here too when the woman next to me nudges me forward and whispers in my ear, "Girl, own your power and go get that spotlight."

I nod, still trying to get my tongue to remember how to form sounds, and step forward and into Nicola's wide-open arms. "This is Lauren, she's going to be on the podcast panel on the main stage in an hour. Go get your seats now"—she drops her voice to a whisper—"because I just know this woman is about to blow our minds."

Nicola freaking Roberts thinks I'm going to blow minds.

How is this life?!

. . .

"Yes! Snaps and claps for you!" Nicola says to Rani, a beauty blogger who started a podcast that delves into the different beauty standards and practices across cultures.

She's basically a supermodel who is also brilliant and, of course, who I get to speak after.

Lovely.

She passes me the microphone and I take it with shaking hands.

"You're going to be great," she mouths before giving my hand a quick squeeze. And even though I appreciate the intention behind the action, I'm not sure I believe her.

"All right now, Lauren," Nicola says into her microphone, sounding perfectly comfortable and confident. "You're actually new to this entire podcasting and influencer world, aren't you?"

I send up a quick thank-you to whoever is listening for the easy question to work my way in.

"I am, I'm extremely new. I honestly can't even believe I'm here today," I say, and am pleasantly surprised at how steady my voice sounds.

"Well, anyone who has listened to *Mom Jeans and Martinis* or read the hilarious emails you send out every week knows why you deserve to be on this stage."

Applause sounds in the audience, and my cheeks and heart warm at the praise and support. My smile comes easily this time, not forced or fake to cover the nerves. My shoulders relax, and some of the butterflies that have been wreaking havoc on my digestive system fade away.

"Well, thank you." I loosen my grip on the mic. "I really appreciate that."

"So tell us, what made you decide to start a podcast?"

"I honestly didn't decide." I give her the truth I'm sure she didn't expect, but if I'm going to be up here, I have to give it to everyone real. "My best friend is Jude Andrews, who, if you listen to the podcast, you know is also my cohost. She has been just killing it in this industry for years. Her phone was always in her hand, and I could never take a picture of her without getting a full-on tutorial before snapping one. I, on the other hand, didn't have social media at all. But a few months ago, the father of my five-year-old daughter decided that after a couple of years of being completely absent, he was going to get involved in a big way. This big way included taking me to court for full custody." There are a few gasps in the audience, and I nod along with them. Even knowing how this story ends, I still get worked up thinking about it.

"I don't know about the rest of you, but I like to be liked and I hate to rock the boat or cause problems." There are some nods of agreement and raised hands in the audience. "So when my ex decided to leave, I didn't want to do anything to make it worse. As a Black woman, I know the stereotypes that are thrown around. I know how easy it is to dismiss my feelings by saying I have an attitude or that I'm angry. So instead of letting that happen, I let my ex, a white doctor, walk all over me. And what I thought was going to be the thing that protected me and my daughter—letting him see her when he wanted, never pushing child support—ended up biting me in the butt.

"So when I met with my lawyer and it was kinda shoved in my face that by not taking him to court earlier, he could direct the narrative in whatever way he wanted, Jude threw out the idea of a podcast." I pause and make eye contact with a woman who I saw earlier getting her makeup done. "And I immediately shot it down. There was no way she was getting me on a microphone talking about motherhood. Nobody wanted to listen to a twenty-something, med school dropout, single mom of a kindergartner. Nobody." The crowd laughs, and a buzz like I've never experienced shoots through my body, lighting every nerve with excitement that makes me feel like I'm floating. "But then, because Jude doesn't give up on her ideas, she threw the idea out there when I was meeting with my lawyer. And to my shock, my lawyer loved the idea. She worked with a single mom who had been able to create a network of support and an unbreakable image that went a long way in court, so she thought it could do the same for me. I agreed, but only if we could be real about motherhood.

"Don't get me wrong, I love mom influencers. Adelaide's lunch boxes are practically gourmet, and I've labeled and organized every inch of her bedroom thanks to blogs and vlogs. But there are times when watching them makes me feel even more alone than I did before I watched. And I'm a single mom who lived with my parents, so more alone is, like, the bottom of the bottom." There are more laughs, and my nerves are completely gone. I get it. I get why Jude loves it so much. "There was just too much perfection, and to me, motherhood is imperfection. It's imperfect people doing their best to love these small humans and turn them into good, decent big humans. But there's no way to be a perfect parent. No matter what you do, someone will have an opinion. Someone will tell you you're doing it wrong and that you're ruining your kid. Literally, from day one. Natural delivery versus an epidural. Breastfeeding versus formula. Co-sleeping versus a crib. It just doesn't stop . . . ever. And I hate that. We're all trying our best, and just because that might look different to you than the person sitting next you doesn't mean they're wrong. It means we're human and that means we all need support and love."

"Yes!" Nicola yells into her microphone and comes out of her seat to hug me. "Listen," she says to the crowd after she lets me go. "This woman was afraid to be here. She didn't think she had anything to offer and she just took us to freaking church! This is why I asked you to come today, Lauren. You are a testimony to everyone in this room that you don't need to be anyone other than the person God made you to succeed. Speaking your truth is the key to success, and you embody that, sis."

Well, damn.

"Wow. Thank you so much, Nicola." I'm smiling so hard that my cheeks hurt. I don't even care how crazy I look up here. Nothing can ruin this moment.

Nothing.

. . .

"Hold on one second," I say to Rani. "I just want to check my phone really fast in case Jude called."

I slip into the VIP room where all the speakers were told we could leave our purses and jackets while we mingled and did our events.

I find my purse in the cubby where I left it and pull my phone out.

When I see the screen and the multiple missed calls from Jude, that happy adrenaline rush I've been skating on fades fast.

I start to type in my passcode as fast as I can, every worst-case scenario running through my head, when my phone buzzes in my hand, startling me so bad that it goes flying.

I pick it back up, and the panic I'm already feeling compounds by a million when I see the name on the screen.

"Ben?" I ask when I put the phone to my ear. "Is everything okay?"

THIRTY-THREE

. . .

Jude

"The boots my mom got her are in the back of the closet, and make sure she wears a long-sleeved shirt and has a jacket," Lauren tells me for the hundredth time this morning. "And her—"

"Her gloves and hat," I say, cutting her off. I know I'm not a mom or even the most responsible human in the world, but I'm not a total fucking idiot. I can remember that a five-year-old needs a jacket, gloves, and a hat to go play in the snow. "Lauren, seriously. Chill. Get it? Chill. Snow?" I laugh at my pun, but Lauren looks less than amused. "It's going to be fine. I'm going to make sure Addy doesn't get frostbite."

"You're right. I'm sorry. You're both going to have fun. I heard this event is a blast." She twists her hands together. She hasn't stopped fidgeting since she confirmed the Nicola Roberts event. "I'm just freaking out about this panel. I think I made a mistake? I don't know anything about public speaking. I almost failed the one class I took for it."

"Take a breath. You're going to be great. Just like the podcast.

You're going to be your smart, funny, wonderful self and everyone is going to love you. Plus, now they get to see how hot you
are." I grab her hands in mine, partly for support, partly because
the constant movement is making my eye twitch. "Anyway, at
least you get to go hang with Nicola Roberts. I have to spend the
day with Jennifer and the rest of the bitches of Remington. Sabrina is coming, though, right? I need at least one decent mom to
be around."

"Sabrina will be there." Her shoulders relax and the tension
leaves her mouth. Even though I know she's still freaking out, I'm
glad something I said sunk in there. "And you're right, public
humiliation is still better than an afternoon of Jennifer, Colleen,
and Whitney."

I don't even try to hide my eye roll. "You owe me so huge for
this," I say, but I don't really mean it. I'm just glad that Lauren is
finally starting to see her potential and is doing something for
herself.

"You're the best." She leans in and wraps her arms around me.
Careful not to mess with her curls. "Adelaide!" she shouts when
she lets me go. "Come give me a hug!"

Adelaide barrels down the stairs. Lauren braided her hair into
two French braids so her curls wouldn't make it hard to keep her
hat on, and she looks so damn cute. I can't with this little girl. I'm
so obsessed with her that it's low-key unhealthy. I can't wait to
sled with her.

"Bye, Mommy!" She doesn't slow down and collides into Lauren's legs at full speed. Lauren rocks back half a step, and even
though getting struck by a child-sized rocket doesn't look pleas-
ant, Lauren's smile grows wider as she wraps her arms tight
around Addy. "Do good talking!"

"Thank you, sister girl." Lauren laughs a little, dropping to a
squat to give Addy a kiss. "Be a good girl for Auntie Jude, okay?

And have the most fun ever. I'm going to want to hear all about it tonight."

"Okay, Mommy!" Addy drapes her arms over Lauren's shoulder and whispers like a five-year-old, which is to say she's just as loud as ever. "And I'll make sure Jude is nice to the other mommies."

"Thank you," Lauren whispers back with a very rude and large smile.

A car honks from out front, and Lauren stands up, wringing her hands again. "All right." She looks at the door like it might grow fangs and bite her. "I guess this is it. I'll call you when it's over."

"You're going to be amazing. Seriously." I hand her the sweater she laid on the back of the chair. "Just enjoy it. I have a feeling this is going to be the first of many events for you."

She nods once and pulls open the door. "Wish me luck."

"Good luck!" Addy shouts after her, waving until Lauren is tucked in the back of the car Nicola Roberts sent for her.

I close the door, twisting the lock, and look to Addy. "Party time?"

She claps her hands together, bouncing on her toes. "Party time!"

"You go get your boots and jacket. I'll get your gloves and hat. Then let's meet in the kitchen to make hot cocoa for our thermoses." I ignore Lauren's voice in the back of my head telling me not to sugar her up. But this is the benefit of being the fun aunt— I get to give her whatever she wants. "Deal?"

"Deal!" Addy screams, the sugar not even a factor in her energy, and turns to take off up the stairs.

And she doesn't even know about the marshmallows yet.

• • •

"Jude!" Addy's voice rises above all the other squealing and shouting around us. "Will you take me down the hill?"

I thought kids ditched their moms when they were teenagers. But since I'm the super-fucking-cool aunt, I knew I would never get the slip. So imagine how it felt when five-year-old Addy dropped my hand like a bad habit the minute she saw Lake and Winnie.

It hurt.

A lot.

And because I'm grown as fuck, I wasn't allowed to show it. But now that she's back where she never should've left, wanting to spend time with me, I can let all of my excitement fly.

"Oh my god!" I yell back. "I thought you'd never ask!"

Also, adults aren't allowed down the snow hill unless they're accompanying a child. Addy is my ticket to adventure.

"Want me to hold your bag?" Sabrina holds out her hand.

"You know, Sabrina." I hand her the backpack Lauren shoved full of extra gloves, hand warmers, and snacks. "You're not like other moms, you're a cool mom."

"Obviously." She slips the backpack strap over her shoulder. "Next playgroup, are we all wearing pink?"

Lauren is my number one favorite mom for obvious reasons, but it's safe to say that Sabrina is my number two. Anyone who gets a *Mean Girls* reference without added commentary is my kinda person.

"Jude!" Addy yells before I can make another quote. "Hurry!"

I wave at Sabrina before I take off to Addy.

"All right." I'm out of breath when I get to her. Trekking through the snow is like the cold equivalent of walking on sand. I also managed to successfully dodge three snowballs and jump over one very small human who hadn't quite mastered walking in snow boots . . . or maybe walking in general, so it was a journey and I'm not mad at my lungs for the extra effort. "Let's sled."

Addy hands me the string to the sled and then wraps her

mitten-covered hand around mine. She looks up at me, the sun bouncing off the white snow sparkles across her face. The sweet little wrinkles at the top of her nose are even more pronounced with how big she's grinning. "Thank you so much for bringing me, Auntie Jude. I'm having so much fun."

Obviously, she's not my kid. I honestly don't think I ever want a child of my own—and I've always thought that, even before my life went to shit and I realized I have no fucking business bringing another human into this world—but when Addy holds my hand and looks up at me with those gorgeous, innocent eyes of hers, I can't help the way my ovaries twitch. I just love her so, so much.

I know I promised to tell Lauren everything tonight, but right now? Laughing and running around in the snow with a little girl who is everything good in this world? It's hard to remember why I've been so upset. It's like Lauren said, Addy is magic.

"I'm having so much fun too." I squeeze her hand in mine. "I love spending time with you."

"Even with the other mean moms?" she asks, and I realize that Lauren was not lying when she said that Addy hears everything.

Oops.

"I shouldn't have said that," I tell her, trying to be a semi-decent role model for once. "Plus, all the moms are actually being really nice today."

This is not a lie.

The ice around us must have somehow canceled out the ice around Jennifer's heart. She still showed up with Lake wearing matching jackets and boots, but considering the last time I saw them they were wearing Gucci, the plain black jackets and boots with the fur (sorry, Flo Rida, no apple bottom jeans in sight) feels about a million and ten percent less obnoxious. And she's actually letting Lake run around and have fun. We've been here for an hour and she hasn't scolded her once for getting her clothes wet.

And because she's the ringleader of her crew, everyone has followed her lead. They've all been so nice and haven't given me a snide look or backhanded compliment once. It's like a Christmas miracle. Or maybe they made a resolution not to be bitches? That would for sure be one resolution I could get behind.

"If they stay nice, does that mean you'll come to all my playgroups?" she asks as we walk up to the top of the sledding hill.

That might be pushing it a little far, but she looks so hopeful that I can't pop her bubble. "Maybe," I say, and her smile gets even wider. "Especially if playgroup is at cool-ass places like this again."

Addy starts giggling uncontrollably. "Ooooh! You said *ass*!"

Welp. I guess there goes my role model card.

"Shi—I mean, shoot." I just barely stop myself from digging that hole even deeper. "Let's not tell your mom about that."

I'm kinda into this whole babysitting thing. I wouldn't mind doing it more often. Lauren can go out with Hudson or do some speaking events, and me and Addy can go check out all the kids' movies I've felt too creepy to see alone in the theater. It's a win-win for everyone involved.

"Deal," she says . . . but I've seen this gap-toothed smile before, and I know she'll be telling Lauren about my potty mouth over dinner tonight.

We reach the top of the hill, and Addy picks the line right in the middle. She told me it's the fastest spot. I don't know if this is accurate, but I also don't fight it. Once it's our turn, I position the sled right at the line and hold it in place while Addy climbs into the front of the sled. She grabs hold of the string as I climb in behind, trapping her between my thighs and activating those muscles like never before.

"Ready?" she asks, and I can hear the smile in her voice.

I look down the hill, which seems a lot longer and steeper than it looked from the bottom, and try to forget that sledding accidents are a thing. I shouldn't be more scared than a five-year-old, but she doesn't know that her mother will straight-up murder me if anything happens to her.

I take a deep breath and mutter a quick prayer to any higher power that might be listening. "I'm ready!"

Addy starts wiggling her little body, trying to scoot the sled forward. I join in, putting one hand behind us and giving a little shove, and instantly wrapping it around Addy when we surge forward.

"Weeeee!" Addy screams through her giggles.

I just scream.

We fly down the hill, not slowing down until we reach the flat bottom. Addy pops out of the sled like a shot, I—the Pilates master—claw and crawl out of it.

"Look!" Addy points to Winnie and Sabrina, who are both waving at us. "There's Winnie!"

She sprints straight to them while I hand the sled to a waiting kid, and then, I still don't sprint. I walk. Slowly. My nerves feeling so shot that maybe I will need to break out my hot chocolate.

I know I spun the hot chocolate making like I was just being fun, cool Aunt Jude. And I was. Obviously. But I also had ulterior motives. Those motives being I've spent time with this group before and I needed a strong drink when I got home each time. So today, I came prepared in case of an emergency. While Addy was adding approximately a thousand marshmallows to her thermos, I added a splash or two of peppermint schnapps to mine. Not anything that could get me drunk, just to take the edge off.

It's pretty much a flashback to when I volunteered to walk in the Parade of Lights when I was in high school. Just a little something extra to keep me warm, if you will.

Sabrina hands me the backpack. "You look like you lost ten years off your life."

"I've literally never felt so old in my entire life." I tell her the god's honest truth. "No wonder Lauren is always so tired. Is this what parenting is like? Just constant worry and running around after small humans?"

"If I had to sum it up, that's exactly what I would say." Sabrina winks, but I still can't tell if she's serious or not. "All right, girls, everyone is getting hungry, so we're going to take a quick lunch break, okay?"

"Yay! Lunch!" Winnie and Addy both cheer. Girls after my fucking heart.

As with all outdoor events in LA, there's a line of food trucks parked in front. Lauren said I could pack a lunch, but considering the masterpieces she creates in Addy's lunch box every day, I decided I didn't need that kind of pressure. Plus, I was hoping someone would have cheese fries.

"We have to go grab food from the food trucks, then we'll meet up with you." I take Addy's hand in mine, and she only slightly pouts about being pulled away from her friend. "Where are you all sitting?"

"They grabbed a table over there"—Sabrina turns and points to the area off to the side without snow—"but why don't you go and I'll bring the girls. It's easier to do lines without wiggly and indecisive five-year-olds, trust me."

I take her at her word. I've been in the car while Lauren tried to order in a drive-through. Addy changed her mind like ten times and there were only three choices.

"Deal." I release Addy and she latches onto Winnie like a lifeline. Rude. "Lauren packed a few snacks in here." I point to the backpack. "Wanna take it so if Addy suddenly dies of hunger, she can munch on something while I'm gone?"

"Sounds good to me," Sabrina says.

I slide off the backpack and unzip the little pocket in the back to grab my wallet before handing it over.

"All right, Addy." I bend down and get eye to eye with her the way Lauren always does when she wants her undivided attention. "I'm going to get us food and you're going to go with Winnie and her mom. I need you to promise to be the amazing, polite kid you always are. Okay?"

"Okay, Auntie Jude." She aims that saccharine smile at me that means she's going to do either exactly as I ask or the polar opposite. But knowing that she just really is a sweet kid, I think it's the first.

I squeeze her shoulder and stand up, handing the backpack over to Sabrina, who puts it on before taking Winnie's hand and forming a human chain.

I watch them walk away for a second before turning and heading directly for the food trucks.

In a stroke of luck I'm not accustomed to, one of the food trucks does in fact have cheese fries . . . but elevated. Of course, their line is the longest of all. I send a silent thanks to Lauren for supplying me with snacks so I can wait.

But it's a wait well worth it, because when I get to the front, I order nachos that are on waffle fries instead of chips. It goes against everything I preach on Instagram, but this is why I don't post every single meal. After the month I've had, I want some fucking carbs that are covered in cheese, brisket, more cheese, and ranch. I get Addy the mac and cheese that also looks decadent, hoping she'll share with me.

Carbs on carbs on carbs and sledding. The Halloween outing was a dud, but I gotta give it to whoever planned today's outing because this is the best playgroup ever. It's so great, in fact, that I can even see why Lauren contemplated skipping out on what is probably the biggest career opportunity she's ever had to take Addy today.

I glance at my watch to see what time it is. Lauren should be about to go onstage. I know she's probably a nervous wreck right now even though it's for nothing. She's going to be fantastic. She's amazing at everything she does and if I didn't love her so much, I'd probably hate her. I can't wait for her to come home and tell me about all the people who fangirled all over her. She has no idea what this is going to do for her life, and I'm so excited that I get to ride this ride with her.

As I approach the playgroup, I can't help but laugh seeing so much snow in one section and nothing but green grass right next to it. Only in LA. I swear.

But as I get closer, the laughter dies on my lips when I see Addy sitting on Sabrina's lap, all the other moms watching her with concerned looks on their faces.

"Look, sweetie, there's Jude." Jennifer points to me when she notices me. "Why don't you go tell her what's wrong."

Addy climbs off Sabrina's lap and stumbles a little before she rights herself.

I drop the food on the table and rush over to her.

"Hey, sweet girl." I lift her into my arms. "What's wrong?"

"My tummy hurts and my head feels funny."

Even though it's January, I see the sweat forming at her hairline. Her coloring is off, and she has a look in her eyes that freaks me way the fuck out. I try to beat back the panic starting to rise beneath the surface.

"Maybe you just went down the hill too many times?" I say to myself more than to her, trying to think of any reason she would look like this. "Did you eat too many fruit snacks?"

Lauren always has fruit snacks in the backpack, and if Addy found them, there's no saying how many she shoveled back.

"No, I dinnint eat 'em." Her words slur together and her head nods back before it snaps back up.

I lose my battle on panic. I've never seen Addy like this, ever. And it's terrifying.

I think the other moms are talking to me, but I don't hear them. I run to where Sabrina has the backpack so I can get the keys and take Addy to the hospital. I'm not waiting to see what's going on. I find the keys, but as I look up, something catches my eye.

My thermos.

"Oh my god. No no no!" I snatch the thermos off the table. It was full when I packed it, but now it's almost empty. I spin to the other moms, praying one of them drank it. "One of you drank this, right? Addy didn't. She didn't drink this, did she?" My voice doesn't have a hysterical edge. It's full-blown, no-fighting-back hysterical.

"She said you made her hot chocolate. I didn't think there'd be a problem with her drinking some." Sabrina's worried eyes glance at the thermos and then back to me. "What's wrong?"

Oh my god.

My vision goes white, and not from the snow around me.

I don't respond.

I drop the keys and find my phone. Powered on adrenaline and fear, I dial 911 and tuck the phone between my ear and shoulder, barely hearing the operator on the other end.

"I need an ambulance." I rattle off the name of the park we're at and then, following directions, I don't disconnect the phone. It's only minutes, but it feels like centuries until I see the flashing lights of the ambulance coming down the street. Clinging to Addy, I take off running through the snow, not even registering the slush as it splashes onto my pants and into my shoes. I get to the parking lot just as the ambulance pulls in.

"We're here!" I scream, jumping up and down like a mad-woman. Desperation is seeping through my every pore with each passing second. "*Here!*"

Even though I doubt they can hear me, they do see me.

They stop right next to me. One paramedic comes straight to me while the other one opens the back of the ambulance.

I hand Addy to him, following on his heels as he climbs in the back of the ambulance.

"Ma'am!" he yells, and I realize he's been talking to me. "I need you to tell me what happened."

"She . . . I . . . I was gone and they didn't know and . . ." I stop, taking a deep breath, needing my words to come out so they can help her. "She drank alcohol. It was in hot chocolate and she didn't know it was in there. I don't know how much of it she had."

The paramedic shouts something and starts grabbing equipment around us as the ambulance starts to move.

"Auntie Jude." Adelaide's voice breaks through the haze around me. It's quiet and weak and so at odds to the loud, vibrant little girl I always hear. "I'm scared."

The tears I've been successfully holding back begin to fall.

"Don't be scared." I squeeze her hands and whisper the only thing that can be true. "Everything is going to be okay."

She has to be okay. She has to be okay. Dear God, please let her be okay.

I don't stop repeating those words or let go of her hand the entire ride to the hospital. I don't stop chanting them when the ambulance doors open and doctors place Addy's tiny little body on the stretcher. And I don't stop as I run behind them, staying as close as I can without getting in the way. I don't stop as my hands tremble while I find Lauren's contact in my phone and start calling her over and over again, knowing she won't have her phone while she's onstage . . . knowing this is the one thing she might not ever forgive me for.

I don't stop praying or chanting, while my tears come harder as Addy's cries echo around the small room when the doctors place an IV in her arm or while they discuss whether or not she'll need her stomach pumped.

I never stop.

Not until God sends his answer loud and clear.

Not until the curtain pulls open and, dressed in scrubs, Ben Keane runs into the room.

...

THIRTY-FOUR

Lauren

I had a really awful pregnancy.

Terrible, actually.

I knew the statistics. I knew Black women in this country are three times more likely to die during childbirth than our white counterparts. But it wasn't going to happen to me. My dad was a doctor, my spouse was a doctor (or going to be), I thought I was going to be a doctor. Not only was I going to take care of myself, but if anything went wrong, the doctors and nurses were going to listen to me.

And that's what I told myself every day that I chose water over the soda I wanted. It's what I told myself when I went for a walk instead of taking an extra nap. I was going to be the model pregnant woman and it was going to be the smoothest, most perfect pregnancy in the history of pregnancy.

And it was . . . until it wasn't.

When I was around twenty-six weeks pregnant, I woke up and my hands were swollen. And I mean really, really swollen . . . like, crying while trying to pry off my engagement ring swollen. I called my doctor to ask about it, but the on-call doctor brushed me off, assuring me that swelling was perfectly normal. I should rest and keep an eye on things.

So I did.

Then, a few days later I woke up—still swollen—with a terrible headache and called them again. "Just hold off," they said. "You have an appointment next week," they told me.

I didn't hold off. I called Ben and told him what was going on. He knew I was scared I was beginning to show symptoms of preeclampsia and encouraged me to go to the ER. That was all the encouragement I needed. I knew if a doctor looked at me, they'd see what I saw. They'd take me seriously and run tests.

But that's not what happened.

Instead of listening to me, they insisted I call my regular OB and wait for my appointment. The nurses wouldn't listen to anything I said, they ignored my tears and pleas for help. Instead they rolled their eyes and asked me to calm down; they complained about my tone and accused me of being too aggressive. The doctor was worse. He seemed less interested in helping me and more interested in speaking to me in the most condescending way possible.

I drove myself home knowing that my baby and I were going to die.

It wasn't until Ben came home later that night and found me still crying and still in pain that he rushed me back to the hospital and demanded I be seen. And of course they listened to him. Why didn't I tell them what was wrong? Why did I have to raise my voice? If only I would've been a little less angry, they would've been able to help.

Medical gaslighting.

I ended up on bed rest until I had an emergency C-section at thirty-five weeks pregnant. And even though she was born early,

Adelaide came out screaming and fighting. She didn't even need to go to the NICU. She was tiny, but she was strong.

And now, seeing her in the hospital bed, still so tiny and perfect, I'm painfully aware that my fear never went away.

"I still don't understand what's going on." I'm a broken record, I've been repeating myself since I walked into the hospital room and laid eyes on Ben and Adelaide. "She just was going sledding, how did this happen?"

"I don't know, ma'am," the doctor says. "We just know she was rushed in and we were told she had alcohol in her system. Luckily, she reacted well to the glucose IV and we didn't need to pump her stomach, but it was close."

I hear everything he's saying, but I still can't comprehend a single word. My eyes keep flicking from the doctor's kind eyes to Adelaide's sleeping ones. She was laughing and kissing me a few hours ago. "But . . . how?"

At that, Ben, who's been sitting quietly in the corner of the room while his colleagues flutter in and out of the room, snaps.

"Because you live with fucking Jude!" His voice bounces off the walls. His face is bright red as he closes the space between us. "You let that fucking bitch watch our goddamn kid knowing damn well that she's a fucking mess! One afternoon with her isn't no big deal, it's too fucking much! Wasn't she just in trouble for getting into a physical altercation like a day ago? And you let her take our daughter out unsupervised? Are you out of your fucking mind!"

The end of his outburst might be framed as a question, but it most definitely isn't one.

"No." I shake my head back and forth. There's no way Jude would let this happen. She's been in a bad space, sure, but she would never do something that could hurt Adelaide. "Jude loves her, she would never put her in danger."

"Oh, wake the fuck up, Lauren!" He's still shouting, and it's hard for me to recognize the man in front of me. Everything Ben does is measured . . . calculated. I've never seen him lose his cool before. Not ever. "Jude is fucking reckless! Everything about that bitch is selfish, and she's always been like that. Caputo was a fucking idiot for calling your home a sorority house. That made it sound fun. But you're damn straight I wanted your living with her held against you. I knew it was only a matter of time before something like this happened."

"Ben, you know Adelaide is my entire world. You know I would never do anything if I thought it could harm her in any way. Living with Jude has been good for both of us, I swear."

"You swear? You swear it's been good for both of you?" His voice drops to a whisper, and he inches toward me. "Look at our fucking daughter, Lauren. One fucking day with Jude and look at Junie."

My heart catches in my throat as I stare at my baby, IVs in her arm and monitors set up around the bed. My whole life, five feet away from me.

"If you think I'm not going to call Ethan as soon as I leave this place, you're fucking whacked. Things might've gone in your favor last time, but I'm not going to stop fighting until my daughter is out of that fucking house." Ben's phone goes off, but before he answers it, he stares me dead in the eyes and asks, "You understand me?"

I nod my head once. "Yeah, Ben."

He narrows his eyes but doesn't say anything else as he stalks into the hallway to talk to whoever's on the other end of the phone.

"Ms. Turner?" The poor doctor I forgot was in here calls my name. "Your daughter will be all right. As soon as your friend realized something was wrong, she rushed Adelaide here. I don't know what led to this situation, but I do know that your friend did everything she could to get her here. And I realize it's scary, seeing her like this, but she's going to be fine."

I close my eyes and let those words sink in.

Fine. She's going to be fine.

I take a deep breath before opening my eyes and responding with the only two words I can manage. "Thank you."

"If you need anything or have any questions, just call the nurses and we'll get you settled." He puts his hand on my shoulder and gives it a soft squeeze before turning on his tennis shoe and leaving me alone with my girl.

I sit in the chair Ben had pulled up close to her bed, and I don't know if it's the relief of knowing she's going to be okay, being alone with her, or that the shock is wearing off, but as soon as I sit down, it's like the dam behind my eyes bursts and I start crying uncontrollably. My entire body is trembling so hard that I can't even hold her little hand. I try to get my phone out to call my mom and dad to fill them in, but when pushing their contact on my screen is too much, I give up.

I toss my phone back in my purse and try to process how this went from one of my best days to the worst in an instant. But I can't. It's all too much.

And none of it's good.

So instead, I just try to forget absolutely everything.

I don't know how long my eyes are closed before Jude's voice startles me back into the present.

"Lauren? Are you awake?" she whispers.

I can't tell if she's trying to wake me up or hoping that I won't. But other than the twelve missed calls and three frantic voice mails she left, I haven't talked to her. When I got to the hospital, I ran straight to Adelaide's room, and when I got there, it was just Ben. I didn't know if Jude left or what, and to be honest, I didn't think about it enough to care. But now that she's in front of me, I'm so glad.

I have to get the entire story.

"Yeah." I sit up in the chair, rolling my neck twice to try to get rid of the kinks that sleeping sitting upright can give you. "I'm awake."

"Oh good." She's still whispering. Her steps are timid in a way Jude never is, and I assume I wasn't the first person to face Ben's wrath. "How's Addy doing? I've been sitting in the lobby, but it was killing me not knowing what's going on."

"Doctor said she's going to be fine. He said that you rushing her here so fast is part of the reason why." I tell her what the doctor told me and watch as her body slumps with relief. "I just don't understand what happened. I really need you to explain how she ended up here."

She doesn't say anything, she just moves to the other chair in the room and falls into it before standing back up and pacing back and forth in front of it.

"You know how much I love Addy, right?" she asks, and my hackles instantly shoot up, but I nod when I realize she's waiting for me to respond. "Because I do. And you were right about this playgroup being a fun one. We had so much fun. Even Jennifer was in a good mood."

If I wasn't sitting in a hospital room with my daughter, who almost had her stomach pumped because of alcohol poisoning, this might be the most shocking news of the year. But we're here and I couldn't care less about Jennifer's suddenly sunny disposition.

"But you know I usually hate these things." Jude powers on and I brace, because I know how this story ends, and now I have a very strong feeling that my best friend is the reason we're here. "And that's when I have you to bitch with. Without you there, I just knew I was going to be miserable. So before we left, Addy and I made hot chocolate. She loaded hers with marshmallows and I added some peppermint schnapps to mine."

"You did what?" The world tips on its axis and the room spins as my vision fights to right itself.

She ignores me and keeps talking. "I didn't even drink it, we were having the best time and I didn't even need it. But when I went to get lunch, Addy went with Sabrina and Winnie, and when Addy asked for her hot chocolate, Sabrina gave her the wrong thermos."

"Oh!" I laugh, but there's no humor behind the sound. Disgust is the only thing I feel right now. "So this is Sabrina's fault?"

"I mean . . . well . . . she didn't know that—" She trips over her excuses, but I don't let her finish.

"Of course she didn't fucking know! Are you out of your mind?" I try my hardest not to yell. The last thing I want is for Adelaide to wake up to me screaming at Jude. "What kind of person brings spiked hot chocolate to a playgroup?!"

I want to freaking strangle her. I'm not a violent person. I've never even so much as scratched another human. However, right now? Right now it's taking all the energy I have left to keep myself planted in this vinyl-covered chair.

If Jude was smart, she'd back down and start pleading for the forgiveness I'm not sure I'll ever be able to give, but instead, her back straightens and she glares at me. "You know how much I hate going to those things," she says, like this should mean something. "I was doing you a favor. Bringing a drink to deal with the shit you signed up for isn't that big of a deal."

"You offered to watch her! I would've skipped the damn event if I knew you babysitting would lead us to the freaking ER." I ball my hands into tight fists, and it feels like my nails are about to draw blood from my palms. "And so what? If you didn't have fun, you were going to drink your hot chocolate and then drive with my daughter in the car?"

"You're overreacting." She rolls her eyes. "There was barely any alcohol in there, I wasn't going to get drunk."

"Overreacting? Look where we are, Jude! If anything, I'm underreacting by not wringing your freaking neck!" I put my fists between my thighs to try to keep them down. "And now Ben is calling his lawyer, who's probably on the phone right now getting an emergency hearing to gain custody. So on top of the trauma of finding out my daughter was in the emergency room with alcohol poisoning, I have to call my mom and deal with her again."

"Oh, get the fuck over it, Lauren," she says, and I instinctively come out of my chair. "You have to call your mom, who's going to take care of everything for you . . . again. You're gonna call your mom, who might be a bitch sometimes because her daughter dropped out of med school for the biggest douche in all of California, but is still always fucking there for you and supporting you? I don't want to hear about your fucking mom."

I've heard of people who say they had out-of-body experiences, but I always thought they were crazy. Until right now. Because I don't feel like I have control of my body or the words that come out of my mouth. It feels like I'm outside of myself, watching a train wreck that can't possibly be my life.

"Get the fuck out." I point to the door, knowing I need more space between us, but my feet don't get the message. They keep moving toward Jude, who, with a snarl and bitterness etched across her face, looks like a total stranger. "I know we both signed the leasing agreement and I'll keep paying my portion of the rent, but my stuff will be out by the end of the week."

"Fucking wonderful. Can't fucking wait," she spits, her words like acid. "I can finally live like a normal human and not deal with your judgmental fucking eyes watching every single thing I do."

"Judgmental? I've been worried about you for months and you kept ignoring me! Glossing over your freaking problems with alcohol instead of doing something productive. You're a freaking alcoholic and you can't even see it!" I admit the truth that I, too, have been ignoring for way too long. "All you do is drink. It's why your mom won't talk to you anymore, and it's why you should be grateful if you never hear from me again after today. Because, I swear to god, Jude, the only reason I'll ever reach out is because I'm pressing charges."

Out of all the horrible, cruel things we said to each other, she doesn't react until I mention legal action. And for some reason, that incenses me even more. The end of our friendship, the possibility of me losing Adelaide, the danger she could've put herself *and* my daughter in? None of that bothered her. Nothing except something that might make her look bad to the strangers who idolize her online.

"Yes, Jude, press charges." I lean into her space, needing her to hear that this is not a threat, but a promise. "And I don't know about you, but I don't think there are any filters to help with child abuse."

She doesn't say a word. Not an apology. Not a smart-ass joke. Nothing.

Instead she levels me with one more glare before turning and walking out of the hospital room, taking eighteen years of friendship along with her.

THIRTY-FIVE

Jude

Fuck Lauren.

Fuck my mom.

I drop to the floor, and the glass bottle in my hand hits the carpet just before my ass. "Fucking fuck everyone."

It's only been three days since she cleared all of her shit while I was out with Spencer, but I still can't get over how much bigger the place looks without all of her crap cluttering it.

I drain the remaining drops of vodka from the bottle and toss it to the other empty bottles lying in the corner before flopping back onto the beige carpet to watch the ceiling fan as it spins around and around overhead.

My limbs start to go numb.

I keep staring at the fan, trying to separate the blades as they blur together until my eyes lose focus and I start to think that maybe finally . . . finally, I might lose consciousness.

It would be a relief, truly.

Because when I dream . . . I'm not always so fucking alone.

THIRTY-SIX

Jude

Sixty days later . . .

"Have you decided what you're going to tell her?" Chloe asks.

"Yeah." I nod my head and try to stop my leg from bouncing. "I think so."

It's all I've thought about for the last week, since she reached out and asked to talk. At first I thought about not responding, but we need some resolution. And I know for my own well-being, I have to be able to be honest and open. Keeping everything bottled up—no pun intended—led me down a destructive path. If I want to move beyond that, I have to face things even when they're hard . . . especially when they're hard.

"All right, so tell me." She leans forward in the new mustard-yellow chair she bought while I was off on my bender, ignoring her calls to try to schedule me for appointments.

"I'm going to tell her that while I'm glad she called, I can't have her in my life. It's been proven time and time again that we are toxic together and we're better off apart."

She raises an eyebrow and I know she's impressed. Even *I'm* impressed with myself.

"That sounds good, but you know people are going to judge you. Say that you're wrong for just giving up and throwing this relationship in the trash. That you should at least try to fight for it."

"They'd be wrong." I don't hesitate and I mean every word. "Nobody is entitled to take up space in your life if they aren't good for you. My mental well-being is more important than society's expectations. Family, friends, nobody should be allowed in your life if they are toxic."

"Wow, Jude." She looks me straight in the eye and claps her hands. "I'm so proud of you right now. You've put in the work and it shows in the way you talk, the way you carry yourself, and most importantly, the way you smile."

"Thank you." I receive her words and let her praise sink in. "I'm proud of myself too."

And I am.

It's almost unbelievable how far I've come since I called Chloe almost two months ago, begging her to see me again.

I still don't know what made me call her.

Maybe it was because I was tired of waking up hungover on the living room floor. Maybe it was because I was getting tired of waking up at all. Maybe it was because I didn't have another soul I could talk to.

It was probably all of those things . . . and more.

But no matter why I did it, it's the best decision I've made in a long, long time.

Chloe saw me the next day, and the first thing I did was tell her about my falling-out with Lauren. When I mentioned in passing that Lauren called me an alcoholic, she made a face that froze my world. Because even she knew what I didn't . . . or, more accurately, what I didn't want to admit. My drinking wasn't just a fun way to let out stress, it was my crutch. The only way I thought I could deal with all this shit I was going through was to completely numb myself to it. But it really did the opposite. It magnified every problem, highlighted my every weakness, and turned me into a person I didn't even recognize.

I've been seeing Chloe three times a week and going to AA meetings since.

And I'm sober.

I have to feel my feelings and learn to deal with them. As hard as it is, it's also pretty great too. Everything feels deeper, seems brighter, is more alive.

"You have an appointment tomorrow, you know where meetings are, but if this goes bad and you need to talk after, you have my after-hours number. Do not hesitate to call. You are not a burden and I want to support you. Got it?"

She ends every session with this reminder.

Always feeling like I'm just causing other people stress and problems has been my hardest hurdle. I still haven't cleared it, and I don't know when I will. But I do know that I'm making progress every day and that's all that matters.

"Thank you." I stand up, grabbing my purse off the table by the door, accepting that the nerves I'm feeling for what I'm about to do are good. "I'll see you tomorrow."

. . .

I go over what I plan on saying the entire drive to her new place. I was hoping that would help ease the fear of this meeting, but right after I push the doorbell, I start to wonder if maybe this is a mistake.

It's too late for second thoughts though.

Because the door swings open and there she is, looking as beautiful as ever.

"Ju-ju!" My mom's long, lithe body crosses the threshold and she wraps her arms around me. My body goes solid at her touch, but she either doesn't notice or ignores my reaction. With her, both are equally plausible. "I've missed you so much."

I take a small step back, careful to keep a smile on my face as I gently pull myself out of her grip. "Hi, Mom."

"Well." She tucks a stray piece of hair behind her ear and gestures for me to go inside. "Come in! I'm so excited to show you my new place and catch up."

My steps falter as I enter her home.

I was almost as nervous to see this place as I was to see her. Gossip magazines and websites started to report news of the foreclosure a couple of weeks ago. Of course, thanks to Eliza, my mom was able to work with them and spin it in her favor. They painted her as the poor widow who wasn't losing the house so much as she was making the difficult decision to downsize.

I had to go to an emergency meeting when Spencer sent me that article.

Then I had to block Spencer's number a few days later when, after I told her how hard it was for me to see this stuff, she spammed me with more articles about my mom and asked to meet at a bar.

I miss her, too, but I'm hoping that I'll be able to talk with her soon.

"So? What do you think?" My mom's assessing eyes are watching me as I take it all in.

"It's really nice, Mom." And it is.

It's a fraction of the size of our old house but more than enough space for my mom. There's a huge white-brick fireplace in the center of the room and old, beautiful oak beams on the ceiling with a giant circular chandelier dangling in the middle. All of her furniture is new, and the chair my dad always used to lounge in when we'd sit in the living room and watch TV together is long gone.

I really wish she'd given me that chair.

In fact, everything about this house is new. There's not even a family picture lingering on the freshly painted walls. I have no idea how she managed to pay for all of this, but I don't intend to ask.

Her smile is blinding. "I'm so glad you like it. I made some iced tea, let me pour you a glass."

She walks in front of me, not checking to see if I'm following. I trail behind, not saying a word, still trying to come to terms with these surroundings as we walk into her massive, marble-covered kitchen with gleaming new appliances. She points me to an upholstered stool at the counter and I sit while she pours the tea.

"Lots of ice, just how you like it and . . . oh shoot." She puts the glass in front of me before rummaging through the drawer next to her. "Hold on . . . I think . . . there!" She lifts her hand in the air, raising the plastic straw over her head like it's a trophy. "A straw. I know how much you love straws."

I decide not to remind her that I stopped using plastic straws years ago, something she knows, seeing as I've told her so many times I lost count.

I lift the glass to my lips and take a deep gulp. "Thanks."

"And I have some gin if you want to make it a royal tea." She turns and walks toward what I'm assuming is the bar.

"No thanks, I'm not drinking," I say. But that doesn't slow her down.

"Oh please." She waves me off. "A little gin never hurt anybody."

"I'm pretty sure that's factually untrue," I mutter beneath my breath before remembering what Chloe has told me about speaking up for myself and not letting my mom bulldoze me. "Mom, stop," I say, this time with power behind my voice.

She stops and turns to me, the annoyance in her expression there for a split second before she schools her features. "Why are you so testy? You love my royal tea."

"I did love your royal tea when I needed alcohol to get through our time together, but I'm sober now and I don't want gin." I don't mince my words, even though my first instincts in dealing with my mom are to measure every single sentence that passes my lips.

"Sober?" My mom laughs at the word like it's the funniest joke she's ever heard.

Even though I knew this is how this was going to go, I think the little girl in me still hoped my mom would prove me wrong. I hoped she would've used the time apart like I did and worked on herself, maybe realized that all the media attention and material possessions aren't as important as family . . . and considering we're all the family we have left, she'd realize how much she missed me.

I didn't even tell Chloe this, but I think she still knew.

"Yes, Mom, sober." I push the iced tea to the side and stand up. There's no need to extend this meeting any longer. "Because I had a problem. A problem that was getting so big that I took alcohol with me to a playgroup while I was babysitting Addy. Alcohol that Addy ended up drinking and being rushed to the ER for."

I still can't think about that day without getting sick to my stomach. The look on Addy's face as the doctors pushed the IV in her little arm wakes me up every single night. And the way I spoke with Lauren? I know she'll never forgive me.

I don't know if I'll ever forgive myself.

"You did what?" The color drains out of my mom's face, and for the first time maybe ever, I think she gets that I'm being serious. "Jude, if this gets out, do you know what it will do to me? I can't spin something like that. And I'm just starting to get bigger story lines on *Hollywood Housewives*."

Of course she didn't care about the fact that I destroyed my longest friendship or that I hurt the daughter of a woman who considered her to be a second mother.

She's a narcissist, Jude. Time and space will not change that. You have to protect yourself from her, because if you don't, she will drag you down and then step on your battered body to get back up.

I hate when Chloe is this right.

"If Lauren was going to press charges, I think she would've already done it." I don't actually know if this is true or not. I keep expecting to open the door to police officers one day. Honestly, I keep hoping I'll open the door to police officers. It's what I deserve. "And if she does, it has nothing to do with you and everything to do with her protecting her daughter, something you could probably learn from."

Color fills her face, and if her face wasn't so overstuffed with fillers, she would be glaring at me. "Excuse me? What did you just say to me?"

"You heard me, Mom." I take a deep breath, remembering all of the bullet points I wanted to say to her. "Ever since Dad died, you've treated me like the parent in this relationship. You've ignored my mental health and well-being time and time again in order to get what you want. You've manipulated me and used my love for you as a weapon. You've threatened to kill yourself because I didn't have the money to help you. You disowned me because you prioritized working with a magazine over your own daughter."

"You just hate me. You always loved your dad more, and now you hold everything I've ever done against me," she snaps back, going straight on the defensive and not listening to anything that I've said.

Again, not surprising, but still disappointing.

"I love you, Mom." I let my voice go gentle, not bothering to mask the sadness and anger I feel having to have this conversation with her. "I love you so much. It's why I kept thinking that if I did one more thing you asked, you'd turn back into the mom I lost when Dad died. It's why you treating me the way you have has affected me so deeply."

"You can't hold how I behaved when your dad died against me. I made stupid decisions, but I'm not that person anymore. I can't go back in time to fix it. You have to be able to move on."

This isn't the first time I've heard this.

Not an apology. Not a muttered *I'm sorry*. Just her telling me that I have to move on. I have to forgive her.

"I don't have to move on." This is the part of the conversation I've had to work on with Chloe. This is where I knew I would struggle. "I don't have to forgive you."

"I'm your mom," she says, like that means something now. "You have to forgive me, you're all I have. Without you, I'll be all alone. I couldn't survive that."

"You're the one who cut me off three months ago. You're the one who exploited me to the gossip magazines when I told you I needed time. You're the one who took money you knew I didn't have to buy new shoes and keep up with an image you couldn't afford." Saying the things I've been thinking for months . . . maybe even years, feels so freeing. With everything I tell her, it's like another weight is lifted off my shoulders. "And I know you don't want to hear this, but I'm not responsible for you. I can't put your mental health above my own. Not anymore."

She folds her arms in front of her chest and gives her chin a defiant lift. "So what are you saying?"

"I'm saying that it was a good idea, you giving us space, and we should keep doing it." I cross the kitchen, in hopes that she can see in my eyes how hard this is for me. "I'm not in a good enough place to handle our relationship in a healthy way."

"But Jonathon just told Eliza we'd do a photo shoot in the new house."

"That's not my problem, Mom." I ignore the familiar pain knowing she's more worried about what I can do for her than anything else. "You'll have to figure that out."

"I'm your mom!" Her voice is rising and I know the tears are going to come next. "You can't just cut me out."

"You are my mom, but being that still doesn't mean you're owed a spot in my life if you're just going to abuse it."

I wait a moment to see if she has anything else to say, but when she stays quiet, I wrap my arms around her and give her one last hug before I turn and retrace my steps through her new house and out the front door.

I climb into my car and start the engine, but I don't put it in drive.

Even though I'm so proud of myself for doing what I was always too afraid to do and the relief I feel for getting that conversation out of the way is palpable, I'm still sad. Sad that faced with my truth and a future without me, she still couldn't step up and be the mom I needed her to be.

But I know I can't put my expectations on her shoulders, and I'll move on.

No matter how hard it is.

• • •

I thought I was for sure going to need a meeting after talking with my mom, but I think I've known it was coming for so long that it ended up not being as hard on me as I expected.

I toss the mail on my new coffee table and walk into the kitchen, grabbing a sparkling water out of the fridge and sticking my leftover Indian food from the night before in the microwave. Once my dinner is done, I dump it on a plate and carry it over to the couch I found at a really cool secondhand store next to the new Pilates studio I've been going to.

I don't even get my first bite to my mouth when a small purple envelope covered in stickers beneath this week's grocery ad catches my eye.

I snatch it off the table, and my stomach flips when I see Lauren's name with the return address. I rip open the envelope, not knowing what to expect, and tears start to fall when I see the llama-covered birthday invitation with Addy's handwriting all over it proclaiming how much she misses me. My hand instinctively moves to the necklace I still haven't taken off, and I run my fingertips over the inscription.

I didn't think I'd have to use it, but I grab my phone and go straight to Chloe's after-hours number. Because in more ways than one, seeing Lauren and Addy means way more to me than seeing my mom. And I need a plan.

THIRTY-SEVEN

. . .

Lauren

One of the perks of moving back in with my parents is that I get to use their massive backyard to host Adelaide's birthday instead of forking over a small fortune to whatever venue Adelaide wanted this year.

"Mommy! Mommy! The animals are here! The animals are here!" Adelaide screams from somewhere in the house that I still can't believe I'm living in . . . again.

The biggest downfall of this living arrangement is that my parents indulge Adelaide's every whim and are creating a total monster. For her birthday, they paid to have a petting zoo brought into their backyard. Complete with llamas since they're Adelaide's new obsession.

Unicorns are so last year.

Adelaide's words, not mine.

"I'm just saying, these animals destroy Dad's flowers, I'm not taking responsibility," I say to my mom as we prepare the fruit trays to spread out in the dining room.

"Oh, stop it." My mom waves me off as she rearranges the strawberries for the sixth time. "As long as she's happy, Dad can regrow his flowers. He'd probably be happy to have a new gardening project."

This is not a lie, but still. I have no idea what aliens took over my parents' bodies and left me with this easygoing woman who lets Adelaide play with her porcelain figurines.

"Okay." I toss the grapes on the side of my tray and turn to my mom. "Who are you and what did you do to my mom? Because you would've never let me have llamas and a bounce house at my birthday party."

She laughs like what I said was funny and not a deadly serious inquiry.

"We're grandparents," she replies, giving her standard response. "We get to do the fun stuff like spoiling her rotten. Don't you remember when your grandmother took you to Disney World for your birthday for a week when you were ten? Even though Disneyland is right down the street and you wouldn't have needed to fly and stay in a hotel?"

I do remember that. It was the best birthday ever. We went on every ride as many times as I wanted, had all the character dinners, and bought so much Disney crap that my grandma had to buy an extra suitcase for our trip home.

"Okay." I grab the box of crackers and open it to start the cheese trays. "I see your point."

"Exactly"—my mom smirks—"I was so jealous of her that year. I picked you out this gorgeous gold necklace with your initials. I thought you were going to love it, but it wasn't even an afterthought once you found out about Disney."

I drop the crackers on the counter and turn to my mom. "You were jealous?"

"Of course I was. You see what it's like being a parent. You're

always on. Always worried about how what you're doing will affect your child in the long run." She shakes her head and moves
on to obsessing over the grapes. "I know there are some grandparents who have to worry still, but I'm one of the lucky ones.
You're such an amazing mom that I don't have to worry about
anything except spoiling that sweet girl of mine."

Her words stop me dead in my tracks.

"You think I'm a good mom?" My mom has never told me
that before. Not ever. If anything, I always assumed she thought
I was doing a terrible job. Something I've managed to reinforce
again and again lately.

"Of course I do." She tears her focus away from the tray that
I don't have the heart to tell her nobody is probably going to look
twice at, and when she looks at me, her eyebrows are furrowed
together. "Have you seen that little girl in there? That kind of
spirit doesn't just come from nothing. She's able to be like that
because of the safety you provide her."

"But even . . ." I try to think of the right way to ask what I
really want to know. "Even after *everything* that's happened, you
still think that?"

To say that I've been feeling guilty since the alcohol incident
may possibly be the greatest understatement of the century.

Before we even left the hospital, I had to call Kim because Ben
petitioned the court for an emergency custody hearing. I couldn't
even be mad at him. If that had happened to Adelaide when she
was with him, I would've lost my mind. Thankfully, because we
went straight to my parents' once Adelaide was released, the court
denied his request.

I haven't touched the podcast since. No emails have been sent.
I haven't even gone out with Hudson. My sole focus has been
Adelaide. The way it always should've been.

My mom abandons the tray and takes my hands in hers.

"Especially because of that." She looks me straight in the eyes, and I swear I can feel the intensity of her words. "I know I'm hard on you, too hard, if I'm honest. But in these last six years, you've proven time and time again that nothing is going to get you down. And you've done it while creating this little girl who knows the world has no limits for her." She squeezes my hands in hers, and I can't stop the tears that start to fall hearing my mom tell me she's proud of me.

It's all I've ever wanted.

"But after that day." I shake my head; the image of Adelaide's tiny body in that hospital bed is burned into the back of my eyelids. "If I had slowed down, it wouldn't have happened. I was doing too much. I was being selfish."

"Selfish? Lauren, are you crazy?" She lets go of my hands and puts hers straight to her hips before doing the neck roll that promises a good rant. "I've worked your entire life. I hated those damn dance recitals we had to sit through for four hours only to watch you dance for five minutes, and unless it was history, you know I was useless helping you with homework. I wish someone would dare to call me selfish for wanting to have some autonomy outside of being a mother, I'd tell them right where they could shove their opinion."

I snort out a shocked laugh. I've never heard my mom talk like that. "Oh my god! Mom!"

"What? It's true!" She laughs with me for a second before she sobers and her voice drops to a whisper. "I know you're worried about Jude coming today." She latches onto my hand when I try to move away. "But I want you to talk to her."

"She almost killed Adelaide, Mom. There's nothing to talk about."

I didn't even want to invite her. The only reason I did is because Adelaide has been missing her like crazy and cries at least once a week because something reminds her of her Auntie Jude.

After we moved into my parents' house, I started taking Adelaide to a therapist. I was so nervous what the emotional fallout of being rushed out of playgroup and into an ambulance was going to be that I didn't even think moving out of our town house would be a blip on the radar.

Boy was I wrong.

Getting sick, going to the hospital, and getting the IV didn't even faze her. Really, the only thing she remembers is getting lots of Popsicles and Jell-O and unlimited screen time. What was bothering her was her new living arrangement and sudden and total silence from the woman who had played a huge part in her little life.

When she asked if she could at least invite her to the birthday party, I called Ben and we both talked to the therapist together. We came to the agreement that Adelaide's feelings are all that matter and we'd get over our anger if it was best for her. However, if I see Jude take even a single sip of alcohol, she's gone. No questions asked.

"You know I've had a hard time with Jude in the past," my mom says, and if this conversation didn't have me so on edge, I would laugh hysterically at that.

"A hard time? You hated her!"

"No." She shakes her head with so much force that a bobby pin falls from her bun. "I hated her mom and then I thought Jude was turning into that awful mother of hers."

"What?" This is news to me. "I loved Mrs. Andrews!"

"Of course you did, you were a child and she let you all get away with anything if it meant less work for her. Jude always ended up over here because her mom would cancel sleepovers the second a better offer came around."

I don't remember this.

I mean, sure, I remember Jude coming over to my house and us being bummed because my mom made us have a bedtime even on the weekends, but I don't remember Mrs. Andrews ditching us.

"Don't try to think of when it happened. You didn't know." My mom accurately reads my face. "Juliette would call me and tell me something came up, and then I'd make up some excuse as to why you couldn't go to their house, but Jude could come here."

Well, crap. I do remember that happening . . . a lot. I always thought my mom was being an overbearing jerk who just wanted to keep an eye on me.

"And from what I've caught in the magazines I read, Juliette has only gotten worse since her husband died," she says. This conversation is enlightening in more ways than one. Until this very moment, I thought my mom only read autobiographies and law textbooks. Gossip magazines? Who knew! "They're saying she let the house fall into foreclosure and that her manager dumped her because she kept promising to do campaigns with Jude, but Jude isn't talking to her anymore."

If this were a cartoon, my eyes would pop out of my head and triple in size while a screeching-tire sound effect went off in the back. "What? Where'd you read this?"

I obviously knew something was going on with Jude and Mrs. Andrews, but I had no idea it was big enough to cause them to stop talking altogether.

And curse me, even as mad as I am at Jude—and I'm still really freaking mad—it makes me want to find her and hug her and never let her go.

"All the magazines are saying the same thing, that Juliette has been out and about, complaining to anyone who will listen about her daughter turning her back on her," Mom says. "And even though I can't stand that selfish cow, Jude always idolized her. So go easy on her today."

Well, crap.

I was planning to go full-on Elsa today. Now what am I going to do?

I'm contemplating this when my mom proceeds to blow my mind one final time.

"And by the way," she says. "Can you please call Hudson back? He seems like a great guy—way better than Ben—and I would eventually like more grandchildren."

My jaw flops open, but no words come out.

Who is this woman, and why am I just now meeting her?

· · ·

Between the llamas, baby goats, piglets, face painters, and hordes of kindergartners, I still haven't been able to focus on anything except the constant stream of people flowing in and out of the house.

Jude still isn't here.

She RSVP'd yes and I don't think she'd get Adelaide's hopes up for nothing, but then again, we left off on a terrible note and I don't know what to expect.

I'm helping Lake pick out her face-painting design, while Jennifer—who, while I doubt she'll ever be my favorite, has grown on me—is chatting with my mom about the different boutiques where she finds all of the matching outfits for her and Lake. And even though it will be mortifying, I can't help but cross my fingers that my mom will buy matching outfits for her and Adelaide.

"What about the rain—" I stop talking when Adelaide's loud shriek pulls the entire party's attention to her as she sprints across the yard and straight into Jude's open arms.

"Auntie Jude!" She's still screaming. "You came! I've missed you so much! The last time I saw you, I was five and I'm six now! I grew a whole year since I saw you!"

My mom looks away from Jennifer and tips her head in Jude's direction.

"Here you go, sweetie." I hand the booklet with face designs back to Lake. "I think the rainbow would be beautiful. Plus," I lean in and whisper in her ear, "if you say please, they give you glitter!"

Glitter is all the encouragement Lake needs before she's tossing the design book on the floor and shouting, "Rainbow with glitter, please."

I leave the kid corral (my name for it that makes my mom roll her eyes every time I say it) and move toward where Adelaide is still yapping Jude's ear off.

"—and then the last field trip, we gotta go to a chocolate factory to see how they make chocolate for Valentine's Day! It wasn't like *Willy Wonka*, but it was still fun." Adelaide leans in and covers one side of her mouth with her hand. "I was kinda hoping that Declan would turn into a blueberry, so that stunk."

Jude bursts into laughter while I yell, "Adelaide June! That's not kind."

"Well, Declan is mean, Mommy," she says, like that justifies everything . . . and I guess to a six-year-old, it does. "And he wipes his boogers on the desk."

"Gross," Jude and I say at the same time.

Adelaide opens her mouth, no doubt to say I owe her a pop, a terrible thing she picked up at school, but Winnie runs up to her with a bottle in her hand. "Addy, we get to feed the goats now! Come on!"

Adelaide doesn't even spare us a backwards glance before she's off.

And then something happens that I never thought would be possible when I'm near Jude: awkward silence fills the air.

"Um, hey." She waves and rocks back onto the heels of her sneakers. "Thanks for inviting me. I've really missed Addy . . . and you too," she rushes out. "Of course."

"Thank you for coming, she has really missed you. She was more excited to see you than the llama."

"Better than a llama," she repeats, and laughs. "If I ever sign up for a dating profile, I think that's going to be in my bio."

I cringe thinking of what her inbox would look like. "You might want to rethink that one, I think that's just asking for weirdos to DM you."

"Good call. I obviously didn't think that through."

We both laugh for a second before the silence sets in again.

"I think they're going to be feeding the animals for a little bit." I point to the group of kids crowding the different animal stalls. "Do you want to go find a place to talk for a minute?"

"Yeah, sure. That'd probably be good," she says.

I notice the fear that crosses her face, but I don't say anything to correct her. As much as what my mom said about her mom is weighing on my mind, I still feel like I shouldn't give in this easy.

I lead her inside and up the stairs into my old room turned new room. I point to the old computer chair my parents never got rid of and I sit on the edge of my bed.

"You look really good," I tell her. "And not in the way you always look really good, but something is different."

"I quit drinking," she answers without missing a beat, shocking the shit out of me.

I stare at her with my mouth dangling open and my eyes blinking for I don't even know how long before I find my words again. "You what?"

"I'm not going to make excuses for what I did when I last saw you. There are none and I can't tell you how sorry I am that I put Addy in danger and caused you to experience that kind of fear. I was in a really bad place and I didn't know how to handle it." She looks down and starts tearing at an invisible string on her pants. "I yelled at you when I was really angry at my mom. I drank instead of confiding in you and I drank to numb myself from the pain I was afraid of feeling, not knowing how much pain I was causing you and Addy."

"My mom said she read that you stopped talking to your mom and she lost the house? I know the blogs are usually full of it, but what happened?"

"Well they are spot-on for that story." She looks at me, and for the first time in a long time, her eyes aren't cloudy or unfocused. And even though she looks scared and sad, she still looks like Jude . . . not the dulled-down version I'd grown accustomed to. "I told you the first part, how my mom started blowing through all of the money the first time she was a Housewife. My dad took out a second mortgage to cover her spending. But then he died and instead of changing the way she lived, she came to me. Always asking for money, always needing me for some story line, never just calling to be my mom. What I didn't tell you is that when I started saying no, her methods changed. She threatened to kill herself or she'd disown me until she needed me again. It was just a never-ending cycle. And I finally had to stop it.

"After you and Addy moved out, I got in a really dark place, but now I'm seeing Chloe again. We meet three times a week, but are going to start scaling back soon." She unzips her purse and hands me a little token. "And I've been going to AA meetings every week. I haven't had a sip of alcohol in two months."

"Wow, Jude . . ." I flip the token over and look at the other side before handing it back to her. "I'm so proud of you."

"Thanks," she says, and I can feel the nerves rolling off her. "I know you can't just forgive me for what happened. I've been on the receiving end of empty promises for years, I know they're meaningless. But I want you to know that I'm trying. I'm trying to do better, and if you ever can forgive me, I want you to know I will never let you down like this again."

"Jude." I stand up and cross the room to where she's sitting. "I forgave you the second you said you stopped drinking."

I see the moment my words register because her eyes fill with tears.

"I've been taking Adelaide to a therapist for the last couple of months, and the only thing she ever talks about is how much she misses you. If you are taking the steps to be healthy, Adelaide needs you in her life." I stop, thinking how sad and lonely I've been without her in my life these last months. "I need you. Nobody laughs at the stupid crap we find funny. Nobody gets me like you."

"I missed you like crazy." She swipes away the tears falling down her makeup-free face. "All I do is talk to my therapist, go to meetings, and do Pilates. I'm pretty sure I'm single-handedly financing Chloe's office makeover."

"Well, now you can call me." I push the base of the chair she's in and send her sliding away. "We might not be sister wives anymore, but we're still sisters and I'm still team Jude till the day I die."

"And you already know it's Addy and Lauren till the very end."

I got lucky, getting parents I can count on, having a little girl I adore. I was granted a great family.

But I was just as lucky, walking into my third-grade class and finding my soul sister. Because sometimes, family is just what you make it.

EPILOGUE

...

From: Lauren and Jude
Date: June 4
Subject: We're back mother* . . . nope. Our bad, just mothers.

Hey!

Long time no talk, are we right?

Well . . . if you're like us and the new year has kicked your ass from here to there and back again, solidarity, our friends. We're right there with you.

So what's new with us you ask? Where in the fresh hell did we disappear to? Take a seat, let's have a little kiki while we fill you in on the newest updates.

Update #1: Jude is sober! You read that right! The martinis on *Mom Jeans and Martinis* are virgins now. So juice. We drink juice while we record. And no, you California-loving readers, there is no gin involved in this equation.

Update #2: We're no longer sister wives. This might come as the biggest surprise of all. Though we loved the idea of platonic marriage when we first started, it proved more difficult than we anticipated. Some bumps that we might discuss down the road happened and we realized that being sisters is just as good without the wives. Though I (Jude speaking) do miss Lauren's cooking and I (Lauren) miss Jude's willingness to load a dishwasher.

Update #3: Though Lauren no longer has a sister wife, she does have a boyfriend! You read it here first, folks! Our Lauren is boo'd all the way up. His name is Hudson Phillips. He has his own podcast and also does all the tech stuff for us. And he's h-o-t, HOT. Look him up, you'll see. (Lauren says don't look him up. But don't listen to her, I only wrote that because she's sitting next to me and making me do it.)

Update #4: Jude is getting her own Pilates studio!!! She's going to try to play it cool and pretend like it's no big deal, but it is a big deal, HUGE. She has worked so hard for this and has gone through more than most people can even begin to imagine to get here, and I couldn't be more proud of her. Jude says it's just a Pilates room in a gym where she's renting, but that still sounds like a Pilates studio to me, so we're ignoring her and everything I already said still stands. HUGE DEAL!

Update #5: Even though we haven't recorded in a while, we still get messages from people listening to old podcasts. So here is the answer to our most frequently asked question: Yes, J and her daughter L still match all the time. To this day, neither of us have ever seen them together not wearing some version of the same clothes. The best update to this is that Lauren's mom loves it and now buys matching grandma-granddaughter outfits and they also match. Though Lauren and I both draw the line at Gucci.

No child of ours will ever wear Gucci.

So, I guess that's it for now. We've missed you all so much and we can't wait to reconnect.

So, until next time, stay hydrated! 🐟
Lauren and Jude

PS Yes, that's a wave, but there's no water bottle emoji and Lauren said the water droplets are too sexual.

PPS If you unsubscribed because we were disasters and left you hanging for a few months, go back and hit that subscribe button again! Because we're dropping gems and you don't want to miss them!

Acknowledgments

• • •

When I first began my writing journey, I had no desire to write anything that wasn't heavily focused on romance and kissing. But as I wrote these stories, one topic started to make me more excited than the closed-door scenes I was writing: strong women and the friends who supported them.

I didn't know if I would be able to make the switch and I am so grateful to my amazing agent, Jessica Watterson, and my insanely talented editor, Kristine Swartz, for encouraging me to explore this new passion of mine. You both held my hand throughout this entire process and allowed me to tell the story I didn't even realize I was dying to tell. You are a dream team and I could not be luckier to have such literary badasses on my side.

To everyone at Berkley, thank you for giving me another opportunity to live out this incredible, unbelievable dream I'm living.

If you've read my books, you might have an idea of just how much I love all things pop culture. So I had to take this opportunity to thank the girl group that makes my heart go wild, Little Mix. Thank you for not only providing my writing soundtrack by dropping bops that never disappoint, but for being a shining example of friendship and empowerment that we can all look up to. In the words of my favorite sweatshirt by the one and only Jade Thirlwall, "We have to stan."

Suzanne Park and Falon Ballard, thank you both for putting up with my endless messages begging you to be my virtual Los Angeles tour guides and for giving me countless recommendations and ideas for locations in this book. Also, thank you for not judging me too harshly for the ridiculous requests I made.

Lin. I will never, ever quit you. From belly buddies to critique partners. You are proof that mom groups are worth a chance and the only reason I have any faith in social media. Thank you for your patience and guidance and constant encouragement. I'm not sure I would've made it without you at my back . . . in more ways than one. And yes, I fully expect a kind message in your book, so don't forget this.

Lindsay and Maxym, I am so thankful you allowed me into your duo. You are magical masterminds and I'm honored to be able to call you my friends. I'm so excited for all that we will create together . . . and also, retreats and tacos.

This book is about strong friendship and I am beyond lucky to have so many examples in my life. Brittany, Meghan, Jill, and Shay. I know I can always count on you to make me laugh and smile when I need it the most.

Taylor. I mean, what do I even say? You are literally the strongest person I know. An amazing friend, a fantastic sister and daughter, the best mom ever—there is nothing you can't do. Your gentle encouragement has been a lifeline for me. You turned one of the worst weeks of my life into a time when I was able to smile more than cry. Watching you deal with everything you've been dealt with . . . a freaking TRUCK! . . . and still power through has been inspirational to say the very least. And even though you always say no, just know that the glitter bomb offer is ALWAYS on the table.

Abby, what even is there to say? You've stood by my side throughout it all. From Chili's and movies to walking to 7-Eleven on hot summer days to obnoxious Abercrombie pants to fifth-floor Durwood, you've seen it all. Your friendship is the constant I know I can always depend on. Thank you for loving my kids and answering them every time they FaceTime you. You will never, ever be able to get rid of me. Love you forever.

DJ, Harlow, Dash, and Ellis. I wrote this book during a freaking pandemic and you gave me enough space and encouragement to do it. I love you to the moon and back and around again. You are my whole, entire reason for everything. I hope I make you as proud as you make me. I'm the luckiest mom in the world.

Derrick, thank you for going on this wild journey with me and holding down the fort when I inevitably spiraled as the deadline approached. I love you.

Mom. This is so weird. I miss the days when we called each other multiple times a day and met for lunch all the time. I miss the way your laugh was all-encompassing and your smile lit up the room. I miss the way you loved my kids. I miss the good times. I miss you being my best friend. I wish I could have carried some of the grief you got lost behind. I hope you're with Grandma, Grandpa, Paul, and Dad. I hope you're happy and I pray you know how extremely loved you were and still are.

MOM JEANS AND OTHER MISTAKES

. . . . .

Alexa Martin

Questions for Discussion

. . .

1. Jude and Lauren moved in together for not only financial support but emotional support as well. Is moving in with a friend something you would ever consider doing? How do you think that would change your friendship?

2. Lauren is dealing with the aftermath of a failed relationship and learning how to co-parent. What do her actions around her ex say about her?

3. Jude makes her living as a social media influencer. Do you think this is a real job? If you were an influencer, what would you specialize in?

4. Despite what many people think, Jude and Lauren both take pride in being millennials. What generation are you? Do you feel like you fit the stereotypes associated with people your age?

5. Lauren calls Jude her soul mate. Do you believe in soul mates? Do you think they exist only in romantic relationships, or can they exist in friendships as well?

6. There are a few instances of racism throughout the book. Did these instances surprise you? Do you think Jude was a strong ally and handled it well? How have you handled racist behavior you or someone around you has been faced with?

7. Mom groups and playdates take place throughout the novel and cause both Jude and Lauren a lot of stress. With the rise of Pinterest and mommy influencers, do you think the pressure on moms has increased or decreased? How so?

8. Jude finds comfort in drinking. Did you think she had a problem? Did it surprise you? Do you think the normalization of alcohol in society makes it easier for people to use it as a crutch?

9. Motherhood is an important theme throughout the book. Which mother-daughter relationship did you relate to most? Why?

10. Jude and her mom have a very toxic relationship. In the end, Jude decides to distance herself from her mother, even though it's not a decision society usually supports. Have you ever dealt with a toxic family member? Did you feel pressure one way or another on how to handle it?

Photo by Kristie Chadwick

Alexa Martin is a writer and stay-at-home mom. A Nashville transplant, she's intent on instilling a deep love and respect for the great Dolly Parton in her four children and husband. The Playbook series was inspired by the eight years she spent as an NFL wife and her love of all things pop culture, sparkles, leggings, and wine. When she's not repeating herself to her kids, you can find her catching up on whatever Real Housewives franchise is currently airing or filling up her Etsy cart with items she doesn't need.

CONNECT ONLINE

AlexaMartin.com
🐦 AlexaMBooks
f AlexaMartinBooks
📷 AlexaMBooks

Ready to find
your next great read?

Let us help.

Visit prh.com/nextread

Penguin
Random
House